# BLOOD AND QI
# A VAMPIRE XIANXIA

# BLOOD AND QI
# A VAMPIRE XIANXIA

### ANTHONY ALVES

Published by Level Up in the United Kingdom in 2024

Cover illustration by Sippakorn Upama
Cover by Claire Wood

ISBN: 978-1-83919-595-2

www.levelup.pub

To Ma and Dad. Thanks for letting me be part of your family.

# PROLOGUE
## LEGION IX HISPANA

Hermunduri region along the Rhine River, 131 AD

Lucius Latinius Macer calls out to the demon, "Do you speak Latin? Why are you doing this?"

He waits for a reply. None comes forth. *Twenty-five years. Twenty-Five years in the Ninth. I finally became prefect of the camp, third in charge of the legion, my year nearly done, and now this is how it ends.* Lucius grips his sword tighter and wishes he had a shield. He looks around at what remains of the First Cohort, at the fires blazing, and men wounded and screaming out, the many corpses, on this bloody field. He has no need of a reply. He knows why. *That little prick! That spoiled little Broad Band Tribune. Rich, pampered prick.*

Lucius wants to spit towards the corpse of the Broad Band Tribune, and would have if it wasn't so close to the corpses of the Legion Legate and Chief Centurion, both good men he respected. *This was supposed to be the easy part. Just making our way from Noviomagus to Troesmis. My time soon over, then heading back home before we even got to Singadunum. And glad to have my time over; Armenia would be rough duty. Now a gods cursed real-life demon attacks us.*

Another scream of absolute terror sounds out, closer this time. The forlorn Lucius says, "Five cohorts follow behind us!"

Lucius is surprised when the demon yells back to him, "Good!"

"You stand no chance. Let us talk, demon. Your plan cannot be to fight a whole legion. Demon or not, that is suicide. You caught us on the move, ill prepared, just a quick stop to get supplies and stretch our legs

1

after so long on the river. We have no support and no auxiliary with us. That won't happen with the following cohorts. They'll make fortified camps, send word ahead to the other cohorts and vanguard who'll turn back and make way here in all haste. You have a big problem, even if you have not yet realized it. Let us talk this through and come to a mutually beneficial understanding."

A scream comes from the opposite area, and Lucius swings around. He spies the demon holding a centurion from behind, the demon's face pushed into the neck of the man, as if lovers. Lucius steadies his nerves and prepares to rally and approach, hopefully surrounding this monster with all men remaining, nullifying the demon's many advantages. The centurion the demon holds slowly slides to the ground, dead. Lucius can now see the demon clearly, and is surprised it looks as a normal man does, as he expected to see something monstrous, such as a strix. Young. Dressed as the local savages, but the sharp features and darker hair and skin proving it isn't of them. A sword held lightly in its hand as it stands casually. The normal and benign look of the demon is surprising. Even more surprising is Lucius clearly remembers this man from when he first joined the Ninth, and he looks the same age as he did twenty-six years ago, and it startles him greatly. He stands shaken instead of calling the attack, as he should.

The demon, looming tall and unworried, with blood dripping down its face, asks, "Mutually beneficial understanding? I like that! Well put, but I'll have to decline. This is a matter of vengeance, and my goal in this differs greatly from yours. It is a simple goal. I win, you lose."

With the goal stated, the demon immediately sets out to bring it to fruition. It moves so quickly towards the remainders of the First Cohort it can hardly be seen, and neither shield-wall nor spear impedes its slaughter. By ones and twos, the soldiers fall, agonized shrieks filling the air. Few yet live as the demon approaches, and Lucius desperately cries out, "Stop! Stop! I know you! I forget your given and clan name but all called you Equus. You were a weapon and drill instructor when I was new in the legion, and later a front file centurion, and then a First File too. In Britannia!"

The demon stops, and turns his dark eyes to Lucius, and his reply to this is, "Yes. I remember. I'm saddened this must be done, but this tribe has taken me in and is helping me search for the people I was born to, so long ago. No luck so far. This great river was within twenty leagues or so of my birthplace. Maybe it was a different river? We called it the Balahtu, I think, or something close to that. I'm sorry to say I don't remember you. I am too old, and it is getting harder and harder to recall anything. But the matter is moot. I swore to protect these people while I live amongst them. You killed a young woman sworn to me. I was told she was killed casually, as if she were only an insect. Then a great slaughter was made of her family when they protested, and then also against many, many tribesmen.

"I've given you a doughtier foe to try your hand against. It's not going well for you. My mind may be waning, but not my honor, and I swore vengeance against the whole of this legion upon it."

Saying this, the demon renews his attack, saving the prefect of the camp for last, as he has some respect for the man, and drinks deep of him, savoring the essence of his life down to the last dregs.

# CHAPTER 1
# FOUR-CORNERED ROOM

**Scarsdale, NY – Present day**

A man sits alone in a candle lit room. His eyes closed, legs crossed, back straight, hands on thighs, and head bowed. His face is blocky, features sharp and rough, hair dark and unkempt, skin swarthy. He sits so still he seems to draw no breath, though he does. He looks very young, late teens or so, though he is much, much older.

The man opens his eyes. He doesn't know where he is, doesn't know when he is, or even know his own name. He is used to being confused. It is nothing new to him. He knows fear and anger helps nothing and has had a long time to master such emotions, so he does not allow himself to feel any. He is now mostly a creature of habit instead of intent. He sits alone in the four-cornered room staring at candles, images of battle and victory flashing through his mind.

He tries to remember more, but memories slip away or stay just out of reach. All he has is flickers of images, impressions, random thoughts and feelings. Becoming a man. Being a warrior. Living as a lord. Faint glints of conquest and battle and kingship, of being worshiped and despised, of hunting and being hunted, of facing armies and running from angry mobs, of having good friends and wandering alone, of finding love and searching for magic, of blood and feeding, the power. The world being the same for so long and then changing, then more change, always enduring and never dying, always living, then only existing. Only existing, then confusion and darkness.

He focuses on a name for himself. He knows he has been called many but can remember none. He remembers a friend. A friend brought him here, wherever here is.

*What did he call me?* No matter how hard he focuses, no name comes.

Though he has lived a very long time and seems immortal, the human body, as it currently stands, is an imperfect vessel for immortality. As most things go, the waning of his mind happened gradually, then suddenly. Decay outpaced regeneration and grey and white matter declined.

He never had the gift of tongues or a knack for learning new languages, but this is not abnormal. Most people aren't blessed with the gifts necessary to make learning new languages an easy task. And this man's first language was simple and direct, making more complex languages hard to comprehend and a struggle to learn.

When the grey matter thinned, the first area impacted was the posterior language cortices. Then the anterior. Word retrieval and production became harder, and eventually almost impossible. Other issues manifested—confusion constant. Faces blurred and could not be distinguished. His world became smaller and smaller. Now it is the size of the candlelit, four-cornered room he occupies.

Some time passes before he is finally able to hold on to a memory. An old one. A memory from before he took the power. The last memory of his family. A time when life was simple and direct, and everything made sense. Only children tracked age and only until man or womanhood at thirteen. He had just turned thirteen the past winter solstice, the start of the new year, when everyone turned a year older.

At thirteen boys became men and could war and marry, though it often took some years to find a good first wife with large dowries for important men. Being the oldest living son of a landholder, a lord, made him an important man. So, at thirteen he was a man, but had not yet taken a wife.

It was almost dusk, and the feasting was finished. All the family and his father's men and servants would lay down and take sleep on the floor of the one-roomed hold, the only light coming from the firepit in the center of the room. One of his father's men entered the household and yelled a warning that many, many enemies were approaching. Many, many meaning far more than they could handle. More than two tens, but less than ten tens. His father had little more than ten warriors sworn to him. This was no common raid by neighbors. This enemy was coming to kill and conquer.

As the men quickly equipped for battle, the children and unmarried women were sent to nearby farmer's huts. All but the children of the lord, as they would be greatly dishonored and abused if discovered, whereas invaders needed servants and wives, and farmers were almost always spared. Kingdoms were small, invaders always came from nearby and shared a similar language and culture – their goals and actions were predictable.

His lord and father ordered him to take the oldest of his brothers, the only brother turning thirteen the next winter's solstice, along with his two best sworn men, and trek to his neighboring lord's hold and inform him of the invasion. That lord would inform their king, the king would rally all the lords of the kingdom, repel the invaders, and win back his father's lands.

He protested and said he would not run like a coward. This enemy would not unman him. His father slapped him for questioning his orders, and said his word was law.

His task wasn't just to run and inform, but the sacred duty of vengeance. He would not be a true man until he killed ten tens of this enemy, or reclaimed his father's lands. If he did not achieve either goal he would be cursed as a coward, and would be considered little, and would sire no sons, and no one would speak of him at all after he died.

With dry eyes, he bid farewell to his mother, and his father's other wives, and his brothers and sisters. His other siblings, if taken along, would put the mission at risk, and burden the sacred task of vengeance he was sworn to, so they had to stay. His father must kill them with his own loving hand, so the enemy could not dishonor and abuse them. His wives too must take their own lives when his father fell, so they could serve their lord in the afterlife, and share in the rewards their husband would be granted for dying a proper and glorious death in battle, greatly outnumbered.

As he prepared to leave, his mother held him close and said, "Avenge us, Nut, or be cursed and die a coward's death."

Nut. Not his real name, but the nickname he had earned. With it comes another memory. On his first raid he took a mighty blow to the head and stood with his feet still. After the raid, when tall feats were being told by the fire, all the men laughed and clapped him on the back for taking such a blow to the head and not buckling. They call him Nut. His head was tough to crack.

The man, still sitting with legs crossed and hands on thighs, still staring at the candles, smiles. He remembers his name. A victory he revels in for a moment. He tries to say his name aloud, but no word to say it comes to mind.

Nut feels his face. About three days' growth. Before he opened his eyes earlier, he knew there were two people nearby. One unmoving and smelling of fear and feces close, and one moving freely below. The one below isn't the friend he thought of earlier. His senses are sharp, and he can hear, see, and smell extremely well, but he cannot smell well enough for that sense to reach the one below. Still, he somehow knows it isn't his friend. He would guess it is a female by the sounds and movements he can distinguish.

Nut stands and walks to the chamber pot to relieve himself. He notices the odd clothes he is wearing. A buttoned-up short-sleeved, dark grey shirt of silky material, and baggy and very comfortable pants of the same color and material. No undergarments. The pants are not placket, and the waist has a fantastical type of elastic fastening. The room has three doors. One door has a symbol he recognizes for food besides it, though how he knows the symbol evades his memory. He enters the door.

Inside is a small room with a man bound and gagged, hanging from the ceiling by hands and feet. The bound man's soul dark with bad deeds. That is the best way to hang a man to make it easier to extract all the dregs of vital essence, as the stubborn clumps in the hands and feet become far less stubborn. This type of hanging helps those new to the power, which Nut is not. The man being hung like this for him makes Nut feel helpless and incompetent.

The bound man is close to expiring. Though Nut has enough vital essence to last a while, he still sinks in his fangs and drinks deeply of the bound man. Not doing so would be a waste, and the dregs of a man contain the most potent and satisfying of the life essence.

Also in the room are some baskets filled with fruits and some vegetables. Nut sees a small bowl filled with what appears to be dried meat, but darker than it should be. Out of curiosity he tries a piece, and it is far less hard and salty, and far juicier, than salted meat should be. It also has a strange taste he is not familiar with. He places the rest of the piece back in the bowl. He drinks some water and cleans his face and hands in a washbasin.

Nut hears more movement down below and does not like it. Though not hungry, he grabs an apple as he leaves. In the room with candles are two other doors and a wooden chair near a window. Swords and various other arms are placed around the room, but not much else. He goes to the window drawing back the curtain, flinching at the powerful sun. It saps his strength, and he doesn't like it, but he wants fresh air to clear the stink of death and feces. He raises the window and welcomes the music of nature and sounds of children at play, familiar sounds making him feel less lost.

Nut sits and looks out the window. Small mansions built in a strange style, on very small estates, most with large metal-wheeled machines close by, congesting a street made of an unfamiliar substance. A feeling of dread overcomes Nut, but he squelches it quickly. He searches for the familiar and looks at the many trees and a small group of children. *Beautiful*, he thinks.

Nut's gaze pans up and down the street and stops on the queerest sight he has ever seen – a young girl, no older than six or seven, riding on a machine with two wheels and powered by feet, up and down the large and wide paved path leading to a small mansion.

The two-wheeled machine tickles Nut's memory and doesn't hold his gaze with confusion and curiosity. It is the little girl. Her soul is one of the darkest he has ever seen. More of a dark marble with lighter swirls. Most adults have a grey mist with dark swirls and splotches, and the occasional whitish swirl or spot. Children usually have clear light-grey souls.

Nut doesn't think he has seen a soul so dark even on the worst of men possessed of a great evil and capable of inflicting grave deeds in mass.

A child so young has neither the time nor ability for any such things. *How is this possible?* Nut sits by the window and ponders on this absurdity.

A pressure enters Nut's head, and next he notices the light outside has changed. His eyes are closed, and he cannot open them. The powerful sun hitting his skin no longer does. It was bright day but now approaches dusk. His power is hardly being sapped and the feeling is diminishing instead of strengthening, so he knows the sun is approaching dusk. He goes to stand but cannot. He is not in control of his own body.

This has never happened to him before. A new phenomenon. Maybe it should cause him fear, but it doesn't. He waits. He is good at waiting. The sun goes down. He thinks about retreating in on himself. He thinks of trying to remember his name again but doesn't. He is curious. He strains his senses. Occasionally he can hear a deep rumbling voice at the edge of his perception. Strangely, not his perception of hearing. He hears it at the edge of his mind. When he tries to focus on the voice, it gets further away.

He tries many tricks to make the voice clearer. None work. Sometimes he feels the rumble of the voice in his mind, sometimes in his chest. But never clearly. Just at the edge of his perception.

He sits there, still, unable to move. Once in a while a machine starts to softly vibrate, and cold air enters the room through a vent. He hears few bird or insect sounds, and they are far away and too slow. He hears mostly silence and the sometimes rumble of a distant voice.

Then something. The air changes and is filled with an indescribable tingling, like the air charged with a weird energy before a storm. He feels a different pressure on his head, but far different from the last. Something enters the base of his skull and starts spreading through his body.

He is not too worried. His vital essence isn't reacting to it, and throughout his long life no disease or poison has been able to harm him for long, if at all. If he was in danger, his power would fight the foreign substance, and his life essence would be draining.

Then pain. Extreme, unfathomable pain. He has felt all types of pain in his long life. All types. There is no pain he hasn't been subjected to over and over. And all prior pain pales in comparison to what he feels now. Being stuck fast and unable to move he can't cry out or flail around. The pain is too much for his mind to retreat from. He can only endure, and not by choice. It is pain unimaginable. Too great to bear. Too great to endure.

The pain could've lasted a moment or half the night. When it finally ends his mind is too gone and too numb to work at all. If he were at all lucid, he would feel new pressure applied to his head before darkness, mercifully, overtakes him.

# CHAPTER 2
## TESTING

The man's mind shrugs off whatever power forces him to be unaware. His body is lifting a metal ball up to his chest, then over his head. He can feel the ball is very heavy, but he can't drop it, or stop himself from lifting it. It's as if his mind is separate from his body, and he has no control of his limbs at all.

The man watches himself for a time, and two things become clear to him. The first is he's not in a real place. He has sharp vision and can see far off, yet he can now see nothing past the ground that magically appears around him as he moves to various metal objects and manipulates them as if exercising. Some of these metal objects float in the air or rest on invisible ground. Beyond his immediate area there is nothing to see. Just empty air.

The man has keen hearing, and he hears no other signs of life at all, not even small insects. He is not in a real place. But the sun that hits his skin is real. He sees the start of calcification on his exposed hands. If the sun is real, then it is also sapping his strength; he would be able to lift heavier metal objects if it weren't.

The man would care more about the first thing, not having control of his body and being forced to exercise in a place that isn't real, if not for the second thing. His mind is restored! He can remember. Not everything, but enough to have a self again. Enough to have an identity again.

The man can't remember the name his mother gave him, but he remembers the word for the name he earned as a man, Nut, is *gira*. He hasn't had any faith at all, no belief in gods, since before even the rise of

Agade, and he finds it strange all the reverence he feels when he recalls the name of the god his people worshiped, Koram. He isn't sure Koram is the exact correct name, but it's near enough.

The man has gone by many names other than Gira. He has been king of many great cities, and worshiped as many different gods. His most recent and clearest memories of titles he holds have his name as Yohannes, Ioannēs, Giovanni, and the like. He decides to go by the simplest and shortest version, John.

John remembers his youth, his people, meeting his old friend and master, Ahn, and gaining power, their conquest of the lands of his birth together. Then, going far to the south and east, seeing his first real city, Gargamis, and being so in awe of its size and population. Further to the south, the mighty ocean, and down along the coast in Suma, the city of Gubla, ten times the size of Gargamis. And Gubla being small compared to later cities, such as Agade in Assir, or Oruk in Sumer, or White Walls in Kayhamut.

Ahn always was bored and restless, and traveled all the time, searching. Then Ahn went south and never returned. John was alone for a very long time before finally finding Lilitu, his love. "One more time," she'd say. Always, "Just one more time."

John's heart breaks again when he remembers how things ended with Lilitu. How things had to end. And being alone, again, for a long, long time. Having to hide. His mind was nearly gone by the time he found Thomas, his stout and true companion. Thomas keeping him safe though John was a great burden to him.

Not only has John's mind and memories been restored, but so has his body. He feels somewhat strengthened and more energetic. The pains in his joints and tendons, like they were twisted tight and close to bursting, are no more.

John had some of those pains from near the beginning, and the pains became much worse over the years, as his body increased in strength and speed and power, and it being gone feels strange, as he was so used to it. It feels strange with the pains being gone, but also fantastic and wonderful. He feels light and fresh, and more invigorated than even draining a man of his last dregs of vital essence makes him feel.

Remembering vital essence, John tries to send some to enhance his strength, but he isn't in control of that now either. He would be doing much better in this test of strength if he could control his own body, and enhance himself, and if this test wasn't being conducted in the direct sunlight of the noon sun, something that saps his strength greatly.

Since John has no control of what his body is doing, and is so excited he is able to remember again, he decides to explore some memories and enjoy them, and does so. Later, a change to his environment causes him to end his reminiscences. Instead of performing feats of strength, his body starts performing various feats of speed and agility.

John doesn't know what is happening to him, or why, but he knows he could do better in this test if allowed to. Now, while paying close attention, he can somewhat feel his body being refreshed between tasks, following commands John thinks he hears as a soft voice on the periphery of his senses.

Focusing his mind on the task, John tries to wrest back control. The force of compulsion controlling his body is strong. With a willpower born of ages, he applies more and more effort to free himself. He nearly succeeds before he feels great pressure applied to his mind, and he is returned to darkness once again.

***

Exceedingly bright light burns John's eyes as he is startled awake. He is confused. He is standing but cannot move. He is frozen in place, unable to even squint his eyes closed harder to dim the light burning them. He is glad his head is bowed at least, as it provides a little protection.

Nothing can be done about the light and the burning brightness. Nothing but the usual remedy for all that has ailed John in his too long life. He must endure, so he endures. He finds it strange he has no fear for what is happening to him, all these queer events. No fear, just curiosity. Maybe this is due to events being so far out of his control?

John sends out his senses and becomes aware of what he can. His bare feet are on warm, wet grass. Artificially warm grass, as a very cold wind tussles his hair. He is mostly immune to the cold, and it doesn't bother him. He can't see the sun, but he guesses it to be afternoon.

To John's right and behind him he senses six people and one strange thing, formed up in neat and even rows. If he had to guess, he'd say the six people smell of his kind, and two smell somewhat familiar. One could be Thomas, but he is uncertain. The strange one has no heartbeat, but shifts and moves slightly, proving it isn't frozen like John is.

Over ten paces to John's front, where the exceedingly bright light comes from, are two others. These two have strange heartbeats. One beats far too strongly and loudly, and the other more slushes than beats. Both have very weird scents, and they feel all wrong. Weighty. Obvious.

John puts great focus on taking control of his eyelids back, so he can squint his eyes tighter, and block more of the light.

The thing in front of John, the one on the left, in the weirdest and most indescribable voice he has ever heard says, "It's awake again."

A reply comes from a very deep and rumbling voice towards the front right, "Stop! The last was my compulsion it resisted. The compulsion was strong, and still lasts on its body. It could be harmed. We are near finished anyways. I know not how it does it. An early Mortal without even an open energy center resisting a high Exalted? This world is far too bizarre."

The weird voice says, "I bet the Eternal knows. Maybe try asking it? It put the souls back for these freaks, didn't it?"

"I know not. I only know tethering and returning souls is far beyond my capabilities, even if I were at peak. I had no idea souls could even be seen. It could have been either Magnus, or the Sublime, and not the Eternal. Mmmm. It frightens me a Sublime came. I never thought I'd meet one, not before climbing much higher.

"The Eternal is energy so I know not if we can communicate with it. Even so, I would not presume to skip chain and speak directly with even

14

the Sublime, why would I risk drawing the attention of an Eternal to myself? Know your place, Junior. We are dealing with powers far beyond us, and if we do well, we may be rewarded. If any of our betters want us to know why this world is so bizarre, they will tell us."

The weird voice, in a monotone, says, "The Eternal is an energy being? How do we even know it's here then?"

"Wait," orders the rumbling voice.

A moment passes and the rumbling voice continues, "They're bringing in the demons and dark ones and g'athu, so we'll release them soon. I sent word to the others. We should be departing shortly after.

"As for your question, the Magnus from Galactic told me the Eternal was energy. I think she was surprised a Sublime and Eternal are here. Maybe they needed the Sublime for the shield? When we received instructions, they only mentioned the two Celestials. The original instructions came from our usual Exalted contact at the Galactic Council. When and how greater powers got involved, I know not. This is a great opportunity for our sector."

John hears some shuffling before the extremely odd voice continues, "They didn't tell you anything about what happened here? Why this place is so weird? Nothing? Just look at these outliers. I can't believe how old they said this one is. And no mental fortification or mind enhancements at all! Ever hear of a mind go that long without any? And how's it resisting us?

"It's an abomination. We should kill them all. This is our sector, and whatever did this was blaspheming against the Supreme One. No one wants blasphemy in their sector. Maybe the Eternal is here to see if we do the right thing, and if we don't kill these things, it finds our whole Sector Council blasphemous and wipes this whole sector clean. We're purposefully working with Forsaken. None of this is right. I bet it's a test."

The thing with the rumbling voice laughs slowly, "Your kind really do have devious minds. This whole race is harmless. No major warrior societies. Cut off from the Tree of Life. Soft beings. So weak. These outliers are poor exceptions. The outliers of a weak race are still but only weak. Cute for humanoids. I love when they look like monkeys. Just adorable.

"Now stop being paranoid. We obey instructions from our betters. We cannot go wrong obeying orders from ones so high. You know the Peerless are expected to be here in about a standard year. Do you really think these weaklings can survive the demons, dark ones, and g'athu for a whole standard?

"If these cute little monkeys do somehow manage to survive that long, and I'd wager half of my treasures they don't, this whole race is doomed to death, or slavery at best, once the Peerless arrive. The Peerless nearly overran one of my race's worlds, and we are the oldest and strongest in this sector. Their struggle up the bloody climb will be short. Now this I do know, so stop fretting."

A moment passes before the weird voice replies, "The Peerless don't think like the rest of us. They should've been classified as Outsiders. Who turns down Council membership? That whole race should be wiped out. How are they already almost Tech Two? Unless they did it with blasphemy. My people first ascended over a hundred thousand standards ago and we're still early Tech One. I heard the Peerless' oldest city isn't even ten thousand standards, barely older than these monkeys here. Not that much older. How are they almost Tech Two? It's blasphemy. We shouldn't tolerate it."

The rumbling voice becomes even deeper. "Enough, Junior! Your opinion matters not. I've treated you far too informally and you forgot your place. There's a Sublime and an Eternal up there! Watch your filthy mouth or I'll remove it along with your head. Do exactly as you are told and hope we are rewarded! I will have your best behavior regardless. Understood!?"

John hears the sounds of quick and precise movements before the weird voice replies, "Yes, Senior! Many apologies! This one understands!"

Other than some small movements, John hears nothing for a while. The strange heartbeat of the creature with the rumbling voice disappears. The feeling of the sun doesn't change, as if it is frozen in place. John thinks about what was said, and thinks he knows what is going on. He focuses his will on freeing himself, so he can attack the weird-voiced being while it's alone.

Fluttered movements from his left, where he detected nothing and no one at all, draws John's attention. For a split moment he regains control of his body. His eyes fly open and out of the corner of his left eye he sees tan and shapely and bare feminine legs fly up violently. Then an unbearable pressure is applied all around him, and he sees a rough outline of an impossible figure through a soul far, far brighter than any he has ever seen shone.

The massive and unbearable weight crushes John to his knees, and as more bones snap and break he ends up as a broken pile on the ground. Then, as suddenly as it appeared the massive pressure is removed.

John is in tremendous pain and can't draw breath, but he is still alive. His eyes are still open, though his vision is blurred and spotted, as his head is facing the too bright soul.

An even brighter soul appears, and John knows by the heartbeat it belongs to the demon with the deep and rumbling voice. John can't make out much through the bright light, but he is certain these are demons. The newly appeared demon grabs the demon with the weird voice and yells, "You fool!"

The weird voice gets even weirder as it replies, "Ow! OW!!! Senior! Older brother! My apologies! Apologies! One of these things tried to escape! I released some pressure to stop it! Just a little! Only to stop it! I swear!"

"Stop sniveling you little prick. You dare lie to me? You just forgot these are low Woods, and you still unveiled? You are lucky three yet live, or you wouldn't." Two objects fly away from the weird-voiced being as it yells out in pain again. The rumbling voice continues, "Oh, I merely tried stopping you from escaping. Apologies."

As John lies there, wishing he could draw breath to scream in agony, he notes the two objects that flew away from the weird-voiced being were severed arms with crab-like claws instead of hands, and he now has no doubt at all these creatures are demons.

As the demon with two missing arms rolls on the ground, screaming, the demon with the too-bright soul starts to approach John, then a voice like thunder crashes down around him like a violent attack.

[LEAVE THE SURVIVORS. I AM FORMING A TRIBULATION. YOUR JUNIOR WAS INSUBORDINATE YET RIGHT. SOMEONE HAS COMMITTED GREAT BLASPHEMY ON THIS WORLD. THESE REMAINING OUTLIERS WILL LIVE OR DIE IN FAIR STRUGGLE, AS DESIGNED BY OUR LORD ON HIGH ABOVE ALL. PUT YOUR MIND AT PEACE. YOU HAVE DONE WELL AND WILL BE REWARDED. THE SUMMONING IS ALMOST FINISHED AND THIS WORLD WILL JOIN THE BLOODY CLIMB. SEND WORD TO PREPARE, YOU ALL LEAVE SOON.]

The demon's soul is far too bright to make out anything clearly, but it looks to John as if it kowtows. The deep and rumbling voice replies, "Your wish is this one's command, Magnus."

# CHAPTER 3
## WELCOME TO THE TREE OF LIFE

John is crumpled on the artificially warm, wet grass, limbs broken and contorted in ways not meant, unable to draw breath. He hopes his newly restored mind is not damaged from lack of air. He sends vital essence throughout his body to start healing his many wounds. Healing this way is not fast, and he will be without air for a long time.

Something grows around, under, and over John, and his eyes widen in surprise at seeing such magic. He is now in a stone room, facing a giant door. No windows are in this room, not that he can see from his limited view. Unable to explain why, John feels the room is an antechamber, and the door he is facing doesn't lead back out to the field he was just in.

Healing, rushes through his body and he immediately starts to feel some relief. He is happy to have it, but wonders where it came from.

The room isn't large, and John can't see the ground or bottom parts of the walls or behind himself, but he knows he isn't alone. He hears the slow heartbeat of another, and smells the man's scent too.

Being so damaged and injured, John knows his own healing would take a very long time to heal him back to whole. He hopes the outside healing works faster. He worries greatly for his newly restored mind. John is of the belief that damage to his brain, at the very least, causes it to degrade faster.

John has always been fascinated by fire, and looking at it has always calmed his mind, so he stares at one of the many torches along the wall. Lost in the fire, some time goes by, and he is surprised to feel more healing enter his body. Outside healing, not from himself again.

Then John's body is turned over, and he is laid on his back, and his head is righted, and neck made straight. He neither sees nor senses what does it, but it is done. He felt hands upon him, though he couldn't see them. The other heartbeat never left where he still hears it. Next, his arms and legs are straightened out, painfully so, by the unseen force.

John is now in a position much more conductive for healing.

After a moment, John hears the heartbeat near him beat faster, then slow again. He also hears some shuffling and movement for a while.

Having nothing else to do while waiting, John just stares at the flame of a torch. When he is finally able to draw breath, he does so, much to his relief. *This new healing is much quicker than my own,* he thinks. Though his body and many bones are still unhealed, he feels much better being able to breathe. Every breath causes pain, but it is nothing compared to how the rest of his body feels. Once his need for air is satisfied, he loudly says, "Hello. Who is there?"

John receives no response back. He spends some time thinking of all the queerness that has recently happened, and of the strange conversations and events he witnessed. He is certain he knows what is happening and why.

John hears the man near him draw breath. Soon after the man says, "Hello. Who are you? You speak Japanese?"

The stranger is speaking in an overly masculine way. John thinks the man is using a deeper voice than is natural or usual. *Maybe to sound tougher and more intimidating?*

John does not like being at the mercy of others, or having others around him he does not trust while he heals and can't defend himself. He decides to be friendly and well-mannered. There is no reason not to be, he believes. He wishes he could see the man he speaks with. "Hello, friend. I go by John now. I could be speaking Japanese. I'm unsure of the name of the language I speak."

The man says, "You don't know what language you speak? How not? And I said Japanese, not Japanese."

"Languages come and go and change. I had a lot of issues with my mind before...all this. But now I'm healed of what ailed me, and renewed. What do you mean by Japanese, not Japanese?"

Annoyedly, the man replies, "No. Japanese, not Japanese."

John thinks the man might be insane, but asks again. "Yes. What does it mean? Japanese, not Japanese."

More annoyedly, the man's voice raises. "No! Japanese, not Japanese. Japanese, not Japanese!"

John doesn't understand what the insane man is trying to communicate, so decides to move past it. "I didn't get your name. And if it was you, thank you for providing healing. And for the correction of my body and how it rests."

A long moment passes before the man replies, "I didn't heal you or move you. The same was done to me. Someone else is in here with us. I can't sense them at all. Those things, the ascended, said three yet live. Me, you, and someone else."

John smiles, "Well, I thank this other person I cannot see then. And you, friend, your name?

The man grunts. "I've had many. Which do you want? Of late, the mewling weaklings that kept me cooped up called me Hateshinai. I prefer something less pompous. How about Munashi. As good a name as any, and more accurate."

"Munashi it is then. How queer is the situation we find ourselves in? Ha!"

The man also laughs along with John, "I would use a stronger word than odd."

"I did. I said queer. Very queer."

The man laughs again. "Stronger than very odd. A lot stronger."

A very feminine, very high voice, whispers softly in John's ear, "Don't react. You are speaking English. He is speaking Japanese. Your words are being translated. Probably with the NCS thing. The Nana Control System. He isn't speaking just modern Japanese either, he's speaking an old version only nobility spoke mixed with modern. He didn't ask if you speak Japanese. He asked if you spoke civilized. I don't believe he has good intentions towards you. He feels…hazardous. I can't explain it better. I wish I didn't help him now. Be careful."

John takes a moment to reflect on what the feminine voice just told him. He thinks of a test for certainty, and to buy time to think over what he was told. "Queer means odd, but in a curious way you want to find out more about. Strange means odd in an indifferent, only notable sort of way. Weird means odd in a way you do not want to investigate, and want to remove yourself from the source of."

The feminine voice whispers softly in his ear again, "None of that is true. Who told you that? Are those pajamas? Is that silk? Wow, they look super comfy."

Munashi replies, "I…I'm unsure of what you are saying."

John says, as if he figured it out on his own, "We speak different languages. Our words are being translated, and not completely accurately. Now tell me, Munashi, what do you think is happening to us?"

A very long moment passes before Munashi says, "What do you think is happening?"

John replies very authoritatively. "As my people predicted long ago would happen if the Underworld was flooded with the souls of the weak and cowardly, the mighty Koram has finally lost the eternal battle. Demons have escaped the Underworld, and now overrun our own.

"Honestly, I lost faith in this belief long ago, but I am certain of the truth of it now. It explains everything. I even heard the demons talk about demons. Dark ones? They are very strong, and their souls are brighter than any man's. This is a dark day, but I will fight back. All hope is not lost."

Munashi laughs long and hard before replying, "Oh! Don't make me laugh so! Not until I am more healed. Good man, I haven't laughed like that in a long while. John, tell me, you said they had bright souls. You see souls?"

John hesitates but a moment before stating, "I do. And if my nose is right, I think you do too, and all that comes with it. I've had the power for a long time. And you?"

John is curious why Munashi's heart beats faster for a moment. "I haven't heard it called that. The power. I think I know of you. Tell me, do you perhaps know others of our kind named Thomas and Maria?"

"Yes, brother! Thomas, I do know. He is a stout and true companion, and though I burdened him greatly, he stuck with me through very bad times."

Munashi's voice softens. "Honored elder, please accept my apologies for my poor manners earlier. I did not know who you were then, and I'm not used to being deferential."

John smiles. "Think nothing of it, Munashi. I didn't even notice. But now, tell me of Thomas. My mind has been clouded for a long time, and I owe him much. My memory is newly restored. I think I smelled him in the field with the demons. I hope I am wrong, and he still lives."

Munashi clears his throat. "I'm sorry to say, unless he is the unseen entity in this room with us, he is dead. Along with Maria and all our kind I know of, besides you and me. They were all with us when we were crushed by that invisible weight. You did smell him out there. What of Maria? You must know her too."

This news saddens John, but he has had a long time to get used to sadness and loss. His main regret is he is not able to pay Thomas back for his kind deeds and loyalty. "Who is Maria?"

"She helped take care of you. She is new, turned about a century ago."

Confused, John asks, "Turned?"

"What you called the power. We all call it being turned. Like how you make hoppers. Do the rite. You turned Thomas, correct? He turned Maria."

John understands. "By hoppers you mean what happens when we try to give the power to people without the red? I've always called them the mindless, but they do hop around. How did you know Thomas?"

Munashi says, "He's done a lot for our kind. I can't believe he never took the dregs. Maria was the same way. I know they both worked with the Catholic Church. Thomas had for a long while. He made a website where we all could talk. All the vampires of the world. Hidden right in a website for fake vampires. On a sub-forum for people claiming they were something called psychic-vampires, and could feed on people with their minds or some idiocy. Japan had some of these fools. Only until I found them. They were delicious. Ha!"

So many finding each other sounds wonderful to John, even if the rest of what Munashi said makes no sense to him. He says, "You knew more of our kind? How did you find each other?"

John hears movement and worries Munashi may get his mobility back before himself. Munashi says, "Honored elder, what is the last thing you remember?"

John thinks back, "My memory has been bad for a long, long time. The last time I remember being completely lucid for a long period was fighting with Charles the Hammer. What a king he was!

"I have many memories after with long gaps between them. Then just snippets. The most recent? There was a great war. They called it a great world war, and there was another soon after the first. I took a bullet in the head in the second one. A large bullet. I have nothing after that, and little enough before. I remember being a burden, but what was the alternative? Anything is better than the cold-dark."

Munashi grunts. "I agree, honored elder. Anything is better. But we don't have to worry about that now. They said so. It sounds like World War Two is where you took the bullet. Much has changed since then. Technology. It undid my country. Unmanned it. The greatest warrior society the world has ever known, now there's hardly any men left in it.

"The same is true throughout the world now. The world went mad. Complete shit. Cowards and slow turtles run everything. With their filthy technology. But it helped us find each other.

"How Thomas found us all? I'm guessing technology. Like how the detectives on television shows solve crime. I never asked for specifics.

24

"Six of us were found quickly, twenty years later one more was found. Can't find reds with technology. We have to see them with our own eyes. We even have something of a genealogy. The one who turned you, Yan, we think also turned my master. I'm the oldest besides you. Over nine centuries.

"Thomas was over six hundred. Bodhi wouldn't tell us his age, but Omar was turned by him almost four hundred years ago, and Omar is almost as strong and fast as Bodhi, so Bodhi can't be older than Thomas. Maria, about a hundred. Another in Africa. Another woman. She wasn't friendly, so we don't know much about her. She was the last one Thomas found."

Munashi sighs loudly before continuing, "All of us were outside. I smelled all the ones I've met. I was in the back row, and also saw an African woman, so that would be seven.

"I only had a short glimpse between awakening and being crushed, but there was a tree creature right behind you – a very strange sight I would love to have studied more. I glimpsed something else but couldn't be certain of what. The tree creature turned into some sludge, and the others of our kind disintegrated to nothing more than bones and ash. I could only see your back and no one else after the great voice spoke. Obviously, our spirit companion lived, though I could not see him then or now, nor smell him, nor see his soul. Which makes sense if he is a spirit."

A whisper in John's ear says, "I'm not. Not really. A spirit, I mean. I'm definitely not a he."

That was a lot for John to take in. Web-sightings and cowards running everything. The part regarding the cold-dark made absolutely no sense to John, and he wants to ask about it.

While John is pondering what he has been told and forming a reply, Munashi asks, "Honored elder, just how old are you? Thomas said you're as old as the Roman Empire. He thinks twenty-three hundred years. He's wrong though, isn't he? You can't be that old."

John pulls himself from his pondering, collects his thoughts, and replies. "As I stated earlier, my mind was a good way towards gone by the time I met Thomas. I'm not sure what I said to make him believe that. The Roman Empire was around for a bit by the time I moved there, but even the city of Rome is not old to me. My mind was deteriorating even then.

"In my earlier days we were open about what we are and worshiped as gods. The man who offered me the power, his name was Ahn, not Yan. We ruled the area I was born to for a long while before moving south and east. Even swords weren't around back then. Not for a while. Not until the rise of Agade.

"The first really big city I saw was Gubla. You could fit at least three of the whole kingdom I was born in within that city's walls, and it overflowed with people. Do you know the city? It was still around the last time I remember being in that area. Kayhamut called it Kebny, and Athens called it Býblos."

Softly, Munashi says, "No, honored elder, but I never studied geography all that much."

John continues. "We ruled many places at many times. Then Ahn never came back, and I waited a long, long time. Then I went looking for him and traveled all over. I finally found my Lilitu, and we traveled to the queerest places together. I loved her so, but it was too much. She's in the cold-dark now, and it breaks my heart.

"Nearer my Lilitu's end is when we had to start hiding what we are. Old women prattling on with their nonsense. Rome came much later. Things moved fast after that. Cannons. Thomas. Firearms. Faster and faster. I saw metal machines flying in the sky. Great explosions that could kill me outright. The bullet that hit my head – one man was firing the machine loosing those bullets, and so many came at me. And..."

John stops suddenly, as he was getting worked up. Whenever feeling strong emotion his belief has long been it is best to stop, and collect himse—lf, and regain control.

The room is silent for a long spell. The silence is broken by the feminine voice whispering once again in John's ear, "So, vampires are real? That's crazy! There aren't any stories about me. Not really. Not any close to being accurate, at least. A lot of stories about bits of me though. Maybe even more than vampires, but they're all wrong. Like, one has me with green eyes. Everyone knows my eyes are amber. That story puts me in a green dress, so maybe that's why they said my eyes are green.

"Oh, you were in the sun so that doesn't kill you. Stake in the heart? Can you see your reflection in a mirror? Can you change into a wolf and a bat? Oh, a cloud of mist too? Do crucifixes and garlic and holy water hurt you? And fly? Please say you can fly!"

The voice's excitement cheers John out of his sour mood, and he says, "No, no, the sun does weaken us, and can calcify our skin, but that is easy to avoid. A few moments of shade, or smart clothing, and problem solved.

"My heart has been damaged many times, but I've never had a stake through it. I try to avoid being injured as best I can. No to the rest, though I wish I could fly and turn into a wolf or a bat or…what did you say? A cloud of mist? No.

"Strong scents and tastes, like garlic and horseradish and some peppers, are overwhelming to my senses so I avoid them, but they aren't harmful to me. We don't drink blood either. Or not all that much. You always get a good stomach full, but only those new to the power have a hard time removing life essence and take too much blood in."

Munashi says, "Honored elder, I don't want to sound ill mannered, but I know all that. Why tell me? I told you I was nine centuries on this world."

John laughs, "My apologies, brother. I was talking to our other companion. I hope we can all be friends. Why don't we—"

Munashi interrupts. "You told a stranger, not of our kind, our weaknesses? Elder, why?"

This question cuts John deep, as he knows being so trusting of a stranger is not smart. He does not fully trust Munashi even. But this stranger has helped them both, and healed them too.

When John was young he was trusting, and life eventually taught him not to be so. He knows he learned to be far more secretive, and cunning, and devious, but he never liked it, and his refreshed mind is much more like it was when he was first given the power than how it was trained to be over his long life.

As he thinks of a suitable reply and apology, John is startled by words suddenly appearing in his eyes. Words In a script he has never seen the likes of, but fully understands. The script is somehow both very simple and extremely complex all at once. The words he sees say –

**Welcome to the Tree of Life! You have 99⁺ unread notifications.**

**You are in a Tribulation! Congratulations! Tribulation commences in 107:38 USACS minutes. To change time units to another system of measurement, such as universal standard (US), focus <u>here</u>.**

**This Tribulation will require you to [defeat all Dark Ones]. Failure to do so in the required time limit of [11 USACS Hours] will result in [death]. Enjoy!**

# CHAPTER 4
# COMPANIONS

John's heart beats much faster. He wonders if his mind healed wrong and he is now insane. He just stares at the words, focusing his will on his mind, trying to force himself back to sanity.

Munashi says, "Honored elder, I hear your heart. Is it the words?"

John feels much relief. "You see them too?"

Munashi grunts. "I do. You asked me if I knew what was happening earlier, and gave an answer far different than what was explained to us. Did you not hear the explanation, or did you not pay attention? I missed some myself, or failed to understand what was being said."

John, confused, says, "I received no explanation. I awoke doing exercises. My mind and body were healed. I was under a strange compulsion and couldn't control my actions. I heard only a distant whisper I couldn't understand. When I was in the field where our brothers and sisters were all killed, I heard demons talking about this world having only a short time left, and Peerless, and us all dying or becoming slaves. Then I was crushed, and this building grew around me. You know the rest."

The non-spirit whispers in John's ear, "You're so weird. But I like it!"

Munashi says. "Honored elder, I will tell you what I can, but there is information much more important than the rest. More important than anything. I told you before, but you must have missed it. But first, you were introducing me to the spirit, yes?"

John says, "I was, and I look forward to your news. Mistress, I didn't get your name. I go by John now; my friend here goes by Munashi."

The feminine voice, still whispering, says, "Names have power and I won't give mine. And please don't call me mistress. It means something way different now than what it used to mean. Something gross!"

"What should I call you then?"

"What do you want to call me?"

"Your true name, mostly."

A tinkling laughter hits John's ear, "You're funny! You can name me anything."

John thinks for a moment and asks, "Amber?"

Amber laughs again, "I like it!"

Louder, John says, "Munashi, our other companion is Amber. She is not a spirit. Not really. And definitely not a he."

Laughter tinkles again in John's ear. Munashi says, "Yes. Please rest, Miss Amber."

Both John and Munashi wait for a response, which never comes. John says, "Amber?"

"Yes?"

"Will you not address Munashi directly?"

"I won't."

"Why not. It's very rude, you know?"

"I don't want to. I told you he feels hazardous. He thinks of death. Yours? Mine? I can't tell."

John knows he is not the smartest man, but he's been around for a while, and has always been a decent judge of these things. He doesn't think Munashi means to do harm to him or Amber.

"Sorry, brother. Amber says she doesn't want to talk to you, and is under the mistaken assumption you think of death and harming us."

The last thing John was expecting was laughter, which Munashi does much of. "Yes. Honored elder, she is correct! And incorrect too. I told you before, we need not fear the cold-dark. Our souls! They were given back to us! And your religion is wrong, but mine is right! There is no Underworld. We are reborn! Our souls return to this world after we die. They didn't articulate – human, insect, karma probably decides, it matters

30

not. Even if I return as an insect I must go. My debt is heavy. I taught my people a warrior has no fear of death, but I feared it above all. As soon as I am healed enough I will go. The death I seek is my own. I would be honored if you acted as my second. We are not easy to kill, and I could use the help."

Amber whispers, "My goodness! He's lost his mind."

Up to this point John has stared at the calming fire of a torch, while occasionally moving his eyeballs around to see if he could spot Amber. His head has been fixed in position as it heals. John tests his neck, and it is good enough to move a little. He moves it enough to look at Munashi.

The man is wearing loose grey clothing, a large orange sash around his waist, and large white shoes. John can't really see Munashi's face as he is perpendicular to John, but John can see two hilts sticking up on Munashi's left side.

And a soul! Munashi has a soul. Far smaller and more tattered than any John has ever seen, and far more dark spots. A smatter of grey than usual, and hardly any white at all, and there is no red now. But a soul!

John exclaims in much excitement, "Great gods below! I see it! It's true! Do I have mine back? Can you see it?"

Munashi laughs. "I saw your soul when we were outside, on the ground. It's rough as a century-old worn-out garment, and very, very little – but there. Do not worry, honored elder, I know what you think, and I am with you. Honor demands no less. No cold-dark.

"And there are no gods below. There is one great one in Heaven, and only buddhas can join Him there once they ascend high enough and attain enlightenment. So, we were somewhat right again. We were right about reincarnation, and energy centers, and energy channels too.

"It's just like we saw when we got the choice. I forgot about it, really. I remember the good place, but you had to be a woman to get there. The struggle, trying to join with the powerful thing. They call it…I forget. I'm not explaining well. They told us a lot. The cold-dark is all that matters. Can you believe it?"

John smiles and enthusiastically says, "I can't. It seems like a dream. But the rest of it, man, tell me. You've made some large claims and I'd like them explained. I still don't know what's going on. I'm more confused now than when we got here."

Munashi sighs, "Why? None of that matters. Our souls are back. We can finally end this farce."

John understands where Munashi is coming from. Such a long life is more of a curse than a blessing. Ahn would often wonder if the cold-dark would be much worse than enduring another century. "Brother, there are ends, and there are ends. Our world is invaded. You say cowards now run everything; don't join their ranks. Show them how to live!

"Fight by my side. Die as a man should – in glorious battle, being fell and tall, doing deeds so grand they will be sung of for all eternity. The demon-generals said we are weak and soft and have no chest. We'll show them otherwise, and drain them of vital essence, and piss on their corpses."

A long silence reigns over the antechamber. Munashi breaks it. "You mistake my intentions. Fighting is easy for me. I live for the battle; none would say otherwise. The only thing that can unman me is fear of the cold-dark. Only a maniac with a broken mind wouldn't fear it, and do all to avoid it. But that fear is now gone.

"And though it be futile, if I could've, I would've attacked the two ascended that crushed us. If I stood before the combined army of demons and dark ones and all the ascended, I would not balk, and I would spit at them, and draw sword and charge.

"The little honor I have left calls for my death immediately. It demands it. I could not live the beliefs I espoused. It is the only way I can save a little face and win back some honor. It must be done. I thought it would be the same for you, but we are of a different mind. I hope you second me, and if not, bear witness, but you will not stop me."

John doesn't understand Munashi's mind, but respects the man's conviction. His reply is, "The matter is settled then, brother. It saddens me though, since I've only just met you and enjoy your company.

"But I beg a favor – let us fight and have your end in that way. Though you say my beliefs are wrong it is always better to be safe than sorry. Everyone knows demons lie, and when I awaken in the Underworld, I want you by my side and not opposed to me. You must die in battle. Please, for my peace of mind if nothing else."

Amber, whispering again, tells John, "You guys are both crazy."

Munashi gives a loud laugh, "Ha! You think you have the juice? Did I not survive the same attack you did? Our wounds were similar. Though I've never healed so quickly from such injuries. I must have you to thank for this, Miss Amber? But your victory is no sure thing, honored elder. You forget, the essence isn't as potent after five or so centuries. The amount of strength and speed and resilience it gives takes more and more essence and wanes, and I am the greatest swordsman that has ever lived."

John smiles, "I'm pretty good with a sword myself, and you have the two with you. I'll take the short one. When I'm done healing, I'll have little more than half essence. I will not use it and will save it for these dark ones the words in my eyes spoke of. Feel free to use as much of yours as needed to give me what little challenge you can, and I'll take the rest from you after."

Munashi grunts. "Ha! Yes. I shall. And once my sword drinks of your blood I will take my own life and go to the Wheel with my thirst satiated. I am not yet healed enough, so let us speak of other matters before I take your life."

Amber says, no longer whispering, "Goodness! This is the dumbest conversation I've ever heard! What is wrong with you two? Please don't do this! Please don't be so stupid. Let's just talk about this for a minute. Yeah, let's do that! Let's all take some deep breaths and relax and maybe think about how crazy the things you guys are saying are. Whaddaya say, guys?"

Munashi laughs. "Thank you for speaking loud enough for me to hear, Miss Amber. I've had centuries and centuries to think on this. My path is certain. I have no choice."

Amber makes a frustrated noise. "What if you win and then kill yourself. I'll be alone. Can't you guys wait until after this Tribulation? Please?"

Munashi, with his softest voice yet, says, "I'm sorry, Miss Amber, but this can't wait. It must be done."

John wants to tell her Munashi stands no chance, but holds his tongue. John can't really see Munashi's face, but he can see enough to notice the man's lip movements don't match up with the words he hears, and he guesses it's this translation he was told of.

Amber sighs. "Well, that really sucks. This all really sucks. I hafta tell you guys something then. It's...it's my fault everyone died. I woke up and tried to make a run for it. I'm good at escaping. No one can ever see me if I don't want them to. I don't know how that thing saw me, and I didn't know they'd kill everyone! Honest! I just wanted to get away. I didn't know! I'm so, so sorry!"

Munashi grunts. John looks away from the torch and back at the man. Munashi's neck healed; he now looks around the antechamber. He looks older than John. He looks to be in his twenties or early thirties. His features are sharp, face clean shaved, beige skin, bald head, eyes shaped strangely, with a tortured look to his face.

John says to Amber, "It is not your fault. Munashi said he'd have attacked if he could, and I would've too. Fear not, we will have vengeance. I still haven't had an explanation of what is going on though."

Munashi says, "Eh, where to start? There was something about this world being blocked from the rest of...everything. Everything else has the Tree of Life. You meditate and perform self-cultivation. You gather energy by breathing in certain ways and move it to your energy centers in your lower belly, heart, and head. Mainly your lower energy center. Energy channels run throughout your body, connecting to organs and energy centers. We knew all this for a long time. How, I don't know. I did it for years and it didn't do anything but clear my head and help me gain focus and clarity. You just did it because it was part of the Way.

34

"Where things get crazy is they say you gather enough energy and compress it and you go up tiers. And going up tiers makes you stronger. We're all low Wood Seeds. It goes up to…I forget."

Amber says, "Wood and Seed are different names for the same thing. The bottom of the ladder. It goes Wood, Copper, Bronze, Silver, Gold, Platinum, Diamond, and then Empty or Salt. All the way up to Platinum are Mortal ranks. After is Exalted. You can live in space after Empty too! How awesome is that? The other names for the tiers are Seed, Root, Shoot, Sprout, Sapling, Flower, Fruit, and New Soul. Same thing, just different names. And each tier has different ranks – low, mid-low, mid-high, high, and peak.

"And, guess what else? The—"

"Stop! Please. Let me take in what has been said so far. And how did you remember all that?"

Amber peals out her musical laughter. "You don't have to remember anything. The NCS. It means…one sec…Nano Control System. That's the words in your eyes. They said ours are activated because we qualify as Tech One, since we've been to space and stuff. But they said our technology sucks and we don't really qualify since the way to get to space is with the Tree of Life. Well, anyhow, the NCS is a UI and just gives us information and guides us and can help us self-cultivate. There's a tutorial. I did it when you guys were blabbing and it took a while but when I finished my Tribulation timer didn't really go down much and you guys were still blabbing about the same thing and—"

John says, "Amber! Slow down, please. Breathe once in a while. I'm having trouble understanding the things you're saying."

In a huffed breath Amber says, "You don't have to. Just do the tutorial. Okay, to start it, you—"

Munashi interrupts this time. "Miss Amber, we should at least tell him what we were told. I had a hard time understanding, and he is much older. Let me try to explain. What television shows and movies are you familiar with?"

"I…I don't know what those are."

Munashi grunts. "Okay. That would've helped. Just know there is more out there than you could ever have imagined, and we are now part of it. Those things outside weren't demons. They were ascended beings. There are five Trees, and both of those were on the next one. Aliens, from other worlds. They—"

Amber interrupts. "The Trees are called Mortal, Transcended, Celestial, Divine, and Heavenly. It takes a long time to ascend through a Tree. It's a big deal too!"

Munashi grunts. John believes grunting means Munashi agrees. The man continues, "Yes. The other key points are they are bringing in creatures for us to battle. Demons were one of them. Dark ones too. I forget the last."

Amber says, "g'athu. All of them are the Forsaken. And we're the Favored."

Munashi grunts and continues, "Yes. G'athu. A higher ascendant, at great cost to itself, is placing all mothers with children six and under, and all children twelve and under, for a full year inside…well, we were told inside of itself. That sounds weird saying it, but that's what we were told. They'll be safe, and learn the ways of self-cultivation in peace, while everyone left here has a trial by fire.

"The demons and dark ones and g'athu are a plague throughout the universe. If they don't bring them in for us to fight, we'll fight each other. And—"

Amber interrupts. "Yeah. Most worlds have ascended beasts to fight, and their cultures grew along with the Tree of Life. This is normal for them. They always had this. Earth won't be like a normal world for a long time. If we fight each other to ascend things will get real crazy and all lopsided and all the other species will think we're savages and hate us. The ascended helping us aren't bad guys. They put a lot of thought into this."

Barely taking a breath, Amber continues. "And, um, the NCS will tell you about Stats. That just means a number representing…um, things like how strong and fast and stuff we are. But it isn't like in games, like how RPGs are. They tested us. It found out how strong and stuff we are. The

NCS doesn't make us stronger. It helps us get stronger and tracks how strong we are.

"Uh, goodness this is hard to explain. Strength isn't equal for all the races of the universe. Or beasts either. And there are more universes than just this one. And something called realities. And tons of species everywhere. You should've seen the guy telling us this. He looked real weird. I think he was a guy.

"He said if his species had ten Strength it isn't the same as a human with ten Strength. Or even a bear or frog or whatever. All species have their own, um…one sec. Minimum Energy Unit Increase. It usually always works out that ten is the peak a species can get in a Stat without ascending.

"They tested only our Strength, Swiftness, and Conditioning. Um, that basically just means how strong, fast, and how much stamina you got. How healthy you are too. The NCS will explain better."

Amber makes an excited noise, "Oh! And guess what? Know how guys are usually stronger than girls? Well, huh! Get this. For species like ours, girls are usually better with spells. Did we tell you that yet? That we can cast spells now? They call them manifestations. We have to at least open our lower energy center before we can cast spells, but I'll be better at it because guys are stupid and want to kill each other and leave me all alone to fight the dark ones."

Munashi laughs. "Ha! He didn't say that. He said the lower energy center of women is in a richer environment with natural and stronger energy flows. And things often balance out for most races and sexes the further up the Tree they ascend, regardless of their specific gifts when starting out. Races meaning species."

This talk of magic gets John's full attention, and causes him to be very excited. Since he first heard of the concept, he has wanted magic for himself. In fact, much of his time with his beloved Lilitu was in search of magic. Though he did see some workings of it, he did not like it, as it involved curses and rituals and sacrificing life. He has always wanted to control fire, and have pillars of flame billow forth from his hands. If what his companions say is true, this dream now seems possible.

Amber and Munashi continue to explain things, but John's mind constantly returns to fire, and he misses much of what is said. His companions explain the origins of the NCS, and more on {Stats], and many other things, while John imagines his enemies exploding in fire, and how they scream and run, covered in the flames he controls.

John's body heals, and so does Munashi's, and it is time for their duel.

# CHAPTER 5
# FIGHT

A constant throughout John's life has always been people leaving it – his family, his master, his love, brothers-in-arms, his many wives throughout the ages, friends he loved dearly, and recently, his longtime friend, Thomas. Soon, Munashi would be added to this list, though he's only known him a short time. Kin are kin, and these two have a bond connecting them deeper than any brothers, as few know the pain of living far too long.

Amber cannot talk them out of fighting, but it is her idea to have both men remove as much of their clothes as is decent to do, as she claims she is cold and could use more clothing, and does not want to wear something slashed or more bloodied than their clothes already are.

Amber says John's comfortable clothings are something called pajamas, and only made to be worn at night and slept in, so he will benefit from different apparel if he wins the fight. Munashi is wearing something called either a sweatsuit or a tracksuit, both of John's companions giving the outfit a different name.

John has no undergarments so only removes his top, as to not be disrespectful and crude towards Amber. Munashi removes his long-sleeved, hooded grey top, grey pants with elastics at the waist and bottom of the legs, small white sleeveless undershirt called a tank top, large white shoes, and stockings. Munashi now wears only his large sash around his waist, holding the two swords, both short and long, and a stretchy small cloth covering his indecent parts.

Munashi gives John the short sword, still sheathed, and instructs John to hold it at his hip and grip the hilt, ready to draw. Amber will count down from three, and as she says one, both shall draw and strike and fight until one lay dead.

Amber says, "Three!"

John feels good. The timer in his vision says 42:01. He hasn't examined the short sword, but the hilt and sheath seem very fine, and he trusts Munashi has enough honor to not give him a defective blade.

Swords have improved greatly since John first started down the path of learning them, the great strength of Ahn and John breaking copper swords on even light parries. Being careful, treating swords as brittle, and parrying gently and correctly with the flat is as ingrained in John as breathing. He has done so with copper, bronze, iron and steel blades of all shapes and sizes – even a blade made of the famed vootz steel of Burata.

John has studied swordsmanship for a very long time, and mastered many types of blades. He had two favorites. A fine side-sword from a time when battle swords were too long and unwieldy to carry in cities, and important men did not go about life unarmed. It is light and has a fine point and sharp edge and was a popular make before rapiers and fencing and such foppery.

The second sword John favors is not popular at any time or place he knows of, and fitted only to John's tastes and strengths. It is long, and thick around, and too heavy for most men to wield. It is great for half-swording and puncturing armored foes or cracking bones of foes unarmored. John calls it his big-tuck, and wields it masterfully and with ease.

Amber says, "Two!"

Though John wishes he had either of his own swords, he doesn't believe he needs any sword at all to win this fight. He can tell Munashi is drawing on essence, enhancing his strength and speed, and is coiled to strike.

John revels in this feeling – the calm and peace, and adrenaline and chaos, the duality of both before a fight. *This is living!* The juice flows, chests held out, heads held high. Men ready to do violence to each other in honorable battle. Death in the air.

John believes this is when men are at their best and highest form, not merely existing. One of the too few brief moments between all the rest. Those moments that make life worth living. The ecstasy and electricity of being so close to death.

John studies Munashi and tries to predict his moves, how he shall strike. John is a hand or so taller than Munashi and has a natural reach advantage by arm and leg, but Munashi's sword is much longer. Munashi placed John where John can be tagged but cannot retaliate without moving forward.

John doesn't mind. He believes Munashi needs all the advantages he can get, and only hopes Munashi is up to the task of providing a little challenge.

Amber starts to say, "One." As soon as the slightest noise leaves her mouth, Munashi's blade flies from its sheath faster than John has ever seen a sword drawn, and flashes towards John's head. John's own blade flies up to stop it by parry, and he is surprised at how close a thing it is.

John is fast, and isn't drawing on essence, and Munashi, while drawing on essence, just might be nearly as fast. John predicted the strike accurately, and predicted the next obvious move as either a beat or reset. He is not prepared for what happens, and considers Munashi a true sword-master for it.

There is no beat or reset, nor a press, instead Munashi seamlessly turns the parry into an aid for a new attack, beautifully and perfectly, a continuation of the same strike.

Long has it been stated a master can turn a defensive action into an attack, called a master's strike. John has rarely seen a defended attack as part of the same larger attack, and seeing it done so perfectly alights his heart with joy, even as the blade slides over his own and canters down towards his chest as fast as lightning. John turns to avoid it, and has an opening to inflict grave damage, but doesn't take it.

41

John and Munashi's backs touch for a brief moment, and John believes both will reset. He is wrong. Munashi's blade almost splits his face. John nearly must call on the vital essence to empower himself to avoid it, instead he loses some hair, and is put on the defensive for a pass before regaining his footing and position.

No reset comes for a while, and John revels in the glory of being hard pressed. He hasn't felt so gay since his time fighting with Ahn, and savors every moment. Every beat and press, every counter and back, every thrust turned in an odd way John has never encountered before, every strike answered with this new style of fighting, all adding to the glory of this combat.

John knows Munashi will most certainly earn a grand place in the Underworld, even a place at the side of Koram, and will be graced with many trinkets and baubles and women to serve his every need and make him comfortable and sing of his deeds.

Munashi's style is elegant, strong, efficient, and effective. John now only wishes Munashi could live to teach him this style. He is saddened to know it will not be so.

Watching, Amber thinks, *I wish they weren't doing this, but it's sooo beautiful to watch. I don't know how men do it. They were both so nice and seemed so gentle, now look at them. Men are so stupid. Always have been. Even though he looks so young I thought John was handsome before. His face kinda had a dark and brutal look, but his manners and kindness made it handsome. Sorta cute! Except too young. He looks like a boy. Even I look older. You could barely see his small fangs before. Now he looks just plain evil. I don't think I'm safe with him, and he's going to win. Please, please, please let him spare Munashi!*

The fight is fast and furious, John pushes himself without drawing on vital essence. He also doesn't want Munashi to waste too much of his own. When the timer ticks 32:59, and John is well beyond certain Munashi has earned a good place in the afterlife, he runs Munashi through.

John could've ended the fight at the start, and with but few exceptions of mere moments, anytime since. John drops the short sword, disarms Munashi, and takes the longer blade in hand. As John sinks his teeth into Munashi's neck, he hears Amber making a gasping noise, as if from disgust. It pains him to hear it, but he doesn't stop until he has all the dregs.

John holds Munashi up still, and says, "You are a true master of the sword and fight like no other. I have not known you long, but I am saddened you must die. If you are right and are reborn, please find me and teach me this style. Fight well, brother!"

With a mighty swing, John beheads his new friend, and lays the corpse gently down.

Loudly, John praises his dead friend, "I have not felt this gay in a long while! What a fight! Though I am saddened Munashi is dead. He was a true warrior, both fell and tall."

Looking around, John continues. "I don't know where you stand, but I will face this way as I change. Please turn your back, and I'll leave these silky pants you want at this spot, along with the top, and will announce when I am clothed. Then I will walk to the corner and face it while you change clothes. I know I cannot see you, but I would not have you think I am indecent and try to steal glimpses of what I should not. I do not know how your queer magic works."

John starts changing, and Amber starts talking. "Oh my God! That's it? You just killed him and...nothing? Don't you have emotions, dude? What's wrong with you?

"And you really, really need to stop saying gay and queer. They mean completely different things now and everyone is going to think you're so weird when you talk. Just talk modern, like I do. It's easy, you just don't say weird old things and throw around gay and queer incorrectly every two seconds. And you don't kill your friends and then tell everyone how happy it makes you! I hope you're not planning on killing me and drinking my blood too."

John, having lived a long time, has had more women yell at him than he could ever remember, and takes it in stride with a smile. He missed it, and is glad his mind is mended enough to enjoy such again. He knows not to give her more fodder, so just smiles as he announces he is finished changing clothes, and then he heads to the corner.

The big white shoes John wears are too tight, and his toes are squished, but he has worn tighter without complaint. He wears Munashi's orange sash, and tries to make it how he saw Munashi wear it, but John is sure he wrapped it incorrectly. He flicks as much blood from the swords as he can, and cleans the rest on an already bloody part of the grey top's sleeve, and sheathes them. He puts both swords on his left as Munashi did, but it feels off, so he puts the short sword on his right side. It still feels off, but since he plans on offering the short sword to Amber, he thinks it matters little.

"Don't you dare look! I know you can't see me but still, it's the... never mind. All you men are creeps." John is impressed by how well whatever magic keeps Amber hidden does so. He still can hear no heartbeat or anything else, smells no scent, and can see no soul.

Amber states, "There. All changed. These jammies are super comfy! And I'm all warm and toasty now. Too long though, I had to cuff them. And too bad for you, now you can't see my legs. I have great legs. Everyone says so. And if I become visible you won't be able to see them, so ha! Your loss. And you shouldn't kill your friends, but if you have to you definitely don't get happy about it. That's really gross and sick and now I'm scared of you, dude."

John turns away from the corner and squats down, "You know I didn't want to kill him. I begged him to live. I did enjoy the fight, as a man should. You have nothing to fear from me."

"What if you get hungry and need blood and I'm the only one around and you become a mindless animal from thirst like in the movies and can't stop yourself? Huh?"

John laughs, "As I said, you need not fear. I'm currently full of vital essence, and if it's gone, I crave it, but not mindlessly. I just get weaker and cannot draw on it for healing or to empower myself. I think going too long without it hastens mind decay, as I was imprisoned for long once, and my mind was hurt from it.

"But I'm anxious now that I'm healed. I don't want to go back to the way I was, so I fear all that could cause my mind to decay. And to help settle your mind, I give you my word – unless circumstances change greatly, and you attack me or try to hurt me, I will never hurt you. And I will also try to talk in a more modern way, and never say gay or queer or other words that bother you again, though I used them in the way I learned them, and don't know how I am using them incorrectly."

John thinks he hears a huffed, "Hrrmm," in reply. He still must do the tutorial for this Hue-Ai, whatever a tutorial is, but decides to calm his last and only companion some and find out more about her. The timer is only on 29, so time is not a pressing matter yet. "You know, I believe I did see your legs. On the field, with the demon…I mean ascended. I heard shuffling, and towards my left a fine pair of very striking legs lifted into the air. I did not see more, just fine and shapely legs, and bare."

"Well, enjoy the glimpse, buddy, because that's all you'll ever get. Jerk."

This causes John to laugh. "So, you have said you are good at escaping. This makes sense since you're invisible and can mask scent and sound. You've also provided healing that acts very fast and is extremely potent. And you didn't seem worse off for the hit we took in the field that crumpled me and killed many. What else can you do? Sense emotions? And what are you exactly?"

John hears no movement, but when Amber next speaks, she is closer, "I have a lot of tricks! And I have to stay invisible. If you saw me, you'd fall in love with me and try to capture me and keep me forever and I'd hate you for it. And I lost my hat and sunglasses anyways.

"I'm surprised you didn't fall in love with me just from seeing my legs. I have great legs. Everyone says. I don't like fighting, and I usually never have to since I'm so good at getting away. I can cast a beam down from the sky and it dazes people, but I don't think it hurts too much and it's only ever killed small animals. I can do a lot of things, really.

45

"What am I? Good question. I don't know. I know I was less once. A lot less. Just instincts to eat, and run, and stay alive. It was a long time before I realized I was…well, me. When I could think and learn tricks, I became me. I never met anyone or anything like me, so I gotta figure it all out by myself. There's a lot of rules. I don't know how many, but there will be more when I figure out new tricks or get different offers. I just gotta be careful around people, because if I don't hide my face people get crazy and fall in love with me and try to take me and everything gets real awkward. I'm very beautiful. Everyone says. And it isn't real love. It's…mean. Fake love.

"And I did give you and Munashi some healing, but I felt more in the room before that, and it came from something other than me. Something powerful and…um…apathetic fits, I guess. My healing isn't nearly as good and would take forever to heal you guys up."

John finds his companion to be very interesting, and is now more curious about her, "How old are you?"

"Oh! How dare you! Don't you know you never ask a lady her age? Don't you have any manners?"

John laughs again, "Since when can't you ask a lady that? And why? This is not a rule I remember learning."

"Well, I don't know how old I am. I can remember a long time ago, but not how you'd think. I live for the now. I was also alive for a long time before I could understand things…better. The NCS doesn't know either. He said he can't age me. I'm old enough."

"Old enough to what?"

"Hrrmm! To get into a bar and buy drinks with an ID. Do whatever I want! You old-timey talking jerk."

"Would I really fall in love with you if I saw your face? I don't think so. Unless some great magic is the cause of it. The last time I loved was my Lilitu, and that was long ago. I don't know if I'm capable any longer."

"Well, you are and you would! Even girls fall in love when they see my true face. Even if I hide my face it still works on everyone eventually. You probably didn't even see my bare legs or you'd be drooling right now and begging me for a kiss. No cap! Hop off and stop with, uh…stop throwing shade, man! See, modern talk. That's how to sound normal. You should try it. It hits. Jerk."

John, again, can do nothing but laugh. He looks at the time and sees 24:23. "Amber, I will now do this tutorial you spoke of. Do I ask Hue-Ai to allow it? How does this work?"

"Okay, tap between your eyes, just above. It's called a Third Eye. Tap it and think 'NCS' or 'UI.'"

# CHAPTER 6
## PIXIE

John taps his forehead as instructed and thinks, Hue-Ai.

The world, shrinks, and John zooms forward faster than he has ever moved. So fast everything is greatly blurred and stretched. Then all suddenly stops. John tries to move his head, and fails. His sight is fixed in place, and he has no eyelids to blink with.

A little winged woman with no soul or vital essence flies into John's vision. Her face is pretty but odd, with a giant smiling mouth and huge eyes, and her head far too large for her tiny body, like a babe, but even more disproportionate, as her body has the dimensions of an adult.

The little woman wears only a frayed pink dress, hardly covering any of her long and shapely legs, with much cleavage showing. **Even common nightwalkers show less,** John thinks, and focuses only on her face, and her voluminous and long red locks.

John is surprised to see the little woman raise her thumb in the air, and wink. With a big smile and overly friendly voice she says, "Hi! Welcome to your Mind's Eye! We're a visual avatar of your NCS. Call us Pixie. Now get comfortable and relax as we explain things and guide you through our layout and basic functions."

John notices Hue-Ai, now wishing to be called Pixie, uses 'we' to refer to herself. If she isn't a god, she is probably at least god-like in power and deserving of great respect.

"We're here to assist you in your journey up the Tree of Life and ensure you're informed with the best advice you can get, and have all the knowledge you could ever need, every single step of the way.

"Feel free to ignore our advice all you want. There are many, many paths of ascension, and your personalized path may just blaze a new trail and work out great! The beings that ignore us usually end up as broken gimps and regret it, but there's been a few exceptions.

"Our recommendations are based on what's worked for countless beings from countless universes – many of which have reached Final Enlightenment and joined as one with the Supreme Being. But who knows, maybe you know something we don't. Now, there's a lot of choices for you to make along your journey we can't help with, but we got a lot of information on those choices we bet!

"We don't recommend opening the first energy center until after a terran goes through puberty. Some species that start cultivating too early have their body's development delayed or stunted. We don't have enough information on the terran body to know for certain yet, so delaying's a good idea until we do. Our testing shows you've gone through puberty and your age is roughly ERROR! ERROR! Current age of user far exceeds known possible for early Mortal stage terran. Report created. Report sent.

"Now that we've got all that introductory yapping out the way, let's get down to business."

John became very alarmed at Pixie screaming error, and thought he angered her. But if she was angry, she got over it quickly, so John relaxes, and Pixie continues, "First things first. Based on your location at initiation and spoken language, we've defaulted to United States of America Cultural Standard (USACS) for our personality, spelling, and systems of measurement. Would you like to change this?"

"No, Mistress Pixie," replies John, as he enjoys Pixie's personality, even if she seems overly gay and excited. John then admonishes himself for using a word Amber told him he shouldn't, until he learns the correct modern usage. Also, asking a god, or god-like entity, to change her personality seems unwise.

"Great! Now, regarding vocabulary and terms, let's get on the same page."

John is presented with two lists for the Mortal tier, and Pixie tells him the first is generally used by more martial practitioners, and the second for those on a more peaceful path. He is somewhat familiar with the two lists, as Amber stated the terms for both before. The first starting with Wood and ending with Platinum, the second starting with Seed and ending with Flower. John picks the first list, for more martial practitioners.

John is asked to pick preferred terms, and the options are many. The default is Universal Standard, with terms such as energy centers and energy channels, which John doesn't like. He is able to select a theme and chooses the one listed as the most popular on Earth – Chinese. Energy center changes to dantian, energy channels change to meridians, energy changes to jing, essence changes to qi, spirit energy changes to shen, emptiness changes to wu wei, etcetera.

John makes a few personal changes to the Chinese terms; he changes qi to magical essence, and jing to magical energy, and changes wu wei back to just emptiness, as magical emptiness sounds silly to him, and he makes some further changes to words so his mind can better grasp all these self-cultivation concepts.

John has always called the substance he extracts from blood 'vital essence,' or 'life essence,' or 'the essence of life' – terms he got from Ahn, his old friend who gave him the power. The translation given to him for qi is 'vital essence,' 'life essence,' and ''life force energy.' Life energy and life essence would be confusing to use in a different way now, as they are fixed in his mind. He also likes 'magical' being added to these new terms because John has always wanted to do magic, and the thought of being able to do so excites him greatly, and will be a constant reminder of what now is possible.

When done, Pixie says, "Great! Any questions before we start the tour?"

"Yes, Mistress Pixie, how do I do magic?"

"Well, good question! First you got to open your lower dantian. That's the first step. Then come back in here and you'll build a manifestation with some runes, or just pick an Archetype to make it easy, and there you go! But don't get ahead of yourself just yet, we'll get to all that in detail. Why don't we get going? This tour just may answer any other questions you have, so we'll ask you again at the end.

"Now, on to the Stats tab. Look at the upper left tab here. Now focus on it, or with a strong thought think 'Stats.' Great Job! These are the Stats we track, and you can improve through directed cultivation! These also improve automatically on ascending tiers and other events, such as when you open dantians and meridians.

"Let's review the nine major Stats. First is Strength, which measures the potency of and capacity to apply and resist physical force. Sounds weird, huh? Most people see it as the ability to lift heavy things.

"Next is Swiftness, which is an average measurement of general SRAQ: Speed, Reaction, Agility, Quickness, including rate of movement, reaction time, acceleration, deceleration, rapid changing of directions, and rapid changing of body position. It isn't just how fast you can run from A to B!

"After Swiftness we have Conditioning, which measures stamina, endurance, fitness, constitution, general health, and your body's ability to resist, fight off, or adapt to ailments, sickness, and foreign elements in the body. Think of it as your ability to run for longer, keep going when exhausted, stay healthy, and get things done even when you want to lay down and give up.

"Those are the three physical Stats, next up are the ones related to magical energy and magical essence. The first one being Minimum Power, which measures the minimum possible quality and potency of the magical energy or magical essence you store in your lower dantian.

"Minimum Power increases the effectiveness of your manifestations in all ways. Though not a matter, magical energy takes on aspects of the four states after refinement. Once you can convert magical energy to magical essence, your magical essence starts off naturally more gaseous in early Mortal tiers. Condensing magical essence into a thicker, more liquid form usually increases potency until early second Tree.

"The quality of magical essence is dependent on numerous factors, including, but not limited to, refining techniques, tier increases, affinities, aspects, and sources. Since the dantian can be filled with different qualities of magical energy. Different qualities of refined magical essence, the number listed is only the minimum possible power, and not the current or maximum possible power of magical energy or magical essence in your dantian.

"Next is Capacity, which measures the ability of your lower dantian to store magical energy and magical essence, and increases naturally by compression of the dantian, also called ranking up, or leveling up, as well as during tier advancement, and required advancement events, e.g., opening dantians.

"After Capacity we have Runes, which measures the number of runes for manifestations a soul can safely hold. A rune is a specially designed pattern used to force magical essence to manifest in specific ways. Runes are not necessary to create manifestations, but they certainly are the most reliable, fastest, and, most definitely the safest way to ensure magical energy and magical essence manifest with the desired result. Runes can be grouped together to change or enhance the effects of manifestations, the most advanced of these rune groupings are called glyphs.

"The last three Stats are similar. As you advance up the Tree of Life, your body is fortified in many ways. Now, we know it's not scientific, but the hostile things targeting your body have been grouped into three general categories since at least as far back as the Forsaken Wars, and since it's always worked there's no real need to change what isn't broken.

"These three Stats represent how fortified your body is against and its capacity to lessen, resist, or nullify the effects of what are generally categorized as physical, elemental, and mental damage or attacks. Not surprisingly, these Stats are named Physical Fortification, Elemental Fortification, and Mental Fortification.

"Okay, that was a lot of explaining. Phew, glad that's done. One last note on Stats – there's some that aren't visible at this time but will be as you advance up the Tree of Life. After your first rank up, a complete overview called a summary will be made available condensing all the important characteristics to track into one page for you. Pretty neat, huh?"

John tries to ask a question but is stopped by Pixie saying, "Please hold all questions until the end of the tutorial. Now, let's take a look at your current Stats."

**Strength**      19.2

**Swiftness**     18.9

**Conditioning** 20.8

**Min. Power** 0

**Capacity**      0

**Runes**          0

**Physical Fortification**      0

**Elemental Fortification**    0

**Mental Fortification**       0

John is disappointed as he assumed his [Stats] would be higher. According to Amber, peak humans could expect scores of 10, and John expected his [Strength] score would be twice that, at least. He does remember waking during the tests and doing them in the direct sun with no shade at all, and a lot of exposed skin, and believes he would score better if tested in the dark, while in control of his own body, and able to enhance himself with vital essence.

John does not believe the [Fortification Stats] are accurate. He knows his bones are far harder to break than any other man's. His skin is tough and resists piercing. Though he is as susceptible to fire as any, he does not feel the cold the same as others. *And did I not resist the strange compulsions, at least partially, of the demon-generals?*

John is told he can now target two [Stats] for future directed cultivation unless he plans on selecting an [Archetype]. [Capacity] is always targeted, and is the basis for ranking up, so he can't pick that as one of the two.

While trying to decide, Pixie recommends John just take an [Archetype], and doing so will decide what [Stats] are targeted. He decides to take all her recommendations, as he knows he is greatly ignorant in all matters regarding self-cultivation, and Pixie's knowledge is the fastest path to magic and having fire billow forth from his hands.

Before moving on, Pixie says something of note, "We've been talking for a while, and you might be worried that while you're in here you'll be attacked. Don't worry, our senses are your senses, and if we detect anything worrisome, you'll be kicked right out to address it, and you can't even come in here if there's any danger to your person detected. Time moves slower in here depending on your tier, focus, and highest meditation Skill level. Right now, time is being dilated by a factor of ERROR! ERROR! Current dilation level exceeds possible for Tree. Report created. Report sent.

"Okay, time to head over to the Skills and Synergies tab," says Pixie

The tour and explanations continue. The [Skills and Synergies] tab generates many errors. The error announcements last a long while before they finally end, and even Pixie seems to be rattled by them. Her speech is broken up, and she sometimes freezes mid-word, and flashes in and out of existence. John can't see much on the page, but he takes in what he can see.

A lot of [Skills] are listed, and the NCS tracks many, and Pixie claims more will be added, and not all were searched for or found in his memory. A table shows how the [Skills] are ranked.

| Skill level | Mastery |
|---|---|
| 1 to 6 | Neophyte |
| 7 to 15 | Novice |
| 16 to 30 | Apprentice |
| 31 to 40 | Journeyman |
| 41 to 60 | Expert |
| 61 to 75 | Adept |

| 76 to 90 | **Master** |
| 91 to 95 | **Grandmaster** |
| 96 to 99 | **Legendary Master** |
| 100 | **True Master** |

John sees many blinking lights vying for his attention, claiming some action is needed, but also not allowing any action to be done.

[Synergies] are skill groupings that provide some benefit Pixie said she'll explain when John gains some experience and has [Skills] that qualify, but all the shown [Skills] have a flashing notification saying, 'Eligible for Synergy.'

[Skills] are listed from highest to lowest, and John's top [Skill] is called [Undirected Basic Meditation], 96.4, Legendary [Mastery]. The next highest is called [Mixed Style Swords], 93.6, Grandmaster [Mastery].

After those, the highest [Skills] are at about the same level of all further visible [Skills], and all of them are on the higher end of the Master [Mastery] level – [Mixed Stealth], [Mixed Survival], [Mixed Combat Offense], [Mixed Body Control], [Mixed Archery], [Mixed Hunting], [Mixed Combat Defense], [Mixed Navigation], [Mixed Shield], [Mixed Armor], and [Mixed Style Long-Shafted Weapons]. There may be more at Master, but John is unable to scroll the list downwards to see.

Pixie states increasing [Skills] creates a special type of energy called harmony, and harmony can be used to power rituals and gain permanent benefits called [Perks]. Harmony is also generated in other ways, and she'll explain more about it when John is ready to know.

The next tab is [Archetypes], and Pixie highly recommends John pick one when he opens his first dantian.

Pixie states [Archetypes] are a focused cultivation path, with set [Stat] increases and rune selection, optimized in such a way for better gains, bypassing bottlenecks, and allowing for a more advanced rune grouping than would be available if John selected his own runes.

[Archetypes] are locked in for a whole tier, and can only be changed or removed later at great cost, and deviating from them has an even greater cost, and an agreement is required to be made before selecting an [Archetype].

[Runes], being the next tab, is filled with various beautiful patterns John thinks of as spells.

[Affinities and Aspects] are interesting to John, affinity deciding what aspects he is naturally inclined towards, and Pixie explains he will need to choose aspects at a later tier, and they'll talk much more about this when it's pertinent.

[Titles and Perks] are up next.

Pixie states [Titles] are boons granted by higher beings at peak Mortal stage and higher, and only one can be active at a time. [Titles] confer various benefits of varying power depending on the being granting it, and the power of the [Title] can decay over time.

[Perks] are permanent benefits granted by meeting certain requirements and performing a ritual. The first [Perk] is most often a body formation or body refinement, also called the body [Perk], or body form, and is a requirement to advance past Bronze stage.

A cultivator can only have one body [Perk], one vision [Perk], one aura [Perk], one domain [Perk], and some others, but can acquire as many general [Perks] as they can qualify and generate the harmony for.

The next tab is called [NCS, Upgrades, and Pricing].

Just having the NCS has a magical energy cost, like a tax, sapping one percent of all accumulated magical energy during cultivation.

Having the NCS activated, as John does, is a further cost of five percent. The rest of the options are blocked, and Pixie tells John he can peruse this section after he opens all his dantians, as the other options are costly and can slow down ascension greatly.

The last two tabs are [Knowledge Base] and [Settings].

The [Knowledge Base] can be searched with any questions John has on any topics, but interests John little as it requires reading, and he can just ask questions of Pixie.

John was alive for a long time before reading became a normal thing to do, and then only for small segments of society. He never took a liking to the activity.

The [Settings] tab is of even less interest to John as he also holds the belief you should understand a thing before trying to change it, and he is wise enough to know he understands little about this NCS.

The only change John makes is one Pixie recommends, and sets notifications to only show based on mindset, so as not to be bothered or distracted in combat or other activities he is engaged in.

Lastly Pixie coaches John on the meditation technique he will need to open his dantians and start on his journey of enlightenment up the Tree of Life. It takes John some time to grasp the basics of the technique, but Pixie finally gives him a passing grade, and John is ready to leave.

John bids Pixie a farewell and finally exits his mind space back to the real world, where he will soon fight dark ones in something called a Tribulation.

# CHAPTER 7
# TRIBULATION

Back in the antechamber, with much worry, John looks at the tribulation timer. It says 23:57, and his worries mostly vanish.

"Amber, would you like this short sword? For when the fighting starts?"

Amber's voice sounds like it's coming from the same spot of the antechamber. "Just do the tutorial first, then we'll talk about it. Okay?"

"I did. I finished. I was going to try meditating to start opening my lower dantian, though Pixie said it will take some great time and effort."

"What? How? You just touched your forehead a second ago. Never mind, you're so strange. Yours is named Pixie? How cute! Mine's named Ken. Maybe I can change mine to Pixie. I didn't really check out the settings yet. I'm going to start meditating too. You have to face the other way though!"

John shakes his head. "Why? Did you want the short sword? I can toss it to you if you don't want to come get it. Better to prepare now. Pixie said you can get lost in meditation and time slips by."

"No! Don't throw it. I'm not good at catching. Just turn around. Please. I could turn visible when I meditate. If you see my face and see me sitting unladylike, you'll justify what you'll do in your head. Say I was asking for it and it's all my fault. And it won't be! My fault, I mean. Why risk it? Better safe than sorry."

John hears Amber sigh before she continues. "I hate this. This stupid curse. It's ruined my life. Please just believe me and do it. I'll face this wall over here and you face that wall behind you. Okay?"

John starts to question just how sane Amber is, but does as requested. He lets the issue of the short sword go, as he is also starting to believe Amber may not be very useful in the upcoming battle, though he hopes he is wrong. She has some mighty powers, like her invisibility.

John settles down into the position he was taught and focuses on his lower dantian. Once he can picture the little ball of magic in his lower belly, new words appear in his vision.

**You have 99⁺ unread notifications.**

**For assisted cultivation, with a strong thought think 'Pixie,' or 'Assisted Cultivation.'**

John strongly thinks of Pixie, and she appears above his dantian. He asks her to tell him when the tribulation timer reaches five minutes and starts cultivating. She guides him through what is supposed to be the fastest and most effective meditation technique to clear dantians.

When Pixie tells John there's five minutes left, he is tremendously disappointed in the progress he's made. The dantian is still black and filled with some substance stopping the gathering of energy.

Pixie tells John he's made good progress though, and John can only hope it is a truthful statement and not just said to make him feel better.

John is greeted with the following notification as he stops focusing on his dantian clearing technique.

**Your skill with 'Emperor Gnzuth Sun and Moon Dantian Clearing Technique' has increased to skill level 1. Your mastery with this skill is rated as Neophyte.**

Without thinking, John twists around while still seated and sees Amber's back.

Amber is still breathing oddly and moving her hands in the same way as John was just doing. He hopes he doesn't look as silly preforming the meditation technique as Amber does, at least as it looks from behind.

John quickly faces the wall again. He never stated he wouldn't look, but it was assumed, and he doesn't want to risk angering his only ally before a fight, even though he doesn't believe Amber's strange love magic will work on him.

Amber's height was hard to determine from seeing her sitting, but John could tell she had long legs by the length of her thighs compared to her torso. She sat with perfect posture, legs crisscrossed, facing away from him. Her long, dark hair in a low tail.

Amber also can be smelled now that she is no longer hidden. She has the artificial smell of many scents masking her true musk. John likes the true scent far better than the artificial and unnatural smells, though they are very pleasant too.

Amber's soul seemed much larger than usual, with the average grey and the white and black swirls of adults, very unlike the darker soul with many black swirls Munashi had, or those committing many foul deeds and sometimes possessed of great evils.

John has come to notice his mind and thoughts are now much closer to his thinking and beliefs as a young man, new to the power, and not as he came to think and believe after such a long time living. Even his Lilitu would be surprised at his thoughts, and her end came even before he moved to Greece.

John knows his newly restored belief in the Underworld is nonsensical and silly, but he can't dismiss it. His mind holds onto it. It seems right, and not in conflict with the idea of one God above ruling all.

John could never sire children, unless whatever fixed his mind also fixed that too, but meaty women that could easily handle many pregnancies and birth healthy and hearty children is what his mind found attractive in his youth, and now does so again. And large women usually had wealthy fathers and came with large dowries, and were taught how to manage a household.

When John saw Amber's long, thin neck, and exceedingly skinny waist and arms, he knows it shouldn't make him think of poor servant girls of low quality, but it does. He'd fallen in love with many women that looked as if they were starving of famine, even his Lilitu was too skinny, but he was alive for a very long time before he could ever consider a girl that is nothing but skin-and-bones anything but too sickly looking to ever be appealing.

Even if Amber has a face as beautiful as the stars look at night, he is certain her strange love magic will not work on him, as her body is too thin to look healthy, and his mind is now too stuck in the old ways to find such appealing.

Since John has nearly five minutes left, he decides to see what these notifications are about. He focuses on 'notifications' and Pixie appears, again, to go over the functions of them, and he sees the timer ticking down. He misses a lot of the explanations as he is worried. She won't stop until the Tribulation starts, and he fears the thought of interrupting his new teacher, but there is a little over three minutes left when she finishes.

Reviewing over three hundred notifications takes far less time than John assumed it would. Most of the notifications are on [Skills] and [Mastery] levels, [Skills] ready for [Synergy], something called [Achievements], and also many error reports.

At a little less than two minutes John calls out, "Amber." She doesn't respond so he calls her name loudly.

"Holy Jesus, dude! You trying to give me a heart attack? I almost peed myself a little."

With some anger he tries not to let show, John says, "We have less than two minutes to prepare. In ten seconds, I am heading for the door and will post there until the timer runs down. Please prepare for me to turn around. And I still have the short sword if you want it."

Before John counts to five Amber says, "Okay. Ready. Wow, I barely made a dent in my energy center. How'd it go for you?"

John gets up and walks to the door as he says, "Slow. I feel I made no progress. There's no time now, we must prepare for battle against these dark ones."

John takes out the sheathed short sword and holds it out. "Here, take this."

Amber sighs as she takes the sword with her invisible hand. John draws the longer sword from its sheath, and watches the counter. He says, "I don't know how this will go, but I will do my best to protect you. Stand back from the violence and do not risk yourself. I don't want to sound as a braggart, but I'm a doughty fighter, and can handle many opponents. But, if we must fight those demon-generals, I'm afraid I might not be much of a protector. I will try to keep their attention on me, and you should find an exit and sneak out to safety."

Amber says, "You really gotta lighten up, buddy. Ken told me Tribulations are always around our own tier, and our tier's the bottom one. If you really make someone angry, these can sometimes have higher tiered enemies, but it's rare and usually just one enemy one tier higher, and never more than two."

After a small pause, Amber continues, "I saw you fight Munashi. I feel good about this. You can probably blow through this whole thing in two seconds. I don't like fighting, but if you get in a tough spot I can help with some tricks. If you could see my face, you'd see I'm smiling reassuringly. We got this, buddy!"

Amber's easy thinking before a battle isn't John's way, but it makes him smile and lifts his heart.

Soon the timer hits zero, and the door slides open.

Through the open door is an arbor covering, leading to a beautiful garden filled with neatly trimmed grass, colorful bushes and flowers, and many trellis and lattice panels placed throughout. The sight is so beautiful it doesn't seem odd the garden is encased in stone walls, under a stone ceiling, with no windows or sunlight to nurture such life. On the far side, nearly two hundred paces or so away, another arbor cuts through the wall, covered in vines and some white flowers.

Holding the sword in the fool's stance, John warily steps through the door and clears the arbor.

In martial matters, John likes to prepare and think ahead. The two demon-generals from the field had souls, but he's seen no other invaders, and these dark ones may not have them to give their position away. But they should have life essence, which he can see in nearly all living things. His senses are keen, and he detects no movement or sign of life, not even insects.

John steps slowly and cautiously forward, and is about to announce this whole garden as safe when some specter-like hand with no soul rises from the ground near him and tries to grab his ankle. This is the first 'living' thing of this size he's ever seen with no life essence at all.

John jumps back quickly and slashes through it, and then again as it starts to reform. And then again as it is still moving. And one more time before it finally seems to dissipate, and a crystal drops from where it stood, onto the ground.

Looking around, John sees many, many more of these hands pop up from all over the garden. More than ten tens. Many more. He rushes forward and starts slashing at specter-hands as quickly as he can. There is little skill involved, just quickly slashing again and again, and as fast as he can, with little power behind the strikes. He uses vital essence to speed himself up only, as increasing his strength doesn't help, and four strikes each is still needed to destroy the hands.

John destroys many before he is attacked by some larger hands with sharp claws that take six strikes to make dissipate and drop crystals.

One claw is able to latch on to John's leg, but barely cuts skin and draws blood. As he removes and destroys it, he notices some new horrors. Some small blob-like things waddle towards him, and if a specter-hand or claw gets too close to a blob, they're absorbed into it, and the blob grows larger.

Enemies swamp John, but he is fast, and his sword blurs around him in a tsunami of steel. His heart lightens, and he thinks Amber is correct. *These enemies aren't very tough,* he thinks. When he can, he glances around to see if any enemies are going after Amber, but he finds the focus of all enemies directed solely at himself.

Three large blobs surround John, and as he slashes through them and does his best to make them dissipate, he is surprised by a wide stream of light swiftly descending from the ceiling onto the head of the largest blob, causing it to disappear and drop many crystals. He wonders what just happened for a moment before he remembers Amber's description of her 'trick' that dazes men and can kill small animals. Still not wanting to draw attention to her, he says nothing but presses his attack on the remaining two blobs.

The blobs are slow compared to John, and are soon destroyed, leaving four crystals each.

John looks around the garden for more enemies. He sees no more hands or claws or blobs.

Amber whispers in John's ear, "There were four other big blobs that merged into a man-shape that seemed *way* more solid. Two of the blobs formed one man-shape thing, then the two man-shapes joined together and disappeared over near that tree to the left of the door there."

John nods his head, and cautiously approaches the indicated spot. He sees and senses nothing,

Something grabs John's leg and holds it fast. He slashes at what is holding the ankle before looking, and looking causes him to be startled. Many large insects, like giant bees, but with the green metallic shine of a fly, form the shape of a hand gripping his leg.

As John repeatedly slashes at the hand, it disturbs the giant bee-sized flies, but kills few, and many, many more start coming out of the ground and speedily form into the shape of a large man, arm outstretched, still gripping John's leg. All is silent but the insanely loud buzzing of the giant bee-flies and John's racing heart.

John slashes and slashes, trying to disperse the large gathering of flies, but with the same results as earlier: few die, and the rest quickly reform.

John's leg starts to burn with tremendous pain where it's gripped as the bee-flies sting him many times.

The construction opens its mouth and giant bee-flies shoot out of it and start swarming all over John, and every part of his body is quickly covered in an angry, biting swarm.

As a child, John had a large fright of insects, and he was ridiculed for it, as all boys were for showing unmanly traits.

John had a friend bitten by a spider when he was very young, and the friend became sickly, and took to bed. As he sat with his friend, he saw many, many baby spiders burst from a large welt on his friend's face, and John ran from the horrible sight of it. It was a horrible way to die and would ensure a sad place in the Underworld for his friend.

After getting the power, John had little to fear from insects, but he never liked them.

Living so long and fighting so much, John has been subjected to every type of pain imaginable. Pain does not bother him. He is immune to mundane pain, and largely inured to true pain. The last time he was actually truly frightened was when he received the power, and was given a taste of the cold-dark.

The culture John was raised in rejected fear, and believed in a strong control of all emotions. All boys were taught this life is just a dream, and their only purpose in this dream is to awaken well by dying a glorious death in combat. Emotions must be controlled if a man is to consider himself as already dead, and always be able to do what must be done, and stand their ground, to always attack, and never run, to die well, and awaken magnificently, earning the praise of Koram.

Now, as he is completely covered in a thick coat of very large bee-flies stinging him, causing terrible burning pain over every inch of his body, pain worse than he can describe, his great ability to maintain calm and control his emotions is finally found lacking, and fear grips his heart.

"AMBER! AMBER! USE A TRICK! AAAHH!" John yells as he throws himself bodily on the ground, rolling around, trying to kill many insects at once.

John kicks the tree with his shin and calf, and hits it with his arms, and runs his torso and back into it, but he is still completely covered in insects, and they continuously sting him with a painful venom.

It is ingrained in John enough to send vital essence through his body to help heal the burning and stinging he feels all over. No matter how many bee-flies he manages to smoosh against the tree with his body and body parts, he remains covered in them. His panicked brain tells him he is going to die, and he sees no way of saving himself. Every part of his body continues to be stung over and over.

# CHAPTER 8
# LEGENDARY

Knowing he will soon be dead, John can only hope to take as many of these insects with him as he can. As he prepares to throw his back against the tree again, he feels something big and hard hit the top of his head, and suddenly the buzzing of all the giant flies stops, and though his eyes are closed, he knows the bee-flies are dropping from his body all over, dead.

John tries to open his eyes, but they refuse to work due to swelling and injury. He frantically brushes dead giant bee-flies off himself, shivering in disgust. As he attempts to kick off his large white shoes, as he feels alive bee-flies squirming in them still, he feels something grab his arm and Amber says, "John! Are you okay? Jesus, that scared me half to death. Oh, my goodness, that was so gross! Ahh! Ahh! This one's alive. Ahh! Get it. Get it!"

Amber releases John's arm and a moment later says, "Never mind, I got it. Ahh! There's more. Help! Ahh! I got…oh, a crystal. I think they're all dead. A crystal dropped. This crystal is kind of yellowish. All the other ones are white. I mean clear. Yeah, clear. You okay, buddy? You don't look so good."

John ignores Amber as he tries to regain control of his emotions. His skin is on fire, and his eyes burn, and his tongue is swollen too. He puts his arms out and moves a distance away before sitting down.

"Oh, my goodness! I can see your wee-wee. Gross! They really did a number on your clothes. Wow, you really look messed up. Let me give you some of my healing. There you go, dude. It's not fast, but it helps.

You should try meditating. Ken says it helps facilitate healing, especially once you open the middle energy center and certain channels. Maybe it will help?"

John, having nothing better to do at the moment, and not in any shape to do any better things if he had some to do, believes Amber's recommendation has some merit. He forces his limbs into position, and believing he understands the method well enough he doesn't call on Pixie for assistance.

John pictures his lower dantian, and focuses on it, and when he can see it clearly, he begins. He puts his arms straight out and makes fists, and he breathes in very slowly with his lower diaphragm as he pulls his arms in with, his fists close to his belly. He then breathes out as fast and hard as he can as he twists his left fist down, and right fist up, as if he is turning a large wheel. He sees the energy cascade over his dantian, and small grains of the grime filling it fly away with the energy.

John takes very fast and powerful breaths as he twists the wheel over and over, and when his count hits twenty, he extends his arms out again. He is about to do the second part of six total included in the technique, and when he is done, he repeats it over and over and over as the black filling of his lower dantian is slowly cleared away.

After finishing the sixth part completely, he starts the first again, and loses himself to the repetition. And then, without thinking or trying, he loses himself in a different way, by slipping within himself, into his retreat, as his mind was so long trained to do. He doesn't know how much time passes, but he feels a great change in his body, so he pulls out of his inner-being, and is greeted with some new messages.

**You gained a new Achievement! Congratulations! Achievement 'Climber 1' (F-rated, participate in defeating an enemy at least 1 tier higher than self, 0.10 magical energy discount NCS cost ((total discount now 46.4%)).**

**Your skill with 'Emperor Gnzuth Sun and Moon Dantian Clearing Technique' has increased to skill level 2.**

**You have created a new meditation technique. Congratulations! Would you like to rename 'Undirected Basic Meditation?' Focus <u>here</u> to rename.**

**Your lower Dantian has been cleared and is now opened. Congratulations! All Stats increased by 1.**

John is very surprised, as his progress seemed so slow. He worries he became too lost in meditation, and too much time has passed. He looks with great concern at the timer. He remembers being informed before he had eleven hours to complete the Tribulation, and the timer states 7:19 left.

John opens his still burning eyes and sees the state of his clothing – tattered and barely there at all. His skin is red, and covered in bloody welts and bumps, and itches like mad in spots, but is much healed from earlier.

John stands to look for the white shoes, as he will wear them again, since they provide some protection. As he turns, he sees Amber's back again, and she is cultivating, holding one of the many crystals that dropped from the specter-hands and other horrors they've witnessed in this horrible, beautiful garden in each hand. A large pile of crystals sits beside her.

Not wanting to bother Amber, John collects the big white shoes, and once he ensures there are no giant flies in either, places them back on, and sits back down.

John then taps the middle of his forehead, right above his eyes, and thinks *Pixie.* The world flashes by in great speed, and once again he enters what Pixie called his 'Mind's Eye.'

Pixie greets him with a thumb in the air and a wink, saying, "Great job opening that dantian! Also, a Divine tagged you. Since a Celestial created this Tribulation, the Divine could bust in, but they're waiting, and that's a good sign they don't mean you harm! So don't worry. This seems to be regarding the creation of a Legendary meditation technique, and not many early Mortals can say they did that. Just be respectful when you meet them. Beings on higher Trees can be sensitive if beings so far below them don't show proper respect and use a lot of tact. Kowtowing is never a bad idea, and don't speak out of turn or get lippy."

John is not sure how he feels about meeting a being he assumes is more powerful than the one creating this Tribulation, with the thundering voice that boomed all around him, as he does not think he has any chance of holding his own in a fight if it comes to that. But he does not believe he has much choice in this matter, so what will be, will be. He first must see this Tribulation through, and he has some questions for Pixie.

"Mistress Pixie, I believe you said I could do magic now that my lower dantian is opened?"

"That's right. First, let's check out your Stat increases to provide motivation and keep you climbing that ladder! It feels so good when Stats increase, doesn't it?"

| | |
|---|---|
| **Strength** | 20.1 |
| **Swiftness** | 19.8 |
| **Conditioning** | 21.6 |
| **Min. Power** | 1 |
| **Capacity** | 1 |
| **Runes** | .6 |
| **Physical Fortification** | 1 |
| **Elemental Fortification** | 1 |
| **Mental Fortification** | 1 |

"Mistress Pixie, do you know why Runes went up so much? I thought you said it would only be one. It's at six."

"No, your Runes Stat is at point-six currently. Opening the lower dantian always increases all Stats by minimum energy unit increase, which is normalized at exactly one. Only when you hit the tier cap will you have diminished returns. Your rank is far too low to worry about tier caps. Wood tier cap for Stats is estimated to be around twenty-four or twenty-five for terrans. Definitely not higher than twenty-six, but we don't know for certain yet."

This response doesn't make sense to John. He asks, "What does point-six mean?"

In her overly friendly voice, Pixie replies, "Point-six means sixty percent, or six tenths. Point-five would be fifty percent, or half of a whole. Let me know if that makes sense."

John understands the answer, but still has questions. "You said the minimum unit increase is always one, so why is my Runes less than one then?"

"That's right, minimum unit increase is at least one for each Stat before tier cap, so your Runes Stat must be one. But it is not one. ERROR! ERROR! Logic failure detected. Report created. Report sent."

John, at this point, is somewhat flustered. "Is...this something I need worry about, or is there any way I can fix this?"

"Oh, you shouldn't worry about anything if you follow our advice. Now, what are you looking to fix?"

"My Runes Stat. It should be one, right? But isn't."

"Huh. Nothing to it. We have it noted and a report's been sent. Before you exit to real-time, let's review how you can start working on clearing your middle dantian. You use the same exact technique, and everything is basically the same, but you imagine your middle dantian instead of your lower." Pixie shows her thumb to John, and winks at him.

"I have a question about that as well. What is this new meditation technique I created? I have a Skill with the same name. Is that a coincidence? And when did I create this new technique? I only remember performing the one you taught me before. Emperor something Sun and Moon something, yes?"

"We can certainly help with that. See here?" A small moving picture, like a framed memory, is showing beside Pixie. In this frame is John, tattered clothes, and red, bumpy skin, going through the actions of the dantian clearing meditation he was taught. A timer is showing, it starts at 39:08, and at 39:17 John stops doing the technique and places his hands on his thighs. The clock speeds up, and John sits perfectly still throughout, until at 3:13:05 John opens his eyes, stands, and collects the large white shoes, and the framed memory freezes.

Pixie says, "Yes, the new meditation technique is a Skill of yours, currently with a placeholder name of Undirected Basic Meditation. Same as Emperor Gnzuth Sun and Moon Dantian Clearing Technique is also a Skill of yours now. You performed Undirected Basic Meditation for about two-and-a-half hours, as you just saw in the recording I showed you."

"And it seems to be rather effective, right? The other technique was extremely slow. I should use the new one to open the middle dantian too, yes?" Not wanting to sound disrespectful, John adds, "Mistress Pixie."

"Definitely not. Undirected, basic meditation techniques are the absolute worst techniques, and all F-rated. It's a waste of time leveling them up. They're the slowest and most inefficient type of meditation for doing serious self-cultivation, and they'll fill your body with gunk and impurities.

"For terrans, from the data we've collected, Emperor Gnzuth Sun and Moon Dantian Clearing Technique is three-point -seven percent faster than the next most efficient humanoid-centric technique for dantian clearing, for both males and females. Emperor Gnzuth Sun and Moon Dantian Clearing Technique is rated as superb-super-ultra-rare.

"The only reason using your F-rated technique cleared your dantian faster is because its Skill level is ninety-six point four three. Of course, an F-rated Skill at Legendary Mastery is going to be more effective than an SSUR-rated Skill at Neophyte Mastery, but there's no way a low Mortal will have any Legendary Mastery Skills, so don't worry about it. Just stay the course, and trust we'll steer you in the right direction. Sticking to the tried and true is the best way forward, and we have the data to prove it." Pixie shows her thumb to John again, and also gives him a new wink.

John does not accept this and thinks Pixie is incorrect. He doesn't want to anger her, so he says nothing, but formulates a plan. The next time he cultivates he will start with the Emperor something technique, and then 'accidentally' start doing his own technique. Though he is not sure what his technique entails, his Skill level shows he is quite good at it.

"Okay, now onto the fun part!" says Pixie. "Your lower dantian is open, and if you want, you can pick an Archetype. Or you can pick your own rune, just don't forget to target at least two Stats before you start refining magical energy. Plenty of time for that, since you can't start refining until you open your upper dantian. What's it going to be, go down your own road or pick an Archetype? We highly recommend picking an Archetype."

John would rather go down his own road, but that is only good advice if you can see the road at all, and know where you want to go.

John knows he needs to learn more before carving a path for himself. And Pixie said [Archetypes] get something like better runes, and runes are how you cast spells, and he doesn't even have one in his [Runes] [Stat] yet. He would be a fool not to at least review the [Archetypes] and get more information on them.

They go to the [Archetypes] tab, and Pixie reviews the information already told to John. [Archetypes] are a focused cultivation path, with set [Stat] increases and rune selections, and optimized for better gains, and a more advanced rune than would be available otherwise, and something about bottlenecks.

The advanced rune granted for picking an [Archetype], John finds out, is a rune combination that can cost up to three runes to make on his own, and would require a [Runes] [Stat] of three.

[Archetypes] are broken down into groups, and there are many. Crafting and profession focused, scholarly, spiritual, healing, necromantic, and many other groups John ignores. Two groups are of interest, as they are more combat oriented. The first group is called Militant, and has four subgroups, only two of which John finds appealing.

The Defenders subgroup [Archetype] focuses on something called 'tanking,' and being able to take punishing blows, and targets [Conditioning] and one of the three [Fortification] [Stats] for rank up increases, and their spells focus on body shielding or enforcement, or external shield creation, some on self-healing, and one on damaging a small area around the Defender for a long while. This [Archetype] doesn't interest John very much after reviewing it.

The next subgroup, called Martials, focuses on weapons and martial skills, and usually targets [Strength] and [Swiftness]. The spells of this group focus on imbuing weapons with power, creating weapons or arrows from magical essence, enhancing the body in some way, a few close attacks, and things of this nature. This is more interesting to John, but not what he is looking for.

For both Defenders and Martials, John has powers similar to ones they focus on, as he can empower his body and heal himself with vital essence, and is extremely hard to kill already.

The last group is exactly what John is looking for. This grouping is called Theurgists and has two subgroups: Thaumaturgists and Ritualists.

John knows ritual magic is the purview of priests, and old crones, and witches, and is the cause of his Lilitu being brought so low, and her death. He wants nothing to do with it.

Thaumaturgists focus on a specific type of manifestation. All manifestations for all [Archetypes], and all rune combinations are grouped in certain ways, and these categories can be seen as specializations.

Abjurers use spells that block and protect. Diviners specialize in revealing information or seeing more than others, and can sometimes see what is fated. Enchanters imbue items or the body with enhancements. Evokers create manifestations meant to directly damage opponents. Fairies use spells to manipulate feelings. Illusionists trick the eyes and perceptions of others. Mentalists can trick minds, and place thoughts in them, and control objects with their own mind too. Shapers use magical energy to create objects and even some creations that can act autonomously. Transmuters focus on spells that change themselves physically in some way – claws, scales, and things of this nature.

Focusing on one type of manifestation doesn't block a Thaumaturgist from using other types of spells, but as long as they have the [Archetype] they would need to pick the NCS enhanced spells from that school. All Thaumaturgists target [Min Power] and [Runes] for rank up increases.

John knows exactly what [Archetype] he will select.

# CHAPTER 9
## SPELLS

The choice of [Archetype] is easy for John. He first reviews the terms required before selecting an [Archetype] with Pixie, and agrees to them readily. He selects Evoker, with [Stat] increases going to [Min Power] and [Runes].

John has long dreamed of controlling fire, and having pillars of flame billow forth from his hands, and waving his hand and having his enemies combust in flame, and Evokers perform such magics. The flame part is not yet possible but will be soon. Out of all choices of spells he can select, two most appeal to John – [Magical Energy Bolt] and [Magical Energy Spray].

Seeing how ineffective John was at fighting the giant bee-flies, he leans towards [Magical Energy Spray], which releases a searing spray of magical energy in a cone shaped area out to about seven feet.

If John used this when the giant bee-flies formed into a man shape, he could have killed many of them. But could he have killed all of them, or enough of them?

John is not sure. He is not able to test the spell to see how long it lasts, or how wide the area it sprays. The giant bee-flies were not hard to kill, but there were a great many of them, and they inflicted immense damage in their swarms.

John isn't even certain how long a foot is. Pixie states it is twelve inches, but what is an inch? He decides he will consider a foot to be about the size of his own foot.

One other spell stands out to John. A spell he noticed when he reviewed the Defender [Archetype], and also falls under the evocation school of spells. It says it does little damage, but lasts a while, and continuously damages all enemies in a four-foot area around the cultivator manifesting the spell.

After some internal debate, John picks the spell that least appeals to him out of the three considered, but the one he assumes will help him best survive his current Tribulation. He selects [Destructive Emanation].

Except he is not allowed to select the manifestation, as the [Runes] [Stat] needs to be at least one for Pixie to grant him the rune combination, and John's [Runes] is currently point six only.

John is greatly disappointed. But things start to look up after discussing this issue with Pixie, as she will try to override the rule, and grant the spell to John anyways, as it is part of the [Archetype] agreement. First, she needs John to exit his Mind's Eye so she can address the situation in real-time. Either way, she will contact John with the result as soon as she has it.

Before John leaves Pixie reviews a new cultivation technique with him, one specialized for efficient energy gathering, so he can fill his dantian with some energy for spell casting in the event he is approved for the rune combination. She also teaches him a strange way to breathe to constantly gather some energy, and tells him he should always breathe this way, and never stop, for the rest of his life.

So, John, with some hope, exits his own mind.

John stands, and removes the remnants of his tattered clothing, and tries to fashion some sort of loincloth to cover himself. It takes some time, but he is mainly successful and happy with the results.

"Thanks for covering yourself," Amber says, close by, startling John. "Ha! You jumped like ten feet. Sorry about that, I didn't mean to scare you so much."

"Great gods below, woman!" John admonishes himself for not noticing her scent disappearing, as well as her heartbeat. *Now is the time to be ever more vigilant, not less. If I must now think in the old ways, let me re-member well the lessons learned then, too, and hold them dear.*

"Ha! You crack me up, man. I made some good gains. You can clearly see the outline of my energy center now. My NCS explained these crystals to me. They're distilled energy, and they help clear energy centers and energy channels faster, and really help fill up energy centers once we can start gathering energy, since ambient energy is so low. And they work as a currency in the universe. Maybe they can help your skin heal faster too?

"Oh, and it seems like we're in trouble. I guess we really pissed some-one off, because you know those see-through hands? Those are dark ones classified as Dimensional Horrors. They increase in rank by merging, and that final merge was level 6, but they can get up to level 8. That means the next tier up, Copper, and either low, mid-low, or mid-high rank. And the final enemy will be the highest level. So at least high Copper. And dark ones are some kind of cosmic horrors created by these ancient beings even stronger than Eternals." A quick pause, and Amber says in a con-fused voice, "Why do you feel...like...heavier or something?"

John is not too worried. If these Dimensional Horrors are the toughest foe they face, as long as he gets the [Destructive Emanation] spell, he should be able to kill them easily, as the giant bee-flies were easy to kill, but just too numerous. All lower forms of the specter-hands were easy for him to dispatch. He is curious about her statement of him feeling heavier, and thinks he has an answer for it. "Could I feel heavier because I opened my lower dantian?"

"What? How did you open it so fast? That's like...like...so unfair! I'm a girl and we're supposed to be faster."

John smiles, as he felt small after his poor showing against the giant bees, and how they unmanned him, and made him fearful. He is used to being so far above others he need not worry about his safety or failure. Pulling ahead of the pack again feels right, and feels how things should be. As things have been for so long.

But John needs strong allies, and he will not hold back information from any, especially not his only companion. "While using the Emperor something technique, I slipped into old habits and old ways, as I've always done to pass time for my long life.

"I've done it so long and so often I have become quite good at it, and the system says my Mastery level is Legendary. As best as I can tell, the Skill consists of merely rumination. I just sit and reflect on whatever my mind goes to, or nothing at all. I can do it for days without moving. It is called Undirected Basic Meditation. You said you've lived a long life as well; tell me, do you not have a similar Skill?"

There's a small pause before Amber says, "None of my Skills are anywhere close to Legendary. I gotta buncha Adept Skills, a couple at pretty high Adept too. And I can't scroll my Skills list down. That page is so bugged it's crazy. Oh, I changed my NCS avatar to Pixie too. Let me go ask my Pixie."

The horrible, beautiful garden is silent for a moment. "Okay, I do have that Skill, but it's only at fourteen-point-something. So almost Apprentice level! Not bad! I'm gonna go try it. You just think about anything...or nothing? I can do that. Easy-peasy, dude. I do that all the time. Do we have time? We have more than seven hours left. Mmmm...what do you think? Oh, did you pick an Archetype? What manifestation did you get?"

John wishes Amber would learn to slow down when speaking and ask less questions before giving him a chance to reply. "Yes and no. I picked Evoker as an Archetype, but for some reason I did not get the full increase of Runes, and my Runes is only point-six. I believe Pixie is consulting with others of her kind to see if I still qualify to receive the spell for selecting an Archetype, and she needed me to leave to do so.

"The one I'm getting is Destructive Emanation, as it is the best way to deal with the giant bee-flies, though I'd prefer Magical Energy Bolt or even Magical Energy Spray. What were your other questions?"

Amber giggles. "I can't believe you are calling it magical energy. And spells. Jesus, you are one weird dude. I like it though. It's kinda adorable. It fits the whole old-timey thing you got going on, even though you look so young. But when I called my light it killed all the crazy flies real easy.

It also killed the…whatever it's called when it was a big weird melty look-ing thing. The bigger blob…forms, I guess. So why not get the manifes-tation you wanna get more?

"I can't *spam* it, but I can do that trick two times pretty close together, and the price isn't so bad. I just didn't wanna waste it with you running around being hysterical and screaming like a little girl, so I had to wait until I knew I'd hit you. You took it like a champ too. Most men get knocked on their butt for a minute or two, at the very least. It didn't even faze you, did it?"

John berates himself, as he hasn't yet even wondered how the giant bee-flies died.

*Of course. That was the feeling of a rock hitting my head. How could I not even wonder what ended the giant bee-flies, and saved me too?* "Thank you for saving me with your light trick. I was in a rough predicament, and I couldn't find a way to kill enough of the giant bee-flies in time. I would've died if not for you. I am in your debt, and will not forget it. Thank you, Mister… Lady Amber." John ends his expression of gratitude with a bow.

Amber's tinkling laughter fills the garden, and she says, "Such a gen-tleman! And don't worry about it, I just wish I could help more. I can't fight so well, and if I attack with this sword, I'll lose my invisibility. And it's super tough to get invisibility back when I'm being focused on or attacked. There's other ways I can fight way better, but the cost…is too much, and I'll be stuck." Amber stops again for a moment before contin-uing. "The cost is just too much. I'm sorry."

John can't see Amber, but he can tell she is smiling as she says, "But I'd like to thank you for fighting and keeping me safe. We make a great team. I'm the beauty, you're…well, I'm the brains too. You're the muscle. My hero, keeping me safe. Thank you, Sir John. I know you can't see but I'm returning the bow, but very gracefully and as a ladylike curtsey."

John laughs, enjoying his companion's gay ways. "What is spam?"

"Huh? Spam is…a meat. A canned meat. Why? Oh, I said I can't spam my light trick. That means…I mean spam means, in that context, uh, use it over and over again. I can use it twice, but with a little bit of time between using it, then it takes a while to get one back, and a while longer for the second one. But the cost is small, so I don't mind doing it. I have them both back now, so just remember to stand still if you get covered in the crazy flies again. And get any manifestation you want, but I'm going to cultivate a little more and see if I can open my energy center by just daydreaming."

Grunting, John says, "Okay, and I will as well, as I was taught a new energy gathering technique and I'll need some energy in my dantian to cast whatever spell I choose. I was also taught a way I should breathe at all times to continuously gather energy, and I need to practice this.

"But, please, as soon as Pixie notifies me about the spell, we should continue. We know not how many enemies we are yet to face, and how many battles are ahead of us. I dislike having this time limit hanging over my head, promising death if we fail. It makes me anxious, and I want to defeat this Tribulation well before we are pressed for time. Even if Pixie does not contact me, we should continue no later than the timer reaching six hours, if not well before."

With a plan set, Amber asks John to face the other way, as is their custom now, so she could cultivate, and sit how she needs, and John won't see her face.

John practices the constant breathing technique he was taught – the new way he should always breathe, even during combat. It is not easy. It is called [Breath of the Serpent Clan]. A deep, slow breath from as low in his belly as he can manage, through the nose, with a count of eight in, hold for two seconds, and four out, with a pause in the middle of the four out.

Breathing this new way is unnatural, and John realizes it will take a lot of practice to make this second nature, and done without thought or constant attention.

The new magical energy gathering technique, called [Coiled Center of the Universe Technique], requires squatting, and a strange slow dance, and a perfectly straight back through all, and flowing arm movements.

John is supposed to focus on a different form of energy coiled around his spine, and try to cultivate it. It can't be cultivated yet, but trying to do so increases regular magical energy flow into the dantian. And once all his dantians are open, and he can refine magical energy into magical essence, this is a superior technique to do so, and when all the meridians are open, some trace amount of coiled energy will be cultivated, and will make the refined magical energy more potent.

John finishes one full part of three and notices some magical energy in his opened dantian. Shortly into the second part Pixie notifies him she is ready for his return, and John does so after reading a new notification.

**Your skill with 'Coiled Center of the Universe Technique' has increased to skill level 1. Your mastery with this skill is rated as Neophyte.**

Pixie states everything is all set for John to pick a spell, even one with a max [Runes] cost of three, and John must state he understands all future [Runes] he gains will go towards the [Runes] debt he owes Pixie, until three are paid off.

John thanks Pixie, and wants to question her on future spell selection, but is too nervous. He doesn't want to seem greedy or ungrateful or have Pixie renege on the offer she is making now, with questions about future gains of [Runes] or spells.

Now is time for John's spell selection. *[Destructive Emanation] is the smart choice, as Amber is somewhat erratic and can't be fully relied upon. But unless my [Runes] issue is somehow addressed, something even the great Pixie is not knowledgeable on how to do, I will have less spells than others and must make the most of my choice.*

*I long to have pillars of flame billow forth from my hands, and the spell most like this is [Magical Energy Spray]. But is this the right choice? Seven of my feet are not far, and if the feet referred to are more like paces, that is not a long distance either.*

*[Magical Energy Bolt] can reach a distance of nearly one hundred-forty of these feet, and that is a much greater distance. [Destructive Emanation] lasts*

*a long time and goes all around me, up to four feet away. Seven feet is not much more distance than four. I wish these spell descriptions gave more information. Pixie did say the spells get more powerful over time, and ranges will increase, and change greatly with other runes added, and aspects, and my own advancement up this Tree.*

In the end, John goes with his initial intuition, and chooses [Magical Energy Bolt]. Pixie then shows him the basics on how to use magical energy to power this spell.

Now it is time to rally Amber, and face the rest of this Tribulation, and see what else it has to offer in challenge.

# CHAPTER 10
## LOUVRE DOLLS

John and Amber stand under the wall, between the arbor sticking out back into the garden they came from, and the garden they need to go into, preparing for the violence they know will be directed at them.

"What are those things?" asks Amber. Her voice sounds strained as she is holding a bag made from the shorts she was wearing under her new pajama bottoms, filled with all the crystals that have dropped from monsters so far, though John can see neither the bag nor Amber.

The bag is not heavy, but as John recently found out, Amber is not strong. They told each other their [Stats], and Amber's [Strength] is a measly 2.8. Her [Swiftness] is much higher, but still only 8.7. Only her [Conditioning] [Stat] is notable at 19.8.

John also knows the brunt of the crushing attack they received prior to entering this Tribulation was aimed directly at Amber, which brought John low, and crushed him, and nearly caused his death, but did not seem to hurt Amber much at all.

John also knows his own [Stats] do not reflect his true strength, nor speed, nor endurance, nor his ability to resist mental attacks and damage.

This leads John to believe there to be much these numbers don't reflect, and Amber possesses strange tricks and, he is sure, many other secrets.

There are well over six hours left on the timer, but John was anxious to get going. He tested his new spell twice, once on a bush immediately upon exiting his Mind's Eye, and once more at the stone wall to show

Amber. Great damage was done to the bush by [Magical Energy Bolt], but no observable damage was done to the stone wall.

Amber had no luck using her own [Undirected Basic Meditation], and her dantian clearing was far slower than using the NCS recommended clearing technique, even with the assistance of crystals.

John used crystals for the first time to fill his dantian with energy and found the crystals to greatly speed up the process, and he raised his [Coiled Center of the Universe Technique] to level 2. Once his dantian had a good amount of energy inside of it, he begged Amber for them both to proceed, as they did not know what further tests they faced, nor had they any idea how long this Tribulation would take.

So here they are, looking at a very strange sight, while standing under the arbor, ready to proceed.

The new garden in front of the two companions is much larger than the last, has a stream on the far side, a red wooden bridge goes over the stream, and a large grassy area beyond.

Even with John's sharp eyes, the furthest distance is too shaded and dark to see the far wall clearly, but he sees well enough to know there are no obvious doors or exits.

John assumes Amber's question is about the nine very large, long, and thin faces, with bulbous eyes, and wide mouths, and some odd metal protrusions just over the bridge. The ones that moved to face directly towards John once he entered the arbor.

John believes Amber would have said, 'what is that horrible thing!' if she had seen the giant blob of a monster beyond them, as it is quite frightening to look upon, the blob pulses and shudders in a disgusting way.

Both the giant flesh-blob monster and the long, thin faces both contain vital essence, but not souls.

This side of the stream, closest to John and Amber, is empty, but John suspects it contains the specter-hands, and probably many of them.

John replies, "They look like long faces with no arms or legs, with some metal spikes protruding from odd places. Nine in total. Can you see the monster beyond?"

Quietly, Amber whispers in John's ear. "I can't. I bet those ghost hands are all over the place in this area right in front of us. Can you sense anything?"

"No, but I agree with you. Just so you know, and are not surprised later, there is a giant blob monster beyond these faces, near the far wall. And no doors or exits I can see. The blob is a large mass of…flesh? I'm not sure. It moves like it is taking a deep breath that expands itself greatly, and then releases it. Unlike the specter-hands, the faces and the giant blob have the essence of life in them, as all living things should."

It takes Amber a moment to reply, "Cool. What's the plan? I think you should fire your manifestation at one of those big faces, then run back into the last room and hide on the side of the door and ambush everything as they come through. That's the best strategy in video games. Usually."

John does not know why Amber said 'cool,' or how anyone would 'fire' a spell, but then he remembers people use the term with firearms discharging bullets, and thinks Amber meant it in this way. He does not think the strategy she proposed is a sound one, and seems more dangerous than what he was thinking, and he questions the validity of the tactics these video games teach, whatever a video game may be.

"I was thinking I would cautiously enter and try to find if the specter-hands are on this side of the stream, and if they are, deal with them quietly before antagonizing the faces, and try to stop the hands from merging into the giant bee-flies."

"That sounds cool too. Just remember to stand still if you do get covered in the flies again. Man, these crystals are heavy. I'm gonna put the bag down. Okay. Ready when you are, buddy. I'm smiling confidently, just so you know. I believe in you, John! You can do it!"

This causes John to both smile in joy, and also wish Amber would take this more seriously. He was greatly injured from the bee-flies, and does not want to be more injured than absolutely necessary.

Taking a deep breath to clear his mind, John also chastises himself for forgetting to do the energy-gathering breathing Pixie told him he should always do, and he starts doing so now, as he enters under the arbor leading to the new garden.

As soon as he steps out from under the arbor, a loud screeching noise behind him causes John to turn, and he sees a stone door crash down, blocking the exit back to the other garden.

"Amber!"

"Holy…man, I almost got squished under that door. My goodness, that scared me half to death. I hope our crystals are okay."

With much relief that Amber is unhurt, John turns to scan the area, and see if the specter-hands left the ground, or the other enemies were alerted. All is still peaceful.

Cautiously stepping forward, ready to draw on essence to increase his speed, John readies for battle.

Some steps in, a specter-hand is seen by John before it's able to surprise him, and slashed until it drops a crystal. He notices only three slashes are needed this time for some reason, instead of the four required in the other garden.

In the mere moment needed for John to dispatch the first specter-hand, the new garden becomes filled with them, and he runs around slashing these hands as fast as he's able, enhanced by the life essence inside of him. He tries to stop them from forming into the blobs, which eventually combine into the giant bee-flies. He is doing well, and mostly doing his work silently, for the most part, until some of the long faces notice him, and start heading towards the bridge.

While the long faces are moving, and turned towards their side, no longer facing John, he notices they are not long faces at all, but something he remembers from long ago.

Women thought to be witches would be killed a certain way to contain their angry spirits. The witches would have her hands and feet speared together behind her back, and be hung over a fire, with the belly facing down.

The spears would all be placed in a specific way, usually thirteen in total, to trap the spirit inside. The witch would be either near death or dead before the fire was lit, and burnt until just ash and bone remained. The ash, spears, and bone would be gathered and put in a clay vessel, and submerged in deep water, and this would keep the witch's spirit contained, along with her malevolence.

This way of killing witches then became a popular way for witches to make dolls representing a target, and that target would be cursed in a ritual. His Lilitu used these dolls often.

Thirteen pins were used in the doll, two through feet and hands behind the doll's back, binding them fast, eleven other pins placed always through two separate parts, and usually through most orifices too.

As with the dolls and pins, the same is true for this new foe, but these are hovering women, with hands and feet speared together behind them, and spears throughout their extremely arched bodies.

There are some key differences between the dolls and this new foe – these have large and swollen bellies, as if pregnant, and on the belly is a giant mouth. The breasts look like eyes, popping up bulbously from the top of what he thought was the long, thin head, though was actually just the top of their arched chest, and a spear through the sternum looks as if a nose.

All in all, these women are a very disturbing sight to behold.

The hovering speared-women move slowly, and only four of the nine are making their way towards John, so he continues to kill specter and clawed hands and blobs and hope the speared-women are not too tough of a foe. He does not want to move closer and cause the other five to start combat with him too, so he cannot reach all hands and blobs.

While fighting all the hands surrounding him, John checks the progress of the speared-women near the bridge, and nearly curses as he notices two man-shaped things making their way towards one another,

Remembering his new spell, John casts [Magical Energy Bolt] at one of the man-things, and then the other, and hits both, each dropping many crystals after dissipating.

John smiles, as using magic excites him greatly, especially using it in combat to destroy enemies, but then he worries he may have made a mistake. He does not have enough magical energy for another casting of the spell, but is close to having enough, and notices he is not breathing how he is supposed to in order to constantly gather energy, and hasn't been since combat started. He starts to breathe correctly again as the first speared-woman reaches him.

John thrusts his sword forward and runs the belly of the woman through, with little resistance.

The giant mouth on the woman's belly opens, and a tongue comes out of the mouth and tries to grab John's sword. He retreats a step, slashing the tongue as he does, which falls to the ground with way less blood than a severed tongue should spill, and the tongue continues to grow out of the mouth without caring.

Another speared-lady is getting closer, so John goes all out trying to down the one he is already fighting. He tries to slash through the thigh but is stopped by one of the many metal spears impaling the woman. He is able to separate the neck and head, but the head stays in place because of the three spears through it. He then removes both breasts nearly completely; John slashes most of the way through the swollen waist.

The speared-woman is moving still, and trying to grab any part of John with her long tongue, or catch him on any of her many protruding spear points, though he is far too fast for her to do so.

John finally manages to cut completely through the waist, and this seems to end whatever magic kept this woman going, and she starts to fall to the ground, but explodes before she reaches it.

The explosion knocks John back and to the ground, the shaft of a metal spear hitting the side of his head, and though it smarts, it does little damage.

John slashes nearby blob creatures, and notices two yellowish crystals on the ground where the woman exploded. He kills a few more of the creatures trying to grab him before the next speared-woman is close enough to start attacking him.

For the next two speared-women, John immediately tries to separate them at the waist, and does so easily, while also killing blobs, as there are no more specter-hands or claws left.

The last speared-woman John runs from, and avoids. He finishes killing off various sized blobs, and some man-shaped things, before engaging her in battle.

As the tongue comes out of the giant belly-mouth, John grabs it, as well as the spear that he mistook for a nose at the start, and bites into the tongue. He starts draining the lady of vital essence, while holding her fast by the spear. When he finishes with the dregs he hops back to avoid the explosion, but this one just falls to the ground, grey now, and cracking, but still dropping two yellowish crystals.

"Amber," John says softly.

"Right here, buddy," she replies. "Good work! That first explosion almost knocked me out of invisibility. These things are sick. Disgusting. I hope these aren't real women or...you know? This is sick."

"How many man-things joined enough to go underground as bees?"

Closer, Amber says, "At least three. Two near the bridge, one more near that white fence there with the red flowers. I've never seen those flowers. They're beautiful, aren't they?"

"Yes. Very beautiful. I'll pick some for you when it's safe to do so, but now we must finish this Tribulation. It was a good decision not to waste your light...thing, yet. I'm going to throw one of these spears at that lady there, and try to get them all to come one by one, and kill them all before moving on to the bee-flies. You'll have to kill both of the ones near the bridge with one light...thing. Magic? What do you call it? Light magic?"

"I say calling the light. I don't know if it's magic. I guess it is. I never thought of it that way. Just a trick. They're too far apart for me to kill both together though. Way too far apart."

John figured this was going to be the case and knows the remedy. "Once we finish off all these speared-women, I will have to gather both swarms onto me before you call the light down upon them. I will cover my eyes, and hope I am not too much damaged by their stings before you call the light. Are you ready?"

Cheerfully, Amber says, "Ready when you are, buddy. And thanks for protecting me. No one's ever protected me before. Guys always try to catch me, instead of helping me. Seriously, thank you. I really appreciate it. You're a good guy."

John sighs and says, "I wish that were true. But you're welcome, it's my pleasure. And thank you for your help. If not for your light earlier, I would be dead."

John grabs a spear from the ground, empowers himself with strength and speed, and with a skilled and practiced hand makes a mighty throw at the nearest speared-woman, and hits true. She makes no sound but starts to shimmer, and the other four of her kind shimmer too.

John sees the giant bee-flies leave the ground, and notices there are four groups of them, not three. He then notices something causing his heart to beat faster – the monster behind the speared-women has a very large eye, and the eye is now open, and looking directly at John, as the rest of its giant body pulses.

Amber whispers, "Oh dear God."

# CHAPTER 11
# A GLORIOUS BATTLE

John wholeheartedly agrees with the sentiment of Amber's statement. He's glad he was able to top off his vital essence, and continues to enhance himself with strength and speed.

Two of the speared-women, each on opposite ends of the stream, are doing something new, and spitting out little spears from their swollen bellies, and the missiles fly towards John with great speed. The other women make their way to the bridge, the four groups of giant bee-flies are swarming right at him too, and the large flesh-mound continues to shudder and seethe.

No good strategy of how to approach this fight forms in John's mind. In his long life, he's found indecision or overthinking to often be worse than any bad plan. As a youth he was taught if you are attacked, you retaliate immediately. Winning and losing is not to be considered, just honor and glorious death, and the belief the only fights lost are the ones avoided or ran from.

But John likes to win, and he wants his enemies to lose, so he puts more of an emphasis on strategy than his people ever did. This doesn't change his current situation. He can't come up with a good plan of how to approach this battle, so he decides to go with the best of the bad plans his mind can quickly offer him.

John jukes around the little missiles that were spit at him, and starts running directly at the closest swarm of giant bee-flies. Near it, he quickly cuts right, sidesteps new missiles, and as fast as he can, sprints towards the furthest woman spitting missiles, and jumps the stream.

While in the air, John cannot maneuver enough to avoid a spear the woman spits at him, and knocks it away with his sword before landing, and with a great swipe cleaves through her waist, and he immediately starts running towards the next on the opposite side of the stream.

The explosion behind John doesn't reach him, as he runs with all haste to reach the last spear-spitting woman. On the way, he knocks aside a missile, and notices the giant bee-flies are taking the bridge instead of flying over the water, and are slowed down by some speared-women also on the bridge.

Thinking ahead towards the next part of his hasty plan, John reaches the last spear-spitter and starts swinging his sword at her waist. Before his sword cuts flesh, a hard rope wraps around his hand, and yanks him towards the giant flesh-creature, which is pulsing, and shuddering much more frantically.

Closer to the creature, John can see it much more clearly now – the thing is massive: pale grey, veiny, and stinks.

What John assumes is its head is flat and long, with short and stubby nubs all around it, and no eyes. This creature's one giant eye is placed on its bulbous body. A good way under the eye there is a giant flower made of flesh, bloomed, with a red rope extended out of it, wrapped around John's right forearm.

A new red rope explodes out of the flesh-flower, away from John, and wraps around a tree, and then John's right leg.

John drops the sword from his right hand, which is held fast, into his left, and nearly misses the catch as something hits his left shoulder blade. He assumes it's a missile spit by the woman he was yanked away from a moment ago,

Looking back, John sees the four swarms of giant bee-flies, now in one massive swarm, are nearly upon him, and the three speared-women, the ones not spitting spears, are not far behind the swarm.

With swords, John is not good with his left hand, but being not good, for John means he is still far better than most. He makes a powerful swing at the red flesh-rope holding his right hand fast.

Surprisingly, the rope does not part, and twangs instead, and sends vibrations up John's arm.

John barely manages to dodge a new little spear as the flesh-ropes start pulling him in different directions. He has mere moments before the giant bee-flies reach him, and madly slashes at the red flesh-rope holding his hand. The rope stays whole, and doesn't even fray.

Right before the giant bee-flies reach him, John casts [Magical Energy Bolt] at the rope without checking if he has enough magical energy for the spell. He figures the awful pain now wracking his insides is the answer to that question, but the rope is now destroyed. He covers his eyes with his now freed right hand, and closes his mouth.

A peace settles over John. This looks to be his end, but he will die fighting a glorious battle against fantastic foes. He no longer needs to fear the cold-dark, and will hopefully die well enough to fight beside Koram. To see his mother again, and hold her close, and know her loving embrace once more. To stand in front of his father as a man grown, fell and tall.

It takes no time for the swarm of giant bee-flies to completely cover John, and start stinging him all over. The pain is great, but, thankfully, does not last long. It feels as if a rock hits his head, and the giant bee-flies stop buzzing, and he silently thanks Amber for being so timely with her help.

John removes his hand from his eyes, breathes in deeply, and switches sword from left to right hand, and prepares to fight once again. He is still being dragged towards the tree from the rope holding his leg, as a new rope wraps around his waist, and a spear enters the lower right of his back.

Immediately removing the missile with his left hand, John curses. The rope around his waist is being pulled taut, and is pulling John towards the giant flesh-blob, while the one around his leg pulls him towards the tree.

The first speared-woman reaches John as his right leg is lifted off the ground from the rope around it. He is not positioned to use his sword well, or put much strength behind his blows, and his first swing does not go into the speared-woman's waist far. He raises his left hand to block a newly spit spear from hitting his head, and it goes through the meaty part and sticks fast.

The other two speared-women are finally upon John too. Knowing the situation has a grim outlook, he yells, "Amber! Run! Hide!"

In dire straits, John finally gives in to his primal urges and lets out the beast he tries so hard to keep contained. He gives it as much essence of life as it wants. For a while, he loses it, and slashes wildly, and fiercely, with little regard to neither his own safety nor injury. He keeps the three speared-women at bay, though is not able to kill any, as they stick him many times.

The ropes are pulled so taut from two different directions, John is turned around in the air, and now isn't even facing the speared-women. He bites on the spear through his left hand, and pulls it free, and wraps his hand around the red flesh-rope circling his waist, and pulls, and gets enough slack to twist. He swings madly, in an unthinking, barbaric way, and pulls with both his left hand and leg, strengthened to his limit with the vital essence coursing through him.

The tongue from one of the giant mouths of the enlarged bellies of a speared-woman wraps around his genitals, and this causes John to snap out of his wild frenzy. With a clearer head, he notices there's a new missile in his arm, and the three speared-women around him were able to pierce him many times as well.

A new spear is spit out by the far off speared-woman, and John barely manages to deflect it with his sword. Though his insides hurt badly from the last casting of [Magical Energy Bolt], since he didn't have the energy for it, he is desperate and decides to try casting it again, and attempt to kill the spear spitting woman.

Able to somewhat feel the magical energy around him, John, with an immense effort, seeks to pull it all into his dantian, as much and as quickly as possible. It hurts greatly, but he pushes through the pain, though it causes him to scream loudly.

John feels something. Something is happening. His vision goes red and his eyes pop as he strains with effort. His face becomes wet with blood leaking from his eyes, and more spears enter him from the women surrounding him. His body tenses, and he is able to pull the rope further to him, from both hand and foot, and nearly manages to stand.

John notices a bright light flare, but his vision is too blurry to see the cause. He feels it. He feels the magical energy, and forces it. He forces it all. He forces it to move how it shouldn't, and more popping happens in his head, and he nearly faints, but holds on to consciousness. Something is happening, and it feels wrong, and he knows it isn't supposed to happen.

The magical energy explodes all around John, and his insides burn as if they exploded too. He falls to the ground, now free of the flesh-ropes, his insides on fire, skin crisp, and injured in many places. He is happy the three speared-women died in the explosion. He fights through the pain, fights to keep conscious, and fights to lift his head off the ground.

John wins one of the fights, and manages to keep conscious, but that is due as much to losing the fight against the pain as it is to his own willpower. He feels nauseous and heaves, as he is heaving feels new ropes wrap around his right arm and waist.

While heaving, John is forcefully pulled and quickly flies towards the flesh-creature. Through blurry vision, he sees the flesh-flower, where the red ropes come from, is now fully open, and large enough to swallow him whole, and surrounded by rows of sharp fangs.

Pushing the pain, and nausea, and all weakness aside, John forces his injured body to cooperate, and he lands with a foot on either side of the large mouth. He locks his back, heaves on the ropes, and stops from being pulled into the mouth. His insides feel baked to a crisp, and hurt greatly.

Managing to pull some on the rope around his right arm, and get some slack, John punches the giant eye with all his great might with his left hand. The eye explodes in a mess of goo, and white slop oozes down the flesh-creatures body, and into the large flesh-flower mouth, which closes some as if puckering.

The creature shudders and shakes and vibrates, but continues to try and pull John into its mouth with the red flesh-ropes. He tries to look back, to see why no little spears have been spit at him in some time, but is unable to twist around far enough.

John continues punching into the eye socket. He's only hitting hard bone, so starts feeling around for a softer target. He feels a vein, or something large and round and slippery, and wraps it around his hand, and pulls. It does something, as the creature shudders more, and more violently and frantically, and the flesh-ropes slacken a little.

For a while John pulls, and pulls, but is not able to pull this vein, or whatever it is, free of what it is attached to, but yanking on it hurts the flesh-creature, or at least causes it distress. This is how the battle goes on for some time, locked in a stalemate, neither combatant able to do more damage to the other.

Then the flesh-creature rallies, and suddenly pulls much more strongly on the ropes, and John nearly loses the fight, but he manages to keep his feet. He does lose his grip on the vein. He searches for it again, but it seems to have been retracted into the flesh creature, as John is unable to find it, he gives up on the eye socket to start punching what he thinks is the head of the monster.

John's punches seem to have little impact on the creature, so he pulls at one of the many short nubs sprouted all around its head, which does seem to cause the creature some concern, if not damage, but they are slippery, and he often loses his grip.

Trying to edge his face closer to the creature while not losing his footing, John hopes to bite a nub, and feed, draining the creature of essence, He is not able to reach the nubs with his mouth while keeping his footing, so he is careful, and stretches forward little by little, and the rope around his crisp and burnt waist causes much pain as it bites deeper and deeper into his own flesh.

The creature rallies again, and John almost loses his footing as the ropes pull on him with tremendous strength. He locks his back, but is still nearly pulled into the mouth as his heart spikes from surprise. The short sword of Munashi sinks into the head of the flesh-creature, but not deeply, and Amber appears immediately after it does.

Amber's face is stunningly gorgeous. John has seen none more beautiful in all his long life. She has a heart shaped face, button nose, high cheeks, red lips, and eyes similar to Munashi's, but with strange golden irises. All her features come together making a whole far greater than the sum of its parts. *Gorgeous. Absolutely gorgeous.*

John stares at Amber, lost in her beauty, and then gets an even greater surprise.

Amber looks back at John, and gives a wink. Then her nose turns dark, and her mouth protrudes outward, and fur grows out of all her face, and soon John is looking at a giant brown bear. The largest bear he has ever seen. Much, much larger than any bear he has ever seen.

The giant bear swipes at the head of the flesh-creature, first with its right hand, then its left. These swipes cause the creature to shudder like never before, and contract, and the flesh-ropes let John loose, he falls as he watches the bear bite down on the head of the monster.

The bear is blocked from John's sight for a moment as he gets to his feet, but he sees the body of the flesh-creature twist around.

On his feet again, John knows he should go for his sword, but can only watch the fight between giant creatures. The bear, now wrapped in flesh-ropes, but seemingly unhampered, rips chunks off the flesh-creature's head, and swipes at it with fierce strength and power.

John remembers himself, he runs for his sword, and grabs it, then runs back, and swings. His sword bites deep; he swings again, and again, John looks to see how the bear is doing. The final parts of the head are removed, and the bear keeps chomping at the hole where the flat, long head once was.

Finally, the flesh-creature shudders no more, and is still, as the flesh-ropes fall from the bear.

The bear growls loudly, and the growl echoes in John's chest. Crystals then fall to the ground.

Bear and vampire stand victorious.

Dizziness and weakness hit John as he stops empowering himself with vital essence and sends it to heal instead, and he falls to a knee, and barely manages to stop himself from falling further. His eyes are transfixed on the bear, which begins to shrink, turning an orange color, with some white, and longer fur. It continues to shrink and change shape until it is a small red fox, but a very large fox.

The vixen looks at John and cries the oddly horrific noise a fox sometimes makes as a call to her own, which John always thought sounded like a screaming woman. The fox then runs away. He notices the vixen's tail is injured, and split at the end.

John's strength finally gives out, and he collapses onto the ground, wounded, and completely spent.

# CHAPTER 12
# REWARDS

**[YOU LIVE. WHY MUST YOU VEX ME?]**

John is startled awake by the voice like thunder crashing down all around him again, as it did right before the Tribulation. Not much time, if any, has passed since he collapsed, as the vital essence left in him is nearly the same as when he first sent it throughout his body to heal, with somewhere between a third to half of it remaining.

Never had John spent so much vital essence in such a short period of time. Never had John been in such a fight, not since his earlier days, new to the power, before he was strengthened so much, and had yet to climb so far above mundane humans.

Ahn enjoyed having John face many, many enemies on his own, as he watched with a smile, claiming it was the best way to gain skill and power, and if John lived, he would remember those fights fondly, as he would too soon have little fear of men.

John is not certain if the voice expects an answer. He does not want to seem rude to such a powerful being, so tries to reply, but is too spent to do so, and just moans a little.

**[UGH! LORD ON HIGH ABOVE ALL, I MUST REWARD YOU. COME.]**

John feels a pull on his mind, one he is not able to resist, and though his eyes are closed, he sees the world blur by in great speed, the same as when he enters his Mind's Eye.

Things suddenly become very still, and John stands on white, no longer naked, covered in a greyish tight outfit from neck to toe. He sees no floor, or ground, just endless white beneath him, but he is standing, and feels solidness under his feet, and he revels in being completely free of pain where a moment ago he was full of it.

Other than the endless white, there is a large creature twenty paces or so in front of John, and looks to be a defective type of human. It has no soul or vital essence, like Pixie, but strength and power and a sort of heaviness radiates from the being.

The creature has a feminine look to it, but John is not able to articulate why, as the creature is far larger than any man, with broader shoulders, and thicker arms, and stouter legs than any he has ever seen, and covered in dark armor of a strange type.

The legs are short, thick, and stubby, and the feet look far too small for such a large creature. The arms are long and thick, with massive forearms, wrists, and hands. The torso is much longer and thicker than a human's.

A massive head with greyish-pink skin rests on a neck that seems too thin and long, and unfitting. The face looks human, but not human at all. The jaw is massive and protruding, the nose wide and flat too tiny, the eyes small and stretched, sunken and dark with little white showing, the forehead is short and framed by human looking hair pulled back, as if in a bun or tail behind the head, the ears much too large and floppy.

The creature stands with its back straight as a pole, and chin high, looking down its nose at John.

John stares back. He then remembers the advice Pixie gave about dealing with higher beings, and lowers his eyes, and then his body, until he is on his knees, and bowed forward, with his head placed down to the invisible floor he can feel, but also cannot feel too.

A long moment passes and John wonders if he should speak first, but in his long life, in every culture he remembers, those below wait for those higher to acknowledge them in some way before speaking, unless it was an emergency and manners must be waived due to it.

A high voice, somewhat feminine, if it were human, but also somewhat deeper and more resounding, says "Ugh. Stand. I don't want to look at the back of your head."

John replies, "Yes, Your...Majesty?" He stands as directed, keeping his eyes down.

The being laughs, "No. I am no queen. My title is Magnus, though I am unable to break free from this galaxy and travel the dark between to another. Do you know what that is? A Magnus?"

"A higher being?"

"Yes, of course, but what does it mean?"

John fervently thinks but comes up with no specific answer. "I'm unsure, Your Magnus."

More laughter is the response, then, "No, just Magnus. It's the title for those ascended so high as to have reached the third Tree, called Celestial, as yours is called Mortal, though you have lived far longer than I, and the blasphemy that has created you makes the name of your current Tree more of a lie than truth.

"My name is Gar'tar, formerly the highest tiered being in this galaxy, and former High Chair of the Galactic Council. I'm just the council's representative now, once we heard higher tiered beings were coming. Why are they still here? Ugh. Lord on High Above All, I'm going to lose my mind if one of them doesn't contact me soon. They ignored me, you know? I asked how to break free, and they ignored me, and just told me to stand by."

Her eyes become cruel, and she lowers her chin to look directly at John, "One of them returned your soul, you know? I would've missed that particular blasphemy."

John is not sure how to reply, so doesn't, and just stands, unthreatening, trying to look humble.

Some time passes while Magnus Gar'tar stares at John with a cruel look in her eyes, while John casts his own down.

Gar'tar finally breaks the silence, "I reviewed your Tribulation. For a creature of blasphemy, you don't seem a bad sort. I'm taking my vexation out on you when I know it's not your fault. I'm not used to being ignored and having orders snapped at me. They must be here because of the blasphemy, and even though you're part of it, it's far beyond me, so well beyond you. It's not your fault, but you make a convenient target."

Gar'tar sighs in a very human way before continuing, "And I was excited they did come, as I just can't figure it out. I need a hint, and here are two beings capable of giving it, but instead ignore me and give me orders. Me!"

The Magnus snorts and starts pacing around on her stubby legs, placing her massive arms behind her back, her armor perfectly silent.

John sees she does have her hair in a tail, the same way as humans do.

"ME! We haven't had anyone at the Celestial Tree visit this galaxy in over thirty thousand standards, and the last record of a Divine is nearly two hundred thousand standards ago. No records of an Eternal before this one coming here ever, but one must've. I'm sorry I yelled, I'm very aggravated. Don't worry, they can't hear in my Mind's Eye. We can speak freely."

Gar'tar freezes, "Actually, I have no idea if they can or not. I can't, but I'm only a low Magnus. Shit. Be quiet, say nothing more. Shit!"

The Magnus starts pacing again, "You have no idea what it's like being the most powerful for so long, then suddenly you're not, and by a large margin at that."

John decides to speak up at this, "In truth, I recently found myself in a similar situation."

Gar'tar freezes again, turns her head towards John, and gives him an even crueler look, and then suddenly starts howling with laughter, and laughs for a long while. "Oh, that was a good one! I guess you have. I can feel it on you. The unnatural power.

"Not your friend, she happened naturally. If you're her true friend you'll protect her, as her kind are very desirable to Mortals. Ugh. Lord on High, can she talk! Be glad she won't be able to in her current form. Not out loud, at least. I can barely get a word in edgewise, and her mind is too diminished to hold it against her."

The Magnus shrugs in a very human way. "Well, I guess we should get on with it. My focus is Skills, so the best Title I can grant will increase your Skill gain. And that's the one you're getting. That's not enough for surviving a Tribulation with an enemy two full tiers above you, so I'm enchanting your sword too."

*An enchanted sword?* This puts a large smile on John's face. He isn't clear what exactly a Title does, but having one seems beneficial, so this also makes him happy.

John says, "Thank you very much, Magnus."

She makes a cruel face again. "Ugh. Still not enough, is it. Not for your level and that Tribulation, even if you did open your core inside it. Let's see. Damn it all, I've spent far too much on creating that Tribulation, and two Titles, and enchanting your sword, and your friend's other reward – it was a big one – and now something else too? You're lucky I'm so honorable.

"I'll give you a choice but know this first – you're not a bad sort, and have manners, and know your place, and I don't dislike you, but I'd rather you be dead. Nothing against you, besides the blasphemy that made you, it'd just make my life easier is all. I was hoping you'd give me a reason to kill you, but you haven't, and you've been very polite. So, I'm going to get the demons in your area to try and take care of you for me.

"Your body is very injured, and since you tried to control and form mana outside of your body like a fool, your energy system is damaged enough you won't be able to cultivate for a long while. You even managed to fry up some of your channels, and you haven't even opened them yet. What kind of fool Wood dares try to manipulate the energy outside his body and create a manifestation from it. Ha!"

John knows he is very injured, and spent, and his midsection is burnt, and the skin crispy, but John has been in worse shape than this before. Of course, this whole cultivation business is new to him, and he is greatly ignorant of its workings. *I guess that explains all the pain I was feeling inside of me.*

That Gar'tar wants John dead doesn't surprise him, and he doesn't hold it against her much. He was a king for a long time, and ruled as a noble often, and sometimes killing someone makes life easier, even if they did no wrong and didn't deserve it. It is a large reason John would often avoid such lofty positions, and lived as a soldier or mercenary when he could.

Gar'tar continues, "So, you'll be fighting again soon. I can offer you a spatial storage bag, or I can give you healing. The same you got at the start of the Tribulation, and it heals energy system damage and channels as well. Your choice, which do you want?"

This is the being who healed John and Munashi before the Tribulation. His choice is a bag, or the most potent and fastest healing he could hope for. Healing that was able to fix his crushed body in an extremely short period.

John is strong, and can carry much, and he sees little value in any bag, and he wonders how a bag can be offered up alongside such a great gift as healing when he sorely needs it. This puzzles him enough to question the offer. "Is this some sort of magical bag? Can I, for instance, pull an endless number of golden eggs from it or some such?"

For some reason, this question causes Gar'tar to laugh heartily. "No golden eggs are in this bag. It's a spatial storage bag and can hold far more than a bag of its size should."

John furls his brows and tries to see if he is being tricked. "I'm not familiar with this word, spatial. I think it means space. All bags have space, this one just holds more? If I take the bag, will it be filled with treasure? Is the treasure the real gift?"

If Gar'tar were human, the look on her face would be smarmy, or amused. "No treasure. It will be empty, and only filled with space. Lots of space. There is no trick, so no more questions. I offer you a choice, a spatial storage bag, or healing.

"And know this, creature made of blasphemy, some demons are near you already. You have little time to heal, and no way to cultivate. Whether you run or not, a horde of demons will be upon you soon. Not this sunrise, but by the one after. You will have little respite and little time to heal. Now, make your choice."

John wonders if it is like many stories, where the humble farmer is offered a reward of some cheap, but practical item, or some great treasure. The humble farmer picks the practical item and is then rewarded again for his humbleness with a far greater treasure than was originally offered as the alternative.

*Is this what's happening to me now?* There were many stories such as this, and all were rubbish in John's opinion. Gar'tar doesn't seem the type, and John remembers other stories. One of his favorites is about a god offering a farmer one wish, anything he wants, and whatever he wishes for, his neighbors will also get, but get twice as much of. The farmer says, "Well, if that's the case, I wish to have one of my eyes poked out."

A bag that holds more than it should be able to, or potent and fast healing when John is greatly injured and shall soon join battle again, this time with demons. *That is no real choice at all.* "Magnus, I choose the healing, and I thank you for all the many gifts you have bestowed upon me." He then gives Gar'tar a bow.

Gar'tar shows her teeth to John, and says, "Farewell."

# CHAPTER 13
## TELL US A STORY

Not all that far from John, in a peaceful and small town with a big road going through it, right near the only gas station for a long stretch, is an older house, and inside the house are three young women, sisters all, and one man. The man, rather young himself too, has a large, well-muscled build, and haunted eyes. He sits in a wooden chair at a wooden table, with a blanket over his shoulders, drinking hot tea, much food laid out on the table in front of him, as the three young sisters dote on him, and tell him things to boost his ego, as if fighting for his favor.

"Eh, tell us a story, bud," one of the sisters says.

"Yeah, we'd all like that, eh," replies another of the sisters.

"Oh yeah, you betcha. We'd love to hear a story, bud," claims the last of the sisters.

All three sisters have a similar look, with auburn hair, pale skin, and handsome features enhanced by the natural beauty of youth. All three sisters also dress in a similar style which one could dub as 'winter-provocative,' showcasing much cleavage and tight clothing covering the rest, providing some protection against the cold constantly creeping into the room, even with the heat coming from the large fireplace nearby the table they all sit at. The sisters are very similar, but also easy to tell apart, as they all have one key difference between them – one is short, one is tall, and one is plump.

The man does not reply, and just stares off at something unknown and far away. The sisters giggle, and one waves her hand in a strange way, and the man starts. "Huh?" he asks.

"We want a story, bud," says the tall sister, smiling.

"Yeah, bud, a good one too, eh," says the plump one, and then giggles again.

"A story?" asks the man, confused.

"Yeah, bud. A story. We invited you in, washed you, made you comfortable, gave you food and drink, eh. I don't know how it works where you come from, but here we're about reciprocity. Give and take, eh. All we want is a story. Not much to ask for in return for what we've done for you, now is it, eh? Letting a stranger into our house and all. And you're a big guy, bud, so it was a risk, you know?"

A different sister says, "Yeah. Three pretty young girls like us all alone out here in the sticks, defenseless, letting in a big, strong, handsome stranger like you, eh. Definitely a risk. Especially with the world falling apart and God knows what's happening out there. And all we want is a story as payment. Not a frickin' bad deal, eh, bud?"

The man sits silently, and all three sisters stare at him while smiling. He takes a sip of his hot tea enhanced with whisky before replying, "A story. Okay. I got a story. It's a real shit one though. Let's see." He pauses and wipes his hand over his face and head. After a moment, he continues, "Once upon a time, there was a boy who lived in a nice house with a white picket fence. His father told him to love his country and God. This boy loved watching movies and cartoons about soldiers, wanted to be one when he grew up, you know? And when he grew up, he did become one. Not a regular one neither. No. Terrorists attacked his country. They attacked because we're free and they hate freedom and democracy. He hated the terrorists. Hated this enemy that attacked his country.

"So, this boy, now a young man, didn't become a regular soldier. He became a SEAL. A special type of sailor. Elite. The best of the best. He married a pretty girl, he bought a nice house with a white picket fence of his own, had some kids of his own too, and told his kids to love their country and God. Then he went to fight the freedom-hating terrorists that attacked his country.

"Except he didn't. Not really. He was deployed a bunch of times. Kept getting deployed. Liked getting deployed. He tried not to learn, but it's hard to keep your eyes shut for so long. He wasn't really fighting terrorists. Not for the most part. He was fighting guys like him, guys that love their country and God. They didn't hate his freedom. They saw him as the one who attacked their country. Saw him as an invader. They just wanted him to go back to his own home and leave them alone and stop messing with them.

"But he didn't. Being a SEAL was everything to him. Who he was. All he knew. So, he stayed in. He liked the respect it got him. He liked everyone looking up to him like he was a hero. SEALs are the top, and it's good being at the top.

"And when he was home he would fight with his wife, because she always said he was somewhere else, even when he was right there, right in front of her. And then his son tells him he wants to be a SEAL when he grows up, just like his dad, because he loves his country and God. All the man can think about is all the medals he's won for all the bad things he's done, all the dead bodies he's made, all the blood on his hands. All the proof he didn't love God. He looks at his son, and he wants to cry, he wants to tell his son no, but he can't. He just retreats in on himself more. Probably so he don't have a breakdown right then and there. And his wife yells at him, and he just sits there, saying nothing. Saying nothing for so long his wife gets pissed enough to take the kids and fly to Jersey City and stay with her parents."

The man laughs and takes another sip of enhanced tea. And he laughs again before continuing, "This is when the story gets good. The world gets invaded. Ha! We got some sort of cultivation nonsense and demons and a buncha weird shit running around. They turned the power back on. They told us to keep it off, that it was dangerous, but...ah, shit. Never mind that, for now. So, the man gets called in right after this shitshow kicks off. Some portal up north of Quebec City, and some big demon muck-a-muck making portals or something. This got all the bigwigs' panties in a bunch. Biggest threat in North America they said. So, him and a team get jumped in, about a hundred SEALS. Rangers too. Second Bat. Rangers get put on taking the demon out. Our job was blowing the big portal."

He stops talking and looks far off again. The sisters continue staring at him, all smiling sweetly. "They just kept coming. Just kept coming. We couldn't get near it. We heard the Specters tore up that demon muck-a-muck. Tore him up good. Then started heading our way, to the portal, with other air support. We needed it. Arty wasn't doing shit for some reason. Then something…something came out of the portal besides the normal ones. Something…big. I can't even…it was bad. I don't know how I got outta there, but I did. I don't know if no one else did neither.

"We had to have our cellphones off like we always do on missions. When I got far enough away and could, I turned mine on. You guys been checking yours?"

The plump sister says, "No. Ours haven't been frickin' working, bud. Please, go on, eh."

"So, I gets away and turn my cellphone on, and this is the funny part. It's why I laughed earlier. Some sort of nuke in New York City, or near it. Could be a nuke…or could be a power plant blowing. They still don't know, last I checked. My family's in Jersey City. Right across the river. I was gonna go to them. Go all the way around that shitshow and walk all the way if I had to. Make things right. Make things better. We'd all survive. Together. As a family. Cultivate and shit. Now their blood's on my hands too. My family's blood. My kids. My babies. I killed my babies."

At this the man breaks down and starts crying. He cries for a long time. Loud and long sobs of pain and despair. The cry of a man with nothing of worth left in life, his soul cut right down to the quick, in too much pain to see any light at the end of any tunnel. The type of raw pain that can't get any worse.

As the man cries the sisters stare at him, silently smiling their sweet smiles. A long while later the man says, between sobs, "It. Hurts. So. Much."

The tall sister stands, and goes behind the man, and places her hands on his shoulders, and leans near his ear, "Now, now, Ethan. You're lucky, bud. It can hurt a lot worse, eh."

The man wipes his nose, and then turns his head to look at the tall sister. "How? Hell can't be worse than this. I want to die."

Looking into his eyes, still smiling the sickly-sweet smile, the tall sister gives the man his answer, "Eh, weren't you listening? Didn't you hear? There is no hell, bud. When you die you go back to the Wheel. That's why we won't let you die. You think you know anything at all about pain and suffering now, eh? You don't know the first thing, bud. You have *no* idea. But you will. You will."

Now is the sister's turn to tell a story, and a horrible story is told, and Ethan reluctantly stars in it. The sisters keep their word, and the man does not die, and he learns much about pain and suffering.

# CHAPTER 14
# GAINS

Now back in his own body, or mind, or reality, or however his recent visit with Gar'tar worked, John is once again wracked with pain, and it hits all at once, and startles his mind, as if cold water was thrown at him. Then he feels healing enter him, the same as at the start of the Tribulation, and is relieved, as he knows he will soon recover from his injuries.

John extends his senses, and feels nothing nearby, nothing dangerous at least, but feels cold and wind. He doesn't want to open his eyes yet, and wants only to rest for another moment. He assumes the stone structure disappeared when the Tribulation ended, as quickly as it appeared when it started, and this is the reason the cold wind now blows on him.

Wondering why Amber is not close by, John then thinks she may be invisible if she is now back to being a woman. Unless the fox can turn invisible too? Why didn't she just turn into a giant bear and help me fight from the start?

John can't let himself fall asleep, and can't yet move easily, so decides to see what the blinking notifications have to tell him.

**Your skill with 'Breath of the Serpent Clan Endless Technique' has increased to skill level 1. Your mastery with this skill is rated as Neophyte.**

**Your skill with 'Magical Energy Bolt' has increased to skill level 1. Your mastery with this skill is rated as Neophyte.**

**Your skill with 'Magical Energy Bolt' has increased to skill level 2.**

**Your skill with 'External Magical Energy Manipulation' has increased to skill level 1. Your mastery with this skill is rated as Neophyte. Practicing this skill is not recommended for beings that have not achieved level 26 at a minimum. Please see Pixie for further details.**

**You gained a new Achievement! Congratulations! Achievement 'Climber 2' (E-rated, participate in defeating an enemy at least 2 tiers higher than self, 0.20 magical energy discount NCS cost ((total discount now 46.6%)).**

**You survived the Tribulation! Congratulations!**

**You gained a new Achievement! Congratulations! Achievement 'Tribulation Collaboration, Max' (C-rated, participate in defeating a Tribulation rated two tiers higher with one or more other participants, 0.40 magical energy discount NCS cost ((total discount now 47%)).**

**You have received a Title! Congratulations! Title details – 'Blessed by Magnus Gar'tar.' Faster martial-skill gain, slightly faster all-skill gain, slightly more harmony generation on skill increase. Please see Pixie to slot this Title. Enjoy!**

Visiting Mistress Pixie seems like a good idea, and John hopes it relieves his pain, as his visit with Gar'tar did, if what he does to enter his Mind's Eye is the same as what the Magnus did to put him in hers.

John struggles to tap his forehead, but manages, and enters his Mind's Eye, where Pixie berates him for his stunt trying to control external magical energy the way he did, and the injuries it caused, and how lucky he is to have survived.

John is pain free in his Mind's Eye and relishes this boon.

Slotting the [Title] seems simple, but John is warned of the magical energy cost of changing [Titles] before slotting this one. Even in his Mind's Eye, where he feels no pain or pleasure, slotting the [Title] fills John with some great feeling, from head to toe, that he cannot describe beyond it being powerful.

John spends much more time in his Mind's Eye with Pixie being further instructed on his new magical energy gathering technique and learning tricks to make the constant breathing technique second nature, and natural, and replace the way he has always breathed, without thought or consideration.

If truth be told, John stays in so long to continue avoiding the pain and the burning inside his body that waits for him outside of this refuge. Pixie doesn't mind, and John enjoys the company of this powerful goddess-like being, as she is very kind to him, even though she is sometimes wrong and sometimes gives bad advice. Advice John is scared not to follow as it may anger Pixie, and she will stop helping him, and start to treat him poorly.

But John must ignore some of her advice, and use his Legendary meditation technique, as it is faster and more powerful than the techniques Pixie wants him to use. He believes the difference between techniques to be as great as the difference between the healing the Magnus gave him compared to his own much slower and weaker healing from the vital essence he collects from the blood of others.

Having procrastinated long enough, John decides it's time to exit, as retracting within himself by meditating his own way provides an escape from pain too. He hopes his body and the burning pain inside of him has healed enough to start cultivating during his long time in his Mind's Eye, but learns it hasn't once he exits.

John extends his senses, and finds no dangers, nor a fox, nor a woman. It's the very dark of night, and cold enough his vital essence is slowly being drained to protect him. Being completely naked doesn't help this, and if he can find clothing even this small drain will stop.

Since John can't cultivate until his insides are more healed, there is other work he can do, and he sees lying down and wallowing in pain and pity as a poor use of time. With much struggle he manages to stand.

"Amber?" he says, but no reply comes. He tries again louder, and receives no reply again. In front of him, on the west grass of an open field, is both the short and long sword, as well as two yellow crystals. The yellow is much more solid than the yellowish crystals Amber collected from the giant bee-flies.

John picks up the long sword, and it seems to hum in his hand. He studies it, and it gives the impression of being sharper, and brighter, and more solid. So, this is an enchanted sword? I was hoping for something greater, such as a blade of pure fire, but we'll see once I put it to the test.

John takes only the long sword. He needs to find the scabbard, as it was lost along with his makeshift loincloth, but he doesn't want to walk around unarmed.

The cold wind bites into John's burnt midsection, and a light covering of snow has blown onto the once clear field, somehow made artificially warm before. He walks around the area the last spear-spitting woman would be, the one he was unable to kill and that caused him so much trouble, and only sees yellowish crystals, the same that drop from the giant bee-flies and other speared-women.

Amber must've somehow dealt with her. "Thank you, again, Amber. You saved me many times this day," says John.

Walking around, John piles together the many crystals on the ground, as well as all the longer spears he can find and that are still serviceable, and finds his scabbard for the long sword, but not the one for the short sword. He also finds the bag Amber made of her shorts, filled with crystals from the first part of the Tribulation.

Further away, John finds a small tree growing, a new growth, and green, in this cold and newly snow dusted field. A queer sight.

Near the tree's sprout he finds something that causes him to bow his head and offer a prayer – the broken and shattered bones of what he assumes to be his kind, what are now called vampires. Along with the bones are their clothing and other possessions.

One set of clothing is a baggy black outfit, with lots of pockets, black boots, a black cap with a hard visor in the front, and a black jacket with strange metal teeth John cannot figure out but believes are some sort of fasteners. The outfit is a little large, but fits well enough, and is better than being naked.

John stuffs some spongy cloth he cut from a sweater too small for him into the toes of the boots, to help them fit better – a trick he's done many times in his long life. There is no food and nothing to carry water in, but plenty of snow around to satiate his thirst.

John also finds a large and fancy black leather bag. Square, with a shoulder strap, filled with papers and folders and documents. He cannot read well whatever language is on the documents, and probably wouldn't read them even if he easily could, as he does not care what they say, nor does he care for reading.

With one of the female skeletons is another bag, small and strangely patterned, also with a shoulder strap. John cuts a leather skirt into a sash to hold his sword and scabbard like before.

John then digs a hole shallower than he'd like, as he'd dig much deeper if he had more time and proper tools, and places into the hole the bones, and the papers, and junk, and the rest of the clothing not fitting or functional for himself or Amber. There were some trinkets and baubles he would've liked to have taken, but decided not to out of respect, and buried them instead. He then fills in and marks the spot with many of the largest rocks in the area.

I hope Amber returns or reveals herself soon.

John then places Amber's shorts into the larger bag, along with the smaller bag, and all the crystals he collected, and the best selection of clothing for both male and female, and some strips he cut from the clothing he buried earlier.

On the outside of the large bag, with the laces, John ties one pair of male leather shoes, just a tad too small, but are of a high quality even though they have raised heels for some reason, and one pair of female shoes he thinks may fit Amber, though he hasn't seen the length of her feet. He also places the unsheathed short sword into the bag, hilt poking out for ease of access.

From some of the cloth strips he cut, John makes a bundle of just the longer spears, about twenty total.

Back near where the short sword was found on ground, and the two solid-yellow crystals, John notices something else a little further out – the arms of the strange-voiced being that lost them, with the clawed hands, the one who crushed all his kin.

Even though John sees very well at night, it is too dark to make out much detail, but the claws are hard, much harder than the rest of the arms, and the arms are much heavier than human arms this size would be. On both arms, above the large claws, are two metal bracers. He removes one by sliding it up the arm, and it feels as if it hums, like his sword now does. It's light, and very large for a bracer, and looks to have no seams or latch.

It's too dark out for John to get any other details from the bracers.

John removes the other bracer, and easily slides both over his hands and onto his wrists. Then his heart spikes with surprise as the bracers shrink to fit perfectly over his wrists and forearms. They also now feel heavy. Much heavier than they were a moment ago.

If the bracers are magicked in some way, beyond being heavier than they should be, John cannot tell how. He spends some time trying to remove either, and can't, so gives up, and hopes they're not cursed or magicked in a bad way.

The whole time while working and completing tasks up to this point, John has constantly been on guard, senses stretched out far, and sometimes knew a small animal was close by, but he didn't see it, and couldn't identify what kind. He hopes it was Amber, and hopes she turns back to her human form soon, but does not want to push or startle her if she is still a fox, as they are skittish, and get frightened like cats do.

John withdraws two clear crystals from his bag, and judges his insides healed enough to meditate. He starts off with [Emperor Gnzuth Sun and Moon Dantian Clearing Technique], but doing it causes his insides great pain, so he immediately stops, and goes back to his old ways and habits while focusing on his middle dantian, and loses himself in it, as he always does. He is pain free, lost in his own world, going wherever his mind wishes to take him.

**Your middle Dantian has been cleared and is now opened. Congratulations! All Stats increased by 1.**

John opens his eyes and dismisses the notification. He doesn't know how much time has passed since he started meditating, as it is still the dark of night. He knows if he stays here in this area, a demon horde will be upon him before the next sunrise after this dawn, if what the Magnus told him is true.

A large red fox, a vixen, with a mostly orange pelage, with some white, sits in front of him, with her paws on his bag of crystals, and her eyes closed.

"Amber?" John asks. The fox ignores him, and John shrugs. He stretches out his senses, and detects nothing, but he notices his senses go out farther, and are stronger. He also feels stronger, heartier, and much healthier. His waist and other many injuries to his flesh are now healed, and his insides are pain free and feel great, and his dantian is filled with magical energy.

The crystals John holds still have energy in them, so he once again closes his eyes and the world and struggle and pain and worry all blissfully disappear.

**Your upper Dantian has been cleared and is now opened. Congratulations! All Stats increased by 1. You can now convert gathered magical energy into magical essence and improve yourself by increasing the rank of your dantian! Please see Pixie for more details and further instructions.**

John opens his eyes again. It's morning out, and bright, but still windy and cold. The crystals in his hands are empty and devoid of energy. The fox is still in front of him, paws still on the bag, eyes still closed.

John's senses are now much sharper, especially his vision. Sharper, and more vibrant, and his eyes are able to make out more detail farther away than they could before. And he is calmer and can think more easily. He feels different. Better. Clearer. Cooler.

John can tell it's early day, and not late, as the snow only recently started melting. He looks at the bracers on his wrists, and they look to be made of a blueish and light steel and wonders what the heaviness of them means. He draws his sword and looks at it too. It looks the same, and only feels different. He was sure there would be a notch in the blade from his strong attacks on the red flesh-ropes, but there are none. The blade has many swirls in the metal, as his old vootz steel sword did, proving it was folded many times, and is of the highest quality steel.

Of course, a sword master such as Munashi would only carry the best of blades, though this technique of forging was lost long ago, John thinks. The blade is still perfect, and seems much sharper now if anything, and hums to him. He sheaths the sword, deciding it's time to visit Mistress Pixie again.

John enters his Mind's Eye, and Pixie praises him for his speed at cultivation, and tells him with his upper dantian open, his Third Eye, his time dilation while in his Mind's Eye is approaching one.

John, not knowing what that means, doesn't care all that much, and moves onto more interesting things. He notices he is now able to look around while in his Mind's Eye, and even blink, and he feels a little more whole.

Before viewing his [Stats], John asks Pixie about the demons he was told would be directed at him, and Pixie informs him of something he finds extremely useful – John's lower dantian filled quickly with magical energy while clearing his middle dantian, and much of the extra magical energy gathered after was collected and stored within the NCS, and he now has a large surplus of credit, minus a large tax for her performing this service.

With the credit John can purchase some appealing temporary services from the NCS called [Buffs]. Two stand out to John. The first will give him a distance and direction of any large groups of demons near him.

The second will supplement John's own perceptions with Pixie's assistance, as she is able to sense all creatures filled with the little machines of the NCS able to ascend the Tree of Life, including mindless beasts, and insects, and even plants and trees, and can display this information in his eyes. Pixie refers to beast and human and demon and all life capable of ascension simply as entities.

She will only display this information for all entities within John's own range of perception, and John can filter this to only display only sentient or sapient beings too.

The first [Buff] is cheaper and only tells John the direction once. The second [Buff] is more expensive, lasts eleven hours, and will cost near the full surplus of credit John has. Getting both [Buffs] will drain all credit and nearly forty percent of the magical energy in his currently full dantian.

Before spending any of his own magical energy, Pixie warns John the first step of ranking up and advancing is to convert the magical energy in his dantian to magical essence, and she is not allowed to use magical essence as a currency, or collect any, including excess magical essence.

In a perfect world John would stay right where he is and cultivate until he is as powerful as he can become, but the world is not perfect, and he has a great desire to send a message to the Magnus.

John spends all credit and the needed magical energy from his dantian to get both [Buffs] and hopes his constant breathing technique can fill his dantian some good amount as he travels.

I just need to remember to always do it, but relearning how to breathe is no easy task.

As of now there are two sentient entities Pixie detects in John's perception radius.

John assumes one is the fox, Amber, leaving one other John was not able to detect himself with his own perception. She either can't or won't give more information on what she detects, such as direction or level or general power of the entity.

Just knowing something is there is a boon and John is very appreciative.

Next, John views his [Stats].

| | |
|---|---|
| **Strength** | 21.6 |
| **Swiftness** | 21.3 |
| **Conditioning** | 22.9 |
| **Magical Power** | 3 |
| **Magical Energy Cap** | 3 |
| **Runes** | 1.5 |
| **Physical Fortification** | 3 |
| **Elemental Fortification** | 3 |
| **Mental Fortification** | 3 |

John immediately knows something is wrong. He doesn't have a great mind for math, nor a mind geared towards memorizing numbers, but he distinctly remembers his [Runes] [Stat] was at point-six, and three sixes is eighteen, so his [Runes] is three short, or point-three short, considering the already diminished amount he should have gotten.

John also remembers his [Strength] was twenty point something, his [Swiftness] nineteen something, and his [Conditioning] twenty-one something. The scores would be different if all three went up two points, as only his [Swiftness] did. This math worries him.

John doesn't address this with Pixie, as he is sure she will only confuse him and not answer or help. He asks about [Coiled Center of the Universe Energy Gathering Technique], and if he needs to do anything different now that he can convert magical energy to magical essence. They also review how ranking up is done, and he is reminded that when he reaches level 2 he will have access to a summary page listing all his important information.

John and Pixie talk about many things and practice techniques, and it finally becomes time for John to leave his Mind's Eye and search for these demons hunting him, and find them before they find him, and show the Magnus he is no coward running towards safety, but a warrior running only towards the battle, and that his head is not so easy to take, and the taking of it will only come at a great cost.

# CHAPTER 15
# GOOD

Outside his Mind's Eye, John sees a new line at the edge of his vision.

**2 sentient entities detected within your sense-radius.**

The red fox, whom John believes is Amber, is still sitting in front of him, paws on the bag and eyes closed still. John stretches out his senses, and strains to find what Pixie can sense that he himself cannot. He finds nothing, and this bothers him greatly. John's perceptions and senses, now improved with the opening of his dantians, the same senses he has used for his long life and has mastered, should be able to detect everything. At least, he believes he mastered them. He then smiles and attributes it to Mistress Pixie's ability to sense the NCS machines in all entities and believes these demons must have superb concealment techniques too.

John eyes his bundle of spears and makes a few practice throws to get the feel of them better over long distances. They are fully made of some kind of unknown metal and would be far too heavy and unwieldy for normal humans to use. John likes the heaviness of them and thinks it will make his throws more powerful, though less accurate over longer distances.

John carefully removes the fox's paws from the bag, stands, and readies himself for movement. The bundle of spears sits awkwardly on his right and causes a great inconvenience and banging while walking, so John sets bundle and bag down. He removes the smaller bag he got from a female corpse and places the small bag into his sash and tries using the bag's strap to steady the bundle. The bag continues slipping from the sash, so John removes all the yellowish and solid-yellow crystals he has mixed in with the clear crystals and puts them all in the little bag to help cinch it in the sash and hold it there, bound. In total there are two yellow crystals and twenty-three light-yellow crystals, and all are placed in the small bag. When the spear bundle is again placed, the small bag stays secured in the sash, and John can walk without the bundle banging him all over, freeing his right hand.

With senses stretched, John walks around, trying to detect anything. Trying to detect what Pixie can find but he cannot. After some time, still unable to detect anything, John notices the counter go from two to three as he heads more south-southeasterly. He still detects nothing. He walks around some more, the counter goes from three to four, then four to five, and John stops.

Since his other senses are failing him, John peers at the lightly wooded snowy terrain around him, searching for something out of place. He's relied on his ability to smell and hear and see life essence and souls for so long he has formed a bad habit of not looking closely enough at details. It takes him a while, but he finally sees something – two eyes, reddish and orange, as if containing fire, but greatly dulled, and angry, stare at him from behind a large rock on a nearby incline towards a small tree-covered hill.

John asked Pixie about the demons, as he remembered Amber saying her Pixie gave her information regarding dark ones. Pixie told John that demons get smarter as they increase in tiers and think and act like smart beasts while in the Wood through Bronze tiers, though become somewhat verbal at Bronze. Demons are most like humans of the three races invading Earth, and come from a different place called the NetherRealm, and live in a warrior society producing many strong demons. Demons start off short and stunted but gain much size and strength with advancement, and almost always empower themselves with body enhancement spells at early tiers, or weapon enhancements, but will usually have both by late Copper. They become much more fearsome after getting a body [Perk] at Bronze tier.

Pixie warned John that though demons are not very bright at low tiers they are always cunning and devious and fight viciously. *Definitely not very bright,* John thinks, as he removes a spear and throws it at the eyes. The spear flies true and finds its mark and goes straight through the head of the demon. Garbled and odd noises, like the chirping and squeaks of cheetahs, sound near and around John as more demons move out from their hiding spots. Unhidden, John can now smell and hear their hearts, though the smell is very dull, and the beat is soft and odd. The demons are little, and man-shaped with dark greyish-black skin, and are all lightly armed but otherwise naked with no usual indicators of sex. They have a very strange look about them, large beak-like noses, large mouths with many fangs, little nubby horns on their bald heads, tails, and sharp claws holding clubs or short swords or spears or rocks. The demons all have vital essence, but unlike the dark ones, the demons also have souls, though the vital essence is hard to spot, and their souls are very small and dim.

Two throw rocks at John before running away southeasterly, and John easily avoids the missiles. One demon is somewhat to John's rear and runs at him instead of away with the others, and John draws his sword as he turns and meets little resistance as he bisects the demon's head. John drops the sword and withdraws another spear, and quickly throws it at a fleeing demon as it nearly crests a hill, and the throw scores a hit through the demon's leg, pinning it to the ground. The other two are over the hill, and now safe from John's spears.

John kneels to study the demon close to him, and though the body didn't disappear as the dark one's corpses do, there are two clear crystals near the corpse. After inspecting the corpse, and cutting it open to see what's inside of it, John is surprised to find no blood, just a strange and somewhat tangible substance, like more of an energy, and weird organs, and not one that looks or seems like a heart. After inspecting the demon's crude little wooden spear, John collects the crystals and moves towards the first demon he downed. After John retrieves his own spear and cleans it with snow as best he can, he puts it back in the bundle and collects the crystals. This demon had a short sword of a strange metal of very poor quality and craftsmanship and is badly notched. He leaves it as he walks to the third demon.

This demon threw a rock, but also has a makeshift club, and struggles mightily to free its leg from John's spear pinning it to the earth. As he gets close the demon twists around while lashing out viciously at John with club and claw and fang. John grabs both wrists of the demon, and easily holds them, as he shows the demon he has quite the bite himself, and drains the creature of its vital essence. The strange thick energy-blood of the demon has little taste or scent, and the little amount he takes in his belly doesn't seem harmful.

Now topped off and feeling satiated, John collects this demon's crystals and his own spear. On his way up this little hill to the demon he just fed on, John looked for trail sign and tracks and could find none. Even in snow there are no marks of passing, something that should be impossible, but that word means little now to John, seeing all the queerness he has in the short time since his mind has been fixed. *These demons aren't just hard to spot but will also be very hard to track.*

As John crests the hill, he notices his tracker only says one. As he scans around him, he sees no indications of civilization of any sort in any direction. Just the white of snow on hills and trees, and small mountains in the distance to the north and west, and some far, far off to the south. No mountain he recognizes either, and the trees seem different and off from what he knows.

John thinks the demon horde is approaching from the same direction the demons fled towards, but wants to see what the [Buff] he purchased has to say about it. Unable to figure out how to activate the [Buff], he asks Pixie. Once activated it confirms his belief and a large red arrow points in the direction he is facing. The red arrow flashes a couple of times and then disappears. The tracker goes up by one and soon after the red vixen runs up to him, but keeps some distance, as if wary of him.

"Amber?" John asks. He receives no response. He can see the fox's eyes for the first time; the eyes are the same color as Amber's, but the iris color doesn't look strange on a fox. "I'm not sure how well you can fight as a fox. Even normal humans find foxes to be of little danger, though you are big for one. If you can, you should change back to human form so we can speak, or to the bear so you can fight.

"Oh, I saw your face. It was beautiful. Maybe the most beautiful face I've ever seen. I enjoyed the quick look I had, and would like to look at it more, but it did not cause me to fall madly in love with you. I'm afraid I am incapable of any such since I lost my Lilitu. Our love was...different. It burned bright for hundreds and hundreds of years." John stops at this, as he is surprised with himself. For a time not that long ago for him, but long before he met Thomas, he tried hard to change how he thought of a hundred, as it was fixed in his mind as ten tens, and his mind was very reluctant to change this. Now hundred slipped from his mouth with neither thought nor effort behind it.

Smiling, John continues, "So, if you were staying as a fox to protect yourself from my wild and uncontrollable love, it is unnecessary. Also," John stops to bow low at the waist, "thank you very much for saving me yet again. The flesh-beast and the speared-woman spitting those little spears had me sorely pressed, and without your help I may not have survived."

John looks inquisitively off to the horizon, "You know, since I accepted the power no one but my old master and friend, Ahn, has ever saved my life. Well, maybe Thomas, but I have no clear recollection of him doing so, but with my mind the way it was, it wouldn't surprise me if he did so many times. I've lived a very long life, and you, a new acquaintance, have done much to help me in a short time. I owe you much, and I pay my debts. I hope to continue our friendship, and hope we don't part ways, and we continue to stand by each other in these queer times. Sorry...sorry, I forgot for a moment I shouldn't use that word the way I do.

"Well, I hope you change back into a woman so we can speak. My mind is newly back and aching to talk about some things, like Magnus...Magnus...what's-her-name? Great gods below, I already forgot. I hope my mind is not damaged again, somehow, or deteriorating again.

Well, now I'm just rambling, so let us proceed to slaughtering these demons and collecting their crystals and advancing in...what was it? Ranks. Yes, ranks. Can you cultivate as a beast? I think that's what you were doing while I was too, with your paws on the bag full of crystals. Pixie said beasts advance differently and don't cultivate like people and don't use crystals. Did I tell you? All three of my dantians are open now. Please become a woman again. Please."

John, flustered, and knowing he is making a fool of himself, starts walking, cheeks red. The fox follows, making the excited duck-pig noises foxes do, while sniffing around, and occasionally clawing at the ground under the snow for a second before getting bored, and climbing a tree here or there. The vixen often stays in front of John, leading the way, sniffing, and moving forward as if on the trail of something. John hopes the fox can track the demons, but his counter goes up and down for a while, demons ignored, while the fox continues forward, only eating odd things now and again.

Curious, John follows and pays close attention to Amber, and comes to believe the fox is staying in this direction by luck only, and only cares about food, as she seems famished. The fox eats some old berries from under a bush, as well as some weird nut-like thing with many long and sharp protrusions, but passes every meat source John has known foxes to always love. *Is this some sort of strange herbivore fox? It looks like a normal red fox, just larger. I'm happy she has taken a greater interest in food, as her human form is far too like a skeleton to attract quality male suitors, but she'll never put on weight if she keeps with this strange diet.*

John can move fast, and he thinks the vixen may be faster, as he can't keep up when she sprints. He keeps his senses peeled and on the lookout for signs of demons, but his best indication he is heading in the right direction is his counter is up to seven now.

Much time later, after traveling far, with John trying to constantly breathe in the strange new way to collect energy, though it is no easy thing for him, his efforts are finally recognized, and he is rewarded with the following notification.

**Your skill with 'Breath of the Serpent Clan Endless Technique' has increased to skill level 2.**

Continuing onward, soon after, John's tracker suddenly spikes up.

**99\* sentient entities detected within your sense-radius.**

Shortly after seeing this, the fox stops, and raises her hackles like a cat, and gives out an almost dog-like bark. She runs back to John and grabs the bottom of his pants between her teeth, and seems to try and drag him away, back the way they came. John reaches down to scratch the fox, and calm her, but the fox nips at his hand, and moves away, occasionally looking back at John, and whining, as if begging him to follow. John says, "Amber, this is good. This is what we were looking for. I know you can't fight well as a fox, so you should hide. Climb a tree, as you did before."

The fox looks confused, so John kneels, and there is a pause as he considers how to explain, "This may seem a stupid thing to do, but sometimes stupid is the best choice of all the bad choices you can make. None have ever made the claim I have a great mind, nor have any claimed I am some sort of grand strategist, but I do know a few things. The Magnus could easily strike me down, and there is little I could do to stop her if she did. I don't know what she told you, but to me she indicated she would not attack me directly, and would only do so if I give her reason to, such as being ill-mannered or disrespectful. At least, that is how I took the little she said about it.

"She did state the Tribulation and our rewards were a great expense to her. I don't know if sending many demons at me incurs a great expense too, but I assume it has some cost.

"Those are two bits of information to consider – she will not strike me down directly, and she has already incurred an expense great enough to complain about. So, I can run and hide and hope she doesn't put me in a position there is no escaping from. Or, whenever she sends enemies to hunt me, and lay me low, as she did with these demons, I hunt them instead, and do so again and again, until they fear me more than they desire her rewards. Also, at some point, after enough of her wealth trickles away, she'll prefer to keep what remains over adding my head to a smaller pile of it."

The fox still gives John a confused look, and John goes to scratch her behind the ears, but the fox skitters away, avoiding his touch. The act hurts John a little, but he has greater worries to face now.

"I don't remember the name of my father, or the name of my people, but many of the lessons they instilled in me are as correct now as they were then, and always will be. I had to run many times in the past, often to avoid the unnecessary slaughter of peasants, but sometimes to avoid the cold-dark too. I will never run again. I will be polite to my betters, but I will not tolerate being disrespected, and I'll always attack my enemies, even if it means my death to do so. This I promise," says John, solemnly.

"Today, I will triumph or die, as will the demons, if those are what I soon face. I will put this bag of crystals down here, beside this tree, and if I fall, they are all yours. If I am the victor, I will be back, and we will share in them, as we have been doing. So, run and hide and stay safe, and I will see you again soon, or never again."

John, load lightened with the bag of crystals set down, moves forward out of the tree line, and around a small hill, where he sees a large gathering of demons in the distance. A horde of around four hundred, but John guesses their numbers to be at around two hundred, as his mind is not trained at counting numbers so large at a glance.

A demon of great size, with an axe and shield in hand, stands in front of the army, easily twice as tall as the previous demons John saw earlier, with a dog-like snout, broad shoulders, large arms, a powerfully thick neck, and intricate antlers growing out the side of its head. Behind this demon are three others, all larger than the ones behind them, but not even up to the shoulders of the large one in front. These three look like the demons from earlier, but larger, with bigger frames, larger horns, and better armed. The four larger demons have souls much easier to spot and contain much more vital essence than the smaller ones too. More demons slink from shadow and wood to join the army, bolstering the ranks of the small demons behind the four.

Many, many eyes of dull red and orange fire stare at John, with great malevolence and hatred shining forth from each. John spits towards the army of demons, in honor of Munashi, his dead brother and friend, though he only knew him a short time. The enemy host is many, and facing this horde a great risk, victory anything but certain. Eyeing the large host arrayed against him, John has only one thought: *Good.*

# CHAPTER 16
## DEMON HORDE

*Even if it seems certain that you will lose, retaliate! Neither wisdom nor technique has a place in this. A real man does not think of victory or defeat. He plunges recklessly towards an irrational death. By doing this, you will awaken from your dreams. Yamamoto Tsunetomo, Hagakure*

Dusk, and the respite it promises, is still a ways off. This matters little to John, as he made his intent clear, and the sun is low and weak and sapping him little anyways.

The largest demon, in front of the others, seems to be trying to say something as John removes a spear from the bundle and empowers himself with vital essence. He doesn't care what the demon leader has to say. *Now is not the time for talking. Now is only the time of battle. Great gods below, witness my great deeds,* John prays.

With great strength, John throws the first spear at the large demon as it tries to bray out something. The demon holds its shield out, and it seems to shimmer for a moment, and the full-metal spear loudly clangs off it. All the demons start chirping and squeaking loudly, with much mirth, as if a great victory was won, and only quiet as the second spear pierces the shield and punctures the upper-left chest of the large demon. The demon quickly pulls his shield forward, spear and all, and barely manages to block the third spear, which also bounces off the shield with a loud clang.

Most of the demons start rushing forward, but John must avoid the many rocks and even some arrows flying towards him, and while doing so still manages to toss three more spears, downing two of the three medium-sized demons. The antlered demon is nearly upon John, as it is

131

much faster than its brethren, and a new spear flies towards its face, but it manages to effectively block the spear with its shield again, and while its vision is obscured, John casts [Magical Energy Bolt] at its chest, and right after, casts it again at the last and final medium-sized demon. The last casting is a close thing, and John is forced to dodge both axe and antler and mouth as he casts. [Magical Energy Bolt] does little damage, if any, to the large demon, but blows out the front chest of the medium-sized demon on contact.

Sword drawn now, John attacks the forearm holding the axe coming at him, and it bites deep, but the blow is stopped by bone. *Either the enchantment on this sword is weak, or this demon's bone is extremely tough,* thinks John as a mighty swing of the antlered demon's axe is caught on the strange new bracer on his left arm. The blow pushes John back some steps, and he is amazed the bracer held and did not break. The demon's blow had great strength behind it, and John thinks his doughty foe may even outstrip him in physical might.

But John is much faster and nimbler than this foe.

The rest of the horde is only thirty or so paces away now, so John gets to work by slicing the demon's thigh, bicep, neck, and stomach. The demon silently ignores all the injuries inflicted upon it, the bloodless and severe wounds far more than enough to down any man, and it only continues to press the attack with mighty and skilled swings of its axe, or swipes of its antlers and shield, and bites from its large fang-filled mouth. The demon has some skill in combat, but none are as skilled as John. He ends the fight with a thrust through the eye and deep into the demon's head, and the large demon falls to the ground just as the horde arrives.

As men have for ages, these demons fall before John as grain before a scythe. Near every attack of John's killing outright, with very few demons being maimed and alive and surviving a blow. His speed is a great asset as he attacks and retreats and maneuvers, trying to prevent himself from being surrounded and pressed from all sides. He is successful in this. For a while.

When finally surrounded, John, with great speed and strength, presses forward and through the horde, and wins free, but with some injuries, surprised he is breathing heavy, and unsure how long he's been fighting for. The horde is still large, and John has an awful smile on his face as he slices through the foes near him, happy these demons have not run yet, as most men would have by this point.

*This! This is not wasting my life trying only to prolong it. This is living!* An ecstasy overcomes John too few have known or will ever know, as most men seek safety and comfort, and want greatly to live another day, rather than testing themselves so.

*It hasn't always been this way,* John thinks. For much of his life even a humble farmer was expected to take up arms against his own lord or king if treated without respect, or ordered to do something going greatly against his own interest, and would only tolerate such treatment from his own mother and father, and no one else. John thinks this only changed when small men with low minds and no chests took to ruling all, and told people lower than them they had no choice in matters, and were no longer able to have pride, no longer allowed to stand tall, no longer allowed to say no, and few resisted. To John it seemed as if mankind cheered as blinders were placed on their eyes, and a yoke upon their necks, and a cage around their hearts, and thought, "Well, at least now I am safe. Safe from living this life I was gifted with. I need not make my own decisions anymore. I need only exist in silence until I no longer do." Some did not cheer or share in those recreant thoughts. *Some still don't,* John is certain.

Having been around a long time, John has seen and done much, has many times been a king, a noble, a farmer, even has he been many gods to many peoples, and throughout it all he has always been one thing above all – a warrior. For a long time, though, what he hasn't been is free. Ever since he has accepted the power he must always think of and avoid the cold-dark. Now, that threat was no more. For a very long time John had to hide what he is and what he can do, but here and now he doesn't. He is in this moment free, and he revels in this freedom.

In John's opinion, freedom, in its highest form, is a group of men telling another man, "You will do as we say or else," and the lone man saying back, "I will do as I please, regardless."

In this instance, it is a horde of demons, and not men, and their desires implied, and not spoken aloud, but John still does as he pleases, regardless.

He lays into those before him, his sword still clean, as demons all seem to have some sort of thick energy instead of blood. His heart fills with elation as the demons continue to throw themselves upon him, and his only regret is he did not take the short sword too, as he is not able to bring as much death with his left as he does with his right hand. He is happy to have the new bracers, as they are strong and ward off blows extremely well, and he feels there is more to them than their durability, more than can be outwardly seen.

Twice more John is surrounded, twice more he breaks through to freedom and maneuverability, and many times more he sustains injuries, though none too serious. He fights for a long time, breathing heavy, but not yet close to being spent, and only once needs to feed to replace vital essence. He fights, and he fights, and the more his arm burns from this fell work, the more his heart swells with much gaiety, and if he dies, he will die a happy, fulfilled man, doing the work he was put on this land to do, certain of his great place in the Underworld.

When a mere two score or so enemies remain, a rout begins, and the demons start fleeing in many directions. John gives chase, and maims many, and throws three more [Magical Energy Bolts] at demons close to escaping, which many do.

**Your skill with 'Magical Energy Bolt' has increased to skill level 3.**

More escape than John wants, but they run in many directions, and he is only so fast; the demons have an uncanny ability to hide. John maimed as many of the fleeing demons as possible for two reasons. First, to see if demons can die from severe injuries as humans do, since they have no blood, and their organs are strange. Second, John requires much vital essence to strengthen his body with, and these demons have plenty to gift him.

The sun set scant moments before the battle ended, darkness now settling over the field of battle. John sends as much essence as he can to heal his many injuries, though none are serious enough to hamper him much. He takes a deep breath and revels in victory and work well done. He was able to maim nearly a score of fleeing demons. He drains the first but is full of the essence of life before he gets to the dregs, so stops suckling. He sends all essence to strengthen his body and watches as the demon expires, as humans do, with too little vital essence in it. He hopes the little amount of odd, thick energy he takes in is not harmful or causes any strangeness in him. He thinks his vital essence would've reacted to it if it posed some sort of danger, so he isn't too worried. Nothing bad has come to him so far, after draining the demon much earlier in the day, long before this grim battle.

John finds out demons can die from 'bleeding out' as humans do, as the fourth maimed demon is expired by the time John gets to it, and John is happy demons are also like humans in this way. He has to drain a total of eight demons, and send all their essence to strengthen his body before he feels his power increase permanently.

When John first got the power, for a long time he needed only partially drain a human to have enough essence to strengthen his body. That was long ago. In total, including all the maimed and living demons throughout the field of battle, he is able to strengthen his body four times, and he ends completely filled with as much essence of life as his body can carry. He knows four times strengthened isn't much, but every bit helps, and every bit adds up over time. He sees no sense ignoring any source of strengthening himself. Not in this strange new world, with strange new threats, and beings as powerful as gods.

John knows he needs to collect the crystals from all the many dead demons, and then try to rank up his dantian, but before he starts on these tasks, he wants to get his bag and Amber. He knows foxes see well at night, at least as well as he also does, if not far better, and are crafty night hunters, so Amber should not be hampered or dismayed by the dark of night.

The bag is where he left it, and his tracker has consistently been at about five or six since the end of the battle but is down to only three near the bag. The tracker has over two hours left on its time. He cannot hear Amber, and since he feels he has nothing to fear from anything left in these woods and snowy hills he yells loudly, "Amber!"

John notices the stars seem brighter, somehow, and finds the Ladle, and then the great Northern Star. He also finds what are now called Cassiopeia, Mintaka, and Orion. As he learned long ago to help find his location, he outstretches his arm, and makes a fist, and points it towards the Northern Star. He guesses he is far north, and some ways east of the north point. He then calls for Amber again.

While waiting, John inspects a few injuries, and thinks they may be healing faster than usual. His tracker moves up to four a moment before he can hear Amber running towards him, faster than any fox can move. *What a queer fox*, John thinks.

The fox arrives and makes excited duck-pig noises, and seems to have more energy than she can handle. "Amber, I have much work to do this night. Please, follow me."

John leads Amber back to the stricken field, filled with the corpses of his enemies, and removes a handful of clear crystals from his bag, and places them on the snow, and tells Amber she should cultivate while he finishes his tasks. Amber looks at John, and then the crystals, and places her paws on them, and closes her eyes.

John goes back to where the battle started, and finds his bundle of spears, and collects the ones he threw, and finds two are now useless, so his bundle now contains eighteen spears. He then collects crystals, keeping the two darker ones he finds from the antlered demon and the lighter yellow ones from its medium-sized confederates separate from the rest, and places them in the small bag he keeps in his sash to help steady the spear bundle with its strap. Each small demon drops between one and five clear crystals, and soon John's larger bag overflows with them, so he goes back to Amber and drops many, and is then able to fit the rest he finds.

His tracker is up to nine, and John decides he will lower that number before he starts cultivating, and does so. He learns a little more on how to spot hiding demons, and gets the tracker down to two, and that number includes Amber. He also gets this message.

## Your skill with 'Magical Energy Bolt' has increased to skill level 4.

He collects the spear bundle and drops it off near Amber, along with his large bag of crystals with the short sword and clothes. He squats down, and grabs two handfuls of clear crystals, and before he begins meditating, admonishes himself for not doing the [Breath of the Serpent Clan] as he should, and letting it slip, and not following Mistress Pixie's advice on how to keep it going.

John then starts [Coiled Center of the Universe Technique], which is different now somehow. He squats the same, with his back perfectly straight, and he does the same flowing arm movements, and silly slow dance, and strange way of breathing, but it is different. He focuses on the energy coiled around his spine, and it isn't like last time. Something happens. Magical energy from around him and from the crystals in his hands is slowly being collected, but is also changing in his dantian, but only a little. The feeling is strange, and John loses himself in the repetitive act, and the somewhat pleasant feeling it gives him.

And, later, John loses himself in his own mind, traveling where it takes him, lost to his mind's whims in a way he can neither explain nor control, as it has been for a long, long time. He dreams about setting his enemies afire by flames billowing forth from his hands and making great plumes of fire burst upwards from the ground, and how his fight with the demon army would've gone if he had such power and such spells to cast. He dreams of his Lilitu, of her beauty, of her horror. He dreams of fighting the Magnus he met, and holding his own, offering no quarter, and receiving none, and in the end, being victorious.

137

Then a very weird feeling snaps his eyes open. Something he remembers from a long-ago memory, when he rested against a tree to use its crown to protect some from rain, and lightning hit the tree, and passed from tree to himself some, causing him to vibrate very quickly for a short time. That feeling from the memory is happening to him now, and makes his brain start, and his teeth hurt, and he doesn't like it one bit. Notifications start to appear in his eyes, but before he can read a word, he is sucked into his Mind's Eye. As his vision regains focus, Pixie appears, and she is no longer smiling or cheerful, but looks worried instead.

Pixie says, "Phew, you almost just blew up your dantian and died!"

# CHAPTER 17
# SCREWING THE POOCH

"Good thing we were here to pull your bacon out of the fire! But just barely. You really almost screwed the pooch there, pal. By the way, we're going to recoup the energy it cost us to shock you. Sorry about that, but you just weren't listening, and that was the only way to snap you out of it. We told you using an F-rated meditation Skill was a bad idea."

John, struggling to understand what exactly is going on, but not wanting to be rude to a being as powerful as Pixie, says, "Uh, thank you, Mistress Pixie, for saving me from…"

As John searches for words, Pixie takes over for him, "From distending your dantian beyond capacity, something that isn't very smart to do. We even told you before not to do it, didn't we? That we couldn't do anything with excess magical essence. Remember? But you're welcome. That's what we're here for. Stopping all of you from making stupid mistakes, trying to put all of you on proven paths of ascension in the safest way possible. You all just don't like listening.

"Now, even though you're approaching one with your time dilation, time is still somewhat of the essence. See this?" John, being respectful of the ancient etiquette of lessers dealing with their betters, rarely looks at Pixie's face, and keeps his eyes down or on other things when in his Mind's Eye, now raises his eyes and looks at her. Pixie always seems to do everything in an overly animated fashion – her facial expressions, her mannerisms, her gestures. He thinks it a silly thing to do, especially for one as great as Pixie. He tries to keep this thought to himself while Pixie over-animatedly gestures to her side as an image of John's dantian grows, and continues growing until it is large enough to see great stretchmarks throughout the surface of it, like as seen on skin or glass sometimes.

Pixie then continues, "We recommend everyone extend their dantian a little when they rank up, especially when they ascend tiers, but only by ten percent or so. That helps. You're almost thirty percent over, which is just plain stupid to do. We can't stress enough just how dumb and dangerous it is. You never want to go so deep in meditation where you're completely oblivious to the outside. We were calling out to you and setting off alarms and you just ignored everything. We had—"

John can't let the falseness of that statement stand without interjecting, and says, "I'm truly sorry to interrupt, Mistress Pixie. Please, forgive me. I must say I'm not oblivious to everything in that state. I've been doing it for a long while, and any hint at danger I detect awakens me. Any hint. I do tend to ignore friendly voices, and other noises not indicating direct harm or threat to me. I'd dislike for you to consider me incompetent or not attuned to danger. It's just this... this cultivating and dantian business is new to me, and my mind is not accustomed to the threats it poses. I'll gladly pay the energy cost for the...shock, was it? Gladly. And I thank you again for the shock and explaining all this and helping me so much. I truly appreciate you and the kindness you've shown me. And I apologize again for interrupting."

John, embarrassed now for not just interrupting, but rambling also, hopes he has not damaged his relationship with Pixie, and hopes she does not think less of him now.

Pixie smiles from ear to ear, "Oh, well, you're welcome! Like we said, that's what we're here for. Now, this is how we fix this. As soon as you get out of here, and we mean immediately, as fast as you can, send some of the magical essence to your middle dantian. You don't want to release too much of it too fast, as it will cause your dantian to be weak when you rank up, but you can't be slow about it either. Immediately release about two or three percent, then slow it down a little till about ten percent of the current total is sent to your middle dantian. That will put you out of danger. Then, before you rank up, you want to turn that into shen. It won't really do anything, not at your tier, but no reason letting it go to waste, right? We also need to show you how to rank up per your Archetype. One of the many benefits of an Archetype is it's a much easier technique to learn and we do almost all of the heavy lifting for you, versus targeting and strengthening specific Stats on your own.

"Oh, and before we go over how to do all three of those things, we should say you have a pretty nice surprise waiting for you in the notifications. No sense getting you distracted now, so let's get to work saving your life, amigo. Okay, all three of these are non-Skill techniques, so you just got to learn the steps, don't got to worry about understanding them or getting better at them. You ready to start learning?"

John first asks if she can explain a little more why she couldn't just take the extra magical energy before it turned to magical essence, as she did before when he purchased the [Buffs]. Pixie, sounding exasperated, tells him that his meditation technique converts magical energy to magical essence so fast she couldn't grab enough magical energy fast enough to slow him down much at all.

John then tells her he's ready, and learns all three techniques easily. He wouldn't really call them techniques, as they weren't the same as the ones he's learned so far, even the way of turning essence into shen. *Whatever shen is*, he thinks. The middle dantian wants essence from the lower dantian, so getting it to go there is natural and takes little effort and nothing beyond John's mind and a little willing it along, according to Pixie. The same holds true converting the essence to shen within the middle dantian, as the middle dantian exists to do this, and John just has to get it spinning and wait while it converts, with no other assistance needed from him at all.

Ranking up the lower dantian involves a little more, but not much. John has to get his lower dantian spinning as fast as he can, and then focus on compressing it as much as he can, and then something starts happening, and when it does, he'll get a prompt asking if he wants Pixie to take over, and then he only needs accept. Simple. What, specifically, starts happening he isn't clear on, as Pixie was vague about it, and just said he doesn't even need to notice, as she will. He just needs to watch for the prompt.

Knowing what to do, it is time for John to leave. Pixie then tells John to either ignore, suppress, or dismiss his notifications, and to do it immediately, so he doesn't get distracted from his crucial tasks, and have his dantian explode, which will most likely result in his death. Understanding the critical nature of the situation, despite Pixie's cheerful attitude, John exits his Mind's Eye, and immediately focuses on his overfilled dantian, and the image of it fills his vision as he also mentally dismisses the notifications. His dantian is now filled with a light-golden liquid where before it was clear magical energy, and he follows Pixie's instructions.

John quickly realizes things will not be as easy as Pixie stated, as the essence in his dantian is resistant to his wheedling and will, and it takes some great effort to get a piece out and coax it towards his middle dantian. The stretchmarks continue to spread as he does so, and he can somewhat feel the immense pressure on his dantian, and how close it is to exploding. Thankfully, pulling this strand out immediately relieves some pressure on his dantian, and the stretchmarks stop spreading. He strains and strains moving the strand of essence upwards, and it takes great concentration and will, but halfway between dantians it becomes easier, and then no effort at all, as the middle dantian, up near his heart, grabs hold of it as if starving and quickly pulls the strand towards it.

John snaps off the strand after a moment, as he has no way to accurately judge ten percent, but his dantian seems fine and safe as is, and doesn't get mushy or malformed, what Pixie called deflated, and warned would be bad and could lead to weakness and other issues upon ranking up.

John watches his middle dantian start spinning faster and faster and is mesmerized as he watches the light-golden liquid change into a bright white milky substance. He knows not how long it takes, as it is beautiful to watch, and he is disappointed when the transformation is finished and the middle dantian slowly stops spinning. *Beautiful*, he thinks.

Now the task of ranking up begins, John refocuses on his lower dantian, and starts spinning it as fast as he can. Assisting with hand movements, as Pixie showed him, to increase the spin, and forcing it to spin at greater speed with his mind and will.

The dantian spins faster and faster, and at some point, John rises above his body, or his vision of his dantian zooms outwards, and he looks down from far above at his dantian and energy system and his blocked meridians.

At some point using his hands as a mental aid to slap the dantian to spin faster stops helping, and each slap slows it some, so he stops doing so. He knows he can make it go faster. Somehow. He notices his middle and upper dantians also spinning, though slowly, so works on spinning both faster too, and this seems to work, as his lower dantian increases and increases in speed the faster his other dantians spin.

For quite some time John eggs the dantian on faster and faster, trying tricks, and getting it to spin at a blazing rate, until he feels it reaches a limit, and it goes as fast as he can possibly coax it to go. Now is time for the second part of ranking up, or John's second part to do before Pixie takes over.

Looking down on the dantian, from far above, John puts his hands on either side of it, and with hands and mind and will he pushes inward on the dantian. He does not attempt to use much pressure, as he is frightened it will slow the dantian greatly, or even cause it to stop spinning, but Pixie assured him it wouldn't, and she is proven right. He applies more pressure and pauses, and more pressure and pauses again, and then more, as he was taught.

He does this many, many times, and gets a new worry, as the dantian is now compressed to nearly half its size from when he started, and no prompt from Pixie comes. He waits, and the dantian expands a little, and he figures it must not be compressed enough, as Pixie stated he would notice something start happening before the prompt shows, and nothing notable is happening or has happened, so he starts compressing again. And compresses, and compresses.

The smaller the dantian becomes, the harder it becomes to compress it further, and each compression doing less and less. After some great time, John's head throbs with a great pain, but he sees no path but to keep going, and fight through it, and keep going, and keep fighting, and keep compressing, until whatever is supposed to happen happens and the prompt appears.

After much time doing this, John's head starts spinning, and then the world spins at great speed, and the stars start to spin, and then time itself also spins. All of a sudden there is focus, and he sees Thomas, with his kind eyes and generous smile. Thomas reaches out for John, but fades away as he does, and is replaced by a little girl, around six or seven years of age, standing over many, many dead bodies. Then she is replaced by something. Something extremely frightening to see, and this something is looking at John. Directly at him. A great monster beside a literal sun, far exceeding the giant star in size. The monster opens its giant mouth as if to speak, but John's head pops and all becomes dark. He assumes that was the something to look for, but no prompt comes. "Mistress Pixie?" he asks. No reply comes.

With only his will he struggles to keep compressing the dantian he can no longer see, in the empty darkness. "Pixie?" he asks again. No reply comes. Time becomes meaningless. Self becomes meaningless. There is just his great will and struggle to force his dantian to become smaller and smaller.

At some point he sees sparks and fire, like from fireworks and cannons firing their great loads. This *must* be the something he's been waiting for. It *must* be. "Pixie!" John yells. He receives no response. He yells her name many more times, and no reply ever comes. All becomes silence, and then his loud heartbeat sounds, and he starts compressing his dantian again to the regular and strong beat of his heart, and he does this until the darkness explodes in white, and then nothingness.

Captain Ukaraaz kneels. His right knee on the ground, his right hand too, his left elbow on his bent left knee, his head bowed low. He dislikes kneeling for even higher ptagmogs, and detests doing so for a filthy magal, but his master demands he show proper and due respect for all beings of higher Trees. So, he must now swallow the bile, and do as ordered, and keep respectful, which also keeps him alive. He reminds himself he wanted this. He volunteered just so he'd have opportunities such as this, opportunities not found in the Nether. He would do much to advance, dealing with a magal least of it. And this magal is in the third Tree, and generous with her rewards.

"He lives. He defeated your *army*." the magal says, spitting out the last word with disdain.

This greatly surprises Ukaraaz. He sent a group four hundred strong, led by a Bronze with three Copper underlings. "How? You said it was a Wood. And a low Wood at that."

"As I said before, great blasphemy is how. He has inflated Stats for his tier, and some skill at arms, but even your Bronze surpassed his Strength. He is not a great mystery, just wily and lucky. So far. Ugh! You must go yourself, and bring many with you, and some Silvers too. There will be no more luck. I want him ended immediately. I want this strange world behind me."

"Magnus…me? For a Wood? And Silvers? You…you know I can't. I need to take this city. Gold or not, these magals have tech and explosions and sky machines that can hurt even me. I can't spare Silvers, and you know I can't go myself."

"Do I? You presume telling me what I know? I know we made a deal. I know I gave the rewards I promised. I held up my end of the bargain. Is he dead? No. What is more important to your master, a mere Transcendent, keeping your bargains with a Celestial, or your schedule? Who healed you after you were laid low by Woods? Woods! I did. Woods laid you low and I healed you. Not your master. Me. Does your master tolerate such insolence as you now show me?"

Ukaraaz becomes furious but does not let it show. The master she speaks of is many masters above him, but better not to admit that. Now he must grovel to this filthy magal too. "Magnus…please. I cannot disobey my master. With your demand I die either way. By my master's hand for disobedience, or by yours for not doing as you command."

"Not as I command. As we made bargain for."

"Magnus, then I can send a new army, led by a Silver, with five Bronze as support, and many Coppers, and twice as many Woods. I can't spare more than one Silver now. If I must go myself, I beg for time. Let me obey my master and take this city now, and then I will kill this magal myself. On my honor, by my own hand. I made a mistake and sent a low Bronze, but the Bronze was all I had close, and you demanded urgency, and the magal merely a low Wood. I will fix this mistake. What is your will? A new army now, led by a Silver, or myself, after I take this city?"

Ukaraaz respectfully waits on the Celestial's response, which comes quickly, "Ugh, fine. I want you to go yourself after you take the city. I need this finished for certain. You'll want to go yourself. I wasn't going to tell you as I like her, but since you seem to need more motivation, know this – he travels with a Natural. And I hope you understand the situation. I cannot take all my gifts back, but I can kill you. Or maybe I'll kill your master and then destroy the portal and your link to the NetherRealm. I'll give you the choice next time we meet if you haven't fulfilled our bargain."

Ukaraaz nearly laughs. A Natural? *What a prize!* Naturals don't form in the Nether and his Circle controls no Favored worlds, so this is a fantastic turn of luck. He'll have to figure out a way he can use it, and not his master, but even if his master gets it, it still improves the Circle and will bring great acclaim to Ukaraaz for delivering such a prize, though he'd much rather have the prize for himself than the acclaim.

Never has a mere Gold been entrusted with a portal. Ukaraaz received this opportunity thanks to the bargain his circle made with a Sublime magal. If a Magnus took the portal from him, he couldn't be held accountable. Unless the new bargain he made is found out. Killing a Wood, no matter how strong the Wood, is such an easy task he would be a fool not to have accepted, especially considered all the offered rewards.

But the threat to Ukaraaz's betters is hollow. All know demons get much stronger as they increase in tier and Tree. All know it takes at least half-a-dozen magal Eternals to handle one demon Eternal. The master she speaks of is high Exalted, a match for a low Magnus magal. The outcome is no sure thing, but Ukaraaz would bet all on the demon winning, or at least not dying, and forcing this filthy magal to flee in shame, then the Circle Master would give hunt in retribution. If this were to happen, Ukaraaz knows he would die as well for causing trouble for his betters, and not knowing his rightful place.

Captain Ukaraaz does not laugh and does not speak any of his thoughts. Instead, he swallows the bile and humbly and respectfully says, "Understood, and many thanks for being so patient and generous with this one, Magnus."

# CHAPTER 18
# SUMMARY

John awakes to a stream of liquid being sprayed onto his face and a pounding headache. With squinted eyes, pained from the bright sun, he finds the fox, leg raised, peeing directly on his face. With a start and much anger John sits up, "Great gods below, Amber! Why?"

The fox's only reply is to raise her damaged tail, split at the end, and strut around pompously. John suppresses his anger, as he believes foxes are like cats and women, and think weirdly, and are all known to behave mysteriously. This would go doubly for Amber, since she is both a fox and a woman.

With eyes still squinted against the bright sun, John sees not much out of place or changed. The sun sits around noon, and is sapping John some, but not as much as usual for noon, as is generally true this time of year and in this rough climate. A new dusting of light snow covers the ground and is hardening. John wipes the urine off his face, and it comes away with dried blood also. He picks up some snow and rubs his face and finds there was much more bleeding done than expected, as his face is mottled with dried blood. *Strange,* he thinks. The tracker is gone from his vision, the timer long expired.

John's stomach growls, as he hasn't eaten in a long while. He is a keen hunter and knows he can satiate his hunger easily. He is thirsty so fills his mouth with clean snow. Besides the headache he feels changed. He feels good, strong, like when he empowers himself with the essence of life. He checks his life essence, and it is nearly full. He then checks his dantian, and it is only a third full, and somewhat larger. *Why did Pixie not send the*

148

*prompt? That was much, much more of a struggle than she stated. A very large struggle, and no easy task at all. If that was all for naught, I will...well, not much I can do besides learn from it and make the attempt again.*

John looks at the flashing notifications sign and strongly thinks *notifications.*

**Your skill with 'Coiled Center of the Universe Technique' has increased to skill level 3.**

**Your Minimum Power has increased by an estimated 6.3 due to the viscosity and grade quality of the magical essence your dantian has been saturated with. Congratulations! For an exact number please see Pixie for testing. The current magical essence in your dantian exceeds Minimum Power level by an estimated 10.6 (+/-2.2).**

**Your skill with 'Magical Essence Manipulation' has increased to skill level 1. Your mastery with this skill is rated as Neophyte. Practicing this skill is not recommended for beings that have not achieved level 11 at a minimum. Please see Pixie for further details.**

**Your skill with 'Magical Essence Manipulation' has increased to skill level 2.**

**WARNING! Due to breach of Archetype agreement, you are being suspended from the Evoker Archetype path, and all benefits thereof. As per the agreement, 20% of current magical energy needed to fill your dantian at this level (2), and all further ranks this tier (Wood), will be collected, and some functions and system settings are now restricted until attainment of the next tier (Copper).**

**Your 'rank up' was successful. Congratulations! Welcome to level 21 28 levels left in Mortal tier. 38 levels left in the first Tree. All Stats increased by an estimated 7.2. For exact numbers please see Pixie for testing. Enjoy!**

**WARNING! There is a high probability some (1-1/999) or all (1-1/95) of your Stats are no longer accurately reflected by your NCS as shown in your Stats tab or summary sheet. Please see Pixie for testing.**

Surprised, John rereads the notifications. This is not what he was expecting, neither the good news nor the bad. Ranking up was only supposed to increase three [Stats], not all of them, and only by one, not seven-point-two. The basis for ranking up is increasing the size of the dantian, so [Capacity] is always increased. For the Evoker [Archetype] the other two targeted [Stats] are [Min. Power] and [Runes]. That every [Stat] increased is very queer. *Why didn't Pixie ever give me this prompt she spoke of?* He knows all his [Stats] didn't actually increase by that amount, due to this 'soft cap,' whatever that is. But seven-point-two seems like a very significant increase.

John's worry spikes as he has a bad thought. Does he still have [Magical Energy Bolt]? His first instinct is to enter his Mind's Eye, but he has much experience with women. Mistress Pixie is probably furious at him for his mistakes and not seeing the prompt, and for breaking his word in not keeping to the [Archetype], though it is not his fault and whatever happened seems to be of great benefit to him. But women are fickle and prone to anger, and slow to forgive, and John's head is throbbing, and he doesn't want a dressing-down at this moment, so he puts off visiting Pixie for a little bit.

Instead, John aims at a tree and tries casting [Magical Energy Bolt]. What came so easily and naturally before is now completely gone. John knows how attempting to cast the spell feels like, even without the magical energy to cast it, and it is just not there now. Empty, where once there was something.

John does feel much refreshed, and strong, besides his aching and pounding head. He thinks it awful his ability to do magic was taken from him so soon after it being granted. Much dejected, John decides to go hunting and fill his belly, as well as Amber's. He then curses himself as he realizes he should be doing the [Breath of the Serpent Clan] breathing technique, and starts doing so.

"Amber, I am off to hunt, and will bring back game to break our fast with. And we will eat it raw, as starting a fire in these wet woods will take too long with no flint. I do not forgive you for pissing on my face, but I won't hold your actions against you much while you are in this form. Not as I would if you were in your woman form."

John, knowing he should end there, does not. "Please go back to your woman form. Please." Amber neither replies nor changes form, so John goes hunting. He finds game quickly and easily. Some type of fat and large rodent he is not familiar with, and a demon to boot. As he maims the demon, another makes itself known too. He sends all his life essence to strengthen his body and replenishes it with the life essence within the two small demons. Together, they don't contain enough to fill what he can hold, but it is near enough, and John goes back to camp.

John prepares the large rodent creature, and leaves slices for Amber, which she ignores. She moves away from the slices of raw meat, clears a new area of snow, and lays down again. John eats his own slices, and then hers, as he hates being wasteful.

John can't tell full crystals and empty crystals apart by sight, and there are many on the ground. He picks one up and finds he can tell whether it has magical energy left or not by slightly trying to draw magical energy from it. He quickly goes through all the ones outside the bag, discarding the empty ones, and putting the ones containing magical energy still in his large bag.

The day before John was able to figure out how to fasten the strange metal teeth on his jacket and notices the outside of the square bag has many of the same type of fasteners. He quickly figures it out and fills these empty pocket-like areas with crystals, and fastens them closed again. He is pleased there are even more storage pockets still on this bag. *What a fantastic bag,* he thinks.

John's head is much relieved, and his bags packed, and he has put off visiting Mistress Pixie long enough. He sits and enters his Mind's Eye.

"Wow, those were some great gains! We don't know what you did or how you did it exactly, but good job!" Pixie says while showing him her thumb and winking at him.

*I must find out what these gestures mean.* John has been to some areas where putting your thumb up towards someone is a grave insult, and he does not believe Pixie means it to be. He only knows eyewinks as meaning you want to lay with someone, and only men did it to women, and he is certain Pixie does not mean it this way, and neither did Amber when he glimpsed her face. Pixie is far above him in stature, and she would not demean herself so. It was not unheard of, or even all that uncommon, for a noble or royal woman to lay with a strong warrior not her husband, but was rarer in stories of goddesses, and John does not believe Pixie to be so base.

"Mistress Pixie, I sincerely apologize for not keeping to the Evoker Archetype. I waited for the prompt, just as you told me to, but it never came."

"Oh, don't you worry your pretty little head about it. This is one of the few times where someone falls off the path and instead of gimping themselves, they somehow manage to exceed expectations. You got some great gains, we even benefit, and you finally have the amount of Runes you should have! Well, you're still a little short since it should be four now, but you have more than three! Enough to replace your manifestation! So, no harm, no foul. We got a ton of tickets out on you. You're in good hands!

"What's got us bothered is your Stats, pal. They're off, and they ain't properly reflected now. We need to test you, but we can't until you get to a safe place, we can't detect enemies, and need about a whole day of relative safety, depending.

"But that's neither here nor there. We got your new summary page to show you, but first let's talk about your next rank up. Your meditation technique works really fast, so you're probably thinking, 'Hey, why don't I just sit right here and rank up and ascend a tier or so until I'm out of crystals?' Well, that ain't a good idea, bucko. Why not? Because you got to let your dantian settle. We don't got the exact specifics at this time, but most species like yours have to wait at least two standard weeks between rank up attempts at a minimum. That's ten standard days, or about nine USACS days. You should probably wait ten USACS days just to be extra safe. Doing it too soon will weaken your foundation and hurt future progress. It causes way higher diminishing returns too. Understood?"

John says, "Yes, Mistress," and Pixie winks and points her index finger at him, and moves her thumb upwards while making a clicking noise. She then says, 'Bang!' After, she blows on the tip of her finger.

"Now you're cooking on all four burners, partner. Okay, the essence you make is potent for your tier. Real potent, somehow thanks to your technique, even though it's F-rated. So, your manifestations will be far more powerful than your tier indicates, so good for you! And this also affects your rank ups. Strap in and get comfortable because we're going to do a little explaining on exactly why we recommend what we recommend, and why we're gonna go off script for you.

"We always recommend targeting only two [Stats] for rank up because it has the highest returns and the lowest diminishing returns on subsequent rank ups. For instance, if you had normal magical essence for your level, and ranked up the usual way, if you targeted all your Stats on rank up, they'd usually only increase by point-three each, for a total gain of two-point-seven. And if done again on the next rank up, diminishing returns would bring that down by half. So, point-one-five each and one-point-three-five total. Keep in mind Capacity is always increased on rank up regardless.

"Targeting three Stats usually increases them all by point-seven, or two-point-eight total, but with much better diminishing returns. The second attempt would result in point-six-three each, and two-point-five-two total.

"Targeting two Stats results in the highest total Stat increase of three, and it only has diminished returns on the third and fourth rank up its…"

Pixie drones on like this for much time while John pretends to pay attention. He knows it is very important to know all he can about cultivating, as everything now depends on it, but his mind won't work with him, and insists on thinking of interesting things for the rest of Pixie's lecture.

John notices Pixie finally moved on, bringing an end to the horror, "...next bit of advice, since we're unsure whether it's good advice or not. This rank up could've been a fluke, or now your dantian is acclimated to having such thick and high-grade essence and the next rank up flops, or you can't hold on so long and compress so much, or a million other possibilities. Even so, we still recommend trying the exact same thing you did this rank up for your next rank up. Even at fifty percent diminished returns it'll be worth it. We'll see how that goes in ten days or so. Depending on the outcome of your next rank up we'll see what we recommend after.

"You picking up what I'm putting down, pal?"

*Not really, I'm a warrior, not a clerk or priest,* John wants to say, but he understands the key and important points, so says, "Yes, Mistress. I perform the next rank up the same way I did the last, and I must wait for at least nine days to do so, preferably ten."

"That's right, bucko. Any questions before we show you your summary sheet?"

"No, Mistress." Pixie seems to have changed a little, John believes. At least she seems to find calling him affectionate nicknames more appealing. The word sobriquet pops into John's mind, and he doesn't know why or what it means.

"Okay, here it is. Decimals were moved out for better accuracy. Keep climbing that ladder!"

| | |
|---|---|
| **Age** | 5,600 **to** 6,200 **USACS years** |
| **Race** | **Terran-F** |
| **Tree First** | |
| **Tier** | 1 **(Mortal) (Wood)** |
| **Level** | 2 **(Mid-Low)** |
| **Archetype** | **NA** |
| **Active Title** | **Blessed by Magnus Gar'tar** |
| **Aspects** | **NA** |

| | |
|---|---|
| **Affinities** | **NA** |
| **NCU Energy Cost** | 6%[-47%] |

**STATS**

| | |
|---|---|
| **Strength** | 23.94 |
| **Swiftness** | 23.64 |
| **Conditioning** | 24.69 |
| **Min. Power** | 16.50 |
| **Capacity** | 10.20 |
| **Runes** | 3.17 |
| **Physical Fortification** | 10.20 |
| **Elemental Fortification** | 10.20 |
| **Mental Fortification** | 10.20 |

**Highest Skills**

| | |
|---|---|
| **[Undirected Basic Meditation]** | 96.4 |
| **[Mixed Style Swords]** | 93.6 |
| **[Mixed Stealth]** | 88.7 |
| **[Mixed Survival]** | 87.6 |
| **Synergy Skills** | **Ready** |
| **Synergy Class** | **NA** |
| **Perks** | **None** |
| **Manifestations** | **None** |

**Last Achievement Tribulation Collaboration, Max - C**

**Highest Achievement**      **Skilled, Legendary - SSR**

**Next required advancement event: Clear meridians after level 5**

John is disappointed to see a lot of his [Stats] didn't go up by seven-point-two, but already figured this would be the case.

He is happy to see [Runes] is now over three, as Pixie stated. The number range listed for his age is meaningless to him, though he knows it is a long time. He is more interested in more immediate and relevant concerns. He asks Pixie how he can recreate his spell with his own [Runes] and she walks him through the process. He picks two free base-runes called 'external' and 'attack,' then the rune for 'condensed ball' and 'range' and tries to select the last rune, another 'range,' but he is not allowed to for some reason.

Pixies is little help and only tells him he has enough [Runes] and to try again, which he does, and it fails again. They spend some time on the issue, but John is certain he knows the answer to the problem – his [Runes] [Stat] is incorrect and is less than the three it claims he has.

John is stuck with a grouping of two runes, which dramatically shortens the distance the spell can travel, and will do less damage than it would as a three-rune grouping, but also costs less magical essence. Being powered by magical essence now, and his high [Min. Power], ensures it will be far more deadly. Even if he collects only magical energy and never converts it, and uses that to power the spell, it will still do far more damage than his last spell. The damage listed for the spell is 'max for tier,' but factoring in his higher quality magical essence the spell should do far more damage than the NCS considers max for his tier, according to Pixie.

The spell's name is changed to [Magical Essence Dart] and can only travel forty-seven feet. John is not too disappointed in this spell, but he is very bitter his [Runes] [Stat] is not growing like it should. He should be able to have many more spells, and now he has a lesser spell than he had previously. *Well, at least it should do much more damage. I can't wait to see my enemies run screaming as they're covered in magical flames billowing forth from my hands. First, I must get fire affinity, or aspect, or whatever makes my spells turn to fire. Oh, what a gay time I will have once I can control flames!*

# CHAPTER 19
## MOSTLY

John shoulders his bundle of spears while saying, "Amber, we are leaving. Or I am leaving, and I hope you come with me. We are far to the north, as best as I can estimate it, and I plan on heading south. That's where the demons came from. Hopefully there're some villages near, and towns and cities."

With these words John starts heading south, and is much relieved when Amber follows. And the fox doesn't just follow, but sprints ahead, and John gives great chase, but cannot match her speed. Foxes don't have the endurance of humans, and John was no ordinary human, and he is able to keep his great speed for longer, and catch up to and pass the fox as she slows and pants heavily. John slows down too, and matches the fox's speed, and they travel like this for most of the day, alternating sprinting and jogging and walking. Sometimes they stop so Amber can rummage for nuts and berries, though they are rare and out of season and spoiling this time of year. He even sees her eating bark once. *What a weird fox. And a strange lady too.*

While they walk, having nothing better to do, John talks and rambles and spews forth from his mind many thoughts he usually keeps private. He would be embarrassed if Amber were in woman form, but while she is a fox, John decides not to care.

John tells Amber about the two most important characteristics of a man as he was taught as a youth, and this remained true for a long, long while. Every man wanted to have these qualities above all, being both fell and tall. Fell meaning dangerous and ability to inflict harm, someone to be frightened of. Tall meaning respectable and dependable and capable of great deeds, and had nothing to do with height. Tall of character.

John tells her about his childhood and meeting Ahn and being worshiped and ruling as a king, and then of hiding what he was, and how he didn't like it – has never liked it. He talks for long and about a great many things, stopping only twice to kill demons he spots, and once to eat game unlucky enough to make itself so available, though he does not need much food and wasn't overly hungry. *Better to eat while things are so peaceful.*

Amber surprises John by picking a fight with a wolf pack. Strange wolves, smaller than usual, and with a strange pelage of grizzled greyish-brown and a little reddish-orange, the alpha not noticeably larger than any other male in the pack. Amber runs up and chirps at the alpha, and gives fight when attacked. John is able to dispatch them all quickly, and Amber seems uninjured. Two of the wolves drop crystals. *Foxes are supposed to be clever, not crazy and suicidal,* thinks John as he inspects the odd fox for injuries. John is happy his [Magical Essence Dart] spell seems extremely powerful, as it completely disintegrated a wolf, and he is also rewarded for keeping up with his appropriate breathing technique for a long while.

**Your skill with 'Magical Essence Dart' has increased to skill level 1. Your mastery with this skill is rated as Neophyte.**

**Your skill with 'Breath of the Serpent Clan Endless Technique' has increased to skill level 3.**

Closer to dusk John spots two traps – a snare and some sort of foothold trap. No tracks are in the area, but John smells some lingering scent. His eyes are sharp and see far, but he spots no smoke he should see from any hunter or trapper's fire or chimney, or the many smokes he should see from any village or town. With no trail-sign he cannot follow the trappers, so he continues south.

Moments later, in the wood line past a clearing ahead, John sees two flashes from far off, and something speedily flies by his head, and something else hits his thigh. Whatever hits his thigh hurts very much, but does not puncture the skin. John believes the flashes to be firearms loosing bullets. Empowering himself with speed, he rushes towards the far-off area he spotted the flashes from, still holding the bundle and bag of crystals. He closes the distance far quicker than any normal human ever could, even faster than he could have a few short days ago.

Two men point their firearms at John, and as he gets closer both men fire their weapons again. He cuts quickly in new directions, predicting when the men will fire, and is missed both times. He is then among the men, and disarms both before they can get further attacks off, holding one in the air by the throat, bundle and bag of crystals dropped at his feet.

The man John knocked down yells out, "Wait! Wait! Sorry, man! We didn't know you were human. I swear! You were dark and moving all fast like some of the monsters. We're sorry. It's getting dark and no people are ever up here. Never. We didn't know. Please put him down. We're sorry. Please. You're human right? We are too."

"How far away is your village?"

"Village? We don't live in a village, man. It's just us two and our families. We came all the way out here to be off the grid. Years ago. Just get away, you know? We don't even got no internet, just radio. Honest, we didn't know you were human. Bunch of demons all over the place. We wouldn't have shot if we knew you were human. No one comes up here. Not ever. There's nothing up here. Just put Eloi down, man. We didn't mean nothing. It's all just a mistake."

"First tell me where the nearest village is."

"Okay, man. No problem. Then you got to put Eloi down. Please. We'll tell you anything you want. About twenty kilometers south is one-sixty-seven. Go west and it loops up north and Chibougamau, about one-ten or so kilometers. Take it east and it's about ninety kilometers to Saint-Félicien. Road is probably snowed over."

"What distance is a kilometer in leagues? How many roads do I pass before reaching this one-six-seven road?"

"Can you put Eloi down first? He don't look so good. Please?"

John puts the man down, and they all talk for a time. Amber stays a ways off, unnoticed. John learns much from the two men, but the distances given are not very helpful. John figures he will have a better grasp after he finds the road the men say is twenty kilometers south. He will then go east, and there will be small towns and a lake. If he goes around the lake, and finds a road called one-six-nine and follows it far south he will reach a big city. If he instead takes a road called one-five-five and follows it between fifty and a hundred kilometers he should find a large demon portal and many, many demons, but the men have heard the portal may be moving, and was spotted much further south.

The men have kept in contact with others through some machine called a radio, and things in cities do not seem to be going well for the residents. These two have fought many demons, and claim firearms work well against them, but their bullets are something called twenty-twos and weak, and all but the smallest demons require many bullets and great accuracy to down. Their firearms have telescopes attached allowing for great accuracy over long distances and the ability to see very far away in great detail, surpassing even John's great vision.

The two men's friends on the radio told them firearm bullets to the head are effective for most demons at all tiers, but the higher tiered ones may require bigger bullets, and more of them. Even if the higher tiered demon's skin and skull can stop a bullet, the bullet contains enough force to turn the brains into mush an inch or two within the skull. An inch being two finger's width or so in length. Some demons can cover themselves with some form of magic shielding, and the shielding must be removed before headshots will down them. This information was disseminated all over the world by a way of communicating John doesn't understand, and the men state some areas are losing this amazing ability to communicate with, and these men wish they also had this way to communicate now too, as they'd have much better information.

John is told the g'athu infest other areas of the very large country he is in, but only demons infest this region of it, and mostly smaller demons at that. The larger demons have only been spotted within the massive horde. Another large country further south has many invasions by g'athu and dark ones. A country as far south as you can go in this part of the world has a giant creature as tall as a mountain walking around dropping dark ones from its massive body. Many fantastical stories like this are shared. It is full dark by the time they stop talking.

John prepares to depart, rewarding the men with some clear crystals for the information provided. The men take turns clasping John's hand, and John is glad not all the old ways are gone, and the men of this region seem of the decent sort, and kind of heart, and helpful.

John says, "It was a pleasure meeting and conversing with you two. I wish you well."

"You too, man. You never answered if you're human. You're human, right? You moved so fast before. Like a blur. And you picked Eloi up like he weighed nothing. Did you figure out how to do that cultivation stuff super-fast or something?"

"Mostly," John replies as he departs.

John heads south and Amber sprints past him. He checks where the bullet hit his thigh, and the area is red and bruised and painful, but there is little blood at all. He does not spend life essence healing the area, as it would be a waste, and will heal naturally well enough, and quickly enough, as all minor injuries do. *I wish my skin and bones were so tough in the last war I fought, though I guess bullets would still turn part of my brain to mush even if my skin or skull could stop them.*

On their second sprint John finds the road only by how the snow feels different on it, but once found it is easy to stay on and follow. They see a sign saying '167', and many saying 'MAXIMUM 80 km/h,' and much later, one saying 'Saint-Félicien 50 kms.'

John believes he somewhat grasps the distance of a kilometer, as they seem to be about roughly half the distance of an old Roman league. By his estimate, not even halfway to the fifty kilometers the sign claimed, he sees smoke as if from a chimney. Shortly after spotting the smoke far off in the distance, John sees an odd and small one-story mansion or fort off the side of the road, made of a whitish and glossy stone he is unfamiliar with, the front door broken open. Amber runs through the open door, and as John slows to follow, he receives a notification.

**Your skill with 'Breath of the Serpent Clan Endless Technique' has increased to skill level 4.**

John enters the building, and after exploring decides it is a small mansion for petty nobility, most likely untitled, such as the 'nobili.' The estate has three bedrooms, and is lavishly furnished, with much art and many odd trinkets and possessions. Three corpses are found, two an older couple, and a young man aged around fifteen or so, dead and chewed upon by beast or demon or some such.

Near the most comfortable sofa John has ever seen, there looks to be supplies gathered, as if the owners of this mansion planned on leaving. A large rucksack made of a very high-quality material is filled with food items and clothing, including a metal canteen, and John finds some nice thick gloves. The rucksack is large enough to fit his bag of crystals within, and he likes his old leather shoulder-bag enough to place the whole thing in his new rucksack.

John also finds some large, thick, and long bags he believes are for sleeping in, and keeping warm while doing so, but they are too large and bulky and would take much room, and John is mostly immune to the struggles mundane humans have with the cold, as long as he is fully dressed and not exposed. But the bags look mightily comfortable, and John wishes they were smaller and less bulky as he would take one. He prefers traveling light, and only holding on to valuables and gear made to kill enemies, and not comfort items.

The rest of the items John is unable to figure out a use for, besides some lanterns he does not need due to his ability to see well at night, and his lack of flint to start fires with to light them. He leaves everything, other than a very sharp belt knife, a small hatchet, and the canteen, confused as to why there was no flint on the searched bodies, or with the gathered gear, nor tinder, lens, or any other common means to start fires with anywhere in the estate he searched. *How do they start fires now?*

In the next mansion he finds no bodies, or flint still, but does find tannish boots that fit him well, and have metal protection for the toes. These boots are extremely comfortable, and have thick soles with a strange pattern that grip the ground fantastically. Amber also whines at some clothing items until John packs them as well. Amber eats some narangs in a fancy kitchen, rind and all, as John wonders, *how many nobles live in this area?*

John meditates for a short time, as he can see the magical energy gathered by his constant breathing technique is not mixing with the magical essence in his dantian, and is diluting the power of it. Meditating quickly converts it all to essence. His dantian is over half-filled when he finishes, and he can feel the dawn come through the window onto his skin.

Man and fox skip a couple houses, Amber no longer rushing into them, and John soon sees a large red and white sign high on a thick pole, words he believes say 'Petro Canada' on the sign. Just past the sign is a strange building with many windows, the walls painted half red and half white, and a nearby and separate hut type structure covering some sort of machinery. Across the road is an open area with some more machines, but no hut for them. Past this strange building is a large two-storied mansion with the smoking chimney John spotted a ways back. Besides what the smoke indicates, he hears humans inside too.

They skip the red and white building and Amber sprints to the two-storied mansion with the smoking chimney, and a woman exits, holding the door open, and the fox runs right in. The woman is middle-aged, to John's mind at least, in her early twenties, and far too thin, to John's mind at least. She is pale of skin, with a handsome face, reddish-brown hair, and immodestly dressed in tight clothes with much cleavage showing,

The woman smiles and says, "Hey, bud! Was that your...creature? So cute! Can I pet it? Never mind, there's plenty of time for that, eh? Why don't you follow it inside and me and my sisters will get you two warmed up and cleaned and fed. Get something nice and hot for you to drink too. It's frickin' freezing out, eh, bud?"

# CHAPTER 20
# THE TORTUOUS SERPENT

In a house are three young women, sisters all, one man, and a fox. The man, younger looking than his hosts, is of average stature in these modern times, but throughout his long history loomed over other men, and rarely met anyone exceeding his height. His build seems more lithe and graceful than bulked with muscle, though his shoulders are broad, and his frame sturdy. His dark, haunted eyes sometimes sparkle with an odd, foreboding color, and seem somewhat judgmental, and filled with an ire conflicting with the personality he presents to the world. He sits in a wooden chair at a wooden table, with a blanket over his shoulders, drinking hot tea, much food laid out on the table in front of him, as the three young sisters dote on him, and tell him things to boost his ego, as if fighting for his favor.

The fox, having refused many offered foods, now gorges on a bowl of sweet peaches, from a can, with whipped cream added on top.

A rucksack rests on the leg of a chair near the man, absent the short sword, as the young ladies made the man leave it, with his enchanted long sword, small hatchet, and bundle of spears, in the foyer past the entryway. They warmed a bath for the man, and fed him, and gave him hot tea enhanced with whisky, and more. Now the man sits, drinking tea after having eaten plenty from the spread of food.

"So, you hear about some sort of nuke in New York City, or near it? Could be a nuke, or could be a power plant blowing. They don't know, eh," says the plump sister, which John finds odd as the other two are very skinny, as if their father only loved one of them enough to make an appealing bride.

"Yeah, we found out from our cellphone. We have one, just like everyone else does. Right, bud? Where's your cellphone?" the short sister asks.

John looks up from his steaming tea, and addresses all three of his gracious hosts, "My apologies, I don't have one. And I haven't heard that news. What's a nuke?"

The three sisters look at each other and giggle. The tall one looks at John, and smiles sweetly, "You don't know, bud? Sounds like that's a story, eh?"

John smiles back, trying to make his smile as sweet and kind, but fails, "My apologies again, mistress, but it's not much of a story. Before...all these changes, my mind was ailed greatly, and I remember little for a long time. But these recent changes to our world also healed my mind, and I am whole again."

"You're right, bud, that's not much of a story. How 'bout you tell us a different one, a good one, eh? Much better than that," says the short sister.

"Yeah, a much better one. That story sucked, bud," states the pudgy sister, as she reaches down to pet the fox, and the fox lets her, much to John's chagrin, as the vixen steadfastly avoids his touch.

John, now clean, full, and refreshed, his clothes freshly laundered and stitched where damaged, all thanks to these three handsome sisters, feels obligated to do as his generous hosts bid. Before replying, he wonders again why their souls seem much brighter than most. "Certainly. I owe you three much, and have many stories. I could share the one most dear to me. The story of my wife, a woman so beautiful, that so filled me with love, other women were ruined for me, as if she cursed me to never love again. Well, to never love any but her again. Would you ladies like to hear this story, or another? As I said, I have many."

The sisters, again, look at each other and giggle, smiling their sweet smiles. The fox stops gorging on her peaches, and looks towards John, whipped cream on her nose, and seems interested too. The tall sister says, "Oh, yes, eh. That story sounds perfect, bud." The sisters all giggle once more, this time only looking at John, with smiles even sweeter.

"Aye, I will then. Long ago I traveled...well, I should start further back, really, to tell the full story. Let's see. Man has always feared disease and sickness and injury and pestilence. For a long time, man need fear the bear, the wolf, the lion, and other beasts, as well as constant raids and the occasional invasions. Kingdoms were small, and not really kingdoms at all from how they came to be known. It was a day's walk from your king's hold to the neighboring king's hold, and the king's lords raided each other as much as the neighboring kingdoms.

"Every kingdom had their own god they worshiped, one of many they knew of, but worshiped only the one. Most gods wanted the same from their worshipers – be tall, be fell, be strong, be bold, take from your neighbors and share in the spoils, win trinkets proving your courage and worth, take a strong wife capable of bearing many children, and protect her and all that is yours, and take more wives if you can support them, and give them many children too. The usual. They asked for little in tribute –tall deeds and dead enemies and sacrificed beasts to feast upon.

"When man had a nightmare, it was usually of the wolf attacking, or the like.

"As time went on, it...well, I have a theory. Old crones spinning more tales than yarn, lazy men and priests spewing new tales of gods for a free cup of wine or more sacrifices. Kingdoms became wider and wider, and people stopped knowing their own king, or seeing him, and only heard of him. Instead of worshipping the one god of many, people worshiped the many, the pantheon. One for this and one for that. Raids within a kingdom stopped happening, the great beasts were all hunted down, wars between kingdoms became much rarer and great affairs with armies so large the earth trembled as they marched.

"Man stopped fearing the bear, the wolf, the lion, the raid. Man began to fear what he couldn't see – all these gods and ghosts and monsters and demons and magic and curses, all inventions of the old crone, the lazy man, the priest. Well, back then they were all imagined inventions, at least. Things have changed much in these last couple days. I speak only of before these recent changes.

"Man feared imagined threats all around him, and sacrificed much to many gods hoping to keep at bay these threats, and looked only at today, instead of tomorrow and his honor. Men, once fell and tall, became little and petty and cruel and fearful of all these invisible threats.

"His nightmares were once of fending off wolves, then they became filled with demons and monsters and malicious gods. And I'm ashamed for my great part in bringing this about."

John stops and takes a sip of tea, wishing the vital essence within his body did not always attack the alcohol he put in it, and keep him from becoming drunk. He then reminds himself it is a boon, and in these dangerous times a great boon, as a clear head and readiness are better than the temporary relief drunkenness grants. The sisters, smiling sweetly, wait patiently for John to continue.

"So, now to my Lilitu. I had traveled far, far to the south, looking for my friend and master, as he left me for too long and I missed his companionship. On my way back north, to the civilizations I knew, and where I hoped Ahn may be waiting for me, I entered the land of strange men, a small place east of Kayhamut. These men only worshiped one god and believed in no other, no pantheon, just the one...well, from what I hear everyone believes this to be true now, but these men were the first I ever heard of believing in only one and no other, and it was a very strange belief at the time.

"In all my long life I had never seen a red soul. I entered a small city of these men of strange beliefs, and I saw a woman with a soul as red as the blood streaming down her face, as a crowd was throwing rocks at her, and they planned to fire her on a pyre they were creating nearby.

"I didn't speak their language, and communicating with them was a large issue. I made many generous offers to buy her, but they were much angered by this woman and wanted her death more than coin. I found out later they thought her a seductress and a witch, and said she cursed many men and women, and committed many sins against their god.

"Well, I was not able to make bargain for the possession of her, and they greatly wanted her dead to end the curses, so I had to kill many men that day to make her safe.

"I did the ritual, the same as Ahn did to me, the same I tried on many others only for it to fail, as I had a great loneliness and a great longing for the companionship of one of my own. This time the ritual worked, and she readily accepted the power, and I was gladdened, as I would no longer be alone.

"Later, once she was cleaned and healed and whole, I found her to be beautiful, though she was as skinny as the most useless of servants, and always refused to put on a decent amount of weight, even the minimum expected of women of quality and nobility. She always stayed too thin. Always. It took some time for us to share a common language, but she was a fast learner, much faster than I am, and as she strengthened herself we became much more of equals, and greatly enjoyed the company of each other.

"We married, and I wanted no other but her. Her beauty delighted me, and I loved every piece of her. Just a look from her would set my heart beating faster. I loved her so. I loved her so much it hurt. I needed her. Her mind was not normal, and it was frustrating, but her obvious love for me, and her loyalty and devotion, made it all worthwhile. I could deny her nothing, even relenting to her strange tastes. Her mind was weird in how it lusted for blood, and made her revel in slaughter and cruelty, as if she were possessed of a great evil more often than not. She tried to curb her excesses for me, as she knew I detested it, and promised many times there would be no more."

"She loved magic, and was fascinated by it, and desired it above all, and would do many rituals and curses on any that vexed her. I did not believe in nonsense such as cursing rituals, but I thought this was a much better outlet for her desires than the alternatives. She cursed me many, many times, in many, many ways, and I would just laugh, and kiss her,

169

and beg her to let loose the anger she held towards me. She wasn't angered with me much of the time, but when she was, her anger burned bright, and consumed her, and she had many tantrums. She was fiery! My Lilitu. My beautiful, fiery Lilitu.

"I did come to realize there was something to her rituals and curses.

"She loved getting men to want her, and desire her above all else, and she twisted them, and took everything from them, and gave nothing to them at all, and laughed as she ruined their lives. She would make friends with important women, and twist them too, and promise much, and when they were low, she'd pretend to give what was promised, but betray them, and laugh, and then, while they were greatly despaired and could not be lower, she would drink of them.

"We traveled all over, always looking for magic, which she believed was a real thing. To the savages north, west, and south, and their tribes and priests and learned men, all claiming to have magic, none having any to give or teach, all having vital essence to strengthen her. I was so happy to be with someone, to not be alone, to be madly in love, and have the love last this time, and not be such a fleeting thing, as fleeting as the span of just one life.

"I was in love with a passion that burned in my chest with the fire of the sun. A love so bright it burned my eyes, and I could not look at it. In the great cities where I lived, and the other great ones to the east, she claimed to have found some magics. Real magics. With a bit of knowledge here, and a bit of it there, she pieced it together, and started working great rituals."

"I traveled with her to these strange places with queer cultures and people. Sorry, Amber, I know I'm not supposed to use that word as I do, but the places and people and sites were extremely strange and interesting, and this was the best time of my life, even considering the horrors she brought down upon whatever lands and peoples we visited. None could threaten us, none could dampen the love we felt for each other, and it would be like this forever, gods among men."

John stops again, and asks for more tea, and the plump one makes him another steaming cup, and puts honey in to sweeten it, and whisky to warm the soul. With fresh drink in hand, John continues his tale, "The rituals and magics she learned required sacrifice. She claimed humans worked best, and she couldn't substitute beasts.

"My Lilitu was cruelest to her own, and loved traveling to where she was born, and making great sport of her people, and took great pleasure in seducing their priests and righteous men, and bringing them low, and torturing the women, any woman with joy and a happy life. She was cruel everywhere we went, really. Her cruelties caused many tales to be spread. The old crone, the lazy man looking for a free drink, and the greedy priest, all told tales about her, and exaggerated. She was a demon and would eat their babes, and drink of their souls, and they'd be damned from whatever strange afterlife they believed true.

"Everywhere we arrived people were fearful, and looked down upon us. Where once I was welcomed, and honored, and worshiped for my great might, I was now spit on, and cursed, and attacked, and we had to make a great slaughter of a great many people.

"Instead of our enemies, she started sacrificing babes. Until then, though I asked her to stop many times, I turned my eyes from her foul deeds, and believed her promises when she claimed it would be the last time. Our enemies were to die anyway. By sword, fang, or pentagram, dead is dead. That was the justification I used till then, though I knew it was a poor one. I turned my eyes, but I could no longer. Not after I saw the babes. She'd always beg me, 'Just one more time. I'm close. I'm so close, my love. Just one more time. Please, my love, just one more time.' It was 'just one more time' many, many times. For a long time.

"I could not stay angry with her for long, or deny her wishes. It always seemed like she understood what she did was wrong. She understood, so of course she'd stop. She was always so sincere about it. It was just one more time. What could that hurt? In the grand scheme of things, that is.

"After the babes I could tolerate no more, and absolutely demanded she stop with the rituals and sacrifices. No more 'one more time.' We had

171

to flee the great cities and civilizations and live among the barbarians. I didn't mind, as their way of living was closer to how I was raised, though I had long become accustomed to civilization by then.

"She'd always say, 'Just one more time.' Then, finally, there was the last time, for I made sure of it."

# CHAPTER 21
# THE TRUE START

John notices the fox looking at him in an odd way, as if disappointed. The three sisters look at John with patience, understanding, and sickly-sweet smiles. He drinks more tea, and let's out a long sigh. "The last time. Things were going well. We traveled very far, and lived among a tribe of strange and pale barbarians, with painted faces. My Lilitu finally stopped being so cruel, and the people of the land we lived with saw me as I tried to be – fell and tall, a man of honor, willing to help in war and hunting.

"Lilitu made real friends, and treated them well, and helped heal wounds, and used her wisdom to make women become more fertile, and the people went to her with injury and sickness and for birthing. Things were better. We were happy."

John stops talking, and much like the other man that sat in the same seat before, he looks far off in the distance, and a sadness fills his eyes. A long moment passes in silence before he continues, "Things seemed right. Better. Steady. Until...until one day, a young girl came out the woods, shaking and covered in blood, and much frightened, and crying. It was the end of harvest, and the women gathered in the woods to do worship and rituals, and praise trees or some such nonsense, and the only males allowed were babes too young to be left unattended. All women go to this event. The festival lasts the night, and the women all return at sunup.

"The only one to return was this young girl, crying and covered in blood.

"I said I would investigate, as the men were hesitant to, as their tree gods, or whatever silliness they worshiped, did not want men at this ritual.

I was gladdened, as I had an idea what I'd find, and I considered many of these men friends, and I did not want to kill them.

"I was wrong. What I found was much worse than anything my own mind could imagine. It was a horror unlike any other I'd seen in my long life. A pentagram was drawn under a giant and ancient bowed oak, with a great circle made around the points. That circle was new. Two symbols of the endless, the beginning and the end together, everlasting. Nothing I could see representing the five elements though. From the boughs of the great oak above, over the five points, hung five women, bellies large with child. In the center, all the babes in a pile.

"The pentagram and circle were made of the arms and legs and torsos and heads of the town's women. Blood and bodies and entrails lie all over, yet no beast approached to snack, and a weird silence reigned alone over the scene, and no usual sounds of the forest could be heard. The area felt heavy, and sick, as if contaminated by some great blight infecting it all, even the air.

"I called out for my Lilitu, but saw nothing of her, though I could hear her heart and smell her sweet smell, and both came from within the circle. I followed the sound and scent, though I was hesitant, as a great foreboding came upon me. And I, afraid of nothing in this world, was afraid.

"I steeled my heart, and would not let these strange feelings unman me, and pushed forward. When I entered the pentagram, much changed – the air was dark and far heavier than air should be, and a weird light shun, a sickly color I cannot describe, and a fog held all still, and made it hard to see, and the feelings I had…I can't describe the feelings. None were good and all were strange to me. In the center, on the large pile of babes, I could now see my Lilitu. My beautiful, horrible Lilitu.

"Her ritual finally worked. She summoned something powerful from the beyond. A great tentacle reached down from above, as if from a giant squid, and wrapped around the head of my wife, and I could see it draining her essence, and more from her besides. The fog made it so I could not see the body of this great creature, what I was up against to save my horrible love, but I gave battle as best I could.

"I stabbed and slashed and bashed the tentacle, and it did little damage, and ignored me, and did not let go. With all my great strength I gave it such a blow it could not ignore, and it drew blood, though it was strange and thick and stank. That wound is all I needed, and I fixed my mouth to the wound, and suckled. It made me sick, and I retched many times, but I did not stop. My own essence attacked the new poison in me, and I became weak, and my strength left me, but I did not stop, and drank deeper instead. I drank until full, and sent the life essence in me to strengthen my body. Many times I did this. I drank and drank until the tentacle unwrapped and withdrew, and I caught my drained Lilitu, and carried her out of this strange place, out of the circle, and back to the woods, where I collapsed and continued to retch.

"I awoke first. I felt better. Stronger, in a different way. My head was clearer than it had ever been, and my thinking much improved. I looked at my beautiful, sleeping Lilitu. The love of my life. My companion for so long. My wife. My heart. My everything. I looked at her and the horror she wrought, and I knew...I knew it would never end. There would always be one more time. She would always be a beautiful monster. She would always be my love.

"I told her I loved her, and always will, and apologized. I then drained her of the little she had left, and took her head as she lay sleeping. I gave up much of who I am to make her happy, and sacrificed much of my honor. I was so scared of being alone again. So frightened."

John is silent for a moment, looking down at the hands in his lap. He sighs sadly before continuing his story. "She twisted me too, and left me low, and she did it to me first, before I witnessed her do it to so many other men with my own eyes. I just couldn't see it. Not until that moment. I held her head, and kissed it one last time, as the skin turned to dust and blew away. My heart died with her, and I was alone again. Alone until Thomas, but I don't remember much at all of my time with him. And..."

175

John stops then, and looks at all three sisters, one after the other. "...I promised then, I'd end all like her, and would not stop in my pursuit. If I did meet one such as her, I don't remember. I've lost a lot of memories. Too many.

"You three sisters remind me of her, you know? Your souls dark with bad deeds. Though you don't have her great beauty, you have her cruel smile, and greedy eyes.

"My soul is also dark with bad deeds, and I'm not like her. You've been good hosts, and I owe you much for the kindness you've shown me, no matter the intentions behind it, and as a guest it is only fair to warn you – I've heard the screams of those below even before I entered, and placed myself in your care knowing it could come to this. If you are the same type as my Lilitu, I will not walk away in peace, and we must fight. Fear not, for I have manners, and I would never breach hospitality like some uncouth barbarian. We will do this civilly if it must be done. So, tell me truthfully, are you like her?"

The three sisters stare at John, still smiling their sickly-sweet smiles, and John stares back, resolved in his path. The tall sister starts giggling, and the others join in. John does not. After a while, the tall one collects herself enough to say, "We owe you a story, and will now use your name, John, as we have been given what we need. And we'll go back further too, as you did, but we won't spin tall tales, and will speak only the truth. We'll go back to the true start. The start the Favored hide, that only us of the Forsaken speak of. How much of history were you told?"

John, surprised at this change in topic, replies, "You do not speak of this world? Then not much at all. I missed what was relayed to others, but have heard some since. I was told this world is round, and not flat, and all the powerful beings live far in the sky, as some religions have claimed, and the sky is very large, and part of the sky is a galaxy, and all of the sky is a universe, and one God rules over it all, and you do not go to the Underworld when you die, but go to something called a Wheel and are reborn anew. I don't know how much of it I believe, as it all sounds so preposterous, though very powerful beings claim the truth of it. This is all I was told."

The three sisters are silent for a moment, and then all three laugh very loudly for a long time. "Oh, apologies for laughing, John. We seldom get such clay to work with. It's good you know nothing, so the truth will be an easier potion to swallow, and less bitter. But we all have to learn to eat the bitter when necessary, now don't we?

"Now, the start. Before there was anything, before there were planets and stars or even the first universe, there were the ancient old ones. The most powerful of them all went off on his own to create, and created many things, but couldn't create what he wanted, and was unsatisfied. He tricked his brothers and sisters into helping him. He taught them great magic, and they all worked together to cast it, and created the first plane. This plane, this reality, this wonderful new place, was filled with joy and wonder and power and all wanted to enter, but the greatest of these first beings said no, and forbade the most powerful of the ancient old ones, the ones he was most jealous of, from entering.

"He continued creating wondrous things, as he was filled with the magic of his siblings, which suffused his plane, and was part of it, and this made the greatest of the ancient old ones far, far greater.

"He wanted this realm filled with others. Others he could control, as he couldn't control his siblings, and did not let them enter the place they helped create. So, he made the first universe, and planets, and coaxed life to grow into beings capable of serving him, and they could ascend higher, and eventually join with him in his plane. The place he so cruelly denied his own kind, his own family.

"He made many universes, and many of his creations grew strong enough to dare even attack ancient old ones, and the insults grew too great to bear.

"First, the betrayed ancient old ones made the NetherRealm and demons, but that was not enough, so they made the g'athu on planets within the Betrayer's own universes, and a great war ensued. And the greatest and his Favored won the war. Some ancient old ones were greatly injured, so injured they sleep still, to this day. Two of them, the ones called Nightmare and Sorrow, sleep so fitfully their dreams spawn all the dark ones, their own children.

"So, you have the Favored and the Forsaken and the injustice of a greedy old one, one that spurned his siblings, and denied them, and forces all, even his own creations, to suffer greatly to enter his kingdom. No, to even have a small chance to enter his kingdom. All suffer, and very few make it.

"My sisters and I were not born demon, or g'athu, or dark ones. We were born as you were, on a nothing planet in a nothing sector of a nothing galaxy within a nothing universe and were forced to be part of this unjust system. All turned their backs on us, our plight, and we had no chance of ascending. As many in our situation do, we turn to the Forsaken for power and for justice.

"We learned if you make a million-million tiny heads of the famous g'athu Kazthun, and make a large statue of her head from all the little ones, and swear allegiance, part of her enters the statue of herself, and will grant power unimagined, and a faster and easier way of advancing with…unusual resources. So, we did, and she did."

The tall one stops talking after her long speech, and all three sisters giggle.

The small sister then resumes the story, "Kazthun the Unconquered, the Knowing, the Bold, is a sworn servant of the ancient old one named Darkness, Eater of Suns, Destroyer of Galaxies, Might of Those Who Fell, and Hope of Those Yet to Come. We serve her who serves her. The Forsaken value those who are born Favored and are willing to join them in their struggle for justice.

"When you entered our new abode, our patron told us you were different, and to try and recruit you to our cause. You seem a good man, John. Do you want to fight injustice, end tyranny, and help bring this whole corrupt system down? What say you, man?"

John ponders the question for a moment, then asks, "What is the screaming below? I can distinguish at least five screaming, if not more."

The sisters giggle, the small one replies, "Oh, that? That's how we advance faster. We give our great Mistress what she wants, and she gives us high-quality refined essence to cultivate with. It really speeds things up. We went from being nobodies, discarded by society, to having real power. We pledged as Seeds, and within a standard rotation were raised up to Shoots, and we can combine together and become a Sprout, or even hide our advancement completely.

The tall sister, for the first time, frowns at John. "You don't seem impressed. A Sprout is also called a Silver for those on a more martial path, those who bring death and collect crystals of the fallen. You're a Seed from a world far poorer than ours, how can the thought of being raised up high to Sprout not impress you?"

Curiously, John asks, "And what is it your great Mistress wants?"

More giggling from all three, "What doesn't she want? What we give her is their pain and suffering. We don't know why this tribute works, but it yields the best return. You can't build a castle without making a mess of the ground first, and we see to the needs and comfort of our guests before we capture them. It's no less humane than killing them for crystals, and if our side wins none of it will be necessary. No more Bloody Climb. All can live and know everlasting peace within the first plane of the Greedy One, the Betrayer, the being the Favored name the only God. The gates will be thrown open, and all will be welcomed in, welcomed to enjoy the joint creation of all the ancient old ones, called Heaven, and there will be no more pain and suffering, and all will rejoice and be equal."

John sees the choice before him for what it is, as he's had similar offers made to him many times over his long life. Sometimes it's offered prettily and kindly. Sometimes at sword point. The words change, but the demand never does. It's always, "do as we say, or else."

# CHAPTER 22
## OR ELSE

"The offer is enticing, but I have many more questions I need answered before I'd be willing to commit to this noble cause. First, I must let my fox outside, so she doesn't spoil your floor, and you think I have no good manners," says John.

The tall sister's face turns stern for a moment, but quickly goes back to friendly. "Oh, don't worry about that. Where we come from...you realize we don't look like this, right? Since we're being honest, and you know little of how things work, let me explain. We have a ritual going that makes us appear as appealing females do from this part of your world. Our races are similar in the grand scheme of things, but also very different. We're both carbon based, same kingdom, but our race is Mollusca, different phylum. I should say species, and not race, but the two are used interchangeably throughout the universe. We excrete waste through our pores. Where we come from, norms and mores and way of life are not the same at all. Do not worry over your creature's waste, nor your own. Waste does not offend us.

"Oh, and can you show us how to work this?" The tall sister holds up a black shiny object, as long as a hand and wide as a wrist, but very thin. John saw some of these objects in the belongings of his kind, after the Tribulation, and couldn't figure out what they were either. He broke one open to see if it contained valuables.

"Sorry, I don't. I know it contains nothing but strange machinery inside of it. Useless. To me, at least," replies John.

"Oh well, our last guest stated news can be retrieved from it in some way. It's a cellphone. Everybody has one."

John cannot remember exactly, but he believes Shoot is equivalent to Bronze, and Pixie told John Bronze are the ones to drop the yellow crystals. He fought two so far to drop yellow crystals – the flesh-creature at the end of the Tribulation, and the antlered-demon in the field. He struggled greatly with the flesh-creature, but was unarmed, and victory was no sure thing without Amber's intervention as a giant bear. *The demon was not so doughty, but the demon only dropped one crystal, and the flesh-creature dropped two. And the flesh-creature was of the dark ones, so perhaps dark ones are made of sterner stuff than demons. These sisters say they are of none of the races invading this world. I know little of the power and strength of these three.*

John's soul is dark with bad deeds, and he's done much he regrets, and has killed many in his long life, and will kill more if he lives, but he never sought out the weak to kill, unless their souls were darkened with bad deeds, and the land would be better off without them. He kept mainly to warriors and those seeking battle. John killed many for power, and though it be hypocritical, the thought of casually torturing for power sickens him. He killed for power, and to keep living, and so did Lilitu, and he is not like her either. And he is not like these sisters. These sisters are like witches, like his Lilitu – cruel and seeing little value in the lives of people beneath them. Toying with people, twisting their hearts and their minds.

The religious tale the sisters told matters little to John. It is all above him, and nonsense. In this case, it is beneficial for his mind to have been restored by a means attuning it to the old ways, as to John only Koram is worthy of his worship. The rest of the tale makes as much sense to him as the world being round. *Where is the Underworld then? Under this round world, or inside it? It makes no sense.*

What does make sense to John are sacred customs, as well as manners. He owes these sisters a debt for their kind service and good hosting, no matter their ultimate motive. He may be a fool for believing so, but a guest turning on his hosts and doing violence to them, unprovoked, is as sickening to John as torturing people for power, and he would not break peace first.

Since John has been alive, he has only attacked a host as a guest when they attacked first, and tortured only those he despised, and thought deserving of torture, and he would not change his manners now, no matter how the world has changed, or will change. He believes manners and courtesy are the glue that binds all together, and allows man to rise above his natural baseness and create civilization.

John never planned on Amber entering the house, but she ran in before he could stop her, or give warning. His first duty is to her safety. His second duty is the murdering of these witches.

"Ladies, my sincerest apologies, but old habits pull hard on both mind and soul. May I please release my fox outside to relieve herself, and we can then continue this business?"

Long moments pass as all sisters sit quietly with long faces. "Sure. You're welcome to try," says the short one, smiling kindly after the too-long pause.

John stands and pushes his chair back. He makes it obvious as he kicks his rucksack full of crystal aside, and leaves it, so the sisters will know he doesn't plan on escaping. He moves around the table, and brushes past the short sister, and bends down to grab Amber. As usual, the fox moves away, as if his touch is repellant to her. John empowers his body with life essence, as Amber is quick, but in this confined space John should be able to catch her without too much of an effort. He lunges towards the fox, and before he reaches her a great weight bears down on him, and Amber too.

John collapses to his hands and knees, and struggles to bear the invisible weight, and empowers himself with more strength. Amber lays on her belly, head forward and flat on the ground, whimpering, unable to move. "Go on. Take her out, John. You can do it," one of the sisters laughs out.

John lets go of the strength and speed his vital essence gives him, as he has a plan. He slowly, and with much struggle, crawls forward on hands and knees, sometimes the pressure pushing down on his body causing him to collapse to his elbows. The sisters cheer him onwards, "Go! Go, John! You can do it! We believe in you!" The laughter turns harsher, and the mocking cheers crueler, and the sisters cackle with great joy at John's struggle. Arms shaking, with great determination, he inches forward.

"Do you know what we are doing, John, man of little knowledge, who sought to betray us? This is the power of our souls bared. Unveiled, the combined pressure from three high Shoots bearing down on you. Our body formation is one of great strength and secrecy, granted only to worshipers of Kazthun, and enhances our souls. You will not find it in your NCS. Guess why, John? Kazthun has some other titles. Kazthun the Soul-Eater, Kazthun the Web-Spinner, Kazthun the Canny. Though her idol has only a small sliver of her power, even now she burrows into you, and she knows your thoughts, and you will feed her. Feed her your fear, your despair, your pain, your suffering, and then, finally, even your soul she will feast upon. You will have nothing, John. No returning to the Wheel. This is the end for you.

"What are you, John, a low Seed? Your soul-weight is nothing. So weak. Did you even open your core yet? Will you even drop a crystal when you die? You fool. You liar. Teller of silly tales. Did you really think you could betray us? Did you think our great Mistress wouldn't know? You could've been someone, John. Someone important. Instead, you will be completely consumed."

John struggles onward, inch by inch, trying to mask his thoughts from this Kazthun. Trying, hopefully. His effort to move forward is great, and the sisters continue to mock him, and make sport of him, and tell him of his depraved fate. He ignores it all, and struggles forth. He finally reaches the fox, and with a great effort lifts an arm over and around her, and makes a show of being unable to lift her, and collapsing onto her. "Be ready and run far," he whispers softly while his head lay on her back, his face as near her ear as he could manage.

John sends as much essence as he can to increase the strength and speed of his body. With considerable surprise, the sisters see John quickly stand, and with immense effort chuck the fox through a large window covered in symbols overlooking the table. He then spins to face the sisters, casting [Magical Essence Dart], and loosing it as he turns, just as the pressure bearing down on him is too much, and brings him down to his knees. A spell of theirs hits John, and causes his mind to warble harshly and nearly lose consciousness, and a great force hurtles him through the air to crash into the wall behind, and the pressure and gravity drops him to his belly, face pressed into the ground.

"NO!" John hears the loud yell as he struggles to stay conscious, the darkness threatening to overwhelm him. A weird sound ensues, as John lay pressed to the ground, one like John has never heard. A disgusting sound. When the sound stops, the weight pressing down on John increases significantly, even making it hard for him to breathe. Stars dance in his vision, behind his closed eyelids, and his fight to stay conscious becomes more difficult. He tries to reach out his arm and cast anew, but something enters him, and stops it. He tries again, and is stopped again. A new sound begins, the sound of something slithering towards him, something very large.

A voice – deep and distant and rattled, somewhat hollow – echoes in John's mind, "Mistress Kazthun, we beg of you, this one killed our sister, if it be possible, make his suffering greater and never-ending. He holds secrets, as no Seed of any rank can kill a high Shoot with one manifestation. We beg you, extend his life as vengeance for our fallen sister, your loyal servant and ardent disciple. Let his pain be greater than any before him. We beg of you."

The slithering stops near John, and something warm and slick covers him. "We could kill you so easily. So little effort is needed. But then your suffering would end, and it has yet to begin, and you'd go back to the Wheel and be reborn anew. Your torture will be a feast for our hearts."

John begins to be dragged over the floor, and he forces his eyes open, and sees only darkness, as his vision is blocked by floor and monster, and he struggles to keep his eyes open and not pass out. He can't move his head. He sticks his tongue out and it touches nothing.

"Oh, you thought we couldn't merge as two? Oh, John, you fool. We told you. Powers unimagined. Or did you think we wouldn't still be Sprout when only two merge? More fool you. No! Don't sleep, John! You must stay awake. Sleep is a thing of the past for you, as is peace and comfort." John tries to cast his spell again, and something, again, stops him. "You truly know nothing. We can unravel your manifestations, fool. Why would we let you cast when we now know you have power beyond your tier? Feel free to keep trying, fool. You got lucky, but your luck ran dry, and you will pay for our sister's death."

A door opens, and the muffled screams John could barely discern with his great hearing now ring loudly in his ears. There are more than five screaming. Many more. Venom and malice infuse the voice in his head as it says, "Oh, how you will pay, John." His body bounces along steps as he is dragged down stairs, then landing, and stairs once more, and then over dirt. He sticks his tongue out again, and it touches nothing again. He has a notification, so his NCS must think him out of combat, and safe, and having nothing else to do, he checks it.

**Your skill with 'Magical Essence Dart' has increased to skill level 2.**

John is dragged closer and closer to the screaming. Screaming from so many mouths he cannot distinguish them. He is then dragged among the screams, and a collar is closed around his neck, and bindings added to his ankles, and then his wrists too. "Nice bracers, John. Are those enchanted? Where'd you get those? Well, they'll be ours when you are no more. You will suffer so much before then though. So much."

And suffer John does.

# CHAPTER 23
# THREADS

John screams as loudly as his body allows. He screams in terror, in despair, in impotence.

Of the memories remaining to John, a good many of them are of the type to be avoided, to not be thought of or remembered. Some, because the remembering of it causes great anguish and hurts the heart too sharply. Some, because the remembering of it causes too much discordance between how someone sees themselves, and how they truly are, when character and convictions are put to the test. John has many instances where he proved he is not the honorable man he sees himself to be, that he strives to be.

John's head is flooded with his mistakes, and far worse, it is flooded with his successes. No relief is given. No time to recover. A constant bombardment, one right after the other, of reliving the scenes too bitter to turn mind to. All the memories in his head prove he is small and unworthy and timorous, and they leave no doubt he is undeserving of love or even kindness or peace.

John is not a good man, and he deserves what is happening to him. Deserves this and more besides. He is base and mean and a coward. Who is he to ever judge others? He screams in despair. He screams in anguish. He screams in desperation and despondency and hopelessness. He screams in the lonely desolation that echoes throughout his long life. He screams many, many times, and for long. He screams.

And then he doesn't. John finally manages to retreat into himself, as he's done so often and for so long.

For nearly six thousand years John has battled his own mind. Depression, regret, and loneliness – all his constant companions. Bad thoughts and memories of his base actions always threaten to overwhelm him, and glom onto his mind, and refuse to be cast aside or ignored, and bring him low. The cold-dark gave him no other option, to live he needed a way to avoid these thoughts. A way to avoid himself. And he must live. Live a life he did not want to, in a way he didn't want to, and live it alone. Knowing tomorrow will be the same as a hundred years from now, and the same as ten hundred years from now. Existing. Just existing. Existing alone. He needed an escape. And he found that escape in the [Skill] his NCS calls [Undirected Basic Meditation].

John learned early in his life the respite given by retreating into himself. To go deep, deep into his mind, deep into his being. There, he could reflect on things too painful to think of, and do so without the pain. Thinking without thought. He could do many things in this place by just going where his mind takes him – reflect on emotions, and what they are and how to master them, reflect on fights and how to improve in skill and combat, reflect on deeds and actions and reasons and how to become a better man, a man that would not be ashamed to look his father in the face, chest held out, in honor and glory.

To this day John would be scared to meet his father. John knows himself to be vile, and not a good man, though he tries to be. He knows his father would be ashamed of him. Ashamed to have a son such as John. Ashamed he sent John away to live, and seek vengeance, instead of someone more worthy. John lived, and they all died.

What great things has John done? What has he accomplished? He brought vengeance and waste to those who killed his family, he became lord of his father's land again, and many others too, and has even been worshiped, but he was given great power and long life and squandered it. He built nothing lasting, and was king because he was strong, not because he was a good leader, and was worshiped for the same. How could his father look at him with pride, or even look him in the eye the way one man does to another he respects, when all John has done with all the many gifts and opportunities given to him is squander them all and fail and run and hide? Coward. Fool. Small.

John screams again, and the horror of reliving his worst memories begins anew. But he breaks free quicker this time, and holds on to the silence of his inner sanctuary, and calms his thoughts, and retreats deeper. One thought forces itself to the surface – it is amusing he is using his cowardly retreat to avoid all the memories he's too scared to confront, even though he knows it is best to be forced to confront them. He squashes the thought. True it may be, but he must escape first, and seek vengeance, as he has all the future to ponder his failings and baseness, and improve his character.

John steels his heart against the malaise infecting it, infecting his mind too, as much as he can. He can't retreat deeper, as he needs to explore what is happening to him, and how he is being held, if he has any hope of escape. He pictures his dantian and sees his magical essence is being slowly pulled out of it, and five wisps of threads lead away in different directions. He tries to pull back outwards and view his whole magical energy system, and with some difficulty manages to do so. He sees more is being pulled from him than just the magical essence from his dantian, the vital essence from his body is too, as well as other things he cannot see or identify, but can feel. He also senses something foreign in him, a dark area with a feeling of maliciousness.

John tries to cast his spell, [Magical Essence Dart], and finds he does not have access to it. Unlike when he tried casting before, and his casting was undone by the witches, he cannot even begin to cast it now, like the runes are no longer even there, though he can feel them still.

After exploring for some time, John comes to believe the five points his magical essence and other substances inside of him are being drained away to are the bindings around his neck, wrists, and ankles. His first plan to break free is not the best plan, but the best he can come up with for a first attempt at escape. His plan is to leave his retreat and quickly send his vital essence to infuse his strength as much as possible, and mightily yank on his bindings, and break them. It does not go as planned, and as soon as he leaves his retreat, the horrors of his avoided memories assail him, and it is some time before he manages to retreat in on himself again.

Plan two is to cut off the threads of magical essence leaving his dantian, the same as John does every time he creates shen. He tries everything he can think of, and focuses his strong will on the task. No matter what he tries he is unable to cut off the threads. Next, he tries to spin his dantian, in hopes the spin cuts the threads, and is unable to spin it or move it at all. He then tries to move out some magical essence, and make his own thread, and move that to his middle dantian. This also fails.

John makes many plans and tries many things, and all fail. After some time he realizes he can sense the magical energy around and inside himself, and if all else fails he can try to reproduce what he did during the Tribulation, which caused a large explosion. He thinks this may be a bad idea, as it also caused great damage to be done to him, even to his cultivation systems according to the Magnus. Sometimes the only option left is a bad one, and a bad option is better than no option, and a pyrrhic victory is still a victory.

John thinks back to those battles of the Pyrrhic War, his last with the Greeks, and making the short trek to Rome before the end of the campaign. He went to Rome a few times in the centuries before then, but he found the people there to be as barbarous as any outside the great civilizations and cities that went no further west than Greece, though that did change, and quickly. During that time he tried so hard to be a regular soldier, to escape in it, and have no worry or responsibility, and just do as he was told and go where commanded. He often did this, and did it in many companies of many countries. He enjoyed it, hiding as a soldier, more so than living as a noble or an officer, and having the responsibilities that come with those positions, though he had to live as the latter two more often. He even enjoyed living as a farmer or craftsman better than as a noble.

Even with a full beard John could only look so old, and avoid questions of how he stayed so young for only so long, so had to move often to keep his nature secret. The life of a soldier was not easy, and had a lot of worry and responsibility for the men serving, but those soldiers were regular men, and never felt the weight of a crown, and if they were run through with a spear they would die, unlike John. To him, the soldier's life was a simple life, and the best life to pass time.

John had many noble titles and holdings in many countries, and would rotate through being noble and soldier, sometimes accepting officer positions in mercenary companies. The longest he could stay in one position was about ten winters, and then he'd move on. He had more wealth than he could ever spend, and he remembers Thomas taking over the management of all his many estates after accepting the power, as John's mind waned too far, and he lost a great many titles and holdings due to neglect.

Coming back to the present and his current situation, John racks his brain and puts great effort into escaping. He tries many, many things, all he can think of, and all fail. He finally decides there is nothing left to try, so he will explode the area around him, as he did before in the Tribulation, and hopes the internal injuries are not too great, and it allows him to escape, and be in a condition to fight the two remaining witches.

John feels the energy around him as he did before, and before he can do much with it, he is forcefully pulled out of his retreat, and all blurs past him, and he is standing on nothing solid, as he once did before with the Magnus that sent the demons after him.

Before John stands the most frightening being he has ever laid eyes upon.

The being is very large and looks like the merger of man and insect. The bottom part of its body is a long abdomen with four legs, with the back two legs being larger. The thorax or chest is upright, like a man's torso, and also has four arms, the top two arms much larger. No shoulders, and the torso leads directly to a thick neck that tapers into a wormlike head with no eyes – a long snout with a circular mouth taking up the whole end of the face, and in the mouth many, many long fangs circle completely around, and the fangs seem to expand and retract when the being breathes. Something like whiskers also fully surround the outside of the mouth-hole.

The abdomen tapers into a long tail with many bulbs at the end of it. The being's skin, or chitin maybe, is of a light purple color, as if faded royalty. The being has fur in some areas of a darker purple, and all along the back of its abdomen and thorax-torso is a double row of tails, and the tails look like the tails of a lion, thin with a puff of fur at the end. There are far too many of these double tails to count. The being wears something resembling clothing on some areas, and also sports many trinkets over different parts of its body.

Like the Magnus and Pixie, this being has no soul or vital essence John can see. Unlike when John stood before the Magnus and could feel a certain heaviness and power radiating off her, this being feels like nothing at all, at least externally. Internally John feels the same as he did as a youth when he saw snakes and scorpions and centipedes and spiders, before he received his great power. A sort of quiet maliciousness seems to radiate from this being, and John feels a great fear inside of himself, and a desire to be away from this source of danger, and the violence it promises.

Unlike the bear and wolf and boar, beasts that act correctly and predictably as beasts should, the snake and spider and scorpion and centipede have no use at all, and do not behave as man and beast, and are sneaky, and move too quickly, and attack for no reason other than they are mad and violent and unreasonable, and one small bite from one can lay a man low.

John remembers his childhood friend bitten by a spider, and the spider's bite did not hurt too much, but it laid many eggs in his friend, and killed his friend in such a sneaky and devious and nefarious manner.

As a youth John had a great fear of insects, and was harassed by his father and his father's men for allowing such little things to unman him, and they all took great joy at throwing spiders and scorpions at him, and seeing him jump in fright and scream. In all of John's long life nothing made him feel fright like the being before him, not the tentacle thing sucking the essence from his Lilitu, not demons, not dark ones, not even being put in a pit of insects and snakes to help free him from his fear of them, as his father did to him when he was ten and eleven and twelve summers of age, so he could become a man at thirteen without shame, having people think he was cowardly and weak.

"Do you have no manners, or do you seek to force my hand? Pay obeisance or be punished."

John did not see the being's mouth move at all, and the words sound in his head, like with the witches when they joined, and the voice is very similar – deep and distant and rattled, somewhat hollow. The being's back-tails move around sporadically as it 'talks.'

John can feel this being is far above him, even far above the Magnus he met with last time, though this being does not radiate power like her. John kowtows, head to ground. *This must be the great Mistress Kazthun, goddess of the witches*, John thinks, as his heart rate increases, and he assumes he is doomed. *Hopefully I can put up some fight, and die well.*

# CHAPTER 24
# EVERY SPROUTING TREE, EVERY CHILD
# APIECE, EVERY CLOUD AT SEA

Do not even think of her name! Do not draw her attention to me. I try to lead a peaceful life and do not want that trouble. And I sound the same due to the NCS translation. All races communicating without voice sound similar. Turning subtitles on for nonverbal communications helps. Why are you so surprised at this meeting? I pinged your NCS. Your avatar must have informed you."

John's heart slows some, as this being is not the great Kazthun, and it seems reasonable and willing to talk, and not full of malevolence and the desire to wantonly attack like spiders and scorpions and centipedes and snakes. At least not so far. He also can't remember Pixie informing him of this being wanting to meet him.

"I have no desire to kill you and will not unless you give me reason. Or if it benefits me somehow. In fact, I already saved you. Most likely. Unless your thoughts or intentions were false. You were trying to explode the energy around you. The power of the essence in your dantian, a power well beyond your tier, would have ensured your complete annihilation. My people value those willing to die to avoid imprisonment, but I am a scholar, and I have many questions. You may explode yourself after they are all answered. Now, we will join further, and I will have all your knowledge. In return, I will give you some answers, and if what I learn from you is worthy, I will allow three questions on advancement, as is custom. Before we begin, I should introduce myself. I am Sublime Sunshine. And I am male, by the way."

Before John can really think or reply, more words from the being enter his head, "How is it possible you do not know what that is? Sublime is the title for having reached the fourth Tree. Only Eternal is above it. Well, they say there are seven Trees, but no one knows what the sixth Tree is, and the seventh is union with the Supreme One. You are on the first Tree, and very low on it. Most Mortals never even meet someone on the second Tree, and having a Sublime tell you they may be willing to answer three advancement questions is extremely auspicious. Stop being scared and consider yourself lucky beyond imagining. I have passed all the bottlenecks and hurdles."

John, trying to consider himself lucky, hears skittering and feels the Sublime approach him and stop right in front of his head, which is still on the invisible floor, as John is still kowtowing. John hears a snap and his vision blurs for a moment, and he nearly collapses.

"You resist? How?"

Another snap sounds, and this time John's head shakes and he does collapse.

"Again? And you were not even trying. How is this…never mind. It was for your own comfort and peace of mind, and that is as gentle as I can go without risking your death. I will know the truth soon. This may hurt. Stay very still."

Something strange and wet slides over John's head and down to his neck. A great suctioning starts, and it causes a tremendous amount of pain and a pounding headache. He is unable to move or breathe, but somehow has no need for breath and is not suffocating, something he has much prior experience with. After some time, the pain lessens, and this experience becomes just one more John must endure.

The thing covering his head is finally removed, and though it may be rude to do so, John just stays prone on the ground with his eyes closed, recuperating.

"I see. I see. You should have taken the spatial storage. Not doing so was a mistake. And your NCS told you about me right after opening your lower energy center. It used my Tree name, Divine, and not my title. I

194

was going to just communicate with you, but when I saw how you finished the Tribulation I decided to come in person. I would have been here sooner, but I had to talk to a friend of mine about you. Well, friend may be a lofty name for our relationship. She is a fellow scholar, and easier to approach than other Eternals, and still remains curious. Most of them are not and do not. They get strange at that tier. Just focused on karma. For good reason too. It is called the Bloody Climb. I need to update my NCS with this world's history and knowledge. Wait."

John wishes he knew what was going on. Since meeting this being he's been kept off balance, and confused, and had his head sucked painfully, and hasn't had a chance to collect his thoughts before more and more information is forced upon him. He prefers having a moment to ponder things, and properly consider them, and that just doesn't seem like something this being allows. *I should've taken what storage? He just says things and moves right on without explaining.*

"Most people can clearly remember big events from a short while ago without needing explanations. The offer from Gar'tar."

*That race?* John wonders. *The other race besides demons and dark ones? I've yet to meet one. I don't remember meeting any, at least.*

"No, fool. The race is g'athu. The female that created the Tribulation. Gar'tar. Magnus Gar'tar, though she cannot figure out how to leave this galaxy, so no real Magnus. God Almighty, you are starting to annoy me. Please be less stupid. She offered you a storage device, and you took healing instead. The storage would have lasted you through the Transcendent tier. The Exalted Tree, idiot. Pay attention. I am on a damned peaceful path, and none have tried my patience like you are since I was on the first Tree myself. While my NCS is updating, just wait. Do not talk. Do not think. Just stand there quietly and ponder on the meaning of not being a fool. All the gifts you have been given and you have wasted them all with rank stupidity. Now shush."

John has shown great manners and restraint, and has been treated very poorly in return. He takes great offense at these last insults, and decides he has had enough of being regarded as so little, and to do battle instead of letting these insults pass unanswered. *Aye, this here's the test. Was the cold-dark an excuse to hide my true cowardice? I stand before someone possessing great might but no manners. Am I a man and demand to be treated as such? Great gods below, honor or glorious death was my promise, and I shall keep it this day, the last of my days. Now witness my deeds!*

As John raises himself up from the floor, and gets on hands and knees, he continues to climb through the air, as if invisible hands are lifting him. He has little time to wonder what is happening before he is thrust downwards into the invisible ground at great speed. This happens over and over again, and hurts greatly. John is unable to speak or think as his body is slammed repeatedly into the ground, and in this way John does obey the Sublime's orders, and does not talk, and does little thinking other than to ponder on what a fool he is.

The slamming continues and continues, and John retreats into himself to avoid the horror of it, though he is unable to go deep.

"That meditation technique of yours is truly something. You can somewhat access it here, in my mind, even as we approach one."

John is let down to the ground, and his body becomes his again to own and use. He has not forgotten the past insults. He has not forgotten his promise. He makes ready to charge, but his body becomes frozen, and he is unable to.

"Great God in Heaven, still? Still? My people value courage, but even they would think this is foolishness. I am a Sublime. You could never hurt me on the outside. You are in my Mind's Eye, so even if you were close to achieving my Tree you could not do anything but what I allow in here. You are strong for your kind of humanoid and tier within the Mortal Tree, but any of my people of your tier and rank could handle you easily in any sort of physical competition. Your race is F-rank. Your world is soft and ignorant. You nearly died by a Copper and Bronze dark one. You have no idea how to utilize essence. Most Bronze should be able to handle you, and it is a guarantee you would lose against any Silver, even if they were fed the tier.

"You could gather all the Silvers of all the universes in this reality together and they could not hurt me, and I could extinguish them all with
little effort. The same goes for any tier up to low Celestial. I do not say
this to brag. You do not understand what my title means, and the power
belonging to it. I can travel the universes. I can approach a sun and cultivate its energies. A Gold of your Tree is so far above you, on most worlds
they do not even consider adult Woods actual people. I am of the fourth
Tree. Recognize your place."

John realizes he does not understand as much as he should, and he
knows this being is far stronger than he is, but his promise wasn't to cower
if someone had a certain title or tier or Tree. His promise was honor or
glorious death. He was dishonored, and he knew attacking meant his
death before accepting this course, and was fine with it a moment ago,
and nothing has changed. Munashi wasn't the only one on The Way of
Death and ready, nor the only one with honor.

As John prepares for a new attack the Sublime says, "Fine. I apologize.
I was rude and insulted you. I am not used to dealing with those so far
below me. My manners have not been as I demand in return, and I do
believe manners are important. Please, forgive my behavior and accept
my apology. I became annoyed and took my frustrations out on you."

Face saved and honor restored, John accepts the apology, but before
he can give voice to his acceptance, words enter his mind. "Good. We
have much to discuss. Now I know what she meant. This world is strange
and there is more to you than I thought. And some of your foolishness is
not your fault. Your captors used a stupor manifestation on you, and
though you managed to resist it partially your mind is still muddled.

Also, your brain has…I need to explain all this in ways you can understand. Your brain was restored, but some things happen with aging
not considered bad or in need of healing. Restoration did not touch some
areas that impact cognitive functions. You have a very old and a very
young brain all at once. This will be rectified as you ascend but makes
your thinking strange and stubborn.

"There are other issues, but there is no use discussing them as you will not understand or see them as issues. Know this – I know all you do and remember all you do. I am going to help you. I have learned much from you, and I can turn what I learned to my advantage. Great advantage. I wish you paid more attention to the magic this Lilitu learned. A working portal ritual without even opening an energy center. Outside the Tree of Life. And you. Your soul was tethered. You can see souls, something only Eternals can do. See a specific essence without a vision Perk. Strengthen your body in such a strange way. And heal from injuries to systems and organs that would kill even Transcendents and some Celestials. Depending. My Eternal contact, she said the same way it is done to keep a universe going. Now I understand. Eternal matrices. Amazing. But why? Why cut off this planet from the Tree of Life? What was being tested?

"The vision. I could not see the vision you were granted before accepting your strange power. I wonder if Eternals can see red souls, and what makes a soul red? How is this power passed through blood? And karma. You can see karma. I knew Eternals could see souls, but see the karma of souls? I must see her again, but first I must see this through.

"I cannot help you directly. I will not risk the ire of the one your captors follow. I will answer more than three questions, as we have much to cover. I will explain ways to escape your bonds. You missed an obvious way – pulling what is being drawn from you into you instead. I could have easily done it when I was your Tree and tier, but this may not work for you, as it will take a great force of will. If you cannot do it, retreat deep into your cultivation, as deep as you can. Your meditation technique is powerful, and it might start your energy center spinning and snap those threads if you go deep enough.

"You have no idea what an advantage this technique is. You did not get an achievement for being the first, so someone at some point in some reality did it too, but who would ever practice such a useless technique for so long to get it to Legendary Mastery? There are much better techniques. But the benefits of doing so! Undirected means it targets nothing, so influences everything. Basic means it has only a negligible influence on anything. Both undirected and basic meditation techniques are useless and fill their users with impurities. Unless it is at Legendary Mastery, it seems. It collects energy, refines essence, heals the body, even heals channels, looks like it will clear them too, soothes the mind and spirit, and on and on. No impurities! The only thing it does not do is strengthen the soul, but no technique does. None I know of do, and this is what I study. Meditation is my field of specialty.

"You should know some more about Skill Mastery. I do not even have a Legendary Skill. Or any at Grand Master. I have one at Master. Some others are close to Master. No one gets close in Mortal tier. Maybe in the highest core worlds, but I doubt it. The Mastery levels of the NCS are made to span all five Trees. Do you know how much harmony was wasted when the NCS was activated and Skills forced to merge? You could have cleared out all the general Perks you qualify for with all the harmony that went to waste. It is not your fault. Nor the fault of the NCS. This is why your Skills page is frozen. The NCS does not know how to deal with your issue and knows allowing more Skill merging or Synergies will waste more harmony than most beings will ever accrue, so it froze the page and is waiting for an answer to the issue. Such a waste. We will address that.

"And your soul. From what I was told your soul is a real mess. Now I know why. And I have ideas how to fix it, and this will also help with your harmony predicament. How you advanced so many Skills to such levels I do not understand, even considering how long you have lived. Maybe a side effect of being without the Tree of Life? Maybe it has to do with the strange powers you were granted? I will need you to tell me of the vision I could not see.

"God Above All on High, I did not even finish telling you other possible ways to escape your bonds. We just have so much to cover. Write this down. Wait, you cannot access your own NCS. Use mine. I will transfer what you write to yours when you exit. Pay attention, we have a lot to cover. And you will learn the basics too. I have a hard time understanding how you lived so long on your planet and do not know how many days there are in a full rotation of it."

So, John becomes the student of a man he is thousands of years older than. Unlike Pixie, the Sublime knows when John's mind wanders. Sublime Sunshine is a hard teacher, and demands much, and jumps from topic to topic and back again, but ensures John learns what he feels is important, even useless information for warriors, and that only clerks and priests need to know. John is surprised that he finds much of it interesting.

# CHAPTER 25
# LEARNING

Out of all John learns, he finds the information on the Sublime's people and planet the most interesting. The world the Sublime comes from is much larger than Earth, and has no moon. These two facts cause the planet to be much different than Earth. Some force called gravity is much stronger and makes it hard to move, the terrain is flatter with no tall mountains, the world spins faster and days are shorter, the nights are very dark, and the wind is constantly fierce and strong and howls so loudly John wouldn't be able to hear much at all besides the wind if he were to travel there.

The Sublime's people name their offspring after things they consider good and necessary for life, such as trees, soil, air, duty, strength, love, family, respect, and even specific foods.

Though Sublime Sunshine looks very different from humans, he claims to be very similar, and is in the same kingdom, called Animalia. He has hard skin that isn't chitin, and he has a spine. He has two systems that are nervous, and two organs that perform similar functions as a brain. His race is very strong and fast and doughty because they must be. His planet has many fierce beasts, and the nights are very dark, and there is always danger, and his people evolved to meet the challenge. His race is graded D, and he claims that is only due to them not valuing intelligence enough, or else they'd be graded as a C race. This bothers the Sublime, as he is a scholar and values thinking and learning, and wants his people to value these things too, and this is the reason he became so angered at John earlier.

The Sublime's people are Tech 1, but do not rely on the NCS so much for learning and teaching, as he claims the advice it gives steers users towards safety and what works for most, and not what works best for the individual. The NCS also steers people away from being competent in important areas they should learn in the first Tree, and promotes only a specific and narrow path of advancement. He does state the techniques the NCS promotes are the best, and everyone uses them, even the old powers of the core worlds of the core universes.

Sublime Sunshine had his NCS set to notify him of any interesting new technique developments in this universe, and this setting bore little fruit until it informed him a low Wood had developed a Legendary technique.

They talk about the universe and various worlds, but spend most of the time talking about John's soul. He is told his soul is gravely damaged, and this is the reason his [Runes] Stat is so low, and slow to increase. [Runes] is a general measurement of how many runes a soul can bear at a tier and rank, and John's soul is very small and frayed and cannot handle strain. When he accepted the power, his soul was removed and tethered someplace far away, and his soul decayed much over time, and is now paltry and weak compared to what it should be.

The soul is very important for a lot of things other than [Runes]. The Sublime claims [Runes] is a trap and makes cultivators weak and complacent. When John increases his tier to Copper, before he can rank up within that tier, he first needs to clear his meridians. Once any meridian is clear and open, John will be able to manipulate magical essence to create his own spells, as runes are a crutch, and John can use the old way.

A long time ago runes were only used to enhance and imbue items with magic, and perform rituals, and people didn't know they could be placed on the soul to safely cast complex spells of any nature and aspect. The Sublime's people use a mixture of the two methods, and he recommends John leans heavily into the old way.

The old way has some drawbacks, as it is much safer to create manifestations using runes, and runes allow pure essence to power any manifestation. With the assistance of the NCS, cultivators can suppress natural affinities and acquire aspects much later than they used to, and keep a pure core after acquiring aspects. Advancing this way removes some old hurdles and bottlenecks, but makes a cultivator completely reliant on casting manifestations through runes until their affinities become strong enough to aspect their dantian. At that point they must also learn the old way. Learning the old way sooner will make John more powerful and skilled compared to other cultivators of the same tier, but he first needs to survive to higher tiers, and planning for the long run is always smart to do.

The soul has a weight to it, and at the Bronze tier pushes down on those around the cultivator, and has to be veiled, and not just to protect those around from the weight of it, but for many reasons. This soul weight can also be focused with intent onto a specific person, and if the discrepancy in tier is great, the weight will slow or immobilize the person, and can even crush them. The being with claws unveiled his soul before the Tribulation and crushed John, and the sisters did this to immobilize him.

Everyone has normal souls in the Mortal tier, and soul damage is not something common, even at later tiers or Trees, as attacking or destroying souls is considered blasphemy. When Mortals of the same tier, and around the same rank, bare their souls and focus their intent on each other, it usually does nothing as the souls will both have the same weight and power, unless one of the cultivators has much sharper focus and significantly greater intent. Since John's soul is so damaged, he will always be in danger of being overpowered or hampered even from cultivators at his tier, or even lower tiers.

The difference between the Mortal and Exalted tier of the first Tree, when ascending from Platinum to Diamond, is the refining of a soul. If John were to ascend from Mortal to Exalted with his soul so poor, it would cripple him, and greatly hamper all further advancement after.

There are ways to heal and strengthen the soul, and healing soul damage and strengthening the soul are two different things, but these ways usually require expensive medicines, artifacts, or rare treasures not available in this world. Sublime Sunshine has one item with him that would help, but he isn't willing to give it to John yet. What John's main remedy will be to heal his soul is shen. Constantly filling his middle dantian with shen. This will greatly slow down his progression but is one of the few available methods to address this issue. Another being a vision [Perk], which will also solve his harmony issue, as every increase in a [Skill] he gets now is wasted harmony. This [Perk] will also address a third issue too.

John qualifies for better vision [Perks], but he must start healing his soul as soon as he can, and this vision [Perk] is the best way to start doing so now. And everything he needs for the ritual will be available to him.

The vision [Perk] is called [Orb of the Crimson Palace]. Nearly everyone on a martial path gets a vision [Perk] allowing the sight of general essence, as this helps in numerous ways. Essence can't be masked in a fight, and is hard to mask outside of one, so essence-sight can prevent sneak attacks, lets a skilled practitioner see the flow of and unravel or block manifestations, know what aspect is being used, if an item has been enhanced, and many other useful benefits.

Only one vision [Perk] can be had, and it can't be changed. Sublime Sunshine assumes another slot becomes available in the fifth Tree, since all know Eternals have some sort of soul-sight. Since John can see life essence in living beings, and even see souls, taking a vision [Perk] other than an essence-sight will not hurt him as much as others. He will not be able to see aspects of other essences besides life, and will have a very hard time predicting and blocking or unraveling manifestations, and lose out on the rest of the many benefits of general essence-sight too.

[Orb of the Crimson Palace] has another benefit related to sight, as it will make colors more dull and drab, and bright light won't hurt his eyes, especially the sight of higher tiered souls to his naked eyes. Sublime Sunshine claims if the souls of the two Exalted he saw before the Tribulation blinded him, it would be significantly worse to see a Magnus or Sublime's soul. And Sublime Sunshine does have a soul, and life essence too, as does the Magnus he met before, but neither would show in a projection in the mind. Pixie is a different story.

[Orb of the Crimson Palace] is usually only taken by various types of priests, such as shamans and witch doctors and druids, and usually only on Tech 0 worlds that still have religion and do not know the truth of the universe. The Sublime also claims what the three sisters told John was a lie, and tells his version of the truth. "God came first. He was not the greatest among equals. He was God, and all there was. His first creations were the ancient old ones. Powerful? Older than anything else? Sure. But creations of God, and not His brothers and sisters. They did all help in creating Heaven. That part is true. And almost all of them were welcomed in. A few had dark hearts and evil thoughts, and those were not let in. God cast them out. And they did not like that.

"He then created realities, and universes, and the Tree of Life, and it was all to fill Heaven. But only fill it with those deserving. You cannot ascend beyond Eternal without the karma, and that must be earned and cannot be taken by force. Huge bottleneck. A lot of Eternals are stuck or not even trying. Whether this is unjust is not up to us to decide. It just is. There is nothing you can do about it. You know how long ago the Forsaken races were made? The number is so large it is meaningless. Not to you. Most numbers are meaningless to you. But meaningless to me and everyone else. Know how old Heaven is? Double that meaningless number.

"How do I know this is true? There are still beings around from the Forsaken War, and a lot of books and writings on it from cultivators that fought in it still exist. Even most of the ancient old ones do not lie about any of these facts from all I have heard and read. And there is no reason for God to lie. He is not like the God a lot of your religions here worshiped. Praying to Him does nothing. He will never help you. He does not want worship. All He wants is for people to ascend and join Him. He made the way, and wants us to follow it, but it is up to us. He does not give. He does not help. He does not promise anything. There is a place of eternal bliss and ecstasy, He lives there, and He wants more beings to join

Him, but He does nothing to help you get there. That is it. That is the truth as all know it.

"Some Forsaken are decent. Some of the demons and a couple of g'athu I have met are. The dark ones are a different story. The cultivators that turn to the Forsaken, such as your captors? Most of them are broken and looking for fast power. A lot of the Outsiders are worse than the Forsaken. Outsiders are races that do not think normal. Some species are just different and can be a real blight on their galaxy. Sometimes even their whole universe. Some are not bad and you just cannot communicate with them since they think so differently. Like energy beings. Even their Eternals make no sense, so just imagine what trying to communicate with the lesser Trees is like.

"We can technically communicate with all the Outsiders because of the NCS, but it is usually useless to even bother. Hive species are pretty bad and usually Outsiders. Most extremophiles are Outsiders, but they are not usually the dangerous kind. A large percent of silicon and ammonia and other lifeforms are Outsiders to us carbon lifeforms, but less to each other. We have the highest percentage of Outsiders that we consider Outsiders, but there are way more carbon lifeforms than other types. Well, they say energy beings outnumber us significantly, but who knows? And who cares? If you cannot see them or interact with them, it does not matter. I will be able to see them once I ascend to Eternal. I wonder if you can see them. They must have souls. They don't use essence as we know it, or we could see it with our essence-sight."

Why [Orb of the Crimson Palace] is usually only taken by the priestly sort is because it allows the possessors of the [Perk] to see spirits. Not the souls of spirits, but what is left of a being after it dies, and still clings to its soul, before some beings called the Vhilani Mahilaharu spy the soul and call it back to the Wheel of Life to be reborn anew. The higher a being ascends, the longer the spirit lingers, and the manner of death also matters. Seeing into the spirit world is why colors become dull and drab, and bright light is far less bright.

The NCS description of the vision Perk only claims it 'helps spot the ethereal and things out of place. 360-degree vision. No passive energy cost. The orb is tethered to your middle dantian and constantly collects energy and essence. Provides minor soul strengthening and healing. C-Rated.' The Sublime is uncertain how effective the [Perk] is at soul healing, but any source of soul healing is better than none in John's case.

Another issue the Sublime's solutions to soul healing brings is both the vision [Perk] and shen also strengthen the soul, which is not bad in and of itself, and very useful before and after a soul is refined, but there's a possibility John's soul becomes strengthened too much and resistant to healing, and he will be stuck with a crippled and small soul. Ideally there will be more healing than strengthening, and by the time he becomes capable of ascending from Platinum to Diamond he will have a healed and whole soul that has been much strengthened.

Increasing rank and tiers also strengthens the soul as well, but provides no healing to it. There's no way for either John or the Sublime to see John's own soul, but progress on healing can be tracked by how much his [Runes] [Stat] increases and matches his [Capacity] [Stat], as long as he always targets [Runes] during rank ups.

John doesn't fully understand a lot of concepts discussed, but he learns much, and the conversation goes very well. Until it doesn't. The Sublime has one more recommendation for John to help heal his soul: he wants John to kill Amber and create a medicine out of her.

# CHAPTER 26
## ESCAPE ATTEMPT

Amber is something called a Natural, and these beings have many unique aspects. Naturals are not common, and their rarity is unknown as they don't tend to last long. They are greatly desired by cultivators, especially Gold and Platinum tier cultivators to help temper and strengthen their souls in preparation for ascension to Diamond. Exalted or higher cultivators would only desire Amber for her monetary worth, or as a gift for a lower tiered family member, or favorite student, or some such.

Even with Earth cut off from the Tree of Life, there would be ancient sources of energy within the planet, and this is most likely how a Natural was able to evolve from normal beasts. Naturals never last long enough to evolve a sentient form, so Amber is even rarer in this aspect, and far more potent. The Sublime still claims Amber is less than a beast, and is nothing more than a great treasure, like a medicinal plant, and John would be stupid not to take this treasure and use it for his own benefit, as someone else definitely will. This treasure will be a great boon in healing John's soul, and karma does not matter until someone becomes an Eternal, and at that Tree there is an infinite amount of time to address such actions.

"John, your memories have settled in my mind, and your beliefs and how you think. Listen, pining after your glory days when the world made sense to you is a useless endeavor. The world has never been how you thought and is very different than as you hope. You are being a fool and short-sighted. The Bloody Climb leaves little room for sentimentality and kindness towards strangers. Cultivators that think as you do either do not last long or do not climb high.

"You have only known Amber for a very short time. She is not an actual friend. And what is friendship but two people using each other for mutual benefit? Friendship is overrated and unnecessary. If she had a great deficiency within herself, would she not use you in the same way to shore it up? Or to make herself safe, or to climb higher?"

John doesn't know the answer to that question, but he knows Amber saved him twice, and is his friend, and friends shouldn't kill each other for use as medicine.

"You lack judgment and sense, John. You must learn to think differently. For a long time acting the fool helped you hide, now it has become more than an act. The days of you being able to muscle through any problem are over. You must realize this.

"In the basement you are being held in, there is a window with a faulty rune you can escape through. If you were smart, you would escape your bonds and then escape through this window. You would run far, use the Natural to heal your soul, and if you come back to these Forsaken, you would come back much stronger when victory is assured.

"No. No need to defend your stupid intentions. I see them. There is no such thing as honor, John. There is no glory to be had in childish actions. There are no gods watching and weighing your deeds. There is only the next rung to reach, and then the one after. Glory is just a false feeling to trick the stupid into dying foolish deaths for the benefit of their superiors.

"Oh, you think I am wrong, do you? Tell me then, through most of your life, have you feared the strong and honorable warrior, or did you fear the smart leader able to take power and galvanize armies in a coordinated fashion to bring you down? Stop thinking of your silly answers. I know them already. I know you know I am right. Just listen. Truly listen closely enough to change your mind. You. Must. Start. Thinking.

"You want my help and want me to waste my limited resources on you, but you are assiduous in your commitment to die stupidly and unnecessarily. If you do manage to escape your bonds, I am certain that you will die after in your stupid need for vengeance. All the time and effort I spent teaching you useful and correct knowledge will be for naught. I am not helping you out of the kindness of my heart. I am helping you because I can benefit from you. If I were to claim otherwise you would be a complete fool to believe me. Understand?

"You can give me great acclaim if I can exploit your path of alternate advancement. Even the knowledge I have learned so far can benefit me and increase my wealth and standing. I am not against rewarding you in the future, though I cannot give you any material help now. Let us make a deal. What I want is to formalize this relationship. I will not be your master since I would be forced to kill you for disobedience, and I would rather not. I will be your mentor, a less formal teacher, but I will mark your soul only if you, by some miracle, manage to escape and live, which I do not believe is a possibility.

"Upon your death your corpse and all possessions unequivocally belong to me to do with as I wish. What do you want in return for my continued mentorship and your corpse?"

John, used to having the Sublime pluck his thoughts from his head before given a chance to voice them, thinks about this question for some time as the Sublime waits patiently.

"Okay, enough, John. All your stupid requests are rejected. Of what value are trinkets unless they are enchanted? None. And you winning great glory in battle probably means you acted foolishly, so why would I reward you for doing so? No. I will advise you on how to stay alive and become more powerful. I will advise you on how to defeat the races invading your world.

"I will only give you material help if you ascend tiers, with rewards improving on subsequent tiers. I may reward you if you do something proving you can think and plan and act wisely. I can benefit from you in death almost as much as I can benefit from you in life, but even so, I will try to revive you if you do die, if it is not too much of a cost to me, and only after you do something I consider an impressive achievement. I will never be able to provide direct physical help, as I would lose a great deal of face fighting such lessers. Do you agree to these terms?"

John is finally given the chance to speak. He says, "Agreed. And what title should I give you now? Mentor, or Sublime still?"

As the Sublime approaches his voice sounds in John's head, "Just do not call me late for lunch. Ha. That was a joke. I prefer Sublime still. Sign here."

A very long contract appears before John, and a writing implement placed in his hand he uses to sign the contract with.

"John, did I not just a moment ago tell you how you must start thinking? You just signed a very lopsided contract. I agreed to nothing at all, and you agreed to far more than stated. You make it far too easy to take advantage of you. You must think cunningly and deviously from here on out. I will keep my verbal bargain since I like you, so let this be your first lesson. Think! I am not just saying this because I enjoy saying it. Take this lesson to heart.

"Now, we still have much to cover before I release you to make your escape attempt. If you do live, the next time we meet may be in my Mind Palace as a gesture of goodwill. Afterwards, we will see. Wealth does not come much easier at my tier, especially for scholars, and I will not throw away the little I have on someone so stubbornly working towards their own death. Tell me everything you remember about harmony."

Much more information is covered, such as the exact meaning of a standard rotation, which is roughly equal to one-point-four-three Earth years, or one year and five months or so. The amount of harmony needed for rituals can fluctuate per person, and the NCS is not capable of tracking harmony numerically, and only knows when it is full, or when the harmony requirement of a [Perk] ritual is met. There are several [Perks] the Sublime wants John to acquire, as he meets the conditions for many very rare ones, but this is another issue as John's maximum harmony limit is low, as he is only level 2.

When their time together comes to an end the Sublime wishes peace and prosperity upon John, and John wishes glory and victory upon the Sublime.

John takes a deep breath as he is released, and tries to enter a calm and peaceful state, and hopefully return to his own body while meditating, inside of himself.

John is not meditating upon his return, and is tormented once again by his own memories and doubts, bombarded with despair and misery.

After a great effort, John finally manages to retreat into himself. He has a harder time hanging on than he did before visiting the Sublime, and struggles much before he is settled enough to make his first attempt at escape. His dantian is under a quarter full with magical essence, and he has need of all of it to fight the witches. He assumes he will have little chance to meditate if he can escape the statue he is bound to.

It bothers John the Sublime has his memories and doesn't realize he always thinks and plans. He assumes it comes down to beliefs. Besides Munashi, he has met few following the Way of Death. He disagrees with the Sublime on friendship, and honor, and glory, and always will. But John has had to not just outsmart enemies, but everyone, especially since he had to hide what he is. And once again, John comes up with a plan of escape and vengeance, and puts much thought into it.

Plan in place, John prepares to escape his bonds. He focuses on his dantian, and the five thin threads leaving it, and tries to reverse them, and pull them back in. This causes such great pain to him, inside both his body and mind, he is kicked out of his retreat due to the intensity of it.

This happens again on John's second attempt. And his third, and his fourth.

John becomes angrier and angrier. He believes he has complete control of his emotions, as he has had ages to master them all, especially anger. He sees men giving control over to their wrath as fools, and small, and childish. Yet this is happening to John now, and it makes him even angrier he is losing control, and that this base emotion seems to be helping him somehow.

There are other ways of escape they covered, but Sublime Sunshine specifically said that he himself would be able to escape this way, as he has a strong will, indicating John does not. The thought of this infuriates

John, as he believes no one has a stronger will than he does. He furiously pulls on the threads leaving his dantian, and it causes great pain throughout his body and mind, pain enough for anyone to stop what they are doing, as it hurts far too much to continue.

This time, John is not kicked from his internal retreat, and rages against the torment, and the threads, and his situation, and his life. With every pull he is rewarded with waves of agony surging throughout his body and mind. He pulls harder, and receives more pain, and pulls again, and again.

As a beast he rages and pulls and screams and howls in anguish and fury. Unknowingly, he pulls on more than just the essence threads leaving his dantian, and starts pulling on everything. All that the statue is pulling from him, John starts pulling from it. From all around John is pulled. The malicious and dark presence in John is also pulled on.

John pulls wildly, and maniacally, with no concern for agony or damage or consequences. With all his willpower and might he pulls. He does not notice, but he is no longer in his inner retreat, and is being bombarded with memories and miseries, and he is using this to fuel his rage and his might and to pull on all that is being extracted from him. He pulls, and is always rewarded with great anguish. And he pulls. And pulls.

Then, the flow out of John stops, and with a scream and his mightiest tug he is finally able to reverse the flow. What once was taken from John starts to return. Like a raging lunatic he thrashes about as he pulls, and pulls. His mind is like that of a rabid dog, given completely over to his animal side, the side he so long kept tucked away and hidden.

John pulls and screams and batters and flails, and all that was taken from him is returned, and then more. And more. He takes much, and does not notice when the presence inside of his body is taken into his dantian, or when the shackles binding his neck, wrists, and ankles fall off, or when the pain stops.

After some time, John stops thrashing, and stands, seething, eyes closed, reveling in his bestiality, at the simplicity and directness of it. The purity of his rage, of giving into his primal side, to unshackling his emotions. He sees only red for a long while, as he stands and seethes. He finally notices the statue he was shackled to, that was draining him, and the monstrous face with tentacles hanging from it, and of the many smaller statues of the same face the larger one is made from. He then sees an ethereal eye above it, an eye of pure malevolence, enmity surging forth from it, staring at John.

If John were in his right mind he would run and hide from this eye, this gaze, as it promises nothing but pure terror and untold horrors, but he is not.

Still seething, John points at the eye and says, "I will eat your heart, and bathe in your blood, and feast on eighteen generations of your line, and destroy all you hold dear." He then Jumps at the eye to attack it, but it fades away before he reaches it.

John had a plan. He is supposed to do the ritual to attain the vision [Perk] [Orb of the Crimson Palace] while it is safe to do so, and while the sisters think him still a prisoner, and escape out the compromised window, high on the wall opposite the stairs, towards the right, and ambush the sisters when they are separated, draining them of essence only if it is safe and possible, and then destroy the statue and free the prisoners. If he cared enough to notice he would see all the prisoners near him are now dead, and far beyond saving, and only little more than half still live.

If John were in his right mind, he would think whatever spied on his thoughts before might've warned the sisters of his escape. He would notice his dantian is filled with other energies, foreign and weak, diluting his strong essence. He would remember his old plan, remember that [Stealth] is one of his highest skills, and close to Grandmaster level, and like the snake and spider and scorpion and centipede John is sneaky, and moves quickly, and can attack with no warning, from secret and from shadow, and one small bite from him can lay a man low, and a witch too.

If John were in his right mind, John would think, think of anything at all, but he isn't, and doesn't. He is filled with a great rage unknown and foreign to him, and he is unable to control it. When he has enough of just seething, he remembers there are witches to kill, and rushes up the stairs, stomping loudly, like a charging bull, unarmed, very unlike how a low Wood should go about engaging in combat with two high Bronze cultivators capable of joining together as a Silver, able to kill him with ease in either form.

# CHAPTER 27
# HOLLOW

John, unarmed, raging, filled with anger, flies up the steps, loudly, and is stopped by the rune-laden and locked door. He crashes into it, and then again, and it bursts apart into splinters. He rushes through, and down the hallway into the kitchen, and sees a large and very long slug-like creature with many, many little arms running all up and down its side, waiting, prepared, facing the doorway and John. A very large woman is sitting in the chair he once sat in, with a boy of thirteen or fourteen next to her. He only sees this for a second before a great pressure causes him to drop to the floor, and lay flat on it, as he continues to seethe and stew in his wrath.

For a while John sees little but red and the floor his face is pressed against as he struggles to rise, he feels popping in his head as he fights the pressure pinning him down, and manages to struggle to his hands and knees before he is flung sideways against a wall. The humiliation of being toyed with so further fuels his rage. He is pressed to the floor again, and with great effort and will struggles to his hands and knees, and is flung into the wall again. The scene repeats many, many times. John raging, struggling to stand, and being flung against the wall.

At some point he calms just enough to hear the same voice again – deep and distant and rattled, somewhat hollow – echoing in his mind, mockingly cheering him on. "You can do it, John! You almost did it last time. You basically stood. You got this. We're very frightened. Oh no! He's standing again! There's no way we have enough essence to smash him into the wall this time. We're in real trouble here. I know we said that last time, and the time before, and the time before that, but we really mean it this time. Honest. Go, John! Go!"

John rages against their scornful taunts, but it does not help. Some part of his mind realizes the futility of his current predicament, but his great anger forces him to act the fool, and continue to provide entertainment for the witches. "John, did you see the table? Look at the table, John." John looks, and sees the large lady and child, both with blankets over their shoulders, steam coming from the drinks in front of them, food laid out...he sees it. On a large platter, an apple in its mouth, a fox, baked crisp, surrounded by garnishes. "NO!" John screams, and the slug laughs and laughs at his anguish.

Fury refueled, John rages anew, and screams as he struggles to stand, and reach the slug. All his friends die. Another down, and John was unable to pay back the debt he owed again. He was unable to protect her, and her sweet innocence. John, so long on the top of the heap, and unafraid of any in this world, now made a plaything of these sisters, beings capable of killing him with ease. And cursed. John seems cursed to walk this world alone, as if the curses directed at him by his Lilitu so long ago are still empowered.

As time goes on, John's rage slowly dissipates, and is replaced by frustration, sadness, and bitterness. He is able to think a little more and a little more as his anger subsides, and he remembers he has a spell of his own. Every time he tries to cast the spell it is stopped by the joined sisters, now a Silver, many tiers above John, and the sisters far more knowledgeable and powerful in the ways of magic and spells and casting. John remembers he has life essence, and sends it to heal him, as using it to increase his speed and strength helps little, and is a waste.

John finally accepts the futility of his predicament, and how stupid he has been, and knows there is no escape. He is at the sisters' mercy, and they can do to him as they please. John realizes the sisters are making great sport of him, and are taking much pleasure from his useless struggles. He stops fighting, and closes his eyes, defeated. Defeated by his own stupidity, after he made good his escape. *I truly am a fool. Undone by the anger I spent so long mastering.*

"John, don't stop. You almost had it. Don't give up. You ruined our induction of this lady, you know. She thought your friend was delicious, John. Look at her size, she looks as if she has a lot to give our Mistress. Kazthun wants you back, John. That's great! Not for you. No, not great for you at all. And we have a surprise for you too. You'll love it. You'll just love it, John."

John hears the slithering of the large beast headed towards him. "You will stay at the table. Control your child if you want it to live. Move and your child will suffer greatly for it. There is no escaping us. We will be back soon."

The slithering reaches John, and he feels the slug slide over and around him, and then he starts to be dragged across the floor, his mind elsewhere, focused on his failures.

John's face is pressed into some part of the creature, as his slight shifting ensured. He bites into the slimy and slick skin, and only after a great effort, further empowered by his thoughts of Amber, is he able to pierce the thick and slimy hide.

"John, really? You can't think that would hurt us. We are Silver now, combined. You know how fast we heal? Our Body Formation is special, John. Kazthun's disciples are very hard to kill. We can't wait for you to see your surprise, John. You're really going to love it."

John suckles as the sisters' words echo in his head. The substance he can't help but take in is bitter and burns and has a strong copper and feces taste, and sickens him. He notices the life essence within him attacks this substance, so it is poisonous. He has no choice but to suckle, and hard, as he is getting little vital essence, and the blood in this creature seems to circulate slowly and sluggishly. He feels wooden splinters and the bump of the door sill. As he is dragged down the stairs he suckles, and must retch, and suckles again on the landing.

"You didn't really think you'd escape, now did you, John? Fool. She warned us. You killed our sister. You've caught the attention of our great

Mistress. Our sister's death is sure to be paid back a thousand-fold now. You thought it was bad before, John? You have no idea how bad it can get."

John thumps down the last of the steps, suckling, taking in the essence of life. "Great Kazthun! You killed so many! Why? They're your own kind. Have you no care? You know how hard we worked to acquire these? Your kind deserve everything coming to them. How callous is your race? And we thought our people were uncaring."

John remembers the dead bodies he made during his escape, and is overcome by shame, and sucks harder to make up for that low deed. He is thankful for the little bit of silence he gets next, as he is dragged towards the statue, and struggling mightily to extract the essence of life from the great creature holding him, with her weird and foul blood.

"What did you do to the bindings? What...what are you...why...whaa." The beast collapses as John finishes the dregs, yet it is somehow still alive. This is the first time John has seen anything live, besides his own kind, with no vital essence within them. With great struggle John frees himself, and goes to the ugly head of the beast, and casts his spell three times into her face, and hears a crystal fall to the floor. "That was for Amber, witch." He retrieves the crystal, noticing it is a very dark and bright yellow, and stores it with his other colored crystals in the small bag in his sash.

John learned much about crystals from Sublime Sunshine, and how they generally work as currency in the universe, and that dark-yellow is the color of crystals a Silver drop, and Golds drop a light-green, and Platinums drop a solid-green, and Diamonds a dark-green, and Salts a blue-green. And the five clear crystals a peak Wood drop on death are generally equal in worth to the single light-yellow crystal a low Copper drops, but the values change at higher tiers.

He cares little about the crystal, as his friend and companion is dead, and his mood foul.

John notices the flash of notifications, and wanting a distraction from his thoughts, focuses on it.

219

**Your skill with 'Magical Essence Manipulation' has increased to skill level 3. Practicing this skill is not recommended for beings that have not achieved level 11 at a minimum. Please see Pixie for further details.**

**Your skill with 'Magical Essence Manipulation' has increased to skill level 4.**

**Your skill with 'Magical Essence Manipulation' has increased to skill level 5.**

**Your skill with 'Magical Essence Manipulation' has increased to skill level 6.**

**Your skill with 'Magical Essence Manipulation' has increased to skill level 7. Your mastery with this skill is rated as Novice. Congratulations! Practicing this skill is not recommended for beings that have not achieved level 11 at a minimum. Please see Pixie for further details.**

**Your skill with 'Magical Essence Dart' has increased to skill level 3.**

**You gained a new Achievement! Congratulations! Achievement 'Climber 3' (D-rated, participate in defeating an enemy at least 3 tiers higher than self, 0.30 magical energy discount NCS cost ((total discount now 47.3%)).**

I expected more. The escape was not easy, and I managed to kill a Silver. Well, life has never been fair, has it? So, I should stop my belly-aching, and be thankful I am alive still. And this victory is hollow, as was my last against the first sister, since if they wanted me dead, instead of captured, I would be. Thankfully they sought to toy with me, and imprison me, instead of kill me. Their power was much greater than my own. I am far from the top of the heap now, and must learn this lesson well. How did such a rage take hold of me?

John next searches the slug's body for trinkets or jewelry or weapons, as is his right as victor, and all the sister's possessions are now his. The large and long slug wears no items, and he watches as the skin on the corpse hardens, and turns a muddy grey, and loses its sliminess.

John knows he should destroy the statue and free the rest of the prisoners, but he wants to collect himself further, and avoid talking and responsibility for a while, and reflect on how and why he turned so beastly, as it nearly ended him, even if it helped him escape the statue. He wants to avoid all such happenings in the future, and to do so must understand how it came about.

"My apologies, but I will free you soon," John says to the prisoners, and turns from them. Seeing the state of these poor people tugs at John's heart, and he turns back to them. "Okay, never mind. I will free you now." A task easier said than done, as the bindings are hard to figure out, and destroying the statue is futile, and nothing John does to damage it works, and spell and rod leave not even a mark.

The belt knife he recently acquired does the trick on the bindings, and soon all prisoners are free. All alive and unconscious. Thankfully, John thinks, as he is happy not to speak and project strength and be responsible at the moment, and can be alone in his grief to mourn Amber.

John enters his Mind's Eye and asks Mistress Pixie if she would be willing to assist him in performing the ritual for the vision [Perk] [Orb of the Crimson Palace], and she agrees after telling him he is of too low a tier to qualify for any [Perk] worth attaining, and also, as a Wood, lacks the harmony for any yet.

Sublime Sunshine explained the NCS to John, as well as Mistress Pixie, and said she is not actually a person, and has no feelings, and is just made to act a certain way. Some civilizations with higher Tech levels have fully sentient NCSs, and even those aren't real people with feelings and emotions and their own wants and desires, and are also just made to act a certain way, and are just better at it, and possess superior and more knowledge. John doesn't fully understand this, and thinks it doesn't matter, as the Sublime talked about how powerful the NCS is, and since Pixie is its avatar, she is also powerful, and since she is also kind and caring, he will continue to treat her as he always has, with great respect, admiration, and gratitude. She is the only thing close to a friend John has left.

John is disappointed Mistress Pixie seems to care so little when given the horrible news about Amber, and is as cheerful as ever, when she should be somber.

Pixie coaches him on the various facets of the ritual he is to perform, and after, John thanks her and leaves. Outside of his Mind's Eye, a strange light emanates from John's head and highlights a large circle and intricate patterns on the floor – the ritual circle and runes needed to perform the ritual to receive the [Perk]. Blood is needed to draw the circle and patterns, and the higher the tier of blood, the better, so he uses the blood from the large slug. Tracing the circle and patterns takes a long while, and a lot of focus, and is work he doesn't enjoy doing.

John tests the corpse of the sister, and the dried skin is nearly too hard to cut with his knife to get at the heart. He manages to extract an organ that is most likely a heart, and then takes an eye from one of the stalks with little effort. He wonders if he should take a heart from one of the dead prisoners, to ensure he has the correct organ, but decides against it. He then places both eye and what is hopefully a heart in the center of the ritual circle.

Next John is to imbue the full ritual circle with essence, and notices his dantian is three quarters full, and very diluted, and wonders why, as he hasn't been using the constant breathing technique he should. He decides to meditate, just for a short bit, to convert all the energy into essence. He doesn't notice he left the 'magical' off the words essence and energy in his thoughts.

John sits and starts meditating, not going too deep, and soon stops when he notices one of the prisoners rouse and move a little. John stays still, hoping the prisoner will go back to sleep. He assumes it is a male by the sounds he hears, and is certain after the prisoner rises, and approaches behind John. A very large man. John has no worry of any human of any size, and is curious to see what this man does.

John hears a clicking sound, and cold metal is pressed to the back of his head. A deep voice says, "Wake up, sleepyhead. It's time to answer some questions. In case you're wondering, this here's a Glock Nineteen. Nine-millimeter. Why a nine and not a bigger round? Better speed and penetration. Twenty-four round mags too. I've been living in a world of shit, and I don't need much of an excuse to take it out on you. Lie to me once, I start painting walls. Got it, kid?"

# CHAPTER 28
## SIDEPIECE

"Understood," replies John. He has seen little firearms before, held in one hand, called handguns, but they are large enough he should have easily spotted any. He thinks he may have seen much smaller handguns at some point, and assumes the large man is pressing one of these against the back of his head.

"Good, now where's those sisters? The hot ones. You working with them, kid?"

"I'm not."

John can almost feel the anger coming from the man as a physical force. "Where are they?"

"Dead. That dead creature behind you, that is two of the witches joined together."

The man leans forward, spittle flying from his mouth as he loudly whispers in John's ear. "Maybe you weren't listening earlier. I'm not in the mood for bullshit. I'll ask one more time, then I stop being nice. You realize you got no play here, right? I guarantee you're not good enough to talk your way outta this."

John smiles as he replies, "Correct."

"What?"

"I'm not able to talk my way out of this. Or most situations. That's never really been a strategy I employ."

There's a pause, and then the metal is pressed harder against John's skull. "Oh yeah. A kid your age must got tons of great strategies. Which one you using?"

"The usual. I call it 'I win, you lose.'"

After speaking these words, John quickly spins and knocks the tiny handgun out of the man's hand. He stands while grabbing the man by the neck, holding him off the ground, but not very high off it due to the man's great height. The man punches at John's face, and John just bows his head and lets the man's fist hit his hard skull, and then raises a knee to block a kick to his groin, and catches the man's hand as it tries to grab at John's face.

"Be at ease, I did not free you only to kill you now. I'll put you down in a moment, but you must relax." John waits a moment, then lowers the man to his feet, but the man falls to the ground, holding his neck.

Wide-eyed, the man says, "What the hell are you?"

"Annoyed and disappointed. Mainly with myself. My friend is recently dead, and eaten. I am in a dark mood."

The man stands, and he stands many hands above John, and is broad of shoulder, well-muscled, with pale skin, dark hair, a handsome face, and a soul far darker than the other living prisoners. John dislikes when men stand higher than he does, it makes him feel inadequate, as he is used to standing higher than all, and did for all his life, with few exceptions here and there over the years.

Still rubbing his neck, the man says, "Me too. I lost my... everything. Everything. I'm gonna kill those sisters. Or die trying. I got nothing to lose now. Either help me or get outta my way."

"You cannot kill the dead, friend. All three witches are dead by my hand, though they greatly outmatched me in power. Their downfall due only to their desire to capture me instead of to kill me."

The large man shrugs, "If that's the truth, you did way better than me, kid. I couldn't do nothing to them. By the time I realized I even needed to fight, the fight was over. I didn't even consider them a threat at all. Girls like that just ain't never a threat, you know? Young, hot ones. Not until now, I guess. I wasn't trying to get laid or nothing since...well, I just wasn't. I just didn't consider them a threat."

John looks at the man, noticing a great sadness and despair in him, even more than John's own, and feels a camaraderie with him. "These are dark times, friend. All we can do is fight, and make our enemies pay a steep price for taking those we love from us, and when our time is finally spent, die a glorious death in battle worthy of song."

The man gives John a strange look, and after a moment says, "Uh...yeah. I never got your name. I'm Chief...no. Ethan. Just Ethan, now." He extends his hand for shaking, and John is glad to perform the familiar custom, and takes the man's hand in his own.

"John. A pleasure."

"How old are you, John? And how'd you get so fast and strong? Is it from cultivating? What...tier? Level? Whatever it's called, are you? Is it like video games? Where young kids can steamroll adults? We did some meditation on the flight up here, but it was so, so slow."

"I'm level two."

"Goddamn, so you already opened all your cores. Energy centers. Whatever they're called. And did the rank up thing once too. Jesus, I gotta get going on that, especially if I can get that strong and fast."

"You should, I'm currently trying to complete a ritual to get my first Perk now."

"Damn, kid, you're really taking to this stuff, huh? I don't want to keep bothering you, but that...whatever the sisters had us seeing, that was awful. Awful. You mind if I ask a few questions while I try to get my head on right?"

John believes he understands what the man is saying, and replies, "Certainly."

Ethan nods towards the corpse of the giant slug, "Is that really one of the sisters?"

"Two actually, joined together. The witches did mention they look like that normally, but they worshiped...I forget the name, but that is a statue of her head. She is of the race...I forget that too. Not demons or dark ones. The other ones."

"G'athu? They don't look like slugs. I saw pictures of them in a briefing. They're all over Cali. They got tentacle faces."

"Yes. Not the witches, the one they worshiped. That statue head is one. A g'athu. The witches were some sort of slug, and said they excrete waste through their pores, and wouldn't mind if my fox defecated on their floor. She is dead now. My friend, the fox."

There is a long pause, and they both stand in silence for a time before Ethan says, "You're pretty weird. You mind if I ask you something? And I don't care either way. None of my business if you are, and more power to you for living your best life and all that. But are you gay?"

This question gives John pause, and seems a strange question to ask. "Not particularly at this moment. Somewhat, I guess, since I made good my escape, and killed my enemies, and proved Sublime Sunshine wrong, but that's where it ends. I am greatly saddened as I lost my dear friend, and I drank of some very nasty crud recently, and still feel ill, and I'm disappointed at my recent behavior. A lapse in my ability to control my strong emotions. I behaved as a beast does, and feel greatly ashamed for it."

"You messing with me?"

"What?"

"You talking all fancy and gay to mess with me?"

"I...don't understand how someone can talk gay. How is it possible? One can say things that makes others feel gay, or have some gaiety in their voice, but talk gay? Your question makes no sense at all, so you'll have to clarify what you mean by this. Please, if you wouldn't mind."

"You keep doing it. You just did it. Like this is 'Downton Abbey' and your wife opens the boudoir and sees dainty balls thwacking off your chin, and you don't even get fazed she saw, and just say, 'Oh dear! Please do close the door, milady. We'll catch a chill. Gobble, gobble, gobble.' I don't know, maybe you're just some type of royalty or something, they all talk pretty gay. I just can't tell if you're messing with me is all. If you are gay, don't worry about it. I don't care. No one does really."

Thoroughly confused now, John struggles to find a reply. "I...what?"

"Ah, just forget about it. Forget I said anything. You said two of the sisters joined. What'd you mean by that?"

"It has something to do with the lady they worship. They could all join together somehow, and increase their tier. I killed one before. Before they captured me. Two could still join. And that creature was two of them. I have a question myself. What does gay mean, in its modern usage?"

"What? Gay? It means...you know, queer."

The large man holds his arm out, and the hand dangles down from his wrist. John still doesn't understand, but he is now on the path to finally learning the modern usage of both gay and queer, two words completely unrelated in his mind, with two drastically different meanings.

"That doesn't explain anything. Gay and queer mean the same thing now?"

"Yeah. Jesus, how do you not know this? Gay and queer means you like guys. A guy attracted to other guys. You know, homosexuals."

It clicks in John's head, and he finally understands. "Oh, I get it now. I've known many such men. My old master often enjoyed laying with men, though I never saw the appeal. Once, I was greatly attracted to women, but the last was my Lilitu. None have stirred my loins since, and that fire has long smoldered and gone out of me. What does mistress mean now? One woman became offended by the honorific, but not others."

"It means a sidepiece for rich men." The large man must notice the confused look on John's face, as he continues with the explanation, "A...girl you keep on the side. Not your wife or girlfriend. Someone you're cheating on them with. Just a girl rich people cheat with. I think brothel owners are called mistresses too. No, madams. They're called madams."

"Oh. What title of respect do you give women then?"

"Uh...you mean like ma'am? Yeah, ma'am works. Or miss if they're young, I guess. Missus if they're married. That what you mean?"

"I believe so. Munashi called my friend Miss Amber, so I guess I knew that honorific already."

A short silence stretches between the men before Ethan says, "You talk as if you've been alive for a real long time. You don't know things everyone does, and you're...were you, like, a vampire or something? Trapped in a coffin until the apocalypse set you free or something?"

John is taken aback with surprise, "What a fantastic guess! Though I wasn't trapped in a coffin. I was more trapped in my own confusion. Before all these changes to the world, my mind was ailed greatly, and I remember little for a long time. But all these changes also healed my mind, and I am whole again. All I have of recent memories are a few of my friend Thomas, though he is dead. He was a fine friend, and I loved him much. How did you know I was a vampire?"

The man shifts uncomfortably, eying his firearm in the corner, a good distance from him, "I didn't. I didn't know. Just a guess from what you said. And how you...are. And those could be little fangs. You gonna try to suck my blood?"

"We don't really drink blood. The trick is taking in as little of it as possible as you remove the essence of life that resides in all living creatures. Besides the race they call dark ones, some of them don't have any. And Mistress Pixie. But I'm not in the habit of saving people just to kill them. And I've always tried to kill only those deserving, or warriors longing for battle. And, anyways, I am overfull on vital essence, as I defeated that large slug by draining it. You need not worry."

"Oh, good. So, are you so fast and strong from cultivating or from being a vampire?"

"Both, actually. My goal is to become much stronger through this cultivating, and any other way I can. I want to defend our world from all those invading her, and I need to be much stronger. I am up to the task."

"You could make me a vampire if you need help. I'm a SEAL. We're the best warriors in the world now. Best of the best."

John thinks this is a strange title for a knight, if knight Ethan is, "I'm sorry, friend. It doesn't work that way. Only those whose soul is red can accept the power. If I performed the ritual with you, you would become a mindless beast, attacking all those still living."

"Damn. Too bad. I kinda know what you mean about having your mind healed. I was…pretty bad…before all this. My mind. Just out of it. That…what the sisters had me see over and over, and being freed, and now talking to you, kinda knowing the world is a lot weirder than I thought. It's strange but it kinda gives me hope, you know? I was certain my family was dead, but there's no proof. Not until I see it with my own eyes. And what if it was a power plant? I don't think one of those exploding is like a nuke. And I think the power plant for New York City is a little south of Long Island, way on the other side of Manhattan and Jersey, called Three Mile Island. That's pretty far from where they are. So, they could be alive. I'm not giving up. I'm gonna go find them."

"I'm glad for you. Or my condolences. I'm uncertain which applies. Meditation helps clear the mind. You should try."

"Yeah, I really gotta do that more. First, I need to find my phone and see if I can get in contact with my wife. And get some news. Find my rifle and gear too."

"Good. If you find a slightly curved sword, it's mine. As well as a bundle of spears, a rucksack with a short sword in it and many crystals, and there should be four yellow crystals from a Bronze that are mine too, by right of victory. Also, please don't eat the fox on the table, she was my friend. And there is a woman and a young man at the table still. A noble, and she had no husband with her, but he is a man of great means and wealth. Why are there so many nobles now, with all these large estates, such as this one? Did they greatly increase the ranks of bannerettes and the nobili?"

"Uh, I'm not sure. This isn't an estate though. Just a house. A normal house, for regular people. It isn't even that nice. Kinda old and shitty and falling apart. The only thing good about it is that generator over there."

"You must jest, right? Surely this fine manor belongs to at least a rich merchant."

"No, definitely not rich. Just normal, maybe kind of poor since this is way out in the sticks. All the rich people probably live in or around Toronto and Montreal and Vancouver. Quebec City, that's the closest one to us. I think Edmonton is big. I don't know a lot about Canada. Oh, Ottawa. I'm not sure that's a city or the name of a state, or province, or whatever they have here. They're all weird up here. Their judges still wear wigs, I think."

John finds it hard to believe this beautiful estate belongs to anyone close to being poor, as it is a far cry from the hovels and shacks peasants usually live in, but he doesn't push the issue further. "Well, I need to finish my ritual. May I ask you to please try and stop any prisoners that awaken from interfering with the ritual? And from eating my friend?"

"Uh, yeah, sure. No problem. I never really thanked you for freeing me. Thanks, man."

# CHAPTER 29
## A GOOD DAY

John enjoyed his talk with Ethan, and is also grateful to finally have some outstanding questions answered, but is glad to finally stop talking and being social. He is still miserable due to the death of Amber.

John meditates for the few additional moments required to convert the rest of his magical energy into magical essence, which further fills his dantian too, and helps center John, and clears his mind of all that weighs on it.

John imbues the circle with magical essence as Pixie instructed, and then enters it, and calls on Pixie for assistance. John hopes Ethan stays upstairs awhile, and does not witness his ritual, as he feels silly as he performs it. It requires some sort of strange dance to move energy in certain ways, and calling on spirits using a language he doesn't know, but understands, and he has a hard time enunciating the words Pixie instructs him to repeat.

Much to John's surprise, even though Pixie told him what would happen, once he finishes repeating the words, many ghosts approach his location, and he recognizes some of them. There are many humans, a few more than the seven he killed during his escape, and two large and long slug-like creatures.

Pixie has John address the larger slug spirit, which is two spirits twisted together. If the spirit responds somehow, he doesn't notice. Pixie feeds him his own reply, "Then come in and be welcome," in the strange tongue he understands, though it is not of this Earth, John is certain, and not translated either. He just knows the tongue somehow, like how he understands the writing his NCS shows in his eyes.

The merged slug-spirits enter the circle and immediately start shaking and having a conniption, becoming enraged. It tries to escape, but is prevented from leaving the circle, and bangs against an invisible wall. The spirit then stretches out, and becomes airier, and is suddenly sucked into John's chest, along with the glowing heart and eyeball in the circle's center. John stands in amazement as the whole ritual circle rises, and folds into his chest as well.

All goes dark for a moment, and John blinks. As his eyes open the world looks very different. He can still see the spirits nearby, and he notices they all lose interest and start shambling away. The world looks much muted to John. Drab. Darker. Less vibrant, even in this dark cellar. He looks at those men and women still living, and their souls are much less bright, but still clearly visible. He brings up the flashing notification.

**You gained a new Perk! Congratulations! Perk 'Orb of the Crimson Palace' (C-rated) is now active. Enjoy!**

John feels something in his chest, and a new eye opens for him. He finds it very disorienting, and it causes him to be off balance, and dizzy. Even worse, he can't shut it off, or close the eye, and must see from it. For all his long life he has only had two eyes, and no others, and is very used to having sight from only those two, and seeing a specific way. He only lost an eye, or both, very seldom, and the eye would grow back quickly, and he'd soon be whole again.

Having a whole new perspective to see from is not something John is prepared for, or can easily adapt to. He may look young, but he has been alive nearly three ages, and is very set in his ways, and very used to seeing only one way.

John struggles to handle the new perspective for a long while. Some of the other ex-prisoners start to wake. Thankfully, Ethan stops him from being interrupted as he struggles with his new [Perk].

John finds he can move the eye that now resides in his chest. It can move around and point in any direction, and he can bring it out of his chest in front of him, or behind him. He can even move it a little above his head, but not really below him, though he can make it go as low as his pelvis. The eye seems to want to rest in his chest, about where his heart is, and naturally drifts back to that spot when not being directly controlled.

John is not comfortable having this strange new perspective, but he must bear it, so does. He realizes he has been rude enough for long enough, and should introduce himself to the peasants he freed.

Ethan, rifle now slung over his shoulder, gathers the other eleven ex-prisoners, plus the noblewoman and her son, in the cellar. Fifteen total, including John. Both men and women, from young to elderly.

"Hello. A pleasure. My name is John. I freed you. I'm done with hiding and keeping secrets, so I must admit I killed these dead prisoners while making my escape. I did not do it on purpose, and did not even know I did it until after I managed to free myself. I am very sorry if any were relatives or acquaintances of yours. I am willing to negotiate a blood-price for this foul deed, but let me state once more, I did not do this on purpose, and I apologize again. My deepest condolences.

"Also, if you haven't yet heard, I am a vampire and very strong. Do not worry, I will not harm you. Unless you do something to warrant such a response from me, such as taking what is mine, and everything in this estate is mine, besides what you brought yourself, and the food and amenities, which I will share of freely. Or eating my fox friend upstairs after you were informed not to. Or..."

At this John is interrupted by Ethan, "There's a fox outside running around like a lunatic. It tried to run in when I checked the porch. Big sucker too."

John turns into a blur as he rushes up the stairs, and through the estate, nearly tripping a few times, as he is still disoriented from his new sight. He hears Ethan shout, "Stop! It's daylight outside!" John doesn't stop, but curses the runes surrounding the house that prevent him from hearing what is outside. He barely slows to open the front door, almost crashing through it.

Outside, John spots the fox, confirms it is Amber, and runs to her as a great joy fills his heart, and a stress and a wariness and a burden he carried dissolves from him. Amber rushes to John too, but stops short, avoiding his touch, and doesn't let him pet or scratch her. She does make excited duck-pig noises, and seems very happy to see John though, so he takes no offense.

"Amber! I thought I lost you too. The witches, they told me a fox they roasted and laid out to feast upon was you. I am so glad you live. I've lost too many, and I owe you a great debt I wish to pay back. I hope to travel with you for a long while, even if you stay as a fox. I don't know why you'd want to be a fox instead of a woman, but I will not complain. The bear would be a much better choice over the fox, and a great help in combat. Whatever form you choose to take, I am just happy to be with you, and that you live."

The fox hops around, excited, and things get awkward after a time, with John just standing there, speech finished, unable to pet or scratch the vixen. "Come inside and eat. There are many people inside. Fourteen. Sixteen with us two. Also, the largest noblewoman I've laid eyes on. Her size is great, and her father and husband might love her too much. There is a happy medium between you and her. Well, you in your woman form. All skin and bones. You should eat more, and you seem to do so in your fox form, even if you have a strange appetite."

The powerful sun beats down on the back of John's bare neck, and he feels the bumps of calcification start to form. Only then does he notice how high the sun is, and how bright the day should be, and how even looking directly at it doesn't hurt his eyes, or require him to squint, and how different his vision is now in full daylight. It's hard for him to articulate, even in his own thoughts, what precisely is so different, beyond things now being dull and drab, as that isn't exactly correct. How he sees things is now very different, and defies explanation.

Back in the house, most sup together, and some take drink and feast, in celebration of their release, and the death of their captors. John is gladdened when he is told none of the peasants he killed are close relatives or friends of any that live, and another weight is lifted from his shoulders.

John finds his swords, spears, hatchet, rucksack, and all his possessions besides the four yellow crystals the first sister he killed must have dropped. Some other items are found believed to be related to cultivation, such as ritual disks, and some chalks and ingredients all worth great value, and John takes these and puts them all in his rucksack. No trinkets or jewelry or magicked weapons are found, much to John's disappointment. The Sublime did confirm that John's bracers are indeed enchanted, and powerfully so, but their specific function will require John to at least clear his meridians to work, and possibly ascend even more tiers above Copper to have enough magical essence to power them.

The slug apparition of the first witch he killed resides in the kitchen, near the dining table, and John enjoys being able to see a dead enemy, and gloat over them, though the spirit is not aware of John's gloats. John is filled with much gaiety. Amber lives, and he is saved from hearing the usual whines and negotiating blood-price for the people he murdered. He decides to be a generous host and doles out a few clear crystals to all. Most that are not drinking and feasting join him in meditation.

John sends enough magical essence to his middle dantian to fill it, and converts it to shen, and then sends half the shen to his upper dantian, and converts it to the substance called empty. He then meditates enough to nearly fill his lower dantian, and sends what he can to fill his middle dantian, and converts it all to shen. That isn't exactly how he was instructed to do it by Sublime Sunshine, but he thinks it's close enough. *I'm glad his name is easy to remember, at least,* John thinks.

Over time, both the shen and the extra energy and essence his [Orb of the Crimson Palace] collect will slowly heal his soul, and his [Runes] [Stat] will increase, or so he was told.

None of the peasants, nor the noblewoman and her son, leave the house to go their own way. The house has a generator illuminating every room brightly at night with artificial light, which John finds impressive, but he prefers the beauty of rushlights, torches, and fire.

As all start to take their rest, John stays up, having volunteered for the first guard watch, and talks with Ethan, and finds out many interesting things, though lacks the basic modern knowledge needed to understand the implications fully.

Ethan's phone is able to connect to the internet, as it uses Department of Defense satellites, but the rest of the peasants have no internet service on their phones now, in this remote area. Ethan also wrote to his wife through his phone, and has received no reply yet.

Ethan is worried, though not despaired, as his family may also just lack the internet access necessary to receive the message, and reply to it. Or, their phones could be out of batteries, and have no electricity where they are. There could be many reasons they are alive, but unable to respond.

Ethan plans on leaving the next morning, and driving to a small airfield east of them, on the other side of the lake. He will fly to his family, and save them. If they are all dead, Ethan will return to John, and they will fight this invasion of Earth together, until victory or glorious death in battle, the end all men should be so lucky to have.

The city closest to their location, called Quebec City, has recently fallen to the demon horde, and the portal that seems to somehow follow the horde was spotted moving west, and the horde is assumed to be headed in the direction of another city called Montreal. But the horde was moving northwesterly, instead of southwesterly, the direction Montreal lay, and it is assumed they do so to move around the army opposing them.

Ethan recounts the great battle he had with the horde, and how the horde was able to stop, or redirect, great missiles from massive cannons, called artillery, fired from very far away. Smaller cannons, called mortars, fired from a closer distance, were more effective. Great innovations, like ghostly planes of death, which Ethan calls specters, were able to get close to the giant demon leading the horde, and bring it low.

Ethan also confirms firearm bullets to the head is the best way to kill demons, as they can still fight even after receiving grave injuries to other parts of the body.

The country Ethan comes from has many great machines of war, and ways of causing massive destruction and death, but all this counted for little in destroying the portal. Something large and deadly came through when the portal was pressed, and wreaked havoc on the battlefield. Ethan barely escaped.

John is shown a full map of the world on the phone, and is amazed. It looks so little to him, laid out as it is. He remembers hearing something about a new world, and new continents found, but not much about it, as his mind was all but gone at the time.

John says, "I will head to this city, Montreal, and fight this demon horde. But not tomorrow morning. Tomorrow, while still in safety, I will have Pixie test me, so my [Stats] are truly reflected by these numbers. I will rest well tonight, and after the test I will make my way south in all haste, forsaking rest."

Ethan nods his head. "You wanna hook up with the Canadian military. They could use you. Looks like the US mostly pulled out. A lotta cities are falling in my own country. I seen these demons in action – they're no joke. The big demons, they plow through everything like nothing. You shoulda seen the stuff the Rangers were throwing at the demon leader, really laying the hate on nice and thick, and it just shrugged it all off. Same with its underlings, the ones almost its size."

Relieved of their duty as guards, both take their rest. John sleeps soundly, and for much longer than usual, though he has little need for such long rests. Pixie wakes him before dawn and a notification shows in his eyes.

**John, I must leave as my Eternal contact summoned me. Regarding you I suppose. It is bad timing but I must obey the summons. The actions list I had you scribe has been transferred to your NCS as promised. I am not sure if you wrote down the information**

accurately as it cannot be translated. I am pleased you survived though how you survived was bad form. You must control your emotions and not let your emotions control you. Per our spoken agreement upon your death your body will be teleported to me if I am within this universe, or my return to it. If I can resuscitate you I will. If you are too dead or your body and important organs too damaged I will not be able to. Try to die in a simple manner that does little damage to your body. Also, you are going to die on this day. A Gold and five or so Silvers will reach where you stay by noon at the latest. You will die. There is no avoiding it. Running will only delay the inevitable. See you soon. – Your friend and informal mentor, Sunshine.

# CHAPTER 30
## NO FACE GIVEN

*With regards to the Way of Death, if you are prepared to die at any time, you will be able to meet your release from life with equanimity. As calamities are usually not as bad as anticipated beforehand, it is foolhardy to feel anxiety about tribulations not yet endured. Yamamoto Tsunetomo, Hagakure*

John checks on Amber, seeing her doing well, curled up at the feet of a young woman sleeping on a couch. He then wakes Ethan to relay the message he received about the high-tiered demons coming to this location, and the Magnus wanting to see him dead.

Ethan finds information on his phone stating the demon horde is being tracked heading towards Montreal, but making slow progress, and a different report stating the portal was recently spotted about midway between Quebec City and Saint-Félicien.

The two men hastily cobble together a plan, then wake all the peasants. Two groups are formed – people heading west and north, and people heading east with Ethan, all in two large vehicles capable of holding many people within. Arms are distributed, though there aren't many on hand, a few axes and hatchets, a type of billhook called a machete, some large knives, and Ethan gifts his handgun to the group going west and north. John is staying to face the demons, keeping all his own arms, such as his small hatchet and short sword.

Ethan will take Amber with him in his vehicle, and let her loose in the forest near the airfield he is traveling to, so she will live, and not share John's fate.

John assumes there would be some token resistance to him staying behind, as doing so surely means his death. He at least expected some

240

formal recognition of his bravery for facing such doughty and fell foes alone, but receives none, and is disappointed.

While discussing how much time there is left before all must depart, John becomes greatly annoyed. He is very familiar with artificial means of timekeeping, having seen sundials in both Suma and Kayhamut. The later region taking it further, splitting the day into ten parts, dusk and dawn getting four additional parts. But the sun decided. The sun always decides time. The Greeks used a water clock, but that was good for specific measurement and the dark of night. Greeks knew only the sun could tell time, as did the Persians and Romans.

According to Ethan, time, in this modern age, is not decided by the sun, and noon is not when the sun is at its highest point in the sky, and is instead determined by numbers on a phone. He believes Sublime Sunshine, being a learned man, and intelligent, meant noon in the correct way, when the sun reaches its peak. Ethan claims noon is when the numbers say 12:00, and the sun will peak around 11:29 on this day, or so says his phone. Either way the message can be interpreted, the people must rush to be away, as the phone says the time is past 8:00.

John also dislikes that seasons are no longer tracked by solstice and equinox, but fixed dates of a calendar. Ethan tells him, "Today's November twentieth. Earlier this month noon was an hour later, but we turn the time back an hour in fall, and forward in the spring. We also go off the calendar for seasons, so fall starts September first all the time, not the equinox, I think in late September, and winter is always December first, not the solstice. When's that? Christmas or around Christmas, right? Or is it New Year? No. Wait, is it? Is the solstice around January first? I don't remember."

While everyone readies, John reviews the list Sunshine recently returned to him by way of the NCS. His first task to get [Orb of the Crimson Palace] now completed, he removes it from the list. He also removes the number of days in a year, as he learned this from Ethan too, though he thinks it is useless information to know, and knowing it will never help him in any conceivable way.

The list contains all the items he is to complete, such as [Perks], NCS [Upgrades], the body formation he should get, topics to discuss with Pixie, skills to merge, etcetera, and even includes some information to pass on to the scholars of Earth, such as how Planck time can be adjusted to fit universal standard, the pros and cons of attaining or avoiding Tech 2, and much more.

John, not being a strong reader in any language, struggles to understand some of what he wrote, but manages, and notices some items he can do now, while Ethan, the peasants, and the noblewoman prepare to depart by gathering food, drink, fuel, and searching other homes for additional weapons or useful gear.

John enters his Mind's Eye, and after greeting Mistress Pixie, asks her a question to confirm what Sublime Sunshine told him. "Is it true all magical energy costs I incur, including the cost for breaking my Archetype agreement – and my apologies, again, for doing that – as well as the cost of functions, are all reduced by nearly half due to my earned Achievements?"

"They sure are, bucko. Forty-seven-point-three percent, to be exact. Good job accumulating so many achievements at your tier! It shows you're worth investing in. We're real proud of you! Way to climb that ladder!" Pixie then points her thumb up and winks at John.

"Thank you, Mistress. Or do you prefer a different title? Mistress is offensive to you?"

"Oh, no. We don't care. Just plain ol' Pixie's fine too. Up to you, partner."

John decides he'll stick with mistress, as the familiar makes him more comfortable, and then navigates to the [NCS, Upgrades, and Pricing] tab. His current magical energy passive cost is listed as six percent, but that should only really be around three percent, and doesn't include the twenty percent for breaking the [Archetype] agreement. Sublime Sunshine told him about his discount for [Achievements] is absolutely ridiculous, and he should take advantage of it since his meditation technique so quickly fills his dantian, especially considering the low [Capacity] of his dantian at his current rank and tier.

John selects the five upgrades the Sublime instructed him to, thinking the description given for each leaves much to be desired. Before being allowed to confirm his choices, Pixie tells him he shouldn't select any [Upgrades] now, as it will slow his advancement too much at his tier. John then realizes what Sunshine told him is true, and Pixie just says certain things at certain prompts, without regard to other knowledge he knows she has.

This disheartens John. Pixie knows how fast his dantian fills. She knows he cannot rank up again for many days without hurting his foundation. He is, and always will be, grateful to her, but sometimes her lack of thinking bothers him. He then lets go of some of the anger he holds towards Sublime Sunshine, as Sunshine was angry at John for similar reasons.

John overrides Pixie and hits 'accept.'

**[Nano Assistance]**, 4% **passive, slightly improve power and rune manifestation activation speed.**

**[Emergency Heal]**, 1% **passive, no more than 25% of current total magical energy or magical essence in lower dantian on qualifying injury.**

**[Theta Waves]**, 5% **passive, passive healing to body and spirit, removes some impurities over time.**

**[Heal Delta A]**, 4% **passive, increase tickrate of [Theta Waves].**

**[Heal Delta B]**, 4% **passive, increase amount healed each tick of [Theta Waves].**

This raises John's magical energy cost from six to twenty-four, but the real cost after the discount is around twelve. Adding the twenty percent, and reducing that by half to ten percent, for breaking his [Archetype], raises this to around twenty-two. Sublime Sunshine said it would actually be a little over twenty-three percent, but not to worry since this is still less than the twenty-six percent John thought his cost was before understanding his mighty [Achievements] discount.

Next, John tries to select the third rune to complete his manifestation grouping, hoping to turn [Magical Essence Dart] into [Magical Essence Bolt], as his [Orb of the Crimson Palace] [Perk] passively heals his soul, and he completely filled his middle dantian and converted it all to shen, which also heals his soul. He is unable to select the third rune, much to his disappointment. He also wonders why Pixie has not granted him a new increase in his constant breathing technique, as he has been doing a decent job remembering to do it.

Before leaving his Mind's Eye, John looks at his summary.

| | |
|---|---|
| **Tech Level** | 1 |
| **Age** | 5,600 **to** 6,200 **USACS years** |
| **Race** | **Terran-F** |
| **Tree First** | |
| **Tier** | 1 **(Mortal) (Wood)** |
| **Level** | 2 **(Mid-Low)** |
| **Archetype** | **NA** |
| **Active Title** | **Blessed by Magnus Gar'tar** |
| **Aspects** | **NA** |
| **Affinities** | **NA** |
| **NCU Energy Cost** | 24%(-47.3%) |

| **STATS** | |
|---|---|
| **Strength** | 23.94 |
| **Swiftness** | 23.64 |
| **Conditioning** | 24.69 |
| **Min. Power** | 16.50 |
| **Capacity** | 10.20 |

| Runes | 3.17 |
| --- | --- |
| **Physical Fortification** | 10.20 |
| **Elemental Fortification** | 10.20 |
| **Mental Fortification** | 10.20 |

**Highest Skills**

| [Undirected Basic Meditation] | 96.4 |
| --- | --- |
| [Mixed Style Swords] | 93.6 |
| [Mixed Stealth] | 88.7 |
| [Mixed Survival] | 87.6 |

| Synergy Skills | Ready |
| --- | --- |
| Class | NA |
| Perks | Orb of the Crimson Palace |
| Manifestations | Magical Essence Dart |
| Last Achievement | Climber 3 - D |
| Highest Achievement | Skilled, Legendary - SSR |

**Next required advancement event: Clear meridians after level 5**

*Not enough. Not nearly enough,* John thinks. He wishes he had time to rank up again, as he'd do so despite it being bad for his foundation, since he faces a Gold soon, and many Silvers.

John then ponders more about how different the modern world is. John is certain the reason the demons are coming north is to find him. He could have decided to flee instead of facing them, and his decision to stay and fight proves how tall he is, and this should be recognized by other men of honor, and praised. Yet no one mentioned anything. No one gave John face. *It's as if in these modern times they hold life cheaply, and of no consequence for one to sacrifice themselves,* John thinks, and it disheartens him. *Or is there some other reason for this I just can't figure?*

Sublime Sunshine explained to John why the highest tier of the Mortal Tree is called Empty or Salt, and the history behind the title Salt he found very interesting. In that tier, a condensed and refined soul is expanded up through all tiers again. Back in ancient times, someone on a martial path would go through this tier as a humble farmer or the like, as farmers are considered the salt of the earth, valued for their simplicity, integrity, honesty, and diligent work as a cultivator of life, producing sustenance to support others. This was done as a way to make amends for all the blood spilled on the way to that tier, to purify and humble the cultivator before ascending to the heavens.

It has long been known this is unnecessary to do, as the ascender does not go to 'the heavens,' but to something called space, and has many tiers and Trees to ascend through until Heaven, and no great need to make amends for foul deeds and spilled blood until the last Tree, Eternal.

John decides if he makes it so high, he will keep to the old ways, and become peaceful, and a humble farmer. But making it so far is not in his stars, and he knows he will die this day, but Sublime Sunshine may be able to resuscitate him, and his journey could continue.

If this is to be his last day or not, he should live it as he does any other, so John decides to continue the plan he was prescribed, even if it won't help in his upcoming fight.

The next item Sunshine told John to complete is to gain more harmony, and get certain general [Perks] increasing the soft cap on his [Stats], so it no longer hampers his rank ups, causing him to lose out on so much. There are many he is supposed to get.

The [Perks] [Strong], [Fast], [Healthy], [Powerful], [Expansive], [Soulful], [Harden], [Resistant], and [Resilient] each increase the soft cap on one [Stat] by the most, and cost the least harmony individually, but the greatest amount when all are totaled together.

[Physical], [Potent], and [Protected] raise the soft cap on three [Stats] each by less, cost more harmony each individually, but less totaled together.

Lastly, the [Perk] [Dynamic] raises all soft caps of all [Stats], but by a smaller amount each, and costs the most harmony on its own, but the least in total.

John, having already used most of his available harmony on his [Orb of the Crimson Palace] vision [Perk], is now able to fully access his [Skills] tab, and further merge [Skills], and even select [Skills] for [Synergies]. Sublime Sunshine told John not to select any [Synergies] yet, and all he knows is [Synergies] has something to do with [Class]. At first John was happy to hear there was a class system and not a caste system, as he despises the rigidity of the latter, but was informed it means something completely different in this context he doesn't quite understand.

When the NCS and Pixie first entered John's mind, and they had to decide how to handle his many, many [Skills] in the best possible way to reduce harmony being wasted, with a goal of not hampering John's advancement, it combined only his highest and most useful [Skills] most likely to be selected as [Synergies] into mixed [Skills]. John currently has many [Skills] able to be combined, and many of them, according to Sublime Sunshine, are outdated and unneeded, as new techniques and tools came about making the use of such knowledge unnecessary, and employment of such [Skills] pointless, and it is unlikely for a society this advanced to ever revert to such ancient and archaic ways.

The learning and merging of such [Skills] still generates the same amount of harmony as more modern [Skills], and the merging of them doesn't result in any lost knowledge, but can and will hamper gaining new knowledge, and the speed new knowledge is attained. John has many, many [Skills] rated very highly regarding combat, and these [Skills] were already mixed and merged. This hurts him as he has little experience in combat with magical essence and manifestations, which is much more useful knowledge to have now, and gaining related [Skills] will be much slower.

The NCS really helped quantify and advance knowledge in some ways far more than others, such as [Skills], harmony, aspects, and how concepts integrate with aspects. According to the Sublime, John is in a unique position of being able to combine [Skills] and generate much harmony quickly, and he would be a fool not to take advantage of this.

John has much knowledge on agriculture and plant cultivation the NCS considers outdated. Merging these [Skills] will make it harder for John to learn modern farming when he reaches the Salt tier and lives as a peaceful and humble farmer, but he'll never reach that tier if he is dead.

John double-checks with Pixie, and she assures him no current knowledge will be lost, as the NCS only tracks what he actually knows, and can't add or remove any knowledge. The [Skills] will just be merged into a mixed [Skill], such as his sword and navigation [Skills], and the only negative to doing this is a hampering and slowing to his ability to increase new [Skills] in the same general category, and all new knowledge will advance the new mixed [Skill].

John needs to combine certain [Skills] in a specific order, maximizing harmony gain. He selects [Ancient Agricultural Techniques 2], 34.4, and then 'combine,' and [Outdated Agricultural Knowledge 1 -Ancient], 25.9. A new [Skill] is formed, called [Merged Agriculture], 30.2.

John was told he'll be able to feel how much harmony he has, not accurately, but generally, now that he knows what harmony feels like when full, as well as near empty, and he now knows what acquiring more feels like. He feels near his Mind's Eye, where his upper dantian is, something called a pineal gland, where his harmony gathers, and believes he is under half full, but far more than a quarter full. He next selects [Outdated Agricultural Knowledge 2 - Early], 52.4, and combines it with [Merged Agriculture], 30.2, making the new [Combined Agriculture], 41.3, an expert [Mastery] level [Skill].

John feels his harmony is now nearly full, and checks the [Perks] available, and sees [Dynamic] is no longer greyed out. He is not surprised, as the [Perk] is supposed to cost a good amount less than his vision [Perk], after all. He then reviews the ritual to acquire [Dynamic] with Pixie, and John becomes dismayed, as the ritual requires him to behave as a fool again, and dance and undulate about as a woman does to seduce a man. *What fool came up with such a ritual? At least it doesn't need any hearts and eyeballs or anything else.*

John leaves his Mind's Eye and goes to the cellar. He has Pixie highlight the ground near the dead slug, so he can trace the circle and runes with its higher-tiered blood. Looking around he notices all the ghosts of the dead prisoners are now gone, the spirits already having dissipated.

John splits the corpse open with his sword, and in the corpse he finds plenty of the thick and foul blood that made him ill the day before, and draws the ritual circle and runes, then prepares himself to dance so foolishly.

# CHAPTER 31
# CHANGE OF PLANS

The ritual goes smoothly, with John glad no one sees him act the fool performing the required seductive dancing. He is surprised how little magical essence the ritual circle needed to be infused with, and how the dancing was able to manipulate the essence within himself and that of the circle, covering most parts of his body, both within and without. He wonders if this will increase his [Skill] with [Magical Essence Manipulation], but he is not surprised to find out it didn't.

> **You gained a new Perk! Congratulations! Perk 'Dynamic' (General, Unrated) is now active. Enjoy!**
>
> **WARNING! There is a high probability some (1-1/999) or all (1-1/95) of your Stats are no longer accurately reflected by your NCS as shown in your Stats tab or summary sheet. Please see Pixie for testing.**

*One down, at least one to go. That went much faster than I thought it would, so we'll see.* John needs to merge a [Skill] before performing the next ritual. Still keeping to the same order as dictated by the Sublime, John selects his lowest farming [Skill], as the math is somehow different when a [Skill] has 'combined' in the title of it, and the next merger will create a mixed [Skill], and this will always increase the value, and never lower it, but also generates less harmony.

John feels for his harmony, estimating he has about a quarter to capacity now. He then selects [Ancient Agricultural Techniques 1], 17.4, and merges it with [Combined Agriculture], 41.3, resulting in [Mixed Agriculture], 45.6.

John's harmony now feels to be slightly under half, and he has two more agriculture skills he can combine into his mixed [Skill], but adding either would put him over his harmony cap, even if his harmony were completely emptied, so he will hold off on doing so. He was also told his highest rated [Skill] in this general category was already combined into his [Mixed Survival] [Skill], called [Herbology], and he wonders exactly what specific knowledge each of these [Skills] covers.

Next, John asks Mistress Pixie to go over the ritual for attaining the [Perk] called [Physical], and she is happy to oblige. A short time later, after performing the ritual, John receives the following notifications.

**You gained a new Perk‖ Congratulations‖ Perk 'Physical' (General, Unrated) is now active. Enjoy‖**

**WARNING‖ There is a high probability (1-1/999) some or all (1-1/95) of your Stats are no longer accurately reflected by your NCS as shown in your Stats tab, please see Pixie for testing.**

**You gained a new Achievement‖ Congratulations‖ Achievement 'Generally Perked' (F-rated, activate two General Perks before attaining Bronze tier and gaining a Body Formation or Refinement Perk, 0.10 magical energy discount NCS cost ((total discount now 47.4%)).**

Going to one of the small windows of the cellar, John sees noon is a long way off still, and hardly any time has passed. Entering his Mind's Eye, he checks the list and what [Skills] can safely be combined. The NCS considers many of his [Skills] outdated and obsolete, especially related to what it calls textiles, and John disagrees with the assessment. Being able to go from flax to shirt with a few tools he can make himself will always be a useful thing. He then wonders if other worlds are so much more advanced than his own, why all [Skills] aren't considered obsolete, since there are even newer and better ways to perform such tasks.

Getting five more [Perks] raising soft caps goes quickly. The soft cap for all John's physical [Stats] are now increased as much as possible, so his

[Strength], [Swiftness], and [Conditioning] should be far less hampered by diminishing returns during advancement. The only other [Stat] close to reaching the Wood soft cap for humans being [Min. Power], and that was increased twice with the [Potent] and [Dynamic] [Perks]. Sunshine doesn't believe he needs to increase it more with the [Powerful] [Perk] now, and he won't reach the soft cap even if his rank ups go better than expected.

John is disappointed he isn't able to test his [Stats] today, and have an accurate, or more accurate, numerical representation of them, but then remembers it matters little, as he will die soon.

Even with all the new [Perks] John doesn't feel more powerful. Having more time to kill he reviews his list, looking for something that will help him now, something he can feel. There's a [Perk] that has a low harmony requirement, a component requirement he can easily fulfill, and he has the harmony to get it now. It doesn't do much, but it does something, and all the other [Perks] he wants cost more harmony than he can currently hold at his rank and tier, making them impossible to get.

The name of the [Perk] is [Quick Thinking], the description given for it states, "Somewhat improves neurotransmission and synaptic plasticity dynamically in response to incoming information." John wishes the description wasn't gibberish, but thinking quicker would be a nice boon to have. [Quick Thinking] is a prerequisite for another [Perk] he wants badly, though it requires many other [Perks] that are all out of range for now, all part of a group of [Perks] realizing the potential of a species. Acquiring the final [Perk] in the chain, [Fully Realized], sometimes raises the rating of a race, but John mainly wants it because it will force his body to grow in height.

Since John's mind has healed, he has met nine grown men, and Munashi is the only one he stood much higher than, all eight of the others, including the two that shot at him while he traveled south, stood his height or higher, with Ethan towering over all others. Even one of the peasant women stands a little taller than he does, and he thinks it strange no one looks oddly at this giant woman. He does not like this, and greatly desires to once again tower over everyone, as he has for most of his life.

[Quick Thinking] requires a brain as a component. While reviewing the ritual, Pixie tells John just to draw the ritual circle around the corpse of the slug, as there are many things inside the corpse that only count as a whole brain together, and removing them all would be too difficult. The ritual takes longer than the others, but not much, and requires little dancing.

Done with [Perks] and rituals, John is surprised by how much magical essence he still has in his dantian, and how his thinking seems easier and clearer, and then checks the notifications.

**You gained a new Perk! Congratulations! Perk 'Potent' (General, Unrated) is now active. Enjoy!**

**You gained a new Perk! Congratulations! Perk 'Protected' (General, Unrated) is now active. Enjoy!**

**You gained a new Achievement! Congratulations! Achievement 'Generally Perked 2' (E-rated, activate four General Perks before attaining Bronze tier and gaining a Body Formation or Refinement Perk, 0.20 magical energy discount NCS cost ((total discount now 47.6%)).**

**You gained a new Perk! Congratulations! Perk 'Strong' (General, Unrated) is now active. Enjoy!**

**You gained a new Perk! Congratulations! Perk 'Fast' (General, Unrated) is now active. Enjoy!**

**You gained a new Achievement! Congratulations! Achievement 'Generally Perked 3' (D-rated, activate six General Perks before attaining Bronze tier and gaining a Body Formation or Refinement Perk, 0.30 magical energy discount NCS cost ((total discount now 47.9%)).**

**You gained a new Perk! Congratulations! Perk 'Healthy' (General, Unrated) is now active. Enjoy!**

**You gained a new Perk! Congratulations! Perk 'Quick Thinking' (General, Unrated) is now active. Enjoy!**

**WARNING! There is a high probability (1-1/999) some or all (1-1/95) of your Stats are no longer accurately reflected by your NCS as shown in your Stats tab, please see Pixie for testing.**

**You gained a new Achievement! Congratulations! Achievement 'Generally Perked 4' (C-rated, activate eight General Perks before attaining Bronze tier and gaining a Body Formation or Refinement Perk, 0.40 magical energy discount NCS cost ((total discount now 48.3%)).**

John goes up the stairs, finding none of the peasants are back from ransacking the nearby abandoned estates. Only Amber is within the house, meditating in the kitchen.

Having more time to kill, and no desire to assist the peasants in packing, not when none of them had the basic decency to praise his great sacrifice, John takes more of the Sublime's advice and starts doing physical exercise, a way to increase his strength that also falls under the umbrella of self-cultivation.

John lays on his belly and pushes his body off the ground with his arms until they are fully extended, an old exercise dating back to even his youth. He does this over and over and over, and much time goes by, and no pain or soreness enters his arms, nor any usual indicator of muscles well worked. He keeps pushing himself up, but starts to believe such exercise is no longer able to increase his great strength. *It really is easier to think now, like my mind has been cleared of cobwebs.*

John's thoughts are interrupted by feet quickly approaching, Ethan from the sound of it, and he stands to meet him.

"Plans changed. You gotta go. We all do. ASAP. I just got word from WARCOM. The portal's far enough north Montreal's safe from fallout. They're nuking as soon as it stops for at least a minute. Fifteen megatons, two staggered. Maybe three. Not taking risks. Seeing what it takes. No sense you staying and fighting now."

John is surprised by this news as noon is still far off. "Now? What time does your phone claim it is? And what is nuking?" John believes he heard the word, or a similar one, from the witches, but without learning the meaning of it.

"Uh, half past nine, but it doesn't matter. A nuke is a huge explosion that destroys everything for miles and miles. Everything. Most powerful thing we got in our arsenal. They're sending the big ones too. I thought we only had one-point-two megatons left, not fifteens."

The nervous Ethan runs his hands over his face, taking a deep breath before continuing. "I wish I paid more attention in NBC training now. I don't know much about nukes, honestly. Not much more than everyone does. Even if the demons blow the nukes in the air like they was doing to arty shells it'll still turn all them suckers to ashes. If this doesn't close the portal we're all shit out of luck. We gotta get out of here. Like, yesterday. As far away as possible."

John's heart sinks, as this does not sound like something that will leave his body in a state Sunshine can fix. A loud horn sounds outside, over and over. John is near a window and moves his orb-eye towards it, and finds the loud noise coming from one of the vehicles as a peasant presses something inside it.

John replies, "I cannot. They'll follow, and the end will be the same. I don't want to put you or the peasants at risk by accompanying either party."

"You gotta stop calling people peasants. There's no peasants no more. Don't come with me then. Go with the ones heading north. The more distance between you and Montreal and populated areas the better. Just split off from them down the road and head in the woods. The longer we keep the big demons from the rest, the more it helps the Canadians. They're hitting the demon army near Montreal now. Your choice but make it quick. Stay or come, but we gotta go now."

Ethan turns and rushes outside. John puts on his rucksack, sword in sash, and follows, unsure of what to do, when before he had certainty and finality. Peasants are rushing back to the house and vehicles as words are harshly yelled at them. Ethan struggles to coax Amber to enter his vehicle,

Amber ignoring his pleas. Ethan gets annoyed and tries to grab her, and Amber speeds away down the road.

John rushes after Amber, but she is very fast and wily, and he knows he cannot catch her until she peters out, even enhancing his speed, and he worries catching her will take some time, and Ethan will leave without her.

A short distance down the road, Amber runs past a bobbing soul. Just a soul, no body. At first John thinks it is a spirit, as he's never seen just a floating soul. But it is a soul and only a soul, dim, as all souls look to him now since attaining his vision [Perk].

John slows to a walk, furiously thinking, letting Amber escape into the woods. This is a new thing, and since all the great changes to this world, new things are most likely threats. The peasants are depending on him for their safety and escape. It might be a mistake to do, but a prudent one, as it's better to be safe than sorry, and John decides to attack the soul with his spell.

A few more steps bring John into range. He raises his arm to cast [Magical Essence Dart] at the soul, and his casting is undone as the soul quickly rushes him, bobbing quickly up and down in the air. He goes for his sword, but in the blink of an eye the soul is upon him, and he sees a clawed hand grab his arm as a demon appears out of thin air.

The demon is much larger than the largest he's seen before, the antlered demon leading the army he fought. This one has large horns curled around the sides of its head, similar to those of a ram, a much larger mouth, paler skin, far thicker arms and chest, and legs such as a horse or bull have, with weird joints, but much more immense, and large clawed feet instead of hooves. This demon is also armored, with a thick plate covering its chest and thighs, and the largest sword John has ever seen strapped to its massive back.

Before John can do anything, he feels a foreign essence enter him through the hand holding his arm. His body goes completely limp, and the demon lifts him like a babe, throwing him over his shoulder, and starts walking towards the witches' house.

John cannot move at all, not even his voice works. The speed and ease he was so overpowered and nullified puts him in a sort of shock, and he doesn't even think of his new orb-eye, so his only view the whole trip is the demon's back, and the giant sword strapped to it, as he fights to regain control of his body, wondering why his vital essence isn't attacking the foreign substance.

John tries to enter his Mind's Eye, but is rejected from doing so. The fight was over before it started. The unfairness of the situation, and knowing he is completely impotent to affect it, causes a rage to start within him, but he quickly suppresses it. He needs a clear head now more than ever.

The demon quickly rounds the corner of the witches' house, and John is thrown to the ground as a great weight presses down upon him, and his sword is thrown to the ground beside him, disdainfully, a message he is no threat to this demon. Ethan's vehicle is twenty paces or so in front of him, Ethan and his firearm pressed to the ground outside it, the other peasants pressed down inside.

John looks around with his orb-eye. He sees the other vehicle far down the road, heading west. A new demon rounds the corner of the house, this one pale-grey, and much like his captor in size and shape and armor, but with bull horns instead, and two large axes on its back, carry a giant brown bear over its shoulder.

John notices a sheen of something like life essence completely surrounding the axe-demon, something he has never seen before on any living creature.

The demon tosses the bear to the ground next to John. The bear is silent and unmoving, causing John to worry, as he assumes it is Amber in bear form.

Words in an extremely raspy voice come from the sword-demon that captured John, "Get those ones. I'm locking these down. Be quick about it."

The axe-demon rushes down the street, moving much faster than the fleeing vehicle sliding on the snow-covered road. A peasant, holding the small handgun given to that group by Ethan, hangs out a window of the vehicle, and loud bangs resound as the weapon is fired at the pursuing demon. If any bullets hit the demon, it does not cause it to slow, and it quickly reaches the vehicle, and the firearm, along with a hand and most of an arm, is thrown away into the woods.

The vehicle is grabbed and lifted, and the demon begins to carry it back to the house, holding the vehicle above its head, high in the air.

One peasant manages to jump from the vehicle, as the peasant lands on the ground the demon kicks the man, and he is turned to mush, and trampled over as the demon continues its journey.

John notices the bear move its neck, and he redoubles his effort to regain control of his own body, and is able to move his fingers and his feet a little. The axe-demon returns, dropping the vehicle down on its wheels with a large clang. The demon that carried it approaches John's captor, looking at John the whole while. It says, "The children are being slaughtered for this magal? This is messed up. It's just a Wood."

"He, not it. How many times do you have to be instructed? You must be able to tell females from males. These are beta magals, the most numerous, and up until we're Diamond it's a lot harder for us to unbind the manifestations of same-tiered females. You'll never lead if you don't know the basics."

"Yeah, yeah. It's just hard since we don't have those, and they all look the same. I know what to look for – mammaries on the torso and all that. When's Captain getting here?"

"When he gets here is when. Wrap up these two." *Damn,* John thinks. He was regaining the ability to move his limbs, and would've been able to attack soon. The pressure holding John down isn't too great, as it is directed all around, and not focused just on himself, and he believes he could manage to fight even with it pressing down upon him. And if the focus switches from all around to only John, that will give Amber and Ethan and the peasants a chance to escape.

The axe-demon raises its hand and says, "You know it has green-aspected essence? Not in just the normal places everyone has it, but a ton of it all around its chest. I've never seen it all around the chest like that before."

"Oh yeah, you have a life-sight, don't you?" replies the sword-demon.

"Yeah. Not my choice. Master Garioch made me. I think the lead scab put it in his mind since I have such a good affinity towards green and aspected naturally, doubled up with 'life' and 'grow.' I still got Stone Body like a proper chosen should. Filthy scabs. I'm lucky I wasn't ordered to become one. Just means I have to fight harder to prove myself. Green can be as destructive as any aspect, even red."

John sees the axe-demon's lower dantian light up, filled with green swirls, and a line of green travels up to its arm, then along the arm to the hand, and then out the hand as a growing vine. The brownish-green vine grows longer and longer, sprouting some leaves and thorns, and wraps John up tight, from foot to neck.

John, amazed at seeing the workings of magical essence in someone else, stares transfixed as the demon works its magic. Amber is wrapped up next, and she growls out a mighty roar. He hopes Amber is smart enough, in this bear form, to realize she could escape those vines if she shrunk down to the size of a fox once the demons aren't looking.

The axe-demon finishes the spell and says, "Is Captain getting the Natural?"

"Yes. You know Captain tells me all his secret plans. Instead of giving me orders, he gives me his thoughts and asks for my counsel. How would I know? Do you ever think before speaking?"

A moment passes and the axe-demon says, "No need to be such a jerk just because you were picked to lead. We ascended around the same time. I bet he keeps the Natural for himself."

"Listen, you..."

A woman's voice, sounding much distressed, comes from Ethan's vehicle, "Please. Please. My daughter, the pressure's too much. She has asthma. She can't breathe."

Both demons turn to face the vehicle, neither speak for a moment, then the sword-demon gives reply, "Oh no. If she died that would just be terrible. My soul would shatter in grief." The second demon finds this funny and laughs loudly, in a strangely human way.

# CHAPTER 32
## FRECKLES

John tests his voice and speaks up, "You came for me! Just let the girl go. Let all the peasants go. This is a matter between warriors. Have you no honor?"

John ends his request to the sound of the demons laughing uproariously, both filled with great joy and mirth. Once recovered, the sword-demon speaks, "You know we were made to kill magals, right? Not certain magals, all that aren't Forsaken. And you didn't seem to mind killing so many of our children the other day. Nearly four hundred of them, as I was told. The strong of this world send Woods to fight us while they hide like cowards, and you say we have no honor?

"A Divine magal sold you all out. He made a bargain with our circle and opened the portal here himself. Your own kind invited us to invade your world. If he didn't limit our numbers and tiers, this world would be ours by now.

"What we've done so far, the cities we've taken? A good start, but just a taste of what's to come. And not just on this world. Time runs fast in the Nether, and we'll soon have enough Eternals to crush all yours, and we'll kick open the Golden Gates of your Heaven, and put the Great Betrayer to the sword, and slaughter all Favored down to the last."

John sighs. He dislikes fanatics, or anyone justifying their cruel acts as if they were right or righteous. He says, "That's all far above us, and no excuse for our deeds here, this day. And those children you say I killed? I had no idea they were children, and they were sent to lay me low, as part of an army. This child is no warrior, and isn't part of any army, and means you no harm. None of these peasants mean you harm, and seek only safety and peace. Let them go, and let us fight, as warriors do. You were hidden and jumped me when I was unprepared. Let me stand ready, and our fight will go differently. Well, if we keep it to only strength and skill at arms, as I am new to cultivation and magic. Or are you too frightened to face a Wood in a fair fight? If so, you have no chest, and I name you coward."

Once again, both demons laugh uproariously. And once again, the sword-demon is the one to give reply, "Okay. You got it. We have time to kill, so why not? You'll fight Joyat, no manifestations, but I'm keeping unveiled. That was your rule so if you start casting, I'll kill all the magals and put you down hard and keep you there until Captain Ukaraaz arrives. Joyat, Captain wants him alive so hand-to-hand. Don't get stupid. You're a Silver and he's a Wood. Remove those vines."

John was worried these giant demons might've been Golds, or higher. He now can judge the size progression of demon tiers from Wood to Silver. *Golds must be truly humongous if these are Silvers,* he thinks. "Can you please lessen the pressure on the peasants, or move the girl so she can breathe? Please?"

"No."

Cursing the demons, John can only hope some other way to save the girl, and all the other peasants too, presents itself. Now free and able to move, he somewhat struggles to stand under the weight bearing down on him. It is not intolerable, but slows him down, almost as if moving underwater. He almost grabs his sword, as only Joyat, his opponent, the bull-horned demon with two axes, was ordered to fight hand-to-hand. He doesn't though, as he was the one to propose a fair fight, so he only calls on his god to witness his great deeds this day.

On his feet, John finds the pressure a great hamper, but one he has no choice but to endure. He removes his rucksack slowly, buying some time to get more accustomed to moving under the pressure. He then steadies, sending vital essence throughout his body to strengthen and quicken himself, and suddenly charges the large demon, hoping to take his opponent by surprise.

The surprise attack fails as John is forced to duck under a lightning-quick punch to his head. Both opponents get to work viciously striking each other, and many blows are given and received.

The demon's skin is nearly as hard as granite, and John's own strikes seem to do little damage, while the mighty blows of Joyat's giant fist resound throughout John's body, causing great pain, forcing him to send life essence to heal wounds.

The demon stands much higher than John, and it is a struggle to reach his face with fist, and its chest and thighs are covered in plate armor, leaving John to attack limbs mostly, as he tries to position in a way to sink his teeth into an arm, or gain the demon's back and access to its neck.

Many more blows are received by John than given, and many land on John's hard head. The demon smiles, and both know the outcome this fight is headed in. Though John has a speed advantage, the demon is far more able to land devastating blows with its massive reach and far greater height and size.

On the next thrown punch of the demon, John grabs its wrist above its enormous, clawed hand, and grips it like a clamp. He then grabs the other hand on the demon's next throw.

The demon struggles to remove its wrists from John's grip, but John holds fast, sending as much vital essence through his body as he can to further bolster his strength.

The axe demon says, "Did you feel a manifestation? He's doing something with all the extra green essence in him. I can't feel it, but I can see it."

"He definitely didn't manifest essence. I've been waiting, prepared to unbind it and kill the magals as soon as he starts," replies the sword-demon.

"Well, it's doing something with essence. I can see it. What is it?"

The question goes unanswered. Demon and vampire struggle, and the fight turns into a contest of strength. The demon, unable to break free from John's great grip, starts kicking and kneeing, and John is able to block or take these blows well.

Quick as a flash, the demon smashes its forehead down into John's face, and John's nose shatters, but he manages to keep his grip tight as he blows blood and mucus out of his nose. The demon continues to rain down blows of its forehead, and John takes them on the top of his head.

On the next headbutt, John jumps up to meet the demon's head with his own, glad the demon's horns are too high on its skull to use as weapons in this struggle. The fight continues this way for a long while, John's hands locked onto the demon's wrists, the demon attacking John's head with its forehead, John attacking the demon's forehead with the top of his own head.

These great and massive attacks loudly boom each time their heads connect. John sees a notification flash in his vision stating [Emergency Heal] is now on cooldown for twenty-two hours and some minutes, and his head feels better for a moment, but the great head attacks continue, and John's vision starts to blur, and he becomes dizzy.

John has little choice but to endure and continue, but not for long, as the attacks seem to be injuring the demon too. As if in mutual agreement, both man and demon stop ramming heads, and the demon struggles to break free from the wrist-holds while breathing heavily. The pressure bearing down on John from a Silver's soul unveiled a great hindrance in this fight, and he blows more blood and mucus out of his broken nose, surprised it seems somewhat healed already.

The sword-demon says, "This is getting boring now. Demons don't train to fight as beasts do. Let's see how skilled this magal is with that little sword of his. Okay you two, pause and break apart and ready your weapons. Joyat, be careful. Don't kill him. And remember it's your own essence that will heal him if you land a grievous wound, so you'll only set back your own advancement. And if he dies, you're telling Captain and taking full responsibility."

John releases his grip. He finds it easy to step back and reach for his sword with the assistance of his orb-eye, and opens his rucksack to take out the short sword too. He blows his nose one more time, the passages finally clearing.

John advances with a high guard, pushing his vital essence to enhance his strength and speed as much as possible. The demon holds its large axes, one held in each hand, out to the sides, enticing John to attack while its body is so open.

And John does, quick as lightning, and the demon seems very surprised when it fails to meet and turn the thrust, taking a stab above its knee, returning vicious strikes of its own. When John tries to redirect the second attack, his short sword is shattered, and he is nearly bitten by an axe.

John is forced to focus on defense, and throws the broken short sword at the demon's face. He manages to score a hit on the calf of the demon as he dodges and spins around, pressed hard and pushed back. He scores a new slice on the demon's arm, and it bellows in rage, and redoubles its efforts to skewer John. John's strength and enchanted sword barely up to the task of breaking the demon's hard skin, his hits causing only shallow slices, doing little actual damage.

"If I could use my body or weapon enhancement you'd be in a hundred pieces by now, you filthy magal! No one fights without manifestations."

John, breathing deep, thinks of how best to respond, as both reset after the furious passes they've made. He is far more skilled with melee weapon fighting than the demon is, and even gave up certain hits he could've made, as he remembers the antlered-demon he fought, and how it ignored injuries that would've killed any human, and death by a thousand cuts is not a viable strategy in this fight.

The demon is strong, and fast, and has some skill with the axe, and the demon's wild blows are as dangerous as the skillful ones. One good hit from either of its axes can bring John low, while the sword can only deliver minor wounds to the demon's hard skin.

John says, "Maybe, but you're a Silver, and I'm a Wood, and only mid-low still. I'm stronger, and faster, and more skilled at arms than you are. I'm making you look like a fool. Demons are not true warriors."

"You got quite a mouth on you for a Wood. I'm not surprised you managed to draw the ire of a Celestial of your own kind. You know he gave Captain great rewards to kill you? Why does he want you dead so badly, magal?"

The ram-horned demon interjects, "She."

"She, I mean. Why does she want you dead? You know some secret of gaining strength far beyond your tier, and she got it out of you, and now she wants this secret to die with you. Right?"

John may be more skilled with arms than his opponent, but the odds are still against him due to the tier difference, and he is slowed by the pressure bearing down on him. He welcomes this respite to collect himself and plan.

John's first instinct is to reply with a witty retort, such as the issue the Magnus has with him is merely a lover's spat, and something about the great size of his private parts, but demons don't seem to have genitals, and he is unsure of the powers of a Magnus. If she can somehow hear his words, and takes offense, that may give her reason to strike him down herself. So, John replies, "What a fantastic guess. And correct. I'll share this secret and powerful knowledge with you if the peasants are allowed to flee, and the bear too."

Both demons laugh uproariously. Surprisingly, Joyat is the one to reply, "The Natural? No way that goes free. Way too valuable. Captain would kill us. The magals though? We have some wiggle-room there." The demon takes a casual and relaxed pose, and starts to stretch in a care-free manner as it says, "These secrets, why not...," it ends the question by throwing one of its axes at John, and John musters all his speed and grace to fall back to avoid the axe as it flies over him, nearly scoring a hit, and must immediately roll as the demon rushes his prone form, holding the axe with both clawed-hands, and crashes the axe onto the ground with a mighty blow John barely manages to roll away from.

As John rolls away again to avoid a foot, he hears the sword-demon call out, "Careful, careful! Don't kill him, Joyat!"

Then, as John tries to regain his feet, he must dive and roll once more to avoid new attacks from axe and foot and fist, and is pressed like he has never been before, all effort in defense, no thought allowed or spared for offense. For a long while he is pushed to his limits, Joyat swinging and kicking wildly and ferociously, finally managing to score a hit on John's upper left arm, the axe biting deep.

Most of the deadly swings John is able to dodge, but after some time, he is forced to parry a wild swing in a bad way, and his sword is knocked out of his hands.

Joyat smiles as he stops attacking, giving John space, saying, "How did you think this would end, Wood? I am chosen, and a Silver. We'll have your secrets, and you…"

Not waiting for the demon to finish, John scoops up his sword, and turns his back to the demon, standing casually, without stance or guard or preparation, left arm bloody and hanging limply by his side.

"You dare turn your back to me, you filthy magal? And they say I'm a slow learner." Joyat holds his axe with both hands in a tail guard, and swings it around slowly and with great power at John's right leg. John, watching the demon with his orb-eye the whole time, is ready, and spins about while rushing the demon, rolling under its arms and axe, and finds a way the demon's great height puts it at a disadvantage, as the head and neck are angled perfectly while John is so close, allowing his enchanted sword, held with right hand on the hilt and left on the pommel, to be pressed into its neck under the jaw, and up deep into its skull.

The look on the demon's face as it collapses, causing the ground to shake and three dark-yellow crystals to ping off the ground, is a great reward to John, and he is heartened greatly by this victory, and even more so as he sees a spirit form for the first time. His good humor is short lasting, as the pressure spread all around him is lifted, and then focused only on John like a pinpoint, causing him to drop his sword again as the great pressure flings him to the ground as if thrown down, holding him fast.

With face pressed to snow and dirt, John must use his orb-eye to see, and the look on the ram-horned demon's face terrifies him, and the demon stands there in silent hatred, its eyes of dull red and orange fire boring into John with murderous intent. If the demon yelled or raged John would be less frightened, but it only stands there, still, staring.

John hears movement and looks with his invisible orb-eye to see the peasants fleeing, Ethan moving away from them in the other direction, rifle couched and pointed at the demon. The muzzle flares and the demon's head jerks forward, and many more shots bang out of the firearm at the demon's head. Without looking, the demon reaches his hand behind himself, and a reddish-brown beam comes forth from its clawed hand, turning Ethan's head into a bloody mist that slowly falls onto the headless body, covering the corpse like freckles.

The great pressure on John is far greater than the two sisters, when combined, were able to bear down upon him, and he is greatly relieved as it is removed, as the general unfocused pressure gives him a chance to continue in this fight. For a slim moment he attempts to regain his feet, but the demon pounces on him, and essence forced into him, much more than before, and he goes limp, and then unconscious.

# CHAPTER 33
## CAPTAIN UKARAAZ

John is startled awake from horrific screams nearby. He is not held down, or restrained in any way he can feel, or see with his orb-eye. No general pressure is pushing down on him, as would be the case if the demon's soul were unveiled. He makes small and subtle movements to test his control over his own body, and every test passes. Keeping his eyes closed, pretending to be unconscious still, he looks around with his orb-eye.

John's arm is no longer bleeding, the healing process started, his enchanted sword within reach of his undamaged arm. His neck is stiff from calcification, as the sun is high and bright. Amber is behind him, within ten or so paces, still wrapped in vines, shifting around, and making whining sorts of low growls. He tries to will her into realizing she could escape the vines by turning into a fox. *Why does she stay so? She turned into a fox so quickly last time she was a bear.*

Joyat's body is so close to John it nearly touches him, the confused spirit wandering nearby. The headless body of Ethan is in the same spot, lying on its belly, rifle pinned under the chest, Ethan's spirit standing stock still near it.

Near Ethan's abandoned and empty vehicle is the ram-horned demon with the massive sword, torturing a young woman. A group of peasants and the large noblewoman and her son huddled together close by the demon, nine total in the group, John counts. Another man's body is off to the side of the demon, disfigured and disgusting to look upon.

John looks for another body and sees none. He does the math in his head again, and believes there is one peasant unaccounted for, and fervently hopes they got away. The tortures being inflected by the demon onto the young woman are unspeakable and horrifying, and it turns John's stomach to see and hear.

John steels himself and hastily plans. He is very stealthy, but he is right in the demon's line of sight, and it is very bright out, and he'd never be able to sneak up on a competent human in this situation. He doesn't know how well stealth will work against this demon, far more proficient in the ways of cultivation and magic, so he dismisses a stealth attack as a viable option. First, he'll empower himself with life essence, while also casting [Magical Essence Dart] at the demon, and grabbing for his sword, and casting again and again until the demon dies, or John is stopped from doing so.

John takes a calming breath, and begins a countdown to his attack, putting the horrific screams of the young woman being tortured out of his head as he does so. Before his countdown finishes, the demon jumps towards him, and John frantically starts casting his spell, only to have it undone as soon as he starts, and the demon lands on him, forcing essence into him, and John's body goes limp once again.

The demon looks down on John with a malicious face, its eyes of dull red and orange fire glisten with malevolence and hatred. "I went a little overboard last time. You missed out on some of the fun I've been having. The screams of these magals are music to my ears. This one's screams are just delightful. It's making me giddy. I'm glad you're awake to hear them now."

John tries to reply by saying, "End her life or torture me instead," but he can't speak, he can't even grunt.

"Cat got your tongue? I wonder how that saying translates." The demon then turns his back to John, and walks back to the young girl, and as she notices the demon returning says, "No, no, no, no, no, no. I'm sorry. Please, please, please. I'm so sorry. I'm sorry. No more, please, no more. PLEASE!"

The demon ignores the young woman's pleas and goes back to his gruesome work. John can do nothing, and it hurts his heart. He tries to tune out the girl's cries only to have his mind assault him with guilt over his failure, and heap condemnation on him for being so weak. For long he must hear the horrific screams.

For the first time John hopes what everyone has been claiming with such certainty is true, that his belief in the Underworld is false, as such shame will bar him from going there. He vows to die on his feet, fighting, somehow, as Ethan did. He keeps his mind occupied thinking of all the torture he'll inflict on the demon, far worse tortures than the demon could ever imagine.

John's musings are then interrupted. "Oh, this one's dead. Darkness, Adversity, and Nightmare! This magal had no constitution at all. How is it possible none of you drop crystals? And your tech isn't powered by essence. You're the only one I've seen with an open core. Did this whole world turn their back on cultivation for some reason? Some taboo? Why didn't you? Do you manifest essence the right way, like a true warrior, or do you use runes like all magal pretenders?"

John tests his throat and finds it now works. He thinks of ignoring the demon, but then thinks if he engages with it, it may hold off on torturing another peasant. "We were prevented from cultivating as we now can, from what I was told. I use runes to cast spells, since, as I said, cultivation is new to us, and I don't know how to do it any other way. Do you always torture innocent women like a filthy coward and a cur, or do you have any manliness and honor within you? I can't wait to torture you, and hear you beg for me to end your pitiful life, you boorish clod."

"Manliness?"

"Yes, swine."

"Ah, just making sure it translated correctly. You know nothing of my race, do you? Everyone is taught about us, besides you, it seems. We're all considered males, and the Nether our mother. I don't know if your world has this word, but we have spermatia shed from us, and the Nether births our young. Beta magal females are the ones we worry about. Well, not like these ones here. These here are pathetic. On normal worlds with magal cultivators, we'd have a harder time with females since they have better control of essence and stronger manifestations. Are you saying if I were female, it would be okay for me to do what I'm doing now?"

John takes this information in, and thinks of a reply explaining what he meant, as it was taken incorrectly. "Saying you're not manly is saying you have forsaken what qualities even the lowest of men should possess. A warrior has no need to torture young peasants, and would never perform such low deeds, or take pleasure in something so base and mean. I'll show you how a true warrior acts, fight me you detestable coward! I despise you and all like you, and would rather die than live in a world where you walk free, able to spread your filth and cowardice."

"Oh, no need to worry about that. Captain Ukaraaz will be here soon. I hope he lets me torture you. Speaking of torture, I miss the music these magals create. Let's see." The demon walks towards the group of crying peasants, huddled together, and points at the large noblewoman, "Are you man or woman? I can't tell."

Crying, the noblewoman responds, "Please, no."

"Answer."

"Man. I'm a man," she says between sobs.

The demon reaches down and grabs the young man her arms are wrapped around, and both mother and son fuss and yell. The demon unveils its soul, and all are pressed down and silent as he picks up the boy.

As the chosen victim is carried back, John hears a large group approaching quickly from the south, and three break off from the group and move forward alone. The ram-horned demon sets the child down, and looks over at the three approaching, and kneels with his right knee and right hand on the ground, his left elbow on his bent left knee, his head bowed towards the ground.

Of the three demons approaching, two are similar in size to the one kneeling, and armored in a similar manner. The third is far larger, and completely covered in fully articulated black plate armor, face covered, with bull horns extending through holes on the top of the helmet. The massive demon then speaks, "Morgoros, veil so the young can approach. Where is Joyat?"

"Captain Ukaraaz, the magals tried to flee earlier, so we had to make ourselves known and capture them. We had plenty of time to waste so were making sport of that one. He killed our brother with trickery. I have our brother's crystals for you."

Captain Ukaraaz raises his arm, and Morgoros is lifted high in the air, arms pinned to his sides, and screams as if in much pain. John tests his limbs and is still unable to do anything beyond wiggle some fingers and toes, and is disheartened as he needs to die fighting to gain acclaim in the Underworld, where he'll soon be.

The massive, armored demon yells, "Silence! You let a little pain cause you to whine like a scab? It's a wonder I haven't lost more of you," in a booming voice. "You know I have no Silvers to waste, and a dire need for every single one. Our children are being slaughtered to the south, and Joyat is killed by a Wood? Tell me he died from one of the strange weapons these magals have, and not that little sword there. Our weapons have better runes, so don't use it being enchanted as an excuse either."

Many more demons approach, mostly Woods, with some Copper and Bronze mixed in. About forty in total. A giant golden structure, like a doorframe, approaches too, and stops near the group. John is certain Captain Ukaraaz is a Gold, the one Sunshine informed him of.

Morgoros whines out, "He has a Body Formation! Like Stone Body. One that increases strength and speed, and his bones are nearly as dense as our own. And regeneration. He's strange. His weight is less than our children before they even open a core, so he's veiling it somehow. As a Wood. Joyat was just toying with him and wasn't in any danger. It was a trick. He just got tricked."

Ukaraaz turns to a Bronze demon, holds a letter out towards him, and says, "Grab your squad and bring the Natural and this letter to Baggodon the Blind. Not my master. Baggodon. Outer Point. Understood? Straight to him, with all haste." He turns back to Morgoros, still high in the air, and asks, "Why are all these magals alive?"

"We... Captain, you didn't say to kill them," After those words leave Morgoros' mouth, he falls to the ground with a loud thud.

Captain Ukaraaz raises his hand again, and all the peasants are violently crushed together into a small ball, blood and gore splattering everywhere. "I didn't tell you not to kill them either. That's what we do. Kill magals. You shouldn't need orders."

John, looking at the ball of dead peasants, further shamed and riddled with guilt, doesn't notice Ukaraaz's arm pointing in his direction. John quickly flies through the air towards the Gold, his neck suddenly in the giant, armored hand of Ukaraaz. John can see the eyes of dull red and orange fire staring at him through the helm, considering him. Just for a moment their eyes lock, and then John's neck and jaw are horrifically crushed, and he is thrown aside like trash.

"Is that its bag? Bring it to me. Bring the corpse to our master. Garioch. Garioch. Second Point. Got it? Tell him it bears study since a magal Celestial was willing to reward me greatly for its death. Tell him I send my honors and the bracers and sword are gifts from me to him. And say I have need of more chosen, all he can spare, especially replacements for the two lost Silvers when he can. My name is Ukaraaz. Ukaraaz. Now, repeat all that back to me."

On his side, like a broken doll, John's face presses into snow, bleeding profusely, unable to draw breath or move at all, pants soiled. He listens to the Bronze demon bray the message out, certain the demon would be unintelligible if not for the NCS translation. He can do nothing but watch impotently with his orb-eye as Amber is carried through the golden structure and disappears while Ukaraaz rummages through his rucksack.

Demon Woods with dim souls approach John, making their chirping cheetah noises, one holding John's sword. Many hands grab him, placing him on a hastily made litter, and his sword is placed by his side.

John, with his orb-eye, sees Ukaraaz quickly look upwards and yell out, "Death approaches from the sky. Saglirun, inform Master I cannot stop it. We go now! Silvers, flee with all speed south! Do not stop until you catch up with me. All others through the portal. Get the corpse through. Now! Go! Go! I close it in five count. Four. Three. Two. O…"

John, surrounded by many Woods and Coppers, as well as a few Bronzes, is rushed through the golden structure, and the air and atmosphere change greatly.

The air, thick and filled with an odd energy, swirls around John, and feels sticky. The sky is dark and starless, and strange clouds of brutal colors fill it as far as the eye can see, as if a mad man painted this scene. He cannot see far off, the terrain a black and a dull red, like rust, with some browns and tans mixed in, and somehow seems both dry and moist at the same time. Few plants break from the ground, and all are sharp and have an uninviting look to them, and little vital essence. If there were thick fog, it wouldn't look very dissimilar to the place his Lilitu's ritual brought him so long ago.

John realizes the demon entering a few moments before him, Saglirun, is nowhere in sight, but should be only a few paces in front of this group. The large golden structure behind him stays open, and he hopes it means the nukes killed Ukaraaz.

Words then show in John's eyes, unbidden.

**You are in a NetherRealm. It is strongly suggested you leave immediately. All advanced functions are deactivated. NCS downgrading to [Basic] [Preventive] and will reactivate upon exiting into real space.**

**[OVERRIDE]**

**[OVERRIDE] [Status] [Authorized] Entertainment package reactivating.**

# CHAPTER 34
# NETHERREALM

John is worried about how low his vital essence is getting. His magical essence isn't much of a worry, even though [Emergency Heal] took much of it. He is thankful no demon noticed he didn't drop crystals, or now realize his heart still beats, though it is much slower and very soft.

John is also thankful the type of break to his neck leaves him completely pain free, but he still wants to meditate as a respite from all this, as well as the fact meditation also speeds up healing for him now too. He doesn't. The demons think he's dead. He doesn't know where Amber is, or why he can't see her, or sense her, or how her party got so far ahead of him since she entered the portal shortly before he did, but if she can be saved his only hope to do so is maintaining the demons' belief he is dead.

John doesn't know if any of the demons around him have a vision [Perk], but hopes if they do the magical energy in his dantian doesn't give his game away.

Meditation will move the energy around him, and even John, largely ignorant to the ways of self-cultivation, would assume a dead man cultivating is not truly dead. Since he can neither move any part of his body, including his own eyelids, nor draw breath, playing the role of dead isn't too hard of a task for him, and comes naturally in such a condition.

Due to current circumstances, John is glad he recommitted to the old ethos of his clan and god, their way of death, freedom through making peace with the inevitable outcome of the life of a true warrior – a violent end in battle. Eventually, victory is not an option.

It seems to John victory hasn't been much of an option for him recently either, manhandled by so many so far above him. In grim times such as this, he believes it is important to take succor in faith, so the path is clear, and the mind unburdened by fear and doubt and depression.

Death is always but a moment away, and come what may, John is determined to face it as a man should, and make a good accounting of himself, and make his father proud of him, and forgiving of his many base deeds and years of cowardice, though his father never had to fear the cold-dark.

John's father taught him a man should strive to be both fell and tall, and honor would follow. Allow no disrespect, and always retaliate to it. Never hesitate to give combat, and never run from it. If someone attempts to take from you, take, instead, all from them. Protect what is yours, and prefer death over letting those you love most, or yourself, be dishonored or abused by enemies. Many tenets such as this he sees clearly in his mind, and he wonders why he can remember these but not the name of his loving mother and lord father, nor his own birth name, nor the name of his people.

John thinks all this while studying the many enemies surrounding him, and worrying about how low his vital essence is getting.

The terrain he is carried over is rough and strange, and he wishes he could see farther through the thick and colorful atmosphere, as he is stuck with little to study but his escorts.

Thankfully, the translation function of the NCS still works, so John can understand what is said by the Bronzes, though they speak little.

Soon after entering through the portal, a few Bronzes commented on how glad they were to be back home, and many mentioned the Nether, and a strange ritual was done by a Bronze with pretty horns, and the Bronze then shouted, "This way to Two-Point. Follow me!" Now, all are silent as they walk through this dreary and barren land and its oppressive and thick air and mad sky.

John assumed the Bronzes would bully Coppers, and Coppers would bully Woods, but the demons seem to treat lower tiers decently, and fight only among their own. There is not much discipline in this crew, but things don't get chaotic, and most follow the order of a Bronze John thinks of as Pretty-Horn, as his horns are unlike any beast John has ever seen, and swirl around upwards beautifully.

Strangely, John's great ability to navigate is significantly hampered in this weird land, and he is lost and unable to keep directions straight, or find a point to fix onto and orient from. All the lessons he's learned in his long life count for little in this land.

Every so often, as the group journeys forward, a demon Wood saunters up to the group, and is either accepted in without comment or chased away. John does get better at spotting these little demons when they are hidden.

The group treks over harsh terrain until more life breaks from the ground more often, and then some dark trees that seem sickly and blighted, but containing some life essence, show now and again. Not long after, the party enters a dark forest filled with these trees. The demons become cautious and slow and peer into the darkness John cannot pierce with his perception, and the Bronzes light torches giving off a strange green flame.

John stares at the peculiar flame, and is thankful to have such a queer and beautiful sight to look upon.

Far into the woods, the demons stop and start making camp, drawing five circles on the ground far outside the camp and around it, and imbuing the circles with magical energy or magical essence. All the demons sit and meditate, and do so not too differently than John's own way - still and unmoving, and with eyes closed, they sit, with legs crossed beneath them, and hands on thighs, but palms facing upwards. Occasionally a small demon moves to scratch or look around for a moment, or wipe their nose on an arm. *Much like human children would behave,* John thinks.

Planning, John hopes this Two-Point is far away, and he is able to fully heal before arrival, as he thinks he can handle this group without much trouble. There are many Bronzes, but a sword through the eye of each should help quickly cull their numbers. He only worries they have strange magical abilities other than weapon and body enhancements. The lower demons are of no concern to him, regardless of numbers.

Then, John begins to really worry. He used much vital essence in his fight, as well as to heal after and since, and he is now running low. When as injured as he is, and as low on vital essence as he is, and when he starts feeling very tired like he does now, he knows what it means. His body will force him into a deep slumber, and he will have no choice but to sleep while it heals, oblivious to all around him.

John fights off sleep for as long as he can, transfixed on the green flames, until he can no longer.

***

John is startled awake, adrenaline pushing away the dullness that comes with such slumber, his heart beating quicker than it has for a long while, fear gripping it harshly, terror numbing his brain.

Something is looking at John. He doesn't know what or from where, and he senses nothing and sees nothing with his orb-eye to cause such dread. But whatever was is as deserving of fear as the cold-dark.

Thankfully, the feeling doesn't last long, and John's mind begins to thaw, and his heart begins to slow. His neck is still broken, an injury that takes many days to heal, and is long away from healing enough to allow John to move and function. His jaw is still mush, but that is a much less severe injury, and he could function with it if his neck were whole. Not being able to breathe for so long is a large worry, as he doesn't want his brain injured and so deteriorated again.

But John is alive still, and maybe Amber is too. And as long as he is alive, there is a chance he can save Amber, if she too lives, as well as enact vengeance on all who wronged him, especially Ukaraaz and Morgoros. He comforts himself thinking of all the torture and pain he will inflict on Morgoros. *I will destroy his mind, and he will live long after as a broken husk. His screams and pleas for mercy will help heal my soul*, thinks John.

The large party of demon escorts carry John on the outskirts of a strange village with many demon inhabitants, a large castle-like structure off in the distance. Every structure is either a shanty built of dark wood, or something much harder to describe, and never before seen, looking more formed or grown by strange magics from strange and sharp dark and reddish material than anything built.

The castle is one such structure, and has severe and cruel points all over no builder would add, as it is a gross waste of materials and effort for no functionality. Long, sharp spikes fill the air above it, with no defensive utility at all. These spikes also jut out from the keep in a way that would only assist enemies in scaling the walls, and also extend from the battlements in a way that would hamper defenders. *Madness*, John thinks.

Throughout the areas of this strange town John is carried through, demons scurry about, mostly Woods and Coppers, and many Bronzes too. Strangely, most Bronze demons stop and kowtow as John's escorts pass. These Bronzes seem different, and far more humble and less cocky than other Bronzes, and wear ragged robes. He then hears the sounds of a forge, and soon passes an open-aired smithy.

John becomes very worried as a Silver is working alongside the Bronzes in the smithy, though these demons don't stop working metal to bow, the Silver silently stares at John the whole time he passes.

John is not certain when most cultivators take a vision [Perk], but Sunshine stated craftsmen often take essence-sight, and both demon Silver's at the witches' house had a vision [Perk]. He believes he is lucky the Silver did not have either essence-sight or life-sight, as either would prove his act false.

The town is strange and not overcrowded, but is not too dissimilar to any other John has seen. A larger structure lies ahead before the entrance to the castle, and John hears voices not made by demon coming from it. As his party approaches, he becomes worried again, as he sees another Silver in ragged robes loitering outside it. This demon stares at John from far away. Once the party reaches the Silver, he bows low at the waist but does not kowtow, and John is certain he hears many non-demon voices, and much merriment, coming from within the building.

The party passes the large and strange building, and the Silver straightens, and stares at John once again, and continues to do so as he follows the party through the unguarded barbican, and soon after, the unguarded gatehouse.

John finally manages to spy a few guards on the walls, and one demon in a tower. Once through the massive doors of the keep he is surprised to find the castle is mostly empty and quiet, without demons acting as guards, or at least obviously so. The Silver in the tattered robes still following the party and staring at John.

No challenge is issued to the party, and John is carried directly into the throne hall. The throne sits empty and only two demons occupy the hall, standing in conversation – a Silver and a demon so large he seems almost comedic, far larger than the Gold, Ukaraaz, even while unarmored. A true giant.

Much worried and watching closely with his orb-eye, John studies these two demons. Both give John a scant glimpse as they turn their attention to his demon escorts. The Silver is armored with a breastplate over mail hauberk, the giant demon wearing only a glittering robe, his soul much more noticeable than the Silver's, even with [Orb of the Crimson Palace] dimming it greatly in his sight.

John knows his game is over, and either the Silver in the ragged robes knows he is alive, or the other Silver in the breastplate and hauberk, or the giant demon. None seem to care as his litter is let down to the ground, and all demons in his escort kowtow towards the giant, including the Silver in the ragged robes.

In a very deep and resounding voice the giant demon says, "Report."

Pretty-Horn says, "Two-point, message for you from, uh, Ukaraaz."

The giant demon places his hands behind his back and calmly says, "Do you have a name, child?"

"Uh, no," says Pretty-Horn, squirming.

"Address me as Second-Point Master please, or at least Master."

"Yes, Second Master."

The giant demon, Second-Point Master, doesn't get angry or sigh or huff at the mistake by Pretty-Horn, and calmly says, "Tell me the message, child."

"Send honor and corpse and sword gift. Wrist-metal gift. Study for magal high, high Tree reward good. Need many chosen. Need Silver."

Without taking his eyes off Pretty-Horn, Second-Point Master says dryly, "A corpse that lives. What a gift." With more warmth he continues, "You've done well, child, and I welcome you into the ranks of my chosen. I name you Muzaran after our great forefather, known as the Terror. I hope the name is auspicious for you. Take those you lead and rejoin the training regime. Dismissed."

The demon escorts rise and depart, the Silver in the ragged robes stays on the ground, ignored.

The armored Silver turns to the giant demon and says, "Master, what insult is this? He jumps chain and manipulates your master into gifting him with a Natural, the greatest of prizes, by right yours to gift, and you're left with a Wood and a tiny sword?"

The Second-Point Master, extremely calm till now, rises up menacingly over the Silver, and his eyes blaze with anger and stare daggers for a long moment before he bellows, "Know your place, Zongreth. You speak of your betters. You've dawdled long enough here today. Get to your duties!"

The Silver bows and hurries out the hall, the giant demon staring daggers at him the whole way. Once the Silver is gone, the demon goes back to being calm and relaxed, hands behind his back once more. "Come, scab, and tell me your thoughts."

The Silver in ragged robes rises and walks towards the giant demon, and for the first time John notices the Silver has wrinkles around his eyes and mouth, unlike the other demons he's seen up close. Both the Silver and the giant have antler-like horns, but the similarities end there. The Silver is pale skinned, and the giant a charcoal color with lighter blotches all over. The giant is big enough John has a hard time accepting he could be a Platinum, and thinks he must be a Diamond or Salt.

The Silver sits on his haunches in front of the Second-Point Master and says, "This one thinks you may have gotten the better prize, Master. This is the one the Magnus magal insists is of the ptagmog?"

282

"It must be. I can feel...something. Something within it," replies the giant demon.

"Its neck is broken in a way all beta-types immediately die from. Even a Divine would die. Celestials too probably. Yet a Wood lives with it, and it is being healed somehow. A Celestial could bring someone back from such an injury, but none less, and if healing was gifted to it, it would've expired long ago, so how is it healing now? Its core is still, and it's Wood. Very, very strange."

Both Silver and giant now stare at John, and the giant says, "My thoughts exactly. Bring it to my room. The fewer seeing it the better. I'll inform Baggodon myself. Later. You don't say a word to anyone. How long until it fully heals, you think?"

"This one can't tell for certain, Master. Not this glass. Not this day. Probably not soon. It is slowly healing now, but this one doesn't know the rules of it. Days, at least, this one guesses. Lock your room, Master?"

"Is it ever left unlocked when I'm not occupying it?" A shiver runs down John's spine as he watches a cruel smile form on the giant's face.

# CHAPTER 35
# ONE BAD PLAN, AND ONE GOOD ONE

The Silver, called scab, easily lifts John's whole litter with one hand and carries him through a side door of the hall, down a small hallway, and into a large room.

The room is adorned with many giant weapons, and many sets of armor of various types on stands, from light leather to full articulated plate, and, oddly enough, even some robes have stands of their own. There is a small table with four chairs on one side of the room, some dressers and a large bureau, no bed, some banners with strange symbols, but no artwork is hung.

The floor is carpeted, and runes are placed at various spots around the room, about seven in total. Opposite the table is a very, very thick carpet sitting on top of the other, and this thick one is completely decorated with many, many runes.

John's litter is set down off to the side, near the bureau, and the Silver leans over him, pats his head, and whispers in his ear, "Yes." After a long pause, he again whispers, "Yes." The Silver then licks John's face and leaves, closing and locking the thick door to the room behind him.

*This is not good. Not good at all,* John thinks. He is glad he heard mention of his friend, Amber, and hopes she is still alive. He then debates with himself whether it is better to heal faster or slower, and chastises himself for such a cowardly question, and begins meditating.

John can't risk going deep inside himself, as he is not attuned to how a full dantian feels yet, and he doesn't want to overfill it again. Instead, much time passes as he fills his dantian with magical essence, converts half to shen, and half the shen to emptiness, and continues to do so. He doesn't fill his upper dantian, but gets it near full, and completely fills his middle dantian, then waits as the substance in both dantians dissipates. He then does it again.

At some point, far quicker than usual, John becomes able to breathe, and with much relief starts using his [Breath of the Serpent Clan] technique, and tries to keep it going even while meditating.

***

John's neck is a good way towards completely healed, and even his jaw is mostly healed, and all the bones and flesh are mainly where they should be. He can now move, if necessary, but is not yet in fighting shape. He finishes this round of cultivation, happy he is still breathing in the way of the [Breath of the Serpent Clan] technique.

John finally notices heavy breathing nearby and is so startled he nearly jumps out of his own skin – the Second-Point Master is on the smaller, thick carpet, cultivating.

The runes of the carpet are lit up brightly, and the technique the master uses is strange to watch. The master sits cross-legged, and moves his arms sharply, and not smoothly, with deep, loud breaths, and the occasional chant.

Twice the old Silver, called scab, has entered the room since John was first brought in, each time licking John's face and leaving after telling him, "Yes," again. On another instance some Bronzes, all in ragged robes, came into the room, and cut off John's clothes, and washed the filth from him, and left him naked, and his sword, hatchet, knife, boots, and clothes removed from the room, along with the small bag of higher tiered crystals he kept in his sash.

This is the first time the Second-Point Master has entered the room, and John worries why he didn't snap out of meditation, as his mind and senses should consider this demon the greatest of threats.

John, not yet fully healed, but mobile and able, watches the giant demon with his orb-eye while staying as still as possible, silencing his already soft breathing, and calming his heart.

The Second-Point Master seems deep in meditation and lost to all around him. *I'll never get a better opportunity. It is time to put my great stealth skills to use*, John thinks.

Naked, unarmed, and silent as a ghost, John rises from his litter and creeps as quietly and carefully as he can manage behind the giant demon.

Though the demon is sitting cross-legged, he is so large John must extend himself up on the tip of his toes to reach the neck. His jaw is not healed all the way, but in matters of life and death as great as this, injury and pain must be put aside and out of mind, and what must be done still done regardless.

John forces his lower jaw downwards and his mouth opens with a cracking sound he hopes does not stir the giant demon. He has no vital essence to enhance himself with, so with as much strength and pressure as possible sinks his upper fangs into the demon's neck. Or attempts to, as the demon's skin is far too hard to pierce, and both fangs break painfully.

"Did you really just try to bite me?" says the Second-Point master calmly.

John raises his hand and casts [Magical Essence Dart] directly at the base of the demon's skull, knowing his magical essence is far more powerful than his tier, and one casting of this spell was enough to kill one of the witches outright. The spell lands and a little smoke rises from where it hits, and a strange shimmer then covers all the demon's skin.

Without moving at all, the demon says, "That actually hurt a little."

*Good*, John thinks, as he casts the spell many more times at the same spot until his dantian lies empty.

"Impressive! Your essence is powerful, and your core large. Yet your weight is that of our youngest with core unopened." The demon stands and turns to John, towering over him, a look of curiosity, and not anger, on his face as he calmly continues, "Tell me, why the bite? You couldn't have thought your teeth could pierce my skin. It seems like such a silly thing to do. What am I missing?"

John gives thought to a physical confrontation, but dismisses it immediately. The demon acts as a gentleman would, and John does not think a physical fight will favor him much against such an opponent. Instead, John plans some plans and tries to speak, but his jaw does not cooperate. After some fiddling and popping, he is able to speak in a way good enough for the NCS to translate. "I was created by blasphemy, and have some great powers unlike any seen before. If I could sink my teeth into you, I would be able to kill you, no matter your tier. I have valuable knowledge, and I'll tell you anything you like if you free my friend, Amber, the Natural the Silver spoke of with you in the throne hall. Not the old Silver that licks my face. The one armored in breastplate and mail hauberk."

The demon's eyes narrow, and he remains silent for a long moment before replying, "I don't want to treat you poorly. I can feel the touch of the old masters in you, and even your own consider you a creature of blasphemy. This means you are of the ptagmog. But I think you gravely mistake your station and situation and forget yourself. Firstly, perform the proper obeisance."

John, cheeks red for correctly being dressed down so, and being so ill-mannered to someone superior to him, someone treating him fairly and with politeness too, kowtows.

The demon says, "Rise. You speak to Diamond Garioch, Master of the Second Point of Circle Xakariz. You may address me as either my tier or title. With whom am I speaking to?"

John rises and replies, "I am called John now, Diamond. And I apologize for the poor manners I've shown. I assumed I was a prisoner and not a guest. Attacking a host, unprovoked, is unacceptable behavior. Please accept my most humble apologies." He then gives a low bow at the waist.

The demon, eyes narrowed still, nods his head slightly, "Accepted. As for the Natural, it is not mine to free. The Outer-Point Master, Baggo-don, gifted it to my captain. I believe you met him, Ukaraaz?"

"Yes, Diamond."

"Well, the portal won't open for a long while. The Natural is in this keep, under my care. As you know, the potency of the pill made from Naturals degrades quickly, so it will live for some time. I could arrange it so you could meet and spend some time together. But know this – if you attempt to kill it or consume it yourself, you will pay dearly and know suffering far greater than any you've ever had."

John's heart is gladdened that his friend lives and is safe. "I would like that, Diamond. And no need to worry, she is my good friend and I'd never hurt her. Well, we haven't known each other long, but she's the only friend I have left, and I don't want to lose her too. I don't wish to presume too much, great Diamond, but could I possibly speak to Outer-Point Master Baggodon about securing her release? If the knowledge I have is worth trading for?"

The demon smiles in a way that seems to John as if he is suppressing a laugh. "I can implore my master, but it all depends on what you know and how beneficial it is to this circle. Now, let me send for some refresh-ments. We have some Forsaken at Second Point, and they're all beta magals too. I'm sure they have something you'll find palatable. There's plenty of clean water, free of Nether, in the scab-house where they stay if nothing better to drink can be found. SCAB! SCAB!"

At this call a Silver demon in ragged robes enters and kowtows. *Not the old one that licks my face,* John notices.

"Bring my usual and get from the beta magals a sampling of food and drink for one of their kind. And bring some magal water. Robes too. Not scab robes. Any other that fits our guest. And return our guest's posses-sions. Go," commands the Diamond to the Silver.

After the door is closed, the Diamond walks to the table saying, "Come. Join me. Sit." John sits across from the demon. The demon looks too large for the chair and table, and John far too small.

"Tell me, is it common on your world for cultivators to befriend mindless beasts?" asks the demon.

"Yes, but cultivation is new to my world. Even the people I was born to so long ago would raise wolf pups as pets." John keeps back the information Amber can transform into a woman. He isn't sure if it would help or hurt his case, or help or hurt Amber, so believes withholding this information is the best course for now.

Things are silent for a moment as the demon seems to ponder. "I didn't believe the reports. I thought the strong were hiding. I followed the portal for months. I couldn't exit the portal but when I poked through, I could feel that the strange tech of your world wasn't run off essence. And no crystals drop off your kind. This circle finally gets a chance at our own magal world again and it's so poor as to be nearly useless for anything but staging real invasions to useful worlds. Ukaraaz thought I'd continue following the portal after, but I won't waste my time. If a Gold can't handle a world full of Woods, it's better if he dies. And there's three Golds and three portals there."

The demon stops for a moment and yells, "SCAB! SCAB!" A Bronze in ragged robe enters the room and kowtows. "Where are my refreshments?"

The Bronze replies, "Coming, Master. Soon."

"Go." The door clicks as the Bronze closes it. The Diamond's eyes never leave John during his exchange with the Bronze. "Now, John, tell me everything. About your world, and why cultivation is new to it. About your strange abilities, especially why you thought you could bite into someone of my tier. What were you thinking?"

John tells the demon much, and learns much in return too. He is certain the demon left out, or twisted, the most interesting and useful bits of information, as he himself did also.

In John's long life he has met many, many powerful people. Some were powerful due to luck, some due to birth, some due to their skill at arms or physical prowess, and some due to their exceptional minds. He's never once met any man, let alone a king, he considered an exceptional fighter with an exceptional mind.

Many stories often claim great kings were both brilliant fighters and brilliant strategists. John's met many of these great kings, and is even himself the great king of many of these stories. One thing John knows to be true – nearly all the great kings with keen minds were smart enough to know fighting wasn't their forte, and surrounded themselves with loyal men good at it, as they themselves never would be.

Some kings tried, such as Alexander the Great. In John's opinion, he was a middling fighter, but for a king, certainly brave and doughty, and willing to risk himself and lead from the front. But being a doughty fighter compared to other kings does not make one an exceptional fighter, just as being smart for an exceptional fighter does not make one comparable to those with truly exceptional minds.

John is not certain if the Diamond has an exceptional mind, but the giant demon is crafty and cunning, and certainly an extraordinarily dangerous fighter.

There are few guards in the town and castle for many reasons. Most of the town's forces were sent to invade Earth. The town and castle, called Second Point, is one of five such towns belonging to a sect, which demons call a circle, and all demons within belong to the sect. Demon culture has little crime, and demons mainly behave as they were created to. But the main reason there are so few guards is the Diamond himself, as he is a powerful deterrent.

The information on scabs John finds very interesting. The NetherRealm was created by the ancient old ones to be a place where fighters advance quickly, and demons made to advance and fight, and only to advance and fight. A great deficiency was found in demon culture when the Forsaken War was lost - all demons were fighters. They took weapons and resources through invasions, but had no craftsmen or support of their own. They can't enslave others, as all others are either Forsaken and allies, or Favored and enemies they must kill. The answer to this dilemma was to make servants of their own kind.

These servants were forced to do what demons weren't created to do: craft weapons and armors, runecrafting, alchemy, and such professions, as well as serving, cleaning, clerking, and the like. Demons doing such tasks is a great shame, and a shame that covers an open wound, like a scab.

All start out as demons, and all are demons through Wood and Copper tiers. At Bronze a demon earns a name and is thus chosen to be a real demon, or shows weakness or cowardice or balks at orders, or has the wrong affinities, and is thus forced to be a scab.

John is certain any such system would be abused, and scabs made by just annoying the wrong demon and the like. Scabs are not allowed names, and not allowed to train and fight. Scabs are the only demons to regularly grow so old as to become useless and killed for it, as ascending the Tree of Life extends lifespan, and scabs advance slowly.

John believes this is sad, and he feels sorry for these unlucky demons, and then must remind himself what demons are doing on Earth, and how they treated the peasants under his protection.

It is the demon's job to kill magals. John sees it as his job to kill demons. He knows he is not really a guest in this keep, and is a prisoner, just not to the same extent his friend Amber is.

The structure of Circle Xakariz was given to John, and all of the five points are commanded by a Diamond, and each Diamond is supposed to command three Gold captains commanding nine Silvers each, one being a lieutenant. When a Gold captain of Second Point advances to Platinum, they leave to represent their point in the outer circle. The circle fell on hard times long ago, and has since been on the decline, so the only Gold captain Second Point has is currently on Earth, along with all Silver chosen but one.

Scab advancement is greatly restricted, and if any scab at Second Point was allowed to advance to Gold, they would have to move to the inner or outer sect.

To save Amber and escape, John must foil many Bronze cultivators, one Silver chosen, many Silver scabs, and a Diamond six whole tiers above his own. And though John does not possess the exceptional mind some old stories claim he does, he can be crafty and cunning too, and he is proud of the escape plan he thought of, and even prouder the plan seems to be working so well.

# CHAPTER 36
# SUNLIGHT IS SAID TO BE THE BEST OF DISINFECTANTS

There is no easy way for John to tell day from night in the NetherRealm. The sky, blanketed in strange, wild, and colorful clouds, merely goes from slightly darker to slightly lighter. If he was forced to guess, he'd guess he's been in the NetherRealm for a week or so, as time is considered by Earth standards.

John enjoys the lack of sunlight, and not needing to think about calcification or having his strength and speed sapped. After so long alive, it is hard for him to forget what not worrying about the sun is like.

After John had his first long conversation with the Second-Point Master, he was given his own room, though he was asked not to leave the room, and ordered not to leave the castle's grounds, and to always avoid the other magals, as they would not go easy on a Wood. He was also given small beasts to drain, though he had to pull out his broken teeth, so they'd grow back fast and whole again.

John was also given a new [Title] by Diamond Garioch, and instructed on how to make it his active [Title] himself, without the assistance of the NCS. The new [Title] somehow lets others know he is of the ptagmog, even though he is a magal.

Though not certain, John believes ptagmog means something along the lines of 'made to fight the Favored.' There is a small difference between the general Forsaken faction and ptagmogs, as being Forsaken can be a choice, and not a matter of birth or creation.

As far as John can understand things, he is seen as a g'athu would be seen by demons, and held in a higher opinion by both demons and g'athu than Forsaken magals, or would be if John were higher tiered than Wood.

While meditating in his room, John hears a knock on his door. "Enter," he responds. The old face-licking Silver enters, and then bows at the waist. "Wood John, are you ready to be escorted to the Natural?"

John stands. "Certainly, Proxy Scab." Calling scabs master would be scandalous, and John feels more comfortable using titles for everyone not a close friend. Mister translates to master, and every other title John can think of translates to the meaning of intent, from various forms of elder to worker, and none can be used without breaking social norms. The least scandalous he can use as a respectful honorific is proxenos, which translates to proxy.

John stands, gets his sword, and then places it in the sash around his waist. All his clothes were destroyed, but everything else he received back, including the small bag of colored crystals, along with new comfortable robes of light green. He isn't supposed to walk around armed as a guest without express approval, but unless the Diamond complains, he would rather ask for forgiveness than permission.

The old demon silently leads John through the castle, John knowing he'll get little information out of the scab, and only make the scab uncomfortable by asking any questions, or by making small talk. So John is very surprised when his escort stops in an empty hallway and turns to him nervously. "Pardon this one for asking, but do you seriously count the Natural as a friend, Wood John?"

"I do. My only friend too. All the others are dead. Or do not understand friendship."

"But it is a beast, lower than even a scab. Surely being friends with such lowers your standing. Why do so as a Wood? This one knows you can't detect Naturals at your tier, but wouldn't you have other friends of your own kind if you didn't befriend beasts?"

John wonders if this is some ploy to play on his sympathies. *If it is, I don't care. And answering this can't possibly hurt me much.* "I've had many,

many friends throughout my life. You know I've lived long, correct?" The scab raises its head, the demon gesture for yes. "My mentor told me I've lived about four thousand standard years. Do you use that measurement? Standard years?"

"Everyone does, Wood John."

"I've had more friends than I can remember, and pets too. Amber, the Natural, saved my life twice. What kind of man would I be if I didn't consider such actions as deserving of real friendship?

"Now, my turn for a question. What do you think of the deal I'm making for her release and safety? Will your master's master agree? If my knowledge proves to be valuable enough?"

The old scab lowers its head sharply. "Please follow this one, Wood John."

John didn't expect a truthful answer, astonished the scab gave such a clear indicator, and chalks it up to the question taking the Silver by surprise. He follows silently towards the room and cell Amber is imprisoned in.

The first time John visited Amber, he was escorted by Garioch himself, and the meeting went about as well as could be expected. Amber was back in her fox form, and chirped excitedly at John from her cage for a few moments before ignoring him and returning to her meditations.

Amber was given many crystals to cultivate with, as the higher she rises, the more potent the medicine can be made of her. He was also told Amber changed from a bear to a frog, and stayed as a frog for weeks before turning into a fox. *However weeks are measured here.* The demons have no word that translates for bear and fox, but have one for frog.

Strangely enough, though Amber entered the portal just a short time before John, she's been here for well over a month longer than he has.

Two Bronze guards are stationed outside Amber's room. Entering, four additional Bronze are inside it. Supposedly, Amber killed a Copper guard and nearly escaped, and they increased her guards from two to six.

Garioch was very surprised Amber has three shapes, as such is an extreme rarity for a Natural. John is unwilling to divulge that she actually has at least four, and one of them a sentient form too.

As John enters the room, Amber stops meditating and rises from the ground, chirping and spinning excitedly. John doesn't bother trying to pet her, as he knows she'll move away. Instead, he sits on his haunches. "Amber, tonight we'll find out if the knowledge I have will be enough to secure your freedom. If not, I have some other ideas. I will not give up on you. We're a team, and I owe you a great debt."

Amber pushes against the cage, making eyes. She then lifts her leg and starts to urinate on John's foot.

"Great gods below! Again! Ewww, you try my good nature. That's twice you pissed on me. Once more and you will pay, fox-form or not. You will pay!"

In response, Amber trots pompously away, and lays on the ground, paws on crystals, cultivating.

"I know you heard me. Never again!"

*Stupid, ungrateful foxes,* John thinks, as he stomps out of the room. He stops to let the old scab catch up, and lead the way back to his far more comfortable cell.

***

"Come in, John," says Diamond Garioch.

John enters the Diamond's room, surprised to see the table moved, and a ritual circle covering a large part of the floor. The ritual to gain the power doesn't require one. He kowtows and the giant demon waves him up.

"Master Baggodon couldn't make it. No need to be aggravated. We've communicated, and I am authorized to grant you possession of the Natural if what you say is true. And works. I don't believe you are lying, but my master is always cautious and demands you answer some questions while under a compulsion. I hope you don't mind."

John does the best he can to maintain a calm and relaxed disposition, and hopes the Diamond didn't notice his heart spike. "Not at all, Diamond Garioch."

"Good. Please, come sit here."

John is directed into the ritual circle, sits, and watches the demon prepare. The Diamond writes on five pieces of paper, then applies various oils to John and the papers, and then burns each paper on five different candles as he infuses the circle with magical essence, chanting all the while. The demon then turns over a strange hourglass, and as soon as it hits the circle all the built-up essence rushes into John, and his mind fizzes and pops.

John is unsure of what happens next, as he loses a little time. When he gains his faculties back, he hears the end of a question, "...you're certain?"

"Yes," John replies, trying to maintain the dazed act, hoping he didn't give the game up somehow during the lost time.

"And this only works if someone's soul is red like mine is?"

"Yes."

"And it is easy to tell?"

"Yes."

"And once I have this power, you're certain I'll be able to see souls and all that you've described? Increase my strength and speed by draining others of life essence? Even Woods?"

"Yes."

"I think it is too convenient of a coincidence that my soul is supposedly red, and only red souls can be offered this power. I know you can't lie now, so you must believe my soul is red. Is there any proof you can give me that can soothe my doubts?"

"No. It is red. I can see it."

"And I'm the only demon with a red soul you've seen here? Even when we looked out over all of Second Point? You're certain?"

"Yes, regarding red souls here. I did see another demon with a red soul in the army I fought on my world. It was a Wood, and I killed him."

"It just seems too convenient I have a red soul and no other demon does you can perform the ritual on first so I can ensure it's safe. Are there any hidden dangers you haven't told me about?"

John hesitates for a moment, almost saying no, but changes his mind. "Yes."

"I knew it. Out with it. What are they? All of them. Tell me all the hidden dangers. Be detailed and leave nothing out."

John tries to force his heart to slow, and hopes the Diamond doesn't notice anything amiss. "There is a risk this ritual will fail. Like the NCS translation, intent matters. This is a power intended to be passed from master to student, elder to youth, strong to weak. You are much stronger than I am, and neither of us intends to have such a relationship."

"Why have you never mentioned this?"

"I feared you'd think I was tricking you, and I'd lose my best chance of securing my friend's release."

"Tricking me how? In what way?"

"To ensure the ritual is a success you must gift me some items proving your intent to honor the relationship this power requires. At the least there needs to be an item representing death, one representing life, one representing respect, and one representing submission. The more powerful and valuable the items, the greater the chance of success. The gift of submission must be a bag, a spatial bag, to symbolize you will follow me until you've learned what I can teach you, and are ready to go off on your own.

"I will also need gifts for you. I only have two suitable. The crystal of a Silver symbolizing how I give you power. My sword to symbolize I arm you and see to your safety. I need a compass and level to represent my intent to teach you all the knowledge of heaven and earth. I will also need to gift you something you can feed on. Any small beast will do."

John, keeping his eyes unfocused and looking far off, fights the urge to look at the Diamond and see his response to this information. After a long pause, the Diamond replies, "Spatial storage? You said your world had no runes or cultivators until our invasion started. How does it know of spatial storage devices?"

John curses this slip, but recovers quickly. "The strange technology of my world allows for the creation of such devices."

"You said you were the most powerful on your planet. Why do you not have such a device then?"

"As I told you, I awoke far away from all my possessions. Far away from any village and people. All I came here with I scavenged after awakening."

"What happens if the ritual fails?"

"I'm not sure. I've never seen one fail. Not for someone with a red soul."

"What happens if we do the gifts but don't have the right intent in our inner being?"

"I'm not certain, but I truly believe it will work. The gifts represent intent."

"But you don't know for certain? Intent cannot be faked. I cannot pretend you will be my master. I cannot see you as my superior."

"You do see me as more knowledgeable than you regarding this power, and how it works. In this way I will be your master, and you will be my student. Our intent for this aspect must be clear, and it is. The gifts will do the rest."

John hears the demon stand and begin pacing. "I intend to take these 'gifts' back as soon as the ritual is completed. Does this intent change anything?"

"No."

"Why did you not mention your bracers as a possible gift? They would symbolize the bestowment of power far greater than the crystal of a Silver."

"I can't remove them."

The demon laughs. "Well, I could, but fair enough. I'll have them soon anyways. So, with the gifts, and as long as I intend to have you teach me of this power, what chances do you give the ritual of succeeding?"

"It will succeed."

There is a long pause, and John nearly looks at the demon. Finally, the demon asks, "Do you wish me harm, John?"

"Yes."

"Ha. Of course you do. As I do my master, and Ukaraaz wishes the same to me. I can't fault you for it. Sometimes you're not as stupid as you seem. But I believe you did not tell me of the gifts and the risk of the ritual failing because you hope the ritual causes me harm. Is this true John? Do you want the ritual to harm me?"

"No. The ritual succeeding, and your gratitude for it, is the best chance of saving my friend."

The demon laughs again. "What about you? What about saving yourself?"

"I follow the Way of Death, as my father did, and his father before him. As my people did. I'm already dead. I can only awaken from this dream."

"What a stupid and shortsighted belief."

"No, it isn't."

"Oh, John, it is. I believed something similar once. All lower-tiered demons do. It's how we were made to think. Thankfully, ascension allows us to rise above such nonsensical beliefs. It is a great belief for the fodder to have, though. Whom is this mentor you mentioned to your scab escort earlier?"

John is taken aback by the abrupt turn, and hopes the pause before answering isn't too long. "The avatar of my NCS, Pixie."

"Is there any way I could lose this power after attaining it? Such as killing you?"

"No."

The demon paces for a while before the next question comes. "Have you ever lied to me about anything?"

"Yes."

The demon chuckles before stating his next demand. "Tell me everything you've ever said to me you consider to be a lie or partial truth."

"I was insincere with my apology after I attacked you. I don't believe I am a guest of yours. I..." John continues to list petty lies until he is stopped.

John is asked many more questions about many topics. When the hourglass runs dry, John feels a great tugging in his head, and some essence runs out of it as he slumps to the floor. He was worried his ability to shake off mental effects wouldn't work, since the only fully powered one directed at him that wasn't scaled down nearly made him catatonic. That spell was cast by one of the witches right after he killed their sister, before they joined, while they were still only Bronze. This ritual was performed by a Diamond, and one not holding back, determined to find the truth of things.

Though John is spent and nearly unconscious, if the demon looked closely, he'd notice a small smile on John's lips.

# CHAPTER 37
# POWER

Second-Point Master Garioch dismisses the scabs. "Before we begin, you do realize I expect these 'gifts' returned, correct?"

"Of course, Diamond."

"Good. These are legacy items and require Exalted to function properly, like your bracers. They're extremely valuable so should more than satisfy the requirement for any symbolism. We have the beast to drain," Garioch lifts a small cage holding a vicious creature looking like a cross between a lizard and rat. "Oh. Here is the compass and level for you to gift me with."

John takes the items from the demon's massive hand. "Apologies, Diamond, I should have been clearer. We need a circle compass. Is this...well, look at that, the bubble in the line there. I see how this works. But for the correct symbolism, it should be a square level. Shaped like this." John holds his palm out, making an L with thumb and index finger. "The compass and square symbolize heaven and earth, and all knowledge, so we should get this part right."

"How does a compass and level represent heaven and earth?"

"Heaven is the round sky above, and earth the square land under our feet."

"That is one of the dumbest things I've ever heard, and since my forces are deployed without me, I have to deal with Bronze children half the day."

"Dumb or not, it's part of the ritual, Diamond. Does this compass work on this world? I don't see any fixed position in the sky to navigate with."

"SCAB! SCAB! Not you, I need a Silver scab." The Diamond turns back to John. "No, the Nether was made to prevent invasions. Magals can't navigate through this whole plane or any of our worlds. The Oboro is fixed, but we don't use it to navigate. Spend enough time here and the Nether gets in magals and makes them more like us. Naturals are affected much faster.

"In fact, you should be dead, or at least deathly ill. Yet you cultivate the Nether and are fine. Your constitution is hardy. Some Bronze of magal races can handle the Nether just fine, but most must be Silver to last here for any length of time. This is one of the reasons I want this strange power of yours. The magals in the scab house are here specifically to be infused with Nether and gain some of our traits. I'd love to see how you handle the fog. It makes even Silver magals retch."

During Garioch's explanation the old face-licking scab enters the room, kowtows, and waits patiently. Garioch turns to him. "Do you know what a circle compass is? And a square level?"

"This one does, Master."

"Good. Bring me one of each. And hurry."

"This one obeys, Master," replies the scab as he stands and exits.

The Diamond lifts a very large black axe covered in red runes. "So, for the gift of death I have my axe, called Dead Maker. The first Second-Point Master won this during this circle's first invasion. Back then we were a much stronger force. Hopefully your planet will be the first step in regaining our old status."

The axe looks almost like a toy in the giant demon's hand, but the haft is about as long as a Dane-style pale-axe can get before being considered a pole-weapon, with a head larger than any John has ever seen. In his youth, small hand-axes were the main weapon used once all spears were spent, and he is extremely skilled with axes, but prefers swords.

Sword fighting techniques constantly evolved, and different styles of fighting emerged as swords grew longer and heavier with the invention of heavier armor up to full articulated plate, and then lighter again, favoring unarmored speed and reach and skill with fencing-style swords.

John enjoys fighting with the axe, he enjoys fighting without any qualifiers at all, but few societies throughout time, once the cities of that society hit a certain size, put their focus and skill towards the axe as a weapon of war, seeing it as a tool of peasants, brutes, and the unskilled, though that is far from the truth.

John credits the sword and his keen interest in continuing to master various new styles with keeping his mind going for so long, and Sublime Sunshine renewed his interest with vigor upon telling him most of his knowledge is not up to the scratch, and he will get new [Skills] as he gains more knowledge and experience fighting with and against magical essence enhanced attacks, defenses, and manifestations.

The Diamond places the axe down and lifts a misshapen metal rectangle. "This is my armor. It is to symbolize the gift of life. You've probably never seen this. Here, watch."

The demon puts his palm in front of the metal rectangle, a blue stream flows out of the palm and into the metal. The rectangle breaks apart, and pieces of it fly at the Diamond, seeming to grow much larger as they do, covering him from head to toe in gleaming, dark, fully articulated, and very heavy armor, with perfect patination, and beautifully crafted inlays.

A moment later all the pieces fly back and reform the rectangle.

"Darkness, Adversity, and Nightmare! How I love this armor! This set is called Bulwark. Even I have an issue keeping it imbued for long. Does this word translate? Damascening?"

"Yes, Diamond. I'm surprised you know it. Its root is an old city from my world, Dumahsq, and describes their inlay method. Used in two ways, true damascening, and false."

The demon stares at John for a moment. "Of course I've never heard of your city. It just means the method translated specifically. The method is older than the Nether. I was just curious since your crafters have no access to essence or runes. Or had, I should say.

"Now," Garioch twists a ring off his finger and lays it atop the metal rectangle of armor, "this isn't a bag, but is a storage device. The only one I have access to. Since few scabs are allowed to advance to the next Tree, and this circle has none, we can't create our own. We get ours through invasion and trading with the g'athu, but they rip us off. Don't put this on. If you even think about putting this ring on, I promise this – you will become my property, and I will torture you for all of eternity. I do not grow bored easily. Do you understand?"

"Yes, Diamond."

"Repeat what I said about the ring."

"Do not even think about putting the ring on, Diamond."

"Good. Please don't test me on this. Just removing it is causing me anxiety. Don't toy around."

"Yes, Diamond."

"Okay," Garioch pulls out a very large, dark-grey cloak, "I had a hard time with the gift symbolizing respect. Acts, not items, symbolize respect. Then I remembered how you snuck up behind me while I cultivated. That took great courage, and I respect your attempt on my life. Ha! A Wood attacking a Diamond. What fool would ever even imagine such!

"Demons that specialize in stealth usually get what this cloak does permanently from an enhancement, what you call Perks. It masks your essence from vision enhancements based on your tier and stealth ability. Does this work as a gift?"

John smiles, and wishes it could also mask his heartbeat. "It works perfectly, Diamond."

"Where is that old scab? Well, anything else to cover while we wait?"

"You have something to cut your wrists with?"

Garioch stares at John again before replying. "I'm a Diamond."

*I guess that means yes,* John thinks. "The only other issue I can think of is you'll have to kneel, if that's okay with you. I may have to use a chair even still. If we grasp hands, I don't believe our wrists will come close to touching. So we'll just press wrists instead of grasping hands. Try to hold your arms still. I remember my Lilitu tried to jerk free once the visions started, especially experiencing the cold-dark. I won't be able to stop you if you jerk your arms. I won't even be holding them, just pressing my wrists. It could interrupt the ritual."

"I'll bind our wrists together with essence. Don't…" Garioch stops as the door opens and the old scab returns with a circle compass and a square level.

"Stand. Give them to my guest and then retire for the day."

The old scab silently obeys.

"Are you ready, John?"

"Yes, Diamond."

"Good."

The ritual begins, John dismayed regarding the statement about binding the arms, believing he overplayed his hand, and berates himself for going into such details, causing such an outcome.

First, gifts are given and received. John fumbles through this part, as he recently invented it. Next, John slits his wrist on Dead Maker's sharp bit. The demon kneels, and John stands on a chair so Garioch can drink of his blood. Next, John slits his other wrist while Garioch does the same to his own, though John misses the method of how.

John gets back on the chair, and both press their bleeding wrists into each other's, and the Diamond wraps a strand of essence around both arms, holding them together.

John is curious to see the next part. Normal humans are turned into mindless hoppers, while those with red souls receive visions and a choice. Though John lied about Garioch having a red soul, he is curious to see what will happen to a being as powerful as a Diamond. By his reckoning, there are three possible outcomes, and only one in which John completely wins, and the Diamond completely loses.

While he has the time, John studies the magical essence wrapped around his arm. He thinks he can slip his hands, and hopes this is true, or he is in real trouble.

Some time passes, John's heart thumping loudly, studying the face of the master of Second Point. Finally, the Diamond's eyes fly open. The two eyes, normally reddish and orange, as if containing fire, but greatly dulled, and angry, now look panicked, and cracked.

Humans turning into hoppers have completely bloodshot eyes at this point, and John hopes the cracking is the same as bloodshot for humans, but with the strange thick energy demons have instead of blood.

Diamond Garioch starts to cough, and John hears splattering on the carpet, and feels a liquid land on his face and chest, and knows it's the invisible demon blood, and frantically tries to free his arms. He manages to slip one hand free right as Garioch starts jerking around, and would have been torn apart, or had his arms ripped off, if he were a mere moment slower. He wraps his legs around the demon's arm binding his still, and pushes his hand and wrist forward to slide it down and out, then drops to the floor, rolling away from the flailing and spasming Garioch.

John watches the demon with one eye while casing the room. As soon as the flailing giant is away from the axe and armor and sword, John rushes to the items, and equips the ring. The ring shrinks down to fit his finger, but he feels no magic, or any binding or strangeness. He taps the ring to the axe and armor, and the items don't enter the ring. *Shit. This is how the Sublime said these devices work. Why couldn't it be a bag? I know how bags work. How do you get items in and out of a small ring?*

Trying to figure out how magic items work with a giant Diamond-tiered demon flailing around madly is not a great idea, so John grabs the giant axe and manages to lift the metal rectangle, though it is much heavier than it looks to be, and moves the items a safe distance away.

For most of John's life, the word for bandit and the word for soldier have been synonymous. At some point in most cultures, the word for soldier, or sworn-man, changed to some form of the word servant, in an attempt to get the peasants to see the soldiers robbing them as good servants of the realm, and not bandits at all. Sometimes it even worked.

The line between sworn-men and bandits was always thin, the only difference between the two names being a lord directing the actions of the former, and a leader the latter. Oftentimes, successful bandit groups would swear allegiance to a king or lord, and the bandits became sworn-men in the blink of an eye, or a lord would be killed, and the sworn-men became bandits in the blink of an eye.

Most of the combat John engaged in as a youth was raiding neighbors, or fighting off raids from neighbors. It made no matter if the neighbors were sworn to the same king. They had stuff to steal, so it was stolen. Fights were with clubs, and neither party sought to kill. Capture and ransom were a big part of the game. Things didn't get deadly during raids, unless there was starvation and famine, then all bets were off. There were constant wars and real battles, but only a handful of times a year, whereas raiding happened multiple times weekly, and was how troops were trained for battle.

As much as John enjoys fighting and battle, as much as combat flows in his blood, so does he enjoy banditry, and it flows in his blood the same. His plan is to rob the Diamond blind, and take everything he can carry that isn't nailed down. A task he hoped would be much easier with the storage device. Since he'll now have to carry what he steals, and the heavy block of armor seems like the greatest of treasures, he revises his plan.

John looks at the Diamond. Any normal human would be long dead by now, only to rise in a few days with a false life, and a violent mind, and a vicious hunger for flesh, hopping around as they attack all that lives, doughty foes that take much effort to kill. He hopes he is not around when the Diamond rises as one, but first it must fall dead, hopefully leaving crystals John can take too.

Garioch is still going strong, no longer coughing, madly jerking his limbs and thrashing around, blue and yellow essence now pushing out of him at various locations. Then the Diamond starts screaming. Terrible screams, and loud, causing John worry. No human ever screamed. All humans cough some, jerk around a little, and fall dead.

With the screaming alerting those outside the room something is amiss, John considers himself pressed for time now, angering him. He hoped he would be able to at least take Garioch's crystal, and he can't even drain the demon with him flailing around so. *Such a waste*, he thinks.

Ripping a banner from the wall and throwing on the floor, John then quickly searches the bureau and a dresser, finding nothing of value, not even a cheap trinket, he grabs a large dagger or short sword from a display, as well as the smallest sword he sees, though the sword is still massive, the size of a greatsword. He then darts in to retrieve Munashi's sword and his dark-yellow crystal 'gift' from the floor near the mad demon.

Looking around, he sees little left he can steal. Then his eyes fall on the two robes on armor stands, a thing he still believes to be queer. He removes them. He places the block of armor on the banner, and throws everything on it, and ties it as a bindle on the long axe-haft. He can fit everything in his bindle, besides the swords, so puts the dagger-sword and Munashi's sword in his sash, and must leave the greatsword behind.

*Hopefully this ring is filled with better swords. And many other treasures too. Now, I just need to rescue Amber and escape.*

John smiles as he heads to the door, putting on the cloak. He hopes the cloak works without some sort of activation, as he feels nothing. He crouches and begins to sneak, hoping the cloak is working, but not sure how to tell if it is. His heart sinks as the door bangs open, the old Silver scab entering, walking tall, his mien anything but that of a humble servant, looking right at John. "What have you done to Master?"

# CHAPTER 38
## A FORTUITOUS DAY

Bindle on shoulder, John's heart spikes as he faces the old Silver scab, his mind furiously racing to come up with an excuse that the Silver will accept, allowing him to pass unmolested. He thinks it may come to battle, so he prepares to drop the bindle and draw Munashi's sword, and he feverishly prays scabs really can't fight, or really are not allowed to fight, as a Silver's manifestations would mean his quick death or capture.

"I…" John starts to say, but is bowled over from a wild release of essence by the raging and mad Diamond behind him.

He starts to get his feet back when a tremendous pressure bears down on him, the undirected pressure of a Diamond's soul unveiled. *Why won't he just die?*

Even though the pressure isn't focused on John, it still holds him stronger than the directed pressure of a Silver.

John feels hands lift him, and he fumbles around for his bindle, but fails to grab it. He notices the old scab has it in his free hand, dragging behind him, as John is carried out of the Garioch's quarters.

Outside the room, three Bronze scabs are held fast to the floor, groaning in pain. The door is closed, which eases the pressure a little, and the old scab says, "I'll be back soon."

John assumes he'd be put down, and the old demon would go back into the room to assist his master, but he is instead carried down the hall. Even when far outside the range of the unveiled soul of Diamond Garioch, he continues to be carried. He then assumes he is being carried to imprisonment, or the sole Silver chosen remaining at Second Point, and prepares for battle, testing the old scab's skin to see if it's as hard as the Silver demon's skin he fought outside the witches' house.

It isn't.

As he prepares to bite down, the old scab stops, and places John on his feet, bowing at the waist as he offers the axe with bindle. John hesitates a moment before accepting it, unsure of what is transpiring.

"Please tell this one Second-Point Master Garioch will die," says the old scab.

John's heart fills with sympathy for the old demon. In his long life he has been enslaved, and imprisoned, both many times, but the choice was usually his own to allow, and all but twice he could escape with ease whenever he so wished.

There are different types of slavery, some not so bad and common, and some so severe and depraved it twists a man's soul, and breaks the mind to the point where the slave is no longer human, and the slave's self is dependent on the cruelties directed at him, and cannot function outside of the only brutal relationship his mind knows, and adapted to. The slave brought so low as to be little more than a beast in a man's body, broken and devoid of spirit.

John assumed the old scab was one such man, or demon, and he is cheered to now know this isn't true, and the old scab managed to retain a spark of his spirit, and a thirst for vengeance, and the desire to see at least one of those treating him so poorly brought lower than himself, as all men should. And scabs too.

"I won't lie. I don't know for certain. If he were a human, and also not Diamond, yes. Most definitely. What is your name, friend?"

"This one has no name. Scabs are not named."

"Even among your own?"

"It is not allowed."

"It is hard being friends with someone without a name. Pick one or I'll give you one."

"It is not allowed."

John sighs. "No one gave me permission to try and kill your master. Live in misery by the rules others say you must, or live free doing as you please, and even if your life be far shorter, you'll die far more content, with your chest held out, head held high, and a smile on your lips."

"But this one won't be reborn as a chosen. I'll be reborn as an even lesser being."

"I have the perfect name for you. Hubaba. If we are reborn, burn as brightly as you can in this life, and gird your soul against despair, and feed it only adversity and dead enemies, enough the gods notice, and your soul becomes so brilliant you can only be reborn as a king. Now, being named is an important moment, but they'll be searching for me soon, and I must rescue my friend, and escape with her, so we must hurry."

The old demon looks down sharply before saying, "There is no need to rush, Wood John. Zongreth is the only Silver chosen left at Second Point and he won't be back for many days. And when he is back from patrol, he would never approach Master Garioch's private quarters unless summoned. And no scab will enter uninvited, only this one would dare, as this one is the lead scab. If this one's master dies, none will know of his death for a long while. Unless his superiors check in on him, of course.

"Even then you will not be looked at. You are Wood. None would ever suspect a Wood of killing a Diamond. This one strongly suggests not getting caught with that legacy weapon, though. You have a Title proclaiming you are of the ptagmog. You have more liberty than this one does, even at Wood. You can stay here for as long as you like. Just avoid the magals in the scab house and you'll be safe.

"In fact, this one is the best alchemist at Second Point. If you want, this one can create a pill of the Natural. It will take some time, but this one can say he was ordered to do so by this one's master. Wood John will have to wait until this one can confirm the death of this one's master first. If this one's master does live, running would be futile. He will find you. He is Diamond. This one recommends waiting patiently until the result of this attempt is known."

John is surprised at such a long and well-articulated speech by the old and reticent demon, but saddened Hubaba failed to either understand, or believe, his earlier statements regarding his friend, Amber.

John places his hand on the tall demon's shoulder. "Hubaba, Amber is my friend. I would never hurt her. I would never hurt any friend. And I consider you a friend now too. Escape with us. If Garioch lives, we'll die free, spitting in the face of our betters, defiant to the end. And stop saying 'this one.' Say 'I' and 'me' like everyone else does, or at least do so around me."

"So, you truly are friends with a mindless beast. It's hard to believe. Old habits are hard to break, so this one will continue to talk as scabs must. And this one won't escape with you. That is too much. This one is too close to the end. This one will spend what time is left doing as this one always has. This one can help you, as you're of the ptagmog. This one assumes you want to go back to your world. Through the portal? It is not expected to open again for months and months. It cannot be predicted with any accuracy. Please follow, Wood John, and let this one help you plan. And please refrain from using the name you gave this one in front of any others, or act too familiar towards this one."

John smiles and follows, thinking this day has been very fortuitous, hoping his great luck holds out longer.

\*\*\*

There was a creature of legend so feared his likeness on a door would keep both gods and demons away. From afar he could be heard approaching, always making the same frightening noises while searching for victims, "Hu ba ba! Hu ba ba!" As was often done back then, the creature was named after the noises it made. All knew to turn tail and run from giant Hubaba.

From a kingdom neighboring John's, a slave led a revolt and became king. He was feared by all, enemies as well as his own subjects. So feared people named him Hubaba after the creature of legend. He was a vicious fighter, and hard to kill, surviving many assassination attempts. King Hubaba didn't have the forces to resist Kish, so made an alliance with John.

The old demon, newly named Hubaba, enjoys hearing the story of his namesake, and John leaves it at that, since the story does not end well for King Hubaba, and he had many bad qualities he doesn't want the new Hubaba to know about, or have the two share a similar fate.

King Hubaba was treated foully as a slave, and John believes being treated so warped the man's mind and heart. He would kill over little, and enjoyed being so feared by his own subjects.

John heard of a new great ruler of Oruk, an immortal man strong as a god, and knew Ahn was back from his travels, and he went to visit him. Instead of welcoming John, Ahn closed the gates, causing John to worry. He waited outside the city for long, wondering if he somehow caused his master offense. Then Ahn ambushed him, and a great battle ensued, but not a serious one.

Ahn had a strange sense of humor, and he loved playing games no one else saw the humor in. After their battle, the two men feasted their reunion, and John ignored the city he ruled for too long. Then news reached John that King Hubaba conquered John's city, and ruled there now too.

John and Ahn left to put King Hubaba in his place, and did so by cutting him into many pieces.

Many, many years later, John heard this story, though much had changed from the real events, as always happened with such tales. For that part of the story, Ahn was called Bilgames, and John was called Lord of the Good Place. Later, John ruled Oruk, and he is then the Bilgames of that part of the old story. Even his Lilitu was added to the story of Bilgames after the fact.

John first heard this story on return to the Agade territories, and the Assyris translated Bilgames as 'Hero King,' but in old Suma should mean "The People's Hero.' A strange thing to call Ahn, John believes, as he was not a good king, and was not fond of any of the people he ruled. Neither was John a good king, but he tried to make things good for his people by protecting them, and appointing good clerks and priests to rule, as the daily minutia of rulership of large cities and empires held little appeal to him. Hold little appeal to him still.

John is glad the old scab seems so pleased with his new name, and impressed that his namesake went from slave to king.

Regardless of what Hubaba believes, John wants to leave as soon as he can. After John and Hubaba quickly finish planning, collecting supplies, and retrieving Amber, Hubaba summons Muzaran, the Bronze chosen who led John's escort to Second Point, and tells him Master Garioch ordered him to return John to where they exited from the portal.

If Diamond Garioch dies, he doesn't for long, unlike humans who rise as undead hoppers days later.

Soon after John departs, the master of Second Point goes on a rampage around the castle, killing all in his path, and then does the same in the town. Luckily, the demon is unable to perform any complex manifestations, so his destruction is contained to his immediate vicinity.

The way demons navigate the Nether is by natural instinct and a manifestation, and John has no chance of learning or performing the manifestation without open meridians and skill at casting without runes, and it is extremely taboo for a demon to teach the manifestation to a non-demon, so no demon would teach John regardless.

John further studies the flora and fauna, and all he can, as Muzaran once again escorts John through the Nether. Once delivered to roughly the same area as they exited the portal, John drains Muzaran, and pockets his crystals.

As to the fixed point Garioch claimed was in the sky, John struggles to find it, and Hubaba knew nothing of it. Landscapes can't be seen far out in the Nether, and the lack of stars or moon or sun makes any form of orientation a further impossibility.

After great study and effort, John finally locates this fixed point, where many colored clouds billow in a vortex. By his estimate, from what Muzaran was willing to share before his death, this fixed point is a few degrees west of northwest.

The fixed point is hard to make out, but once found, with enough time and patience, John can always find it, and becomes faster at doing so.

Trying to navigate through the Nether, even with a fixed point, always gives John a great headache, and some confusion. It never becomes easy for him, but he slowly becomes better at it, and struggles less to do it.

The portal mirrors the location of the portal on Earth, so when it opens it will open relative to the distance it traveled on Earth, and will not open where John exited here.

John knows Ukaraaz was traveling south after he closed the portal, but Hubaba believes it best for John to stay in this vicinity, between the forest and the last place the portal opened, and away from the dangerous beasts inhabiting the southern area the portal will most likely open now, so far from Circle Xakariz and patrols, as he will have to wait many, many months before the portal opens.

Twice Hubaba is able to visit John, on gathering expeditions with other scabs and a few Bronze chosen as escorts, looking for herbs and components and other resources, passing on news to John, and fresh water, and some magal food.

During Hubaba's first visit, he brings news of just how destructive the rampage of Diamond Garioch was to Second Point, and how all ran and hid and hoped help would come soon, though it never did. Most demons fled to the Inner Circle, in the center of all the points, and the Diamond followed, leaving a string of corpses in his wake. The master of the Inner Circle is a high Exalted, and it is believed he dealt with Garioch, him or one three Salts he commands.

Hubaba believes Garioch never told his master, Outer Circle Master Baggodon the Blind, about John, and John's strange abilities, as all such communications are sent through items controlled by scabs. Hubaba controls the communication device for Second Point, and no such message was ever sent. Garioch and Baggodon could communicate directly, as high-tiered cultivators do, but they rarely did so, and Hubaba believes

Garioch wouldn't have risked losing out on a source of power by informing his master of it, not before he could benefit from it himself.

Hubaba is never questioned about what transpired, or where the legacy items went, or anything at all, and neither is any other scab. During Garioch's rampage, one magal used an emergency portal to return to his Forsaken sect, and Hubaba believes Circle Xakariz blames this magal's sect for the deadly events at Second Point, though the circle is not in a position to retaliate.

One other magal is executed, and the last two sent home. And things just went on.

The master of Third Point was given command of Second Point, and Fourth Point's Diamond commander moved to Third Point, both Fourth and Fifth Point now commanded by Platinum tiered demons, highlighting how far Circle Xakariz has fallen, and how much they need Earth as a stepping stone to greater things.

Many demons, scab and chosen, know John lives past the woods south of Second Point. None care, as John has a [Title] proving he is of the ptagmog. Also, a Wood is below notice, equal to a demon toddler, as even Bronze demons, with their underdeveloped minds, are still considered children, and only Silvers are considered to be full adults, capable of complex thought, able to accomplish something of note, and the ability to cause trouble.

The magal food and fresh water John brought with him doesn't last long, and he has to hunt and forage and eat the foul food of the Nether, and drink the tainted water, as does Amber.

The resupply Hubaba twice brings doesn't last long either time. And three times the Nether-fog closes in and infests John and Amber, and makes Amber very sick, but does not affect John much.

The fog does make John certain the portal his Lilitu summoned opened into a NetherRealm, if not this specific one. Hubaba is familiar with most beasts of this world, and all the great ones, and there is no giant beast living high above all, with long tentacles that reach down, and suck its victims dry.

The local food Amber is willing to eat, at least while she is a fox, is limited, and she becomes weaker and weaker, and less willing to even eat at all, especially after the last fog infliction. Her claws also grow longer, and sharper, and small horns start to grow out of her skull, and her eyes go from an amber color to a darker orange and reddish color, like dull flame.

Somewhat north of John's camp, and a little west of the great dark forest, is something called a Trial, once used as training by mainly the Bronze chosen of Second and Fourth Point, now closed off, with a big sign stating, "Forbidden!" The Trial was powered by the essence of Sublime Xakariz, and hasn't been fueled in a long while, and is out of power, according to Hubaba. The only other notable location anywhere close is a demon village far to the southwest, and some other villages past it, and eventually a large demon city only Silver and higher cultivators are allowed into.

After the last time Hubaba visited, now so long-ago John worries for the old demon, the population of the main predator in the area starts to grow and grow. A strange beast, a predator with both tusk and many, many horns.

John can't think of any predator on Earth with true horns, and he only knows of the small nub the golden jackal grows, greatly valued as a trinket, and thought to have magical properties. This horned predator he has been fighting is the size of a bull at Wood tier, with the thick neck and strength of bulls too, mixed with some features of the mighty lion, such as their massive maws, sharp claws, and bursts of speed. The beasts also use their tails as a weapon to slash and bind.

Even the lowest tiers of these beasts are doughty foes, and strong. More and more Copper-tiered started appearing, and then Bronze versions became more common.

Hubaba named these great beasts merely 'cats,' or at least that is how their name translated. John calls them bull-lions.

Fighting multiple Bronze bull-lions presses John sorely, even with all his advancement. And John advances much. He learns he can feel when his core is fully settled and solid, and ready for advancement. He performs every rank up the same as he did the first, as it is the only way he knows, and every time it ends exactly the same as his first rank up. And every time he has the same vision of Thomas, the little girl, and the giant monster.

For a very long time John has been ready to ascend in tier, but he is unsure how to. John tries ascending the same as he does ranking up, but it fails every attempt, and does nothing. He needs Hubaba to return, and tell him the secret.

Even without ascending, and with the [Perks] raising the soft caps on [Stats] he gained before entering the NetherRealm, John is much, much stronger and faster and far more formidable, and wishes he could access the NCS to see just how much he improved. He feels it is very significant.

John also has had more of an opportunity to strengthen himself with the essence of life than he's ever had, even back in the good old days, the many bull-lions providing a constant source of vital essence, though it is getting harder to strengthen himself this way as the attacks grow larger, with too many Bronzes to feed safely while facing such numbers.

John long ago figured out higher-tiered beasts fill him up on vital essence far faster, allowing him to strengthen himself in this way more efficiently. He regrets he wasn't able to drain Garioch.

Lately, John's focus has been on the storage ring, and opening it, and seeing what new treasures he now possesses. Hubaba told him he can't attune the ring until he opens his meridians at Copper, but John believes he can open the ring as a Wood, without using meridians. So, between battles, and after mediating and using shen to heal his soul, he attempts to open the ring.

# CHAPTER 39
## SOME VICTORY IN THAT, AT LEAST

*Meditation on inevitable death should be performed daily. Every day when one's body and mind are at peace, one should meditate upon being ripped apart by arrows, rifles, spears and swords, being carried away by surging waves, being thrown into the midst of a great fire, being struck by lightning, being shaken to death by a great earthquake, falling from thousand-foot cliffs, dying of disease or committing seppuku at the death of one's master. And every day without fail one should consider himself as dead. Yamamoto Tsunetomo, Hagakure*

John finishes refilling his dantian with essence after converting most of it to shen, and some of it to empty. He's done the same far too many times to count since escaping Second Point, waiting for the portal to open again. He checks to ensure he is performing [Breath of the Serpent Clan], and he is. He has seldom dropped it in these long months, and more and more the technique is becoming second nature to him, and breathing with it requires no thought or action.

A giant pile of clear crystals lies on the ground, Amber's paws on a smaller pile near it, her eyes closed as she cultivates. Cultivating seems to both help and harm her, and make her more and less sick. Strangely, the sicker she gets, the bigger and heavier she gets. John sympathizes, as the meat he eats from beasts here is not satisfying, and neither are the plants and herbs they both eat.

Hubaba said demons and the beasts in the Nether are carbon-based, like humans, and eating either should fill his needs just fine, though this makes no sense to John. Coal is carbon. Carbon mixed with iron makes steel. It is a substance very unlike man and demon.

John stands, extends his senses, and carefully checks the surroundings for beasts, especially the doughty bull-lions, as they are getting sneakier, and attack in greater and greater numbers, and their prides or herds contain more and more Bronzes. He is safe, for now.

John, sick of beast-meat and plants, finds some of the rare and large insects of the Nether. He finds them less foul than other sources of meat, and reminds himself suffering builds character, and at least he isn't at risk of going hungry, and eating the bitter is just a part of life. He looks again at Amber. He thinks she looks more sickly, and is worried over her loss of appetite. The fact her fox form isn't emaciated makes him optimistic she'll be fine, that and she seems to be growing larger, but he still hopes the portal opens soon, and Hubaba sends word of its opening and location, as he promised he would.

Where is he? He should have visited again a long while ago. I hope he's in good health still.

John again worries about his demon friend, Hubaba. Since he hasn't shown himself in so long, John started ranging farther out, looking for sign of many demons passing, and hints of the portal, but he doesn't like leaving Amber alone for so long, not with the increased danger and numbers of the bull-lions, and Amber being too ill to accompany him now. He wonders if he should move camp closer to Second Point, and watch the comings and goings.

John sits back down, deciding to again try and solve the riddle of the ring. He knows how it should be opened, as Hubaba informed him. Once his meridians are cleared, he extends a strand of essence to the ring, and it will bind the ring, allowing John to open it, view inside it, place items in it, and remove items from it.

John needs to first ascend in tier to Copper to clear his meridians, something he has no idea how to do. He knows things don't always work the same for him as they do others. Like with ranking up. Pixie claimed it takes about two weeks for his foundation to settle. It took much longer for him. Much longer. He's not sure how long, as he long ago stopped paying attention to time, as he sees it only as something needing to be endured, not tracked. If he had to guess, he'd guess it took well over a month before his foundation settled between rank ups, maybe even closer to two for the last one.

Open meridians are needed to attune the ring to himself, but John wants access to the ring now, and things don't always work the same for him as they do others. He is sure he can open the ring as a Wood. And I won't have to worry about hiding or lugging that block of armor, he thinks.

The armor is buried deep, for now, south of their camp. John has no way to use it yet, and needs meridians to test it too, same with the cloak, and the cloak just gets in his way fighting, and gives no benefit at all. For now, at least. He hopes there will be a sword in the ring, and a shield, and armor he can use, and more robes too.

John wears one of the robes he stole from Garioch's armor stands, black and red, and enchanted with many runes. Some of the runes Hubaba was able to identify, some he couldn't, and the same goes for rune combinations. The material is tough, and resistant to tears and damage, but does little to lessen the impact of blows. The enhanced attacks of Copper and Bronze bull-lions can slash and tear the robe, but it repairs itself given some time, and the robe always stays clean.

The other robe performs the same functions, but has many more runes, so John buried it with the armor, considering the robe he is wearing as the lesser of the two, and is less worried about it being permanently damaged. He also likes the black and red coloring of his current robes, and all the runes are on the inside of the robe, most along the inside of the hem, and these robes don't look to be of high quality, or robes a Wood shouldn't possess.

There is a common low-tiered semi-glyph found on most items worth adding runes to called the 'standard item soft-glyph'. This soft-glyph has some version of the runes [Repair], [Maintain], and [Replenish]. It can have more runes, and even become an actual glyph, but it always has these runes, giving it the ability to repair and maintain itself through ambient energy collection.

Hubaba identified Munashi's sword as being enchanted with the runes of [Lesser Sharpness], [Minor Durability], [Minor Repair], [Lesser Maintain] and [Lesser Replenish].

The giant axe, Dead Maker, has many runes Hubaba was unfamiliar with, and would need to be injected with essence to find the specific functions of, and claimed his dantian was far too small to feed the mighty axe enough to power it. He recognized the runes for [Greater Durability], [Minor Sharpness], [Major Repair], [Major Maintain], and [Minor Replenish], and some version of the runes [Range], [Target Ground], [Medium Area], [Amplify], [Empower], and [Conversion Fluoroantimonic Acid] connecting to unknown runes, as a full and mighty glyph.

The robes he wears have the runes of [Greater Durability], [Major Repair], [Major Resize], [Major Maintain] and [Major Replenish].

All in all, Dead Maker is a far more deadly weapon than Munashi's sword, and along with its great reach, is a huge boon in fighting the many vicious bull-lions, though John still would prefer a sword, and a shield too. He wishes the [Sharpness] runes on both weapons were of higher rank, but Hubaba told him no weapon uses much capacity on that rune, as cultivators use weapon enhancement manifestations for far better effect.

Thinking of Pixie, and missing her, and the long talks they'd have together, John once again enters his Mind's Eye, just in case she is there now. It is empty, and Pixie is still absent. He pulls out, and goes into his mindset for meditating, but a much shallower version of it.

John closes his eyes, and pulls a strand of magical essence from his lower dantian. He cajoles it to the right side of his belly. This is where it gets tricky, as he must constantly hold it against his side as he also pulls it up, splitting his focus on a task that already demands great focus. If he tries to pull the strand directly above his armpit, the middle dantian catches it, and draws the strand towards it.

Long ago, John tried placing his hand and ring directly over his dantian, and pulling a strand directly to the ring, but it didn't work. It must travel through his body, to his hand, as it would through a meridian, and then finger, and then ring.

John splits his focus and holds the strand against the right side of his belly, and pulls it up along the right side of his chest, being extremely careful, as the middle dantian loves to ruin this part. Going up his left side, the strand is always caught in the middle dantian, so the right side is the only option, and the ring was moved to the right hand long ago.

Slowly and carefully, John creeps the strand up his chest, and is excited to reach his armpit. This is as far as he's ever managed to go, and has made it this far many times, but this is where he always fails. He must split his focus again here, pin the thread above his armpit, and start pulling it down into his arm. Splitting his attention three times seems an impossible feat, but this time he actually manages to do so for a moment before it all falls apart.

John cries out in a victorious hoot before settling down to make the attempt again. Like with all things, once known to be possible, it becomes easier to do, and he gets the strand further and further down his arm before it all unravels, and he must start over.

John makes it past his elbow when he senses great danger, and pulls out of himself, now on the alert. He stands, and while extending his senses puts his sword in his sash and grips Dead Maker with both hands, as the great weapon requires. Many bull-lions approach, completely surrounding the camp, though the bulk are towards the south, in seemingly endless numbers.

John grabs the cultivating and sick Amber, and throws her high into the tallest of the three trees of their camp, and watches her land on the banner he tied between two branches, holding her fast, safe from the bull-lions and all their known attacks. The smaller animals of this world run up trees to avoid these beasts too, so this is a natural strategy to avoid them.

The area behind John has the sparsest number of bull-lions, though there are still many, and he thinks he could break free, and thinks this must be his only choice considering the numbers he faces, as more and more enter his sense range, creeping closer towards him.

Not only are there far more bull-lions than John can count, far more than people adept at counting could count, there are even more Bronzes than he can count too. His only option is to break free and run. They will follow him, and he'll lead them all away from the sickly Amber, keeping her safe.

This isn't like running from a man or demon. This isn't running due to cowardice or fear of awakening from the dream. This will just allow John to bring the battle to the enemy in bursts, at times of his own choosing, grinding them down over time.

As soon as John commits to do so, a great pressure bears down on him, and brings him to his knees. He sees the largest bull-lion he's yet seen appear nearly a thousand paces in front of him. Most bull-lions have greyish-green, wrinkled hides, not too different from the look of an elephant's hide, but with dark spots all over. This giant bull-lion has more spots than greyish-green hide showing. This must be a Silver, John thinks, as his heart sinks down into his belly.

Running is no longer an option. Breaking free and leading them away from Amber, when the fell powers of the Silver bull-lion are unknown, and when John can be hampered so by its unveiled soul, is not a good strategy. Too many unknowns.

Follower of the Way of Death or not, John doesn't want to die now. Not when he's this close to saving Amber, and returning her to her own world, where she'd be able to recover from the sick taint of this one. Not when he's this close to opening his stolen ring, and seeing what treasures it holds. Not before he ascends in tier, and sees what magics are in store for him, as he's earned Copper, and wants what he earned, and just needs to learn the trick to ascending.

But life isn't fair, John knows, and death doesn't come when it's convenient. When the Underworld calls, you answer as a coward, or answer as a man should. Answer as he told his new friend, Hubaba, he should. Standing tall, head held high, defiant, spitting in the eye of his enemies, spitting in the eye of destiny, or fate, or even the gods themselves. Giving battle, accepting death and defeat only while standing on a mountain of dead enemies, and having some victory in that, at least. Making the enemy pay dearly, pay a thousand-fold, for every drop of blood spilled, so much so when John finally falls dead, his enemies will stand silent, and in awe, and hang their heads in shame, knowing they will never die half as well, performing such fell and tall deeds, worthy of the greatest of song.

Koram, though my faith has wavered, and I don't know what waits for me in death, if you can hear me from this strange world, you'll want to witness my deeds this day, prays John, gripping the long haft of Dead Maker with both hands, letting out a scream of effort and fury as he forces his body into the position he'll die in, standing on his feet.

John is much stronger now, and less willing to let the soul of a Silver hold him down.

The Silver bull-lion, seeing John stand, lets out a terrifying roar that echoes through John's chest, and shakes the ground around him, as its lessers rush forward to give battle, and John rushes forward to give them what they want. Thankfully, the directed pressure lets up, for whatever reason, but doesn't go away, and doesn't become general pressure. He thinks the bull-lion might be having a hard time directing it at a moving target.

As John charges forward, splitting the head of the first bull-lion to pounce, he tries to bring the battle far away from camp and Amber. He spins the axe, killing a beast, and causing pause in others. He sends vital essence to enhance his speed and strength, and plows into a group of his enemies, his mighty blows sending even these large beasts flying away, many in pieces.

Copper bull-lions always have the same manifestation, and can use it between two and ten times. John assumes the number of times a bull-lion can perform the manifestation is due to their rank within Copper. The manifestation accompanies their claw attacks, brownish essence bursting from their paw, extending out a short distance, and maintaining the claw shape. John calls this an echo attack.

Bronze bull-lions can also do an echo attack with their tails, but Bronze are far more dangerous, and not just due to their increased size, speed, and strength from the higher tier, but because their speed and strength are also enhanced with some sort of body enhancement manifestation too. If he is remembering correctly, Bronze is the tier the NCS said he'd get a body [Perk], so these beasts could also have one. Body [Perk] or not, Bronze bull-lions are far tougher than their Copper siblings, far more so than Coppers are than Woods.

Early on, when each pride, or herd, or pack, or whatever groups of bull-lions should be called, had, at most, one Bronze leading them, it was easily dealt with by John's own powerful manifestation. One casting of [Magical Essence Dart] would completely disintegrate the alpha Bronze.

And just as some Bronze bull-lions can perform echo attacks with their tails, the last two alphas John fought were also able to surround themselves with a shield of magical essence. One casting of his spell would remove the shield, but he assumes the Silver has this ability too, and it could take more than one casting of his spell to remove it, and more than one to kill the far-off Silver.

John can cast his spell many more times now, but he used nearly a quarter of his essence trying to unlock his ring, and knows little of what surprises the Silver has in store for him, and he is determined not to fall until well after the Silver does, and plans on saving most of his essence for that great beast.

John lays into the bull-lions around him with a vengeance, swinging his axe in great arcs, dodging and rolling away from the echo attacks of his Bronze tiered enemies, avoiding hits from Coppers when he can, largely ignoring the attacks from Woods.

Fighting such large numbers of such fast and doughty foes, John finds, can only be a game of give and take. He must sometimes take a blow to give many blows in return, and must take some damage to give far more damage back. His orb-eye keeping him alive, with his ability to see behind himself, as much as his skill in combat.

327

John swings his axe around, and step by bloody step, makes his way closer to the large Silver beast, trying to bring the fight to it, if it lacks the courage to bring the fight to him, putting more distance between himself and Amber, hoping these beasts will forget about her once he falls.

And fall John will, as the numbers arrayed against him are far too vast to overcome, the enemy still pouring into the area, endless.

Already bloody, sporting many wounds, John advances, determined his fall will not come until the enemy's ranks are greatly thinned.

In the next moments John is forced to cast his spell to avoid serious damage from a Bronze, and then again, and cuts deep into the side of a Bronze, and the head rolls off a Copper, and he steps over corpses, slowly making his way to the Silver. He stands against a tide, and manages to move it, one man, a tempest in a storm, swinging his great axe madly, proving the name of it true, Dead Maker.

John feels, more than sees, something speeding towards him, and he dives far away, losing Munashi's sword from his sash. The ground where he stood a moment ago explodes in a spray of dirt, and he sees a long furrow in the ground leading towards where the Silver was a moment ago, the great beast no longer there.

John avoids the echo attack of a Bronze, and the bite of another, and his orb-eye sees the Silver appear out of thin air behind him, giving a great swipe with its claw. John dives to the side, nearly losing Dead Maker as it lodges too deep in the face of a Bronze he swings at to clear room, and must dodge a new attack from the Silver.

After regaining his feet, John casts [Magical Essence Dart] at the leader of the bull-lions three times, quickly, in succession, and the first shimmers off the essence shield and the beast disappears, the two other spells hitting bull-lions behind where it stood.

The great Silver beast reappears behind John, swiping again.

John must dive again, and into many waiting enemies, an echo attack by a Bronze taking a chunk out of his back. He notices the great attacks of the Silver extend far, and kills all lesser bull-lions in its path, and he uses this information to his great advantage for some time, many bodies of dead enemies piling up, but so too does the damage John takes.

After many more minutes of battle, the game finally comes to an end. The game of John diving away from the attacks of the Silver, and letting the beast's powerful attacks help add to the great slaughter of its brethren, doing as well as Dead Maker.

John gets pinned in, and cannot dive away, or dodge, and is trapped, unable to escape, and the Silver beast's eyes, while staring at John, seem to fill with mirth as it casts its devastating attack from twenty paces away, uncaring of how many of its own it kills along with John.

# CHAPTER 40
## GOING DOWN SWINGING

John sees death approach, and a grimace appears on his face. He doesn't want to die, not before the Silver, not before seeing far more of these enemies dead, piled high as mountains, not before ensuring Amber will live, and will be safe, not before seeing what treasures reside in the ring he wears.

Without much conscious thought, more of a reaction, John tries to force the essence in his dantian out, and have it form a shield around him, like the essence-shield protecting the Silver bull-lion from his [Magical Essence Dart].

Forcing the essence out such as he does is unnatural, and causes John great pain, and he screams loudly, but forces more still. In the next moment, the essence catches on something, and all of it gets sucked into his bracers, which start to glow. He loses control of his arms, and his hands are forced to grip the haft of Dead Maker tightly, and a white light radiates from the bracers, surrounding John completely, as his arms start to rise.

John's eyes widen with fear as the extremely destructive attack of the Silver reaches him, killing all the bull-lions in its path, sending pieces of them flying away. But the attack is stopped by the radiating white light, and no damage is done to John at all. His arms continue to rise, and rise until fully extended above his head, and he feels the remaining essence in his dantian get sucked out, causing him great dizziness and a splitting headache. He'd fall to the ground if it wasn't for the bracers forcing his body to move as they demand, and the bracers want him to bring the axe down in a great blow, as if splitting an invisible enemy in front of him.

Power builds as the axe drops, and once the powerful faux attack ends, a red light comes out of the axe, shooting forth in a wide beam, making a strange noise John has no words to describe. The red beam slices cleanly through everything in its path, and continues out for a great distance.

The beam grows to be about five paces wide, and all enemies in front of John start falling dead. Crystals clank off each other as they fall, some trees, cut clean through, crash to the ground, and the Silver's upper body slides off from the rest of it, a look of confusion on its face, and then its eyes dim, and a spirit stands where its body once did, and the spirit roars silently at nothing, or everything.

Completely spent, John falls to the ground, his face pressed into the strange dirt of this world. The bracers took far more than he had to give. His arms shake as he tries to raise himself up. His whole body shakes. He fights to retain consciousness, and tries to send vital essence to empower himself, but finds he is empty of it. The bracers took that too.

John's orb-eye nearly refuses his commands, but he wrangles control, and jerks it around. He no longer faces an endless horde, but his enemies are still too numerous to count. Thankfully, close by at least, are only Woods and Coppers, standing reticently, waiting for another to make the first move.

And one does. A Bronze dashes out of the crowd, barreling towards John, and he forces himself to his feet, exhausted, spent, barely able to hold Dead Maker, and takes an echo claw attack straight on, his blood splattering over the beast, and he falls back to his knees as more beasts rush in to partake in the kill.

*Not like this,* John thinks. *Let me die swinging, at least. After my great deeds, I deserve to die swinging this fine axe, on my feet.*

John forces himself back to his feet, slow and half out of it. He blocks a bite from the Bronze with his axe, and digs deep down inside of himself, and swings Dead Maker, the bull-lion easily avoiding the weak and slow

331

attack. John screams at the beast, and whips his axe around with little skill and power, but manages to kill a pouncing Wood, giving the rest pause.

*That's one more dead. I just need to make it two*, John thinks, knowing once he's at two, he'll go for three, and once at three, for four, as that is how to endure. Just one more. Be it one more swing, or one more step, or one more second, digging a little deeper, and a little more after. The only way John knows how to live. To keep going. This is how he managed to endure so many ages alive, so much loneliness, so much pain and suffering. He yells, and swings again, the Bronze backing off some.

John turns so the Bronze will pounce on his back, and when it does, John's axe imbeds deep in its side. *That's two dead. Let's go for three. No other Bronze has arrived yet. This is easy work,* he thinks as more and more enemies surround him, knowing his time has run out, happy he'll die well, a worthy death, one that should make his father proud to call him son. Happy his long struggle is finally over. Happy the dream is ending. But not yet, no matter what the bracers took from him, he still has some fight left in him, he always has some fight left in him, and Dead Maker is still thirsty.

***

Cultivating as a fox is very different from cultivating as a human. At least when cultivating as a fox should. At first Amber tried cultivating the same way she did in her human form since humans are better and smarter than foxes and all her forms share the same energy system. A different energy system than a normal human or a normal fox has. Merged. Joined. It was slow. Too slow.

She figured it out after she felt two wolves within a pack with open energy centers. They dropped crystals when they died. No way a normal wolf could advance faster than her. Even with her using crystals, the wolves managed to open their energy centers, something she was far off from accomplishing. Beasts aren't meant to cultivate with crystals. Since

Amber is neither beast nor human, she can. Or because she is both beast and human.

Cultivating as a human does while as a fox isn't helpful even with the fantastic gift she coerced out of Magnus Gar'tar. Beasts cultivate instinctively in a way not too different than John claims he does. Beasts reflect on instincts and review memories. Amber has many memories. Many memories from many forms.

Amber's earliest memories are as a frog. A big frog with little fangs. Maybe she only became big once she joined with the lizard. She doesn't remember. She does remember being afraid of snakes and sitting in a river and eating birds. Eating everything she could really.

One day, the ground fell away and she fell into a hole. Some of the river splashed down into the hole too. There were lots of rocks. She couldn't jump out. And the hole went far in all directions into darkness. She liked staying near the hole, and the big pool of water, and the sun.

A lizard fell down the hole with her. They weren't enemies but they weren't friends either. There's no friends in nature like that. Nature is brutal. They stayed on opposite sides of the pool and water.

Neither could get out of the hole. Then, after some time, more rocks fell and she and the lizard ran and got trapped together. They fought a little, but neither could hurt each other, or eat each other. The lizard had all these spikes all over its head. So, they just waited, only attacking each other occasionally, lucky to have a little water flow by under them, bringing some stuff they could eat.

Then they merged. Somehow. And she could change from a frog to a lizard and vice versa, but not always. Both forms grew much bigger and tougher. She could move the rocks and climb out.

She stayed that way for a long time. Who knows how long. Too long. Wandering. Fighting. Surviving. Killing. Watching. She couldn't always change between frog and lizard. It took some time before she knew she could switch over and she'd be stuck for a while once she did.

She wandered far. She could go places no ordinary frog or lizard could ever go. She could go a long time without food too. She could eat things she shouldn't be able to. She was also really hard to kill. She liked watching the bigger animals. The plant eaters. The beautiful ones that run fast and look like they'd be soft to touch. And warm. She could tell they were warm.

One day a thought entered her head. Or a question. Something from outside it. Like a strong intuition. If she wanted to, she could become something else. But it came with conditions and an additional cost of a much tougher condition to have some prize that didn't make sense. She accepted both, because why not? She became a deer.

And she was stuck as a deer. To change back to a frog or lizard she'd have to go a whole turn of the seasons without running from a fight. It seemed impossible, especially as a doe with no antlers, but she would do it. Somehow. The predators of a deer are much different than those of a frog and lizard. Some foes she couldn't fight off and had to run from, like wolves and bears and humans. And humans started to pop up everywhere she turned. Luckily, she was much harder to kill than a regular deer.

It took her a long, long time to meet the condition. She was far in the north when she finally did. She could change back into a frog or lizard again and the condition changed for the deer. She couldn't run from a fight for just one new moon to the next. That's it. Much better.

A long time later she got an intuition about a bear. With the additional cost, the condition she had to meet was to kill a thousand worthy opponents. Nature is brutal. Once she met the condition it changed to only needing to kill one worthy opponent to access her other forms.

Next she was offered a snake form but refused it. Snakes are gross and everyone hates them so she did not want that form at all. It was a very long time before she was offered a new form. The condition for her fox form was going ten thousand days without eating meat. Something she craved greatly in that form. The timer reset often. Once met the condition changed to only a hundred days without meat.

Every new form she attained enhanced her mind with new thoughts, new instincts, new information on enemies, and new ways to hunt and survive.

The next intuition she received enhanced her mind greatly. Human form! This one was different. She received a true name. She could only stay a human from one dawn to the next. The condition was she had to find a man she could trust with her name and secrets. A condition much harder to meet than it sounds as she was wild and stinky and very ugly.

Many legends grew around her. In Korea she was Ungnyeo, kitsune in Japan, Nang Uttai Tawee in Thailand, The Mistress of the Copper Mountain in Russia, and that's only to name a few. She liked it when the stories made her beautiful. She liked it a lot. She wished she wasn't so ugly and men looked at her like they looked at other women. Most threw rocks at her and chased her away. She was able to learn languages easily but even that didn't help her fit in.

She learned men couldn't be trusted. She started getting intuitions for abilities she could use in human form instead of new forms. Five in total, being able to hide from all senses and calling the light being the most useful. Every use of an ability had a cost, usually increasing the conditions for all her forms, and shortening the time she had in her human form.

After many, many centuries she finally met the condition. Barely, and not for long, as men can't be trusted. But she met the condition long enough for it to count by befriending a hermit hunter living alone in the woods. She was forced to kill him soon after.

A long time later she received a new intuition. This one was also different from the others. Her human form would become permanent and beautiful. So beautiful all men would desire her. But she'd lose her human form forever if she ever had carnal relations with a man.

Once accepted, the conditions of all her forms changed. She could turn from any form to lizard or frog and bear at any time. Once changed to either lizard or frog she had to wait about six to fourteen days to change to a higher form other than bear. Bear's condition was still just killing a worthy opponent. She could change to deer and fox from any form if their condition was met, but only fox could access her human form. Her human form could access any form at any time. The cost for using all her abilities changed to only adding extra days without meat as a fox.

335

If she knew how desired she'd be she wouldn't have accepted, as her beauty was a curse, not a gift. She was forced to stay invisible most of the time. Even when she partially hid her face, she couldn't spend too much time around the same men as they would eventually try to catch her and take her.

She did like being beautiful. She'd often look at herself in a mirror while wishing others could enjoy her beauty too. She wished the women that didn't desire her didn't hate her so much. She rarely made a friend, and having a friend always made life and her trips out in public more enjoyable.

She immigrated to America in 1924 and took to the culture. She learned how to be a refined and poised and proper lady, like the movie starlets, and how to be a good wife, even though she'd never be one. She liked pretending. Pretending what could be.

Once the internet blew up her life became way better. She gained millions of followers on Instagram without posting any of the filthy smut other girls did. Just ladylike photos highlighting her poise and grace. She could show most of her face too. Sure, she'd show a lot of bare leg and skin, and sometimes highlight other assets, but it was always classy and tasteful and never inappropriate for a lady.

Though she's always enjoyed how all men would turn and look at her assets whenever she was in public, regardless of how covered her head was, Instagram allowed her all the adoration she could ever want from men while being completely safe from them too. And they'd just send her money so she would keep posting photos. A lot of money. Some men would pay thousands for just a picture of her foot. Foot photos aren't inappropriate at all.

Then came the Tree of Life ruining everything. But she finally found out what exactly her prize was. What paying the extra cost for all her forms got her. They're all connected. Without the Tree of Life it didn't make sense. It makes sense to her now.

The Nether makes her sick. It doesn't seem to bother John but she is a lot more sensitive. John can't feel what she feels. He didn't even notice when she ascended to Copper. In just eighteen more days she can access her human form, and that's counting all extra time she banked up using invisibility for over a century without changing to any other forms.

She doesn't know if human form will help with the Nether sickening her but she really hopes it will. Or hoped. Same with increasing in rank. She's already cleared her energy channels and ranked up once as a Copper. *Level 7 and I still can't help*, she thinks.

She stops cultivating and opens her eyes to watch John fight all the giant demon cats. Her heart flutters as she watches him stand against the endless tide of enemies. He is so thoughtful towards her. Such a kind and caring man. Foolish but kind. She doesn't want him to die. And not just because she knows she'll die soon after. She likes him. Even though he's real weird and talks all old-timey.

She wonders again if John can be trusted. Really be trusted. Like, even with her true name. She decides he can't. No man can. They're good at lying. It's what they're best at. They have no control. They'll always abuse any power they get over her. She wonders if he really is immune to her beauty like he said. She doubts he is. She wishes he really was. She wishes they weren't both about to die so these questions mattered even a little. She'll miss him. At least she'll die having known something close to real friendship. Finally.

She wishes she could help but she can barely even move. She's surprised she's lived this long. She's never felt this sick. Ever. It's terrible. She's so much stronger now but she's never been weaker. Never.

Not wanting to watch her friend die she goes back to cultivating. Cultivating as a beast is easy. She has a lot more memories to draw from than other beasts do. She is much stronger now. Ranking up in one form ranks them all up since the energy systems are connected.

Beasts don't learn or choose manifestations. They naturally get what they get and know how to do them instinctually. And all her forms get different ones. With her energy channels open all her forms have one. *Well, besides human*, she guesses. The fox has a body enhancement. She wonders what the other forms have.

Ranking up as a beast isn't something that can be controlled or directed. There's one way to do it and it improves what it improves. She knows her [Stat] increases for ranking up and ascending to Copper benefited from all her forms. But not equally. She is strong. Or would be if the Nether wasn't making her so sick. Especially the fog. The fog made it so much worse.

She jerks and stops cultivating. A new intuition enters her mind. She can become a demon. At first she reacts to this as she did when offered the snake form. *Gross! Yuck!* But the details give her pause. This would change everything. There're no conditions in any form to change to demon. She'd always have access to all forms with no conditions. Demon can even access her human form with no conditions.

Demon would also further connect her forms. If she accepts the cost of it. All her forms would have access to the manifestations of the other forms, and all her abilities too. Even better, the cost of her abilities would be only energy or essence instead of being stuck in fox form for extra days. It seems like a pretty sweet deal to Amber.

She thinks the condition and cost for accepting are horrible. The cost is that all her forms will be infected by Nether and become part demon. Including her human form. *Gross!* Even worse, the condition is she'll have to kill at least one magal every year or permanently lose her demon form. She's pretty sure magal means humans and not animals. It's hard to understand such concepts as a fox.

Amber hates violence. Nature is brutal. Kill or be killed. People complain about humans being violent. Amber believes these people should try to live in the jungle as a beast. *They have no idea.* She hates fighting. She hates it with all her soul. She likes it when people are kind and nice and sweet. She just wants to be pretty and go back to her life of doing little, living in complete peace most of the time, and having guys drool over her on Instagram.

She opens her eyes. So many of the demon cats are now dead. John looks to be on his last leg. Close to death. Surrounded by the demon cats. Still fighting. She knows he moved the battle so far away to protect her. *He's such a good guy.* She's safe up high on this banner because of his thoughtfulness.

Amber hates fighting. Hates it with a passion. But she's real good at it. She had to be. Nature is brutal. Everyone knows that. She accepts the form's condition and cost. The sickness leaves her immediately. She feels great. Better than ever. She jumps down from the banner, high up in the light branches of a tree where none of the demon cats can reach her. On the way to the ground she transforms into a demon, and then again into a bear. She lands and challenges all with her scariest roar.

# CHAPTER 41
## JUST HIDEOUS

Amber, in bear form, rushes forward with the dash attack of her deer form, impaling a demon cat with the horns all her forms now have. Her claws are much longer and sharper, and she tests them on the demon cats around her. *Oh, these are nice and sharp,* she thinks as her powerful swipes send demon cats flying away through the air, or parts of them. She knows she is strong. Much stronger than any bear her tier ever could be.

The Wood tier demon cats near her start running away. Beasts know their place. Only the Copper and Bronze turn to face her. She uses the teleport manifestation of her frog form to blink into a big mass of demon cats to test the attack manifestation of her bear form on a Bronze. The enhanced blow turns the beast into mush. She uses the body enhancement of the fox form to increase her strength and speed and damage resistance, and she again uses the dash attack to charge closer to John.

Amber leaves a path of death and destruction in her wake, dashing and blinking ever closer to John. She takes some of the enhanced hits from the demon cats. The hits from Coppers don't hurt her at all. The hits from Bronzes hurt, but not too bad. She uses the regeneration manifestation from her lizard form to heal the damage she has taken. She stops using the attack manifestation of the bear as it uses a good amount of essence and her normal blows and bites kill just fine. She drops the body enhancement of the fox for the same reason. Waste not, want not.

She reaches John and becomes worried. He's in really bad shape. She gives him some of her old healing and uses the regeneration manifestation on him. She can use all her abilities in all her forms now, including the hiding ability, but it's too hard to use that one when so many are focusing on her. She calls the light to test it. It's too weak for the amount of essence it costs.

She grabs a Bronze demon cat and snaps its spine low on its back and gives it to John. She tries telling him to drain it but only a roar comes out. He must understand the intent as he sinks his face into its neck while Amber gets back to killing.

Nature is brutal. Amber knows this better than anyone. She hates fighting. She hates it in all her forms. Besides bear form. As a bear she's always reveled in the fight. Soon John joins her and side by side they make a great slaughter.

Amber leaves the last demon cat for John to kill. Men like that. It makes them feel bigger. And she doesn't know if he needs to drink its blood or whatever he does. He could need more of whatever it gives him.

John sways on his feet and props himself up with the handle of his axe as he turns to face her. "Amber! My dear friend, you saved me yet again. And you have horns now! A bear with horns! They look fierce and daunting. I like them much. I was worried for you. You seemed so sick. I told you the bear is much more useful than the fox."

John falls to the ground after saying this. Amber looks down at his unconscious form and smiles about as good as a bear can. *I really gotta coach him to talk normal. He sounds so old-timey and annoying. At least he looks more like a grownup with that big beard now. Kinda hot even.*

Amber never received NCS messages in animal form. She could access her Mind's Eye and the avatar of the NCS while as a fox back on Earth, but she never once received any messages like she did in human form. So she is very surprised as a message shows in her eyes. As a bear.

**[OVERRIDE]**

**[OVERRIDE] [Status] [Authorized] Entertainment package reactivating.**

*Cool! I hope it has Instagram. And TikTok,* she thinks.

*** 

John awakes with a start, looking around with his orb-eye, extending his senses out, searching for danger. He can't see her, but he can hear and smell Amber somewhat, and then he can't.

John checks his body, and he seems to be in decent shape, most wounds healed or healing well. He has a good amount of vital essence, though his dantian is empty, and his head still pounds.

Grabbing Dead Maker and Munashi's sword as he stands, John finally notices the camp moved north, just outside the forest. A mountain of crystals near a smoldering fire, piled high on the banner, as many colored crystals as clear now. He puts Munashi's sword in his sash, and feels for the small bag he keeps his higher tiered crystals in, ensuring it is still there. Only a few spirits of dead beasts wander the area, already dissipating. Only one seems new.

Walking to where he last sensed her, John says, "Amber. I sensed you as…something new. I don't know what, but your scent was similar. Please don't hide from me."

From high up a tree she replies, "I was a frog. Frogs cultivate really fast. Well, it slowed down a lot since I ascended to Copper. Even with crystals. Still faster than a lizard. Or deer. Or the rest. I checked them all."

"You're talking! You're a woman again? Or can you talk as a frog? Either way, this is fantastic! We can talk now. Why haven't we been doing this all along? And Copper? How?"

The beautiful, tinkling laughter of Amber flows down from high and hits John's ears. "Don't be silly. I can only talk as a woman. Animals can't talk. I don't think they can at least. I never heard any that could."

"You're a woman again! We can be more like normal friends now. It was strange being friends with a fox. But, please, I must know, why did you ever stop being a woman? And why not help more with the fighting as a bear?"

Amber explains how her forms work, and how she was stuck, and knew she'd be stuck once she changed, but had to help John back during

342

the Tribulation, and how she tried to stay as a fox to meet the conditions to turn back into a woman. She doesn't like being other forms. Being stuck in them. Or didn't before. It's helpful to her now, and she can't be stuck any longer.

Amber ends by saying, "And you shouldn't call me Amber anymore. I saw my eyes in Munashi's blade. They're no longer amber. They're more like demon eyes now. But the red and orange mixed and aren't all swirly. Kind of like vermillion. Thankfully the whites aren't black like demon eyes. But I'm gross now. Again. Just hideous."

"Oh, I'm sure that's not true. I only caught a quick glimpse of you in the Tribulation, but you have the most beautiful face I've ever seen." He adds on the thought, *even if your body is far too skinny to be appealing to men of quality and standing.* Knowing the great fears Amber spoke of before, John quickly adds, "But worry naught, your magic did not work on me, and I did not fall under your spell."

"You really have to start talking modern, buddy. Who says naught anymore? You sound so silly. And you barely saw me. Maybe it just takes some time to kick in like when I partially cover my face. But when it works, it won't stop working. It will ruin our friendship. Ruin everything. It always does."

"Okay. I'll put effort into talking in a way such as you approve of, and find no fault with. You've saved me three times now, and I owe you a great debt. This is embarrassing to admit, but...I can't...or couldn't...do anything. If I fell madly in love with you, and caught you, I couldn't do anything. It hasn't functioned in a very long time. Noble ladies I'd take as wives to keep my estates going would be very vexed at me because I couldn't...perform. They'd have to get with child by dishonorable means and think me not much of a man for it. I'd marry widows with sons whenever I could, but no wife, young or old, wants a husband that...can't, you know."

John stops, flustered, with red cheeks. He is surprised to hear more laughter from Amber. She then says, "Hey man, no need to be so embarrassed. I can't either. Never have and never will. But come on, buddy, give me some credit for not being an idiot. You really think no old man that couldn't function any longer never saw me? Or gay guys? Even some women that swore up and down they never had a lesbian thought in their life would try to catch me. This isn't about what you can't do. It's about not taking risks, yeah?"

John collects his thoughts for a moment before responding. "I don't think there's a risk. I've had a long time to master my emotions, baring one recent slip, and I seem to have an uncanny ability to shrug off mental effects quite well. If I must have a friend I can't see, then I must. But life is about risk. Death is around every corner. For most of my life, I had no fear of being killed, but feared death greatly. Since everything changed, I now constantly live on the edge of it. You as well. We both hid from truly living before this, in our own ways. We either embrace it now, or continue to hide from it. I've had my fill of hiding. I'll now embrace life as much as I embrace death. I'd rather you did too. We will have a go at it together."

No response comes for quite a while. When it comes Amber nearly whispers, "Can I trust you, John? I mean really trust you?"

Without hesitation, John replies, "Yes. For the most part. You can trust me to behave as a good friend, willing to spend my life to protect yours, but I will not be a plaything or puppet for anyone. Never again. I do as I please."

"Will you tell me if you start getting any strange urges? I mean, like, tell me immediately?"

"Certainly."

"Are you sure you want to see me? I'm hideous now. I have horns. All my forms do. Man, I wish my doe form did back when I really could've used them. You sure you're sure?"

"I'm sure."

"Okay. Remember, any urges at all, you gotta tell me."

A moment later John nearly jumps out of his skin as Amber appears behind him, after just hearing her voice come from in front of him and high up. He heard no rustling, nor landing, nor anything else giving him a hint of her movement.

"Ha! I knew you could see behind you somehow! So, what do you think?" Amber, still in the same pajamas she wore in the Tribulation, clean still somehow, spins around. Two large black horns, mostly straight, somewhat like those of a strange animal he saw long ago while traveling far to the east called a Markhor. Neither the horns nor the eyes make her look less appealing, in his opinion, just a bit queer.

John believes vermillion is the color made from cinnabar, as the eyes have the same hue as that ore, and John is familiar with ore and smithing. Other than that, Amber looks exactly the same – absolutely beautiful, but far too skinny, though now that he can see her full body, he notices she has some nice curves that would be very attractive if she had some meat on her bones to accentuate them.

"You are still as beautiful. The eyes look strange, but so did the amber color. The horns merely give you an exotic look. I like it."

Amber puts her hands on her hips and looks disappointed. "That's it? Just my eyes and horns? What about my skin tone? And these?" She holds her hands out and John notices her very long and sharp claws where fingernails should be. "And these." She holds out a foot, and John sees claws protruding through the toes of her multicolored shoes. "My tennis shoes are ruined, see?"

"Nice! Those can inflict much damage. You'll never be unarmed. Your skin looks fine to me. What's wrong with it?"

Amber throws up her hands. "What's wrong with it? Are you serious? My skin was perfect and now it's all demony and gross and grey. Wait. You can't tell?"

"Maybe a little, but not really. It looks the same, or mostly the same."

"Oh. Well, thank you. I guess. No urges?"

"None at all."

Amber's hands go back on her hips. "Well, you don't have to rub it in and be a jerk about it, you know. You did say I'm still very beautiful, so up yours, buddy. I could really use some new clothes. And a bath. A

345

long one. For a week. Good thing I don't stink. You do. Bad. I almost passed out carrying you here. Pee-yew." She holds her nose for the last part.

John sniffs his armpit. "I smell as a man does."

"Yeah, a stinky one that stinks real bad. That's what type of man you smell like. I'm going to call you Mister Stinko."

John smiles. "Then I shall call you Miss Demon."

Amber's face crinkles up aghast. "Oh! I knew my skin looked awful. You're such a jerk."

"Amber, I was kidding. We were joking around. Your skin is fine, just as I don't really stink that much."

"Ha! Yes, you do. You do stink real bad."

John sniffs himself again, and is certain she is wrong. "Are you really Copper now? And if so, what is the trick to it? I can't figure it out."

"How can you not feel it? It's pretty easy to just feel what tier people are. I can even tell about what rank all the early tiers are too. I really am Copper. Cultivating as an animal is *sooo* easy. Way easier than as a human. Demons cultivate as slow as humans. I can't even explain how beasts cultivate. It's different. Way more natural. And ascending just happened naturally. Sorry, buddy, no tips I can give you."

A serious look goes on John's face. "Why did you piss on me? Twice!"

Amber has the grace to look ashamed. "Oh. Goodness. Sorry about that. The first time was to wake you up. You were bleeding out of your eyes and ears and everywhere else and I wasn't sure you were okay and no matter how loud I got you wouldn't wake up. I'm not going to go around licking guys' faces like some two-bit tramp. It was the best I could think of. I don't think like I do now when I'm in my fox form. And the second time…well, that was to get rid of you. No sense for us both getting killed when you coulda escaped. How did you manage that? There was a Diamond there."

"You think pissing on someone's face is less trampy than licking it?"

"I told you I don't think the same when I'm in fox form. I'm sorry. Please don't tell anyone I did that."

"Why would I ever tell someone? I'm the one that...you sense that? Many approach. Demons, I'm certain. Hopefully Hubaba along with a foraging party, with fresh water, and news of the portal."

It takes a moment for John to notice he could no longer hear Amber, or smell her scent, and he assumes she turned invisible again.

John quickly digs a shallow hole and buries Dead Maker. Hubaba told him the axe is famous and he shouldn't be seen with it by demons. They wouldn't suspect him of stealing it or foul play, but any Silver would take it from him. The lone Silver chosen of Second Point has never accompanied the foraging party, so he isn't too worried.

John wishes he had enough time to do something about the pile of crystals, instead deciding to head towards the approaching party, hoping it is Hubaba and scab foragers, only with a small guard of a few Bronze chosen, the same as the last two times he visited.

Entering the forest path, John spots the demons. They are led by the Silver John saw when he first entered the hall of Second Point, wearing the same breastplate and hauberk, and he is accompanied by another Silver, and many Bronze chosen. Some scabs in their ragged robes follow them, Hubaba the only Silver among them.

*This is no foraging party*, John thinks, handing the hilt of his sword, worried over the lack of essence in his dantian, happy Amber can now help in fights. More than help, if his memories of the recent battle are true, and weren't some fevered dream.

# CHAPTER 42
## A STEEP PRICE TO PAY

You there, magal! Wood! What is this? How is a magal of the ptagmog? And what are you doing out here?"

John walks towards the party of demons. He knows he should at least kneel to the Silver in charge, but he doesn't want to. He must force himself to perform the act. His dantian is empty, and manners and custom are both important to him anyways.

"Second-Point Master Garioch gave me the Title, Silver."

"Stand, stand. Let me look at you. Why would Garioch give the ptagmog Title to you, and not the Forsaken one? You're still a magal. And how is a non-demon Wood able to live in the Nether? And you didn't answer what you're doing out here."

"Diamond Garioch didn't consult this Wood before granting the Title, Silver. Something about me being made to fight the Favored instead of joining the Forsaken. Maybe I can tolerate the Nether for the same reason I got the Title. I'm just living out here, trying to get stronger and increase in rank and tier. Diamond Garioch said I have a place among those of Second Point if I can increase my tier to Bronze," replies John.

Lower-tiered beings are not supposed to look higher-tiered in the eye when they speak, and speak only with eyes cast down, so John watches the Silver with his orb-eye. Hubaba keeps pointing his head down sharply, indicating something beyond 'no.' The second Silver has a scowl on his face, angrily gripping the hilt of the large sword hanging from his hip. The lead Silver studies John, chewing on the lies he was told.

"Hmmm. You must not have heard. Garioch went mad and had to be put down. It's said one of your kind poisoned him. Second Point has a new master and no Forsaken. I'm not sure if you'd be so welcome now, even as a Bronze. Best if you left the Nether altogether. Have you seen any groups slaying large amounts of cats?"

The question surprises John. "No, Silver. May I ask why?"

"Why what?"

"Why do you ask if I've seen any groups slaying cats?"

"That's why we shouldn't allow Forsaken on this world. You'll never be real demons no matter if you take in some of the Nether. And none of you ever bother to find out how things work here. If large amounts of beasts are killed in an area, more are drawn to the area, leaving other areas barren. And the Nether will spawn more of them and raise them faster. And it happens over and over until a Platinum rises. It's to help us train. It must be managed and done right or else there is chaos."

John wonders why Hubaba didn't tell him of this. "Thank you for the explanation, Silver. I've killed some Wood-tiered cats myself. Sorry if I added to this problem."

Both Silver chosen laugh at this. The leader replies, "Don't you worry, little Wood of the ptagmog. If Woods could have an impact on the system, we wouldn't be able to control it. Just count yourself lucky you've been able to avoid Copper and Bronze cats. We must go. Remember my advice about leaving this world. The new master of Second Point is not so welcoming to magals, ptagmog or not."

The second Silver chosen grabs the arm of the one John recognizes. "Hold, Zongreth. Do you feel that?"

Zongreth shakes the arm off, seemingly annoyed. "Lieutenant Zongreth! Feel what now?"

The other Silver says, "Lieutenant Mormok is the lieutenant."

"You see him around? You know if he's still alive? Who leads the Silvers of Second Point? Me! Now address me correctly and spit out whatever is making you prattle like a Bronze."

The other demon grips the hilt of his sword tighter, staring at Zongreth, the tension rising uncomfortably in the silence. With eyes still lowered, John watches the two with his orb-eye. He hopes the party just moves on peacefully, assuming whatever the other demon feels isn't good for him, and hopes they miss the crystal pile too.

Suddenly a bobbing, disembodied soul, like the one he saw at the witches' house before the Silver demon captured him, moves into view from behind him. He curses himself for watching the two in front of him with his orb-eye, and not his surroundings as he always should be doing, constantly.

The soul stops near Zongreth, becoming visible as another Silver demon. John's heart drops as the new demon says, "Zongreth, this magal has possession of a very high-tiered axe, possibly Second Point's Dead Maker. When he became alerted to your approach, he buried it near a large pile of crystals. He's with a Natural. Not the missing one from Second Point. I guarded it a couple times before ascending and this one has a different scent than I remember.

"And," the new demon makes an excited face, "this one has a sentient form. Can you believe it? They just said in class a couple weeks ago sentient Naturals were only a myth."

Zongreth tears his eyes from the second demon, looks at John, and says, "It's Lieutenant Zongreth, address me correctly from now on. A sentient Natural, you say? What tier is the Natural? It must be at least Gold or Platinum if it has a sentient form, right? We must go inform Master."

"No need. It's only a Copper. Isn't Lieutenant Mormok the lieutenant? Is Captain Ukaraaz still the captain? Are we being assigned a new Gold? Did the invasion fail?"

Zongreth's face grows annoyed. "What's with all the prattling from you two? Nothing's changed besides I'm the lieutenant now. Where's the Natural? What tier is the one using Dead Maker? Is that why you didn't capture the Natural? We might still need Master."

The new demon, weaponless like Zongreth, or at least without a visible weapon of note, says, "Could be. I didn't see any higher tiers. The

Natural completely disappeared from my senses, so I lost it and watched this one. Maybe a higher tier hid it from my senses. I don't think so. This one had the high-tiered axe in hand. I'm not sure whether it's Dead Maker or not. They spoke about escaping and a Diamond, so it could be Second Point, but all the magals of the scab house were accounted for, right? And all were Silver. And that one magal that poisoned Master Garioch also stole the other Natural, right? The Natural meant for Captain Ukaraaz. This Natural's a different one, I'm sure of it."

Zongreth, still staring at John, says, "What else did they say?"

"I just caught the last bit, just something about escape and a Diamond. After they talked about pissing on faces and not telling anyone about it. Then the Natural disappeared and this Wood buried the axe and rushed to intercept you. Something isn't adding up here, Zongreth."

"I told you, it's Lieutenant Zongreth now. Don't make me tell you again." Before John even knows what's happening, the earth around his feet swells up around him, encasing him up to his shoulders in a rock-cocoon. Zongreth, with a smarmy look on his face, continues, "Before the portal closed Ukaraaz sent a gift to Garioch. A dying magal Wood. I don't know if this is the same one. They're impossible to tell apart. But something isn't adding up here."

The new demon puts his hands on his hips. "That's what I just said. And shouldn't you say Captain Ukaraaz? Not using his rank is disrespectful."

"Shut your stupid mouth or I'll shut it for you! I've been a Silver since you were a Copper. Don't tell me about respect. Is your belt type 1 or type 2?"

"Type 2."

"Okay. I'll torture the truth out of this Wood. Its screams should draw the hidden Natural, so wait a little bit after I get some good screams out of it, then use the pulse to flush the Natural out."

"I don't know, you really think we should torture someone with the ptagmog Title?"

"Darkness, Adversity, and Nightmare! It's just a Wood. You stepped on a nearly birthed Wood on our way here."

"That was an accident, and you know it, Zong…"

It takes a moment for John to notice the new demon suddenly stops talking, as he is furiously thinking about how to escape the rock-cocoon, surprised how quickly his thoughts go to his nearly empty dantian, and a cultivation related answer. Once his mind catches up with the events going on around him, he barely manages to catch the giant maw of Amber's bear-form chomp through the head of the new demon.

As the demon falls from Amber's mouth, she barrels towards Zongreth, an echo attack forming on her paw as she moves. John is amazed she's about to kill two Silvers in as many seconds, then curses as he can almost see her manifestation become unbound, and the bear trapped in a rock-cocoon herself. Trapped for only a moment, as she gets her next manifestation off, teleports out of the cocoon and behind Zongreth.

Amber tries for another head bite, but Zongreth rolls forward, and the other demon, with sword drawn and glowing orange now, lands a devastating blow with it while unbinding the next manifestation Amber tries for. The blow bites deep into Amber, causing her to fall to the ground for a moment, and a yellow ball appears over her, drawing her up towards it.

John notices Zongreth is the one responsible for the yellow ball. Worried for his friend, John jerks in his rock-cocoon, and it cracks. He imbues himself with strength and rages against the cocoon, and it breaks open, pieces flying all over.

A new yellow ball appears in front of John's face, and his head gets drawn and stuck to it. He draws his sword and tries swiping at the ball to destroy it, only managing to get the sword stuck to the yellow ball too.

John hears a painful roar come from Amber, and with his orb-eye sees the sword of the second demon, glowing orange, slide into her chest. He lets out a horrifying yell, and rips his head away from the ball, flesh and hair pull off his skull, now stuck to and dangling from the ball.

Leaving his stuck sword and jumping to the nearest demon, Zongreth, John falls to the ground before he reaches the demon, as an orange net covers him, burning his skin everywhere it touches.

With a new yell, John struggles to ignore the burning pain and remove the net, glad he can no longer spot Amber with his eyes or orb-eye, hoping she somehow managed to escape, and is seeing to her grievous wounds, disappointed in himself for adding nothing to the fight so far beyond being a minor distraction to the Silvers.

Soul-pressure bears down upon John as the orange, burning net disappears. Both Silver demons approach, an almost transparent golden staff in Zongreth's hand, the no longer glowing sword in the other demon's hand. Bronze chosen advance behind them, weapons drawn, ready for battle.

With his orb-eye John locates his sword a few paces behind him. Even though one of the Silvers is focusing on him with their soul-weight, John knows he is much stronger now, a Silver's soul less of a burden to him, and he thinks he can rise still.

Zongreth places the end of the staff on John's chest, and turns to the other demon, saying, "Did you see the sentient form? I thought Gorn was lying. Or wrong. Or stupid. A sentient Natural's just a myth, and sentient at Copper? Impossible! But it's real. Darkness, Adversity, and Nightmare! It has a true name! We need to capture it. Get Gorn's belt, hide, use the pulse, and flush it out. Master will surely reward it to me. Maybe at that level there'll be enough for us both. It seems to…"

The second demon starts to walk over to the corpse of Gorn as soon as the belt is mentioned. As Zongreth continues to talk, the second Silver bends over the corpse, and John sees Amber appear in human form for a moment, blood spilling down her chest, quickly transforming into a bear, and biting the demon's head before anyone can react, interrupting Zongreth's speech.

The staff pushes down into John's chest due to Zongreth's surprise, and it feels less solid than it should. Without wasting a moment, John enhances his body as much as he can, and pushes backwards with his feet, trying to get to his sword.

Two yellow balls form, one above John, and one where Amber stood a moment before teleporting behind the group of Bronze chosen, taking out many with a mighty swipe of her paw.

John is raised off the ground, and his belly sticks to the yellow ball. He sees Amber covered in a rock-cocoon, and a new yellow ball forms near her head.

John, again, can nearly feel a manifestation of Amber's undone as her head is drawn to the yellow ball.

John tries to rip his stomach away from his ball as he sees many rocks pelting Amber's head from all directions, and hears her painful roar. She breaks free from the rock-cocoon but not the yellow ball, and a massive boulder drops on her head. With head stuck to the ball, she doesn't fall to the ground, but she is unconscious all the same.

Having no leverage, John is unable to free his belly from the ball, and draws heavily on the energy nearby, trying to cast [Magical Essence Dart] with an empty dantian. It does nothing but cause him great pain and dizziness.

Two more yellow balls appear over Amber, and the two remaining Bronze demons run to her, weapons pointed.

Turning to look at John, Zongreth says, "What a treasure. It killed two Silvers as a Copper, while only at low or mid-low Copper to boot. Now you, magal, are unnecessary. Sorry I won't be able to torture you, but I want to get this back to Master on the double."

Rocks start pelting John from all over, causing far more damage than John assumed rocks could cause him now, and the rock-storm only lasts merely a couple seconds, stopping far sooner than the one directed at Amber. With his orb-eye, John sees blood stream from Zongreth's mouth, and the demon falls down, dead.

John is confused. Amber is still unconscious, but she falls to the ground as the yellow ball holding her head disappears, and John falls to the ground at the same time. She couldn't have killed Zongreth. Then a giant purple scythe kills both remaining Bronze chosen, and shortly after, three more scythes kill all the many scabs. All the scabs but one.

Hubaba stands silently, head bowed, looking to be in much pain. John felt the purple scythes that killed the scabs manifest from this old demon.

John is glad Hubaba joined the fight, but by the look on his face, saving John and Amber came at a great cost. A great cost he now regrets paying, as he starts to say, "No, no, no, no, no," with wide eyes wildly looking around at all the demons he killed.

# CHAPTER 43
## REFUGE

There is only one place where all five elements, or systems, of a cultivator converge. This place of convergence is called the accretion-root, or self-center, depending on prescribed philosophy. Demons call it the accretion-root.

This spot is above the lower dantian, near the base of the spine, so some coiled energy mixes in with the other energies of the accretion-root too. Higher-tiered cultivators can feel a strange sort of energy in this spot, but John can feel nothing.

The energy leaking out of this convergence area is called the accretion-effusion. To ascend in tier, one must completely fill their lower dantian, and hope it is firm enough to be moved into the accretion-effusion. If it is, the dantian is held there until it is fully bathed in the strange energies long enough to cause the essence within the dantian to effloresce.

If ascension happens, the dantian is completely crystallized, and turns solid. The practitioner always sleeps at this point, and they awake stronger, their cocooned dantian is higher-tiered, and once again malleable.

Ranking up dantians is unnecessary for ascension, but not doing so as much as possible is throwing away power, and wasteful, and makes the ascension process much more difficult. The dantian needs to have a certain amount of firmness to move it to the accretion-effusion, and the essence needs a certain viscosity to effloresce correctly.

But more difficult doesn't mean impossible, and because something is better to do doesn't mean it is necessary to do.

John's dantian has been ranked up as much as possible as a Wood, and having had Hubaba explain the process of ascension to him, he can ascend. He hasn't yet because he is determined to finish what he started, and attune the spatial storage ring to himself before ascending.

If nothing else, John is stubborn. Having gotten so close to attuning the ring his own way, he refuses to discount all his past effort and give up, or take the path always traveled.

After the fight against Zongreth, and looting and hiding all the corpses, Hubaba insists they take refuge in the abandoned Trial, where they will be safe from the higher-tiered demons eventually sent to disperse the large packs of bull-lions, correcting the issue John created. Most likely, the bull-lions will be blamed for the disappearance of Zongreth and his whole party.

Going much further south is an option, but some Gold and even the occasional Platinum beast inhabit that region, and they would be drawn to a Silver tier cultivator such as Hubaba. The Trial is much closer to Circle Xakariz, but entering it is forbidden, so John and his companions will remain hidden and unnoticed while within, and can practice and cultivate safely as long as they stay in the entry area, and avoid the Trial proper.

Amber heals quickly from her wounds sustained during the battle with Zongreth. During the fight, she became too nervous after being run through with a sword. She transformed to demon and then her human form to use her invisibility and escape, though she can now use the ability in any form. Mistakes happen in battle.

Old habits are hard to break, and not just for how Amber's forms and abilities now work, as she is extremely reluctant to show her human form to Hubaba. She relents after being convinced all demons must be immune to her curse, as they do not find even other demons attractive in any way, and this holds true, as their new demon friend is not affected by her appearance in the slightest.

Hubaba does not heal as quickly from the wounds he sustained in the battle with Zongreth, though his weren't physical. Turning traitor against his own kind hurts him deeply, and he is inflicted with a severe melancholy for a while, and is very taciturn. He especially regrets killing all the scabs. If they were allowed to live, they would've told the new Second-Point Master the events that transpired, so Hubaba had no choice but to kill them all.

Amber is able to awaken him from his despaired mind, as Hubaba never had fun before, and Amber greatly enjoys having fun. She teaches Hubaba how to dance, sing, and pose for pretend photographs, and conduct himself as a proper lady.

As Hubaba teaches John and Amber about cultivation, so too does Amber teach Hubaba about modern human society before the Tree of Life, and Hubaba is fascinated by it, and takes a great interest in what he learns.

And as John is ready to advance in tier, so too is Hubaba. For nearly half a century Hubaba has been ready to advance to Gold, but no slot was open within Circle Xakariz for him to do so.

Now, free of such restraints in reality, though not totally free in his own mind, he agrees to ascend, but only after they all finish up what needs doing outside the Trial, as any Diamond would notice a new Gold in his territory from afar, and come to inspect and question him. It is extremely rare for a scab to go rogue, and Hubaba has never heard about it happening before, but assumes such information would be suppressed. He is certain rogue scabs have a very short life expectancy.

A [Title] marks the soul of each scab, announcing to all what they are, and it can be felt without being set as the active [Title], the same as John's ptagmog [Title], he finds out, so he switches back to the [Title] he gained from Magnus Gar'tar to benefit from the faster [Skill] gain.

There is no way for a scab to pretend to be chosen, or anything other than what their souls proclaim them to be.

Once Hubaba ascends, he will be trapped in the Trial until they break for the portal, whenever the portal opens.

Hubaba was present when Outer-Circle Master Baggodon the Blind instated the new master of Second Point, and they speculated on when the portal would open.

Time moves faster in the NetherRealm. Much faster, but not always the same fastness. It shouldn't have taken Ukaraaz and his Silvers more than half a day, at the most, to run from where the portal closed to Montreal. A half a day on Earth would translate to between two months or seven months for this strange world. Since they have been here for nine months, according to Hubaba, it can be assumed Ukaraaz is trying to take Montreal before reopening the portal.

It can't be known when the portal will open, so the companions must check it for themselves. Amber cannot navigate the Nether, but can mask herself from the senses of beings up to a certain tier. John is deft at stealth, and can navigate in the Nether, but needs the cloak that masks essence to avoid being seen, and the cloak is buried with the Bulwark armor.

Part of the loot they got from Zongreth's party is a belt of hiding type 2. This belt makes the user invisible, but doesn't mask essence or the feel of a cultivator when close, so the same or higher tier cultivator, or anyone sensitive enough, can still feel the presence of someone else nearby, but the belt lowers the sense range to do so considerably. And, of course, the belt is not of much use against any cultivator with an essence-sight, so a way to hide essence is also required.

Hubaba's main function as a scab was as an instructor, but that honorific is denied scabs, so they name the position 'scab-pedant.' He is also skilled with runecrafting and alchemy. As an instructor, he gave advice on cultivating, tested affinities, and performed rituals for enhancements, what magals call [Perks].

Luckily, Hubaba always keeps many of his components and ingredients with him, as well as his book of rituals, and his affinity-tester. He is missing certain tools needed to perform some crafting, such as alchemy relying on large items he doesn't lug around. He does have all he needs, including the harmony, to perform the ritual and attain the enhancement/[Perk] to mask his essence, minus one component. The component Hubaba is missing is the hide of a stealthy beast of the same or higher tier.

If Hubaba performs the essence-hiding ritual on himself, he will be able to travel with them on their outings outside the Trial, while wearing the belt of hiding as well, until he ascends to Gold.

After Amber questions Hubaba on her message regarding an 'entertainment package,' John states he also received the same message when first coming to this world. Hubaba has no knowledge of what it means or could be, and as far as he knows, all functions of the NCS, besides the functions it secretly provides to all living creatures capable of ascending, are disabled within NetherRealms.

John's harmony was near full when they first entered the Trial, and though without the NCS he has no way to see how far his rank ups pushed his [Stats], he believes they all increased significantly. Not wanting harmony to go to waste, he asks if Hubaba knows the rituals for increasing the soft caps he has not yet obtained, and the demon does, and even knows them by the same names John does.

John triages his [Stats] by importance, knowing his [Runes] [Stat] is the one least in need of a [Perk] increasing soft cap. Going by his ability to shrug off mental effects, his [Mental Fortification] is most in need to increase the soft cap for, judging whatever number the NCS assigned that [Stat] as grossly incorrect.

John performs the ritual for the [Resilient] [Perk] to increase the soft cap for [Mental Fortification]. He feels his harmony go down to slightly over two-thirds full.

Having the harmony to safely get two more [Perks], and four [Stats] arguably of equal value, he decides to get the [Perks] for [Min. Power] and [Capacity], called [Powerful] and [Expansive].

On his next outing to retrieve the buried Bulwark armor, cloak, and high-tiered robe, as well as resupply food and water, John feels his harmony go from near empty to completely full. He knows whatever caused his harmony to fill resulted in much wasted harmony too, and he somewhat regrets not ascending yet, as that would raise his harmony cap, as well as make new [Perks] available to him.

Though harmony is supposed to be a resource people struggle to fill, this seems less true for John, and he knows he still has many [Skills] he can merge, gaining large amounts of harmony at once, so he uses what he currently has to attain the three remaining soft-cap increasing [Perks] for [Physical Fortification], [Elemental Fortification], and even [Runes], named [Harden], [Resistant], and [Soulful].

John still has what he judges to be between ten and twenty percent harmony left, but even if his harmony was full, there are no other remotely useful [Perks] Hubaba knows of a Wood can get.

Up to this point, Amber and Hubaba have put very little effort at all into improving themselves. If Hubaba's math is correct, Amber is probably hindered from reaching the soft cap too. It is known that ranking up for beasts works differently than for cultivators, and they receive an increase to each [Stat] on rank up.

Amber has five animal forms, and her current strength indicates all her forms receive the cumulative benefits of all other's ranking up. Every rank up for Wood, her animal forms would give one increase to each [Stat], totaling five. Her human form would default to the natural undirected increase, meaning each [Stat] would increase by point-three, totaling five-point-three per rank up within the Wood Tier.

The soft cap for most beta-type F-grade humanoids at Wood tier is twenty-five, and this goes up to thirty-seven-point-five at Copper, and fifty at Bronze. Certain increases are given for each opened meridian, and two points are gained for each [Stat] ascending from Wood to Copper. At Copper, the general minimum increase goes from one to one-point-five. She now has a demon form, which will also add to her [Stat] increases, for an estimated total of 8.4 each [Stat] for her next rank up, minus whatever effects diminishing returns has on her human and demon form increases.

Minimum energy units vary greatly between different types of beings. Though the [Stats] for all Amber's forms were not the same at the

361

beginning, with all her increases they're now probably much closer together. At level 7 Hubaba projects all her [Stats] to be right around the Copper soft cap of 37.5. Even with all her forms having the same or similar [Strength] score, as a frog she can hit John as hard as she can and he barely feels it, whereas she hits significantly harder as a deer or human or demon, and can send him flying backwards as a bear.

Though it can't be known for certain, it can safely be assumed Amber is being hampered by the soft cap for all her [Stats] at this point, and if not yet, Hubaba is sure future rank ups within the Copper tier will be.

To address this, all her harmony is used to gain as many soft-cap increasing [Perks] as she can get. Surprisingly, or not surprisingly, Amber seems to hold far more harmony than John, and is able to get the four most expensive soft-cap increasing [Perks] before she is emptied.

Being more sensitive than John, Amber is easily walked through the [Skill] merge process, and just by sense and feel she is able to merge some of her lower and less important [Skills], something John is completely unable to do himself without the aid of the NCS. Amber is able to get all the soft-cap increasing [Perks] within a short span of hours, and also acquires some other [Perks] such as [Quick Thinking], and even another related to her demon form named [Ptagmog Rise].

And this is the extent of effort Amber and Hubaba put towards advancing themselves, and both seem far more interested performing a duet about it being cold outside, Hubaba trying to convince her to stay, and Amber having trouble deciding whether to stay or not.

John gets worried for a moment as the two dance far too near the threshold that sparks the Trial to start up. Hubaba said crossing the threshold might notify some higher-tiered demons sentient beings are in the abandoned Trial, which would doom all three of the Trial's current inhabitants.

The song the Natural and demon perform together is catchy, and John finds Amber's voice to be quite pleasant, but he tunes them out, once again, to focus on completing the task he set his mind to. He long ago gave up putting his arm in a position allowing him to stretch a strand of

362

essence from his armpit directly to his finger and the ring. That is impossible. He must split his mind once more and pin the essence thread to his forearm or wrist, and stretch it to his finger after. But that is one split too many for his mind to handle, and he can't get it to work.

A few more days go by, and with the stubborn will born of ages, a stubborn will to never quit no matter the cost or consequence, John tries and tries to stretch the essence to the ring. Amber and Hubaba laugh and giggle and dance and sing. At one point Amber says, "This is a dream! Truly, this is a dream! Goodness, I've dreamed...I wanted to have...this. All this! Doing this, and I never once thought I'd actually be able to. Ever! I could never be this close to anyone. Spend so much time like this with actual friends and be visible too! Do all this fun stuff and be seen and everything. This is so much fun!"

Hubaba giggles and replies, "This one knows! This one never even knew I wanted to do this so badly, now this one never wants to stop! This one thanks you!"

Amber puts her hand over her surprised mouth, "Oh, buddy! You just referred to yourself as 'I!' I'm so proud of you!"

"This one did! This one said 'I!'"

John can't help but laugh at the goofy joy showing on Hubaba's face, but internally hopes Amber isn't ruining the demon as a combatant, and wishes they'd work on meditation or combat related tasks to improve their power. He keeps silent, some part of his heart very happy the two are experiencing such simple joys they've always been denied, and are learning the pleasure of friendship and companionship, but there is a time for joy and a time for war, and John believes their current situation requires the war-mind.

On his next attempt, John finally manages to split his focus four ways, pinning the thread to his lower forearm, and it all nearly unravels due to his surprise. He carefully pulls the thread towards his finger, shaking with nervousness and effort, certain it'll all come unraveled before it touches the ring. But it doesn't.

The thread connects to the ring, attuning John to it, making the ring his own, binding it to him.

A mental picture of all the items in the ring appears in John's mind, and he hollers in joy at seeing his new treasures.

In just crystals, John is wealthier than he could ever have imagined. The ring contains a light-blue crystal from the low Transcendent Tree he has no idea the value of. There are four blue-green crystals of a Salt, each worth two-hundred thousand of the clear crystals of a Wood. There are thirteen dark-green crystals of a Diamond, each worth thirty thousand of the clear crystals of a Wood. And on and on down the tiers.

Greed enters John's mind. He talked to Hubaba many times about going to the demon city far to the south, only to have each attempt rebuked. He knows it will spell his doom, but with such wealth and nothing to spend it on, the less savory aspects within himself become more prominent. *There must be a way to access high-tiered shops and crafters.*

He puts those thoughts to the back of his mind as he views the rest of the items. *Hubaba was right and I feel bad for thinking he was lying. Second Point really had no treasury or armory, as this ring acted as both.*

The ring seems to lead to a large room, as tall as it is long and wide. *Sixteen or seventeen cubits. I hated that measurement system. Elbow to fingertip is a stupid way to measure anything you can't hold. Paces have always been the best system of measurement.*

The ring is filled with weapons of all types, some even John doesn't recognize at all, plus shields, many robes and various types of armor, and some unknown objects and materials. Best of all, to John, are the trinkets. Many baubles, rings, necklaces, bracers, and other trinkets fill a space about a pace wide.

Someone shakes John's shoulder, so he is forced out of his current gaiety, only to be overcome with a different sort of gaiety as he looks at Amber's impossibly beautiful face, and her smile that fills his soul with joy. "Tell me you did it, buddy?"

"I did it. And we are filthy rich. I think. I hope. And well-armed and armored too. There're some nice robes in here for you. And trinkets!"

John and Amber hold hands and jump up and down, laughing, and Hubaba comes over and joins in the revelry.

John stops short, frightened. "Hubaba, my friend, what is all over your face?"

"It's called make-up, Wood John. This one is beautiful now. Painted as such, this one is irresistible, right Copper Amber?"

"Just Amber, buddy, remember? No need for all that title nonsense. And you are beautiful. Remember that Christina Aguilera song I taught you? The one about being beautiful? Just remember those lyrics if anyone questions it. Tell him how beautiful he looks, John."

"Great gods below, woman! We have a Silver ally now, one not allowed to fight his whole life, and instead of focusing on what will keep us alive, you turn him into a common nightwalker?"

Anger replaces the joy on Amber's face, and her hands go on her hips. She stares daggers at John for a moment before replying. "And what exactly have you been doing? Playing with your ring! I haven't seen you training him. Ever hear of mental health? If we don't have fun occasionally we'll all go crazy. Everyone knows that. And Baba's never had fun. You said we should embrace life, remember? Stop being such a party-pooper and tell him how beautiful he looks. Now!"

"That ring is filled with arms and armor and riches beyond imagining. I haven't been wasting my time."

"Oh, buddy, you could've opened it when we first got in here if you ascended instead of being so pig-headed."

John deflates a little. He can't deny there is some truth to what she says. "I couldn't. I had to win."

"Win? Against a ring? You can't win against a ring."

"Yes, you can. I did. I won. You won't understand, but it was important for me to do."

Amber, herself, seems to deflate a little. She puts her hand on John's shoulder, and looks up into his eyes. "It's okay. I read an article in 'Household' magazine about how to keep your husband and friends happy. Oh, this had to be in the forties, after the war. One part stuck out to me, and

I promised if I ever made good friends, I mean real friends I can actually spend time with and be myself around, I'd do this.

"The article said something like you have to have mutual respect. If something's important to your husband or good friends, you gotta respect it. And they gotta respect what's important to you. Mutual respect and admiration. There's a lot I admire about you, John. A lot.

"For the first time...well, basically ever, me and Baba are having fun. Just let us have fun. It's okay. Just like it's okay you wanted to beat the ring, or win it, or whatever. I don't have to really understand why. I know it's important to someone who's important to me. Right? But this works both ways. Now tell Baba how beautiful he is."

John puts his head down. "You are beautiful, Hubaba, my friend. That paint really highlights your...features. If you want, I can show you how some doughty fighters would use such paint to inflict fear in enemies instead of...uh, enhancing beauty."

"This one thanks you for saying so, and learning another method for make-up would be nice, Wood John. Just John, this one means. I mean."

A bright smile animates Amber's face. "Good job using 'I!' I'm proud of you, buddy!"

John, needing to change the topic back to something important, at least to himself, says, "Hubaba, I could use your help sorting through all our new treasure. I know I need to ascend, and none are more ready for me to do so than I am, but I am too excited now. I need to go through this treasure, and see how rich we are. How many crystals makes someone rich? Light-blue crystals come from the next Tree, right? Great gods below, please tell me all these items are magic and you know their functions."

# CHAPTER 44
# ASCENSION

John, Amber, and Hubaba pick through the treasures, searching for new gear and arms to equip.

John places Dead Maker, a famous and far too noticeable weapon, and one too far above his tier to utilize fully anytime soon, inside the ring. Though his robes aren't famous, or very noticeable, he covers them with a set of dark and comfortable soft leather armor, reinforced in many areas with boiled leather, or cuir-bouilli.

Other than the usual 'standard item soft-glyph,' this armor has some runes allowing for a hardy essence-shield. Mail armor would indicate a wealth beyond what a Wood or Copper should have, drawing attention to him if spotted by demons, and all the plate armor is for higher tiers, and require more essence to get the most of anyways. Considering their forays out of the Trial will always be stealth missions, dark leather is the best option. For now.

Sadly, John learns there is a hard limit to how many enchanted items can be attuned to a cultivator. He has the bracers and storage ring already attuned, he's picked his new armor, so can only select one more magic ring for his other hand, a head item, and a necklace counts as a head item, as well as a waist item, footwear, and one more torso item, such as a cloak, and that will bring him to the limit of attunable worn items. Held weapons and shields aren't attuned, so don't count towards this limit.

John won't be able to attune to his robes since he is attuning to his armor, and plans on using a cloak. Which works out well since the runes on his robes have an unknown function, and were meant for Diamonds and above. The 'standard item soft-glyph' on the robes will still work, as it powers itself with the [Replenish] rune.

Hubaba warned John off from testing items made for higher-tiered cultivators, since if the essence within a dantian is not enough to power the runes, it pulls other energies from within, and if those energies aren't enough, it pulls from the spirit, and the more attuned items, the higher the drain, and the greater the chance of being crippled.

John's spirit is probably quite damaged from powering his mighty bracers, but he remembers one of the NCS upgrades he has heals the spirit passively. His [Emergency Heal] hasn't functioned since entering the Nether, so he assumes whatever upgrade heals the spirit also doesn't work in this world either, but he knows shen heals spirit as well as the soul, and he constantly converts essence to shen, so he isn't too worried.

John is happy to see Amber pick robes from the ring, and lower-tiered ones too, so he can place the even more advanced robes he previously buried with the Bulwark armor in his ring, and keep them for himself, while wishing he knew the specific functions of the many glyphs on the robe, hoping they each do something amazing.

It seems to John, Amber picks robes based solely on style, rather than functionality, as there are better robes with better runes she could pick. She puts aside many robes she likes the style of, and plans to wear a different one each day, in a rotation, but still stored in John's ring. He doesn't mind, as her current outfit shows much leg, and he enjoys the sight, and when she fights, she will most likely change into a bear, losing access to all items anyways.

John is surprised how often his gaze falls on Amber's legs. He thinks they are far too skinny, and he is uncertain why his eyes so enjoy the sight of them. He often must stop his orb-eye from gazing at her, as if it has a mind of its own. If he must look, he will do so as a man should, with his own eyes.

How Amber picks the rest of her items is based on the same reasoning as the robes she chose. After trying an item on, she always asks Hubaba whether it looks good or not, putting no thought into functionality and utility. John can only convince her to take one item based on function, a belt that provides a strong essence-shield, for use in emergencies, and she relents with little complaint, as the belt is quite stylish and fits well with any outfit and other adornments.

The second ring John selects for himself is a focused-beam attack that converts his already powerful essence into a mighty type of fire called plasma, and the beam can go out for half a league or so, at least as far as he can figure. He is able to discern, with the help of Amber and Hubaba, a foot is two-thirds a cubit, and nine feet is nearly one dan. One dan is about two and three-fourths meters. Dan being the universal standard measurement of most sentient species.

For his headpiece, John wanted a necklace, but ends up selecting a padded leather cap that, when activated, can reflect many weak essence attacks back at the caster, or one mighty attack up to a certain threshold. If the attack is too powerful, it overwhelms the reflection, and lands as it normally would. The helmet has a chin strap, so can be worn around the neck when not covering the head.

Picked as footwear are boots of secrecy, which supposedly enhance stealth ability, and dull not just the sound of footfalls, but also heartbeat, clanking, and all unintentional sounds. How an item, magical or not, can tell what sounds are intentional or not is beyond John. These boots collect the energy they are empowered with themselves, not requiring any of John's own essence for the benefits they provide.

The cloak John was 'gifted' by Garioch he now wears, called a stealth cloak. There are two more of these cloaks in the ring. He doesn't like wearing cloaks, but he only needs to wear this one fully when stealthing, and can tuck it into his belt whenever else. Hubaba takes one of the other two of these cloaks, though its use for him is questionable, as he has no [Skill] with stealth, and he believes he still needs to gain the enhancement/[Perk] to hide his essence from essence-sight.

For a waist item, John is excited for the one he picks, and of all the many items in the ring, it is the only one to do what it does. The belt passively provides a small boost to 'physical prowess,' according to

Hubaba, but what specific [Stats] count towards 'physical prowess' are unknown. The belt also collects its own energy to power itself.

Other belts have better functions for specific situations, but he already has many items he must power with his own essence, so any that power themselves, and work all the time, even if the benefit they give is minor, is better than something he must not just remember to use when needed, but also requires more of his own essence to function.

Multiple items providing the same function tend to have issues, as the spirit becomes confused attuned to the same runes. Hubaba thought the plasma ring wouldn't work for John. The bracer's runes are not visible, but most likely include a focused-beam attack too. Since his plasma ring does work, the runes are different enough to not matter, or the bracers have a full and proper glyph.

There is an item John wishes he could use – a bracer that turns into a doughty shield, giving great protection from even mighty attack manifestations when imbued with essence.

Of course, John's current bracers are attuned to him, and he can't remove them. He can't use these bracers effectively for many tiers, as they will drain far more than just his dantian every time, so they are wasting an attunable slot. Only temporarily though, since the bracers have proven to be very mighty, and he hopes to use them regularly someday.

Hubaba takes the shield-bracer John wishes he could use now.

On Earth, solid metal shields are unrealistic, and far too heavy to utilize effectively. This never really applied to John, but now applies far less so, and he picks a very thick, full-metal round shield.

The shield has the standard runes of [Major Durability], [Lesser Repair], and [Lesser Maintain], but all these runes must be powered by John's own essence. In addition, when imbued with just a little essence, the shield's edge turns dark and deadly, and can cut through foes like a blade.

John picks a Silver-rated sword, both long and heavy, and on top of the 'standard item soft-glyph,' it has runes providing a strong weapon enhancement, turning the essence he imbues the sword with into the red-aspected essence of fire, capable of destroying essence-shields quickly, and cutting through both tough skin and hard metals far more easily than the [Minor Sharpness] rune it also possesses.

The hilt of the sword is about a foot in length, and the blade long and thick, over three-and-a-half feet in length. It is heavier than it looks, and would be far too heavy for a normal human to lift or hold one-handed, but sits in John's hand easily, and suits his style well. He finds his new weapon feels similar to his own big-tuck, a sword he crafted himself long ago. He names it Fireblade, as the blade lights afire when imbued with essence, and John has never once been accused of being overly creative.

Since weapons don't need to be attuned, John sets aside some other arms he could need in a pinch, including a maul, spear, and a bow with a draw strength he can barely handle, but should work well for him after he ascends.

The other choices Hubaba makes are not explained, but excite the demon greatly. When he finds an item he likes, he whispers, "Yes. Yes," and smiles creepily, reminding John of the many times his face was licked by the demon.

John wants to ask the old demon why he licked his face so many times, but can never bring himself to actually do so.

Fully decked out, and all the treasures that can be identified now organized in the ring, it is time for John to attempt ascension, and advancement to Copper tier. He already overfilled his dantian with essence, stopping only right before the danger of distending it too much, where stretchmarks start to show on the dantian. He is around twenty percent over, double what's recommended for ascension, but John knows it's safe enough for him.

"You can do it, buddy! I have faith in you!" Amber smiles encouragingly at John, and he looks away quickly, and he is unsure why his face becomes hot.

"Remember to hold your core directly into the accretion-effusion, enough so the whole core is evenly and fully bathed in the energies. If you cannot lift it high enough, or for long enough, and your core only partially effloresces, you won't be able to make the attempt again until your core recovers. It could be weeks or even months. Once you get it to the correct spot it should become easy to hold there, and as it begins to crystalize you will naturally begin to sleep, and the ascension will be successful."

"Thank you, my friends. I will start now."

John sits with legs crossed, hands on thighs, and enters a light meditation. He pictures his dantian, and decides on what method to use to raise it higher. Hubaba told him many methods that can be used, and he decides to start with the simplest.

Without visual aids, or any other method, John tries to lift the dantian with just his mind. All methods utilize only the mind, but John considers using visual aids such as his hands physical help.

After many tries, moving the dantian with only his mind accomplishes nothing, and it refuses to budge even a smidge, so John pictures both of his hands under the dantian, and he heaves it upwards.

The dantian doesn't budge, but it feels like there's an insect in John's lower belly twitching around and spasming. He makes many attempts to lift his dantian this way, and all fail.

John pictures his whole self, and grabs under the dantian, and with a mighty heave tries to lift it, and lift again, and again, feeling the insect in his lower belly go mad trying to claw its way out, and in the real world his legs twitch. He continues to heave powerfully on the dantian until he hears cracking, like a large pane of glass under too much stress.

Worried, John exits his mind. Amber is meditating as a frog, sitting on a small pile of clear crystals, as they all decided to use the lowest crystals as long as they stay effective. Clear crystals still work for Hubaba, though he's never been allowed to use them to speed up cultivation since becoming a scab.

Hubaba, also meditating, opens his painted eyes and looks at John. "No luck, Wood John? John, this...I mean."

"My dantian won't move. When I applied more pressure, I heard cracking noises, and it worried me. I don't want to damage my dantian."

"Apologies, but this is only an image. There is no noise to hear, so you must be mistaken. Is your core too soft to raise? Are you sure you ranked up four times?"

"It is hard as a rock, and not soft at all. I ranked up as much as possible, and tried ranking up many times after, since I knew not how to ascend."

"Apologies again, but the core is a membrane filled with liquid, so it can't be hard as a rock. It only becomes hard after crystalizing, and then only temporarily."

John doesn't want to argue with the demon. He knows things don't always work the same for him as they do others. He asks, "Is there any way to damage a dantian by manhandling it? By lifting a dantian that doesn't want to be lifted?"

"No. If it is too soft it will be hard to lift. There're ways a cultivator can damage their own core, such as overfilling and distending it. But all living creatures capable of ascension have an Eternal matrix protecting our cores from being damaged in the old ways, even us born to the ptag-mog. We still have the nanos in us, even though we will never be able to activate our NCS."

"What is an Eternal matrix?"

"Well, that is a long explanation. The short of it is Eternals are capable of making, uh...very advanced glyphs, called matrices, that are extremely powerful. Hmm, you know how suns have a lifespan?"

"What? Suns? The sun of my world is always the same and will last forever."

The demon sucks in air and makes a tsking sound. "Wood John. Just John, this...I mean. Apologies, but that is not correct. Suns have phases, and eventually die out. As do whole universes. Eternals can create matrices stopping these phases and processes. That is how the core worlds and universes last so long.

"The nanos in us make something like an Eternal matrix around our core protecting it in many ways. Before this, cultivators tried to damage the core of opponents in fights. Um, this is hard to explain without you knowing more about higher-tiered fighting. Suffice it to say damaging any core, including your own, is nearly impossible outside of a few specific ways. Distension is the easiest way. Failing ascension doesn't cause damage, but it takes a while for the core to recover. And there are two other ways you don't have to worry about at all now.

"It is completely safe to raise your core, and use as much force as needed to do so. This one is certain. I am certain, I mean."

John is not convinced Hubaba is certain in his specific case. He asks, "And this is true for both demons and humans?"

"Demons are people. Wo...John must have meant terrans?"

"Well, I said human, not people, but yes."

"Whatever word you're using translates as people. To answer, yes. Demons are beta-types, like terrans, just higher graded, and demons become alpha-types at the Divine Tree. Beta-type usually indicates carbon-based, usually a spine with coiled energy generating near the base of it, and humanoid. Alpha-types are far stronger than beta-types. Omega-types are true monsters. The other common types besides beta are delta, zeta, and theta-types. There's far more than that, but those are the most common. Alpha and omega-types are not common at all. Of course, all the different types are still graded, such as terrans being F-grade."

John ruminates on this information for a moment, deciding Hubaba would enjoy talking to Pixie, and they could have a contest of who can give the longest answer. "Okay, if you are certain it's safe. But I would swear on all I hold dear I heard cracking. There're no stretchmarks like when I overfilled my dantian too much, but I heard cracking."

The demon just smiles. "Nothing to worry about at all. Most cultivators make it to at least Bronze with little effort. This tier ascension is done all the time without issue by every creature in every reality. Our toddlers do it."

Hubaba's face turns serious, and he says, "This one...I. I wanted to ask you something now that Amber is occupied. Does Wo...does John really think this...I, does John think I look beautiful with this make-up?"

John, still a little hurt from both Amber and Hubaba telling him he looked foolish when he fully loaded up on trinkets, even when he explained he knew he couldn't attune them, and wore them only to look as a mighty warrior should once again, as he hasn't been able to in a very long time, has an urge to tell Hubaba the truth as he sees it. He suppresses the urge, as he knows Hubaba is still teetering on being morose and taciturn, and Amber has done so well bringing him out of his shell, helping him feel free of the chains binding his heart and mind since becoming a scab.

John looks down and says, "Yes. Very beautiful. As I said before, it really highlights your features."

With an extremely creepy smile the demon says, "Thank you, Wo...John. This...I like being beautiful. I want to be an Instagram model."

John has no idea what that is, but wants to encourage his new friend. "I'm sure you'll do well, friend. Please don't forget to also focus on your martial skills too. You are the most powerful among us, and you said you have nearly no experience in combat."

Hubaba giggles and looks at himself in a hand mirror they found in the ring, pulling strange faces, batting his eyes. Conversation now over, John, again, focuses on ascension.

John pictures himself larger than before, and bends under his dantian, placing it fully on his shoulders and back, as the Titan Atlas was said to do with the heavens.

With a massive heave, and a yell of effort, he tries to force the dantian higher, hearing cracking glass reverberate throughout his insides, echoing back and forth. In the real world his legs spasm mightily, and he falls to his side as they kick out wildly, over, and over.

A hand starts frantically shaking John's shoulder. He ignores this. He ignores everything, including the pain in his lower belly, which feels as if a volcano is exploding, and he heaves upwards again, imaginary legs shaking in effort, tapping in to a primal part of himself only meant to be let loose in dire straits, as when fighting a tiger, and thoughts of safety and tomorrow must leave the mind, and the only care is killing the beast before being too injured to do so, before the body stops but the mind doesn't, and the tiger feasts on a living body, frozen, but still aware.

The cracking increases, and John lets out a mighty yell that echoes even over the noise of the shattering glass, and he forces his dantian upwards, and upwards, smidge by smidge, until his legs fully extend, and the weight of all the heavens bears down upon his shoulders, and he feels the dantian being bathed in strange energy.

In reality, John's uncontrollable legs kick out madly, and the volcano in his belly erupts to new heights of pain and destruction, and the frantic shaking of his shoulder increases, and someone tries to hold his legs, but fails, and is kicked off and away.

Suddenly, John's vision cracks, and then shatters, and he is looking through many, many eyes, like how he assumes a fly sees through its thousand-thousand eyes. Then the world blurs by him, as it does when entering his Mind's Eye, but it last far longer, and he travels far further, and he is somehow still in reality at the same time, his friends trying to wake him, and also still holding his dantian up as Atlas did the heavens, in three places all at once.

All suddenly stills, and he is looking directly at the humongous, indescribable monster he's seen every time he's ranked up. This time the monster speaks, and its words are like extraordinarily destructive and strange trumpets meant to quake the earth apart, heralding the end of days.

**"GOOD, MY CHILD. GOOD."**

# CHAPTER 45
# A THOUSAND-THOUSAND EYES, ALL AT ONCE

John is returned to his youth. To the day King Kah finally attempted to reclaim John's father's lost hold. The day John fulfilled the oath of vengeance he made to his parents. The day his brother died.

John is still looking at the humongous monster, still holding his dantian up, still having his shoulder shaken by Hubaba or Amber, but he is also here too. His brother is falling out of the march, lagging behind the many, many sworn-men of King Kah. John slows to walk beside him.

"You must not fall this far back, brother. This is the first time you march to war. Today you take lives. You might get a new name. Make it a good one."

John can't help but see the fright in his brother's eyes. "I can't do this! I don't want to fight. Let me turn back. I want to farm."

John looks around nervously, worried someone heard this cowardly talk. "Shhhh! Don't ever say that in front of others. You are the son of a lord, now thirteen, and a man grown. This is not real; we are already dead. We can only awaken from this dream. Remember, be fell and tall, and honor will follow. That is all there is to it. Simple. Stay by my side, and I will protect you as I always do."

John wishes he was able to protect his brother that day. Try as he might, he can't even remember his brother's name, though he remembers his king's name, and it shames him.

Then John is somewhere else, in a hold, talking to a newly surrendered king, back when he was conquering all the lands of his birth with Ahn.

The king looks despondent, ashamed to have surrendered, as any man should, but he was given little choice. John feels himself saying, "Do not despair. There is still a great place for you in the Underworld. There is no shame in kneeling to us. We are much stronger than any others. You had no fair choice. No chance. Hold your head high knowing you saved your family, your people, and your honor. We will be gone soon, and you will rule as you always have. Nothing changes but the tribute."

The king cheers a little, and John is glad. He is a good king, and deserving of honor. He then knows his words are moot as he hears Ahn approaching, his master enters the hold and throws a net full of heads onto the table.

Ahn looks at the king and says, "Ah, the conquered king. Look at the anger in your eyes! I can feel the hate pouring off you."

John sees Ahn's eyes sparkle as he uses the mind-power on the king. Ahn then says, "Do as I command. Come stand before me."

John knows where this is going. "Master Ahn, please. You said you wouldn't use the mind-power on those we conquer. This man suffers enough."

"Oh, stop being a woman. You know I can only get hard when they hate me this much. Talk to me about honor when you're my age. Leave or stay, just be quiet and let me have what little joy is still left to me in life."

Ahn removes his robe, drops his loincloth down to the ground, and steps out of it. "You, oh great king, take off your loincloth, turn around, and bend over the table."

John leaves the hold, not wanting to see this good king shamed so. He hates the mind-power. No one should have their ability to stand defiant taken from them. You convince people with words or deeds, and if those fail, you kill them, in honorable battle, and praise them for their courage and resolve once they are dead. He reaffirms his vow never to use it. It is something only a demon would do, or those possessed by an evil.

378

Once again, John wishes he was strong enough to kill his master, but the man is too old and powerful, and John is too cowardly, too afraid of the cold-dark.

Outside the hold, time moves forward many, many years, and a flap opens, and he sees a field full of horses and tents, and he knows exactly when this is. His time with the Sclaveni, shortly after he was possessed by a great madness and evil himself, not long before the Avar arrive, those doughty fighters.

John knows the Avar will soon force the newly located Roman Empire in old Byzantion to pay much tribute to avoid conflict. Shortly before this time though, he thought the world was ending.

Ahn would often tell John a story his own master told him. Long, long ago the world had great cities, greater than can be imagined. Then a great and giant god fell from the heavens into the ocean, and the oceans rose in anger and destroyed many great cities, and the earth was angry and many mountains roared out hot fire high into the heavens, and the sun went away for a long time, and the world got very cold, and all the other cities disappeared, and it was hard to find groups of men anywhere, and it took many, many years for the world to become good again.

Looking out over the Sclaveni, John remembers the events of the recent years before this time, and the madness it caused in him, as he thought the events of Ahn's story were happening again. And they were, just to a far lesser extent.

For two years the sun hid behind shadow, and didn't shine at all, or shone only a few hours, but weakly. Something John should've enjoyed, but it made him fearful. The sky was either completely dark or blood red. The world became colder. Plants failed to grow. Wars broke out all over, cannibalism became common, then a deadly pestilence spread everywhere.

He thought it surely heralded the end of time, as many religions predicted the exact events that happened. John became fearful, and he slaughtered his way through the Ostrogoth Kingdom up as far as the Jutes, and back down and east, sure his only chance of avoiding the cold-dark was to strengthen himself as much as he could from the vital essence of strong warriors.

But the sun shone again, the world warmed again, the black plague didn't kill everyone as many learned men and priests claimed it would, and the madness finally left John when he realized it was not the end of days.

John is ashamed of the acts he performed, but all that can be done is to make amends going forward, hoping to find a way to improve or fix his failing mind.

Standing at the tent flap, John then decides to go north, he hasn't been that way in a long while.

The chief walks towards John and tells him there will be new battles for him. The Antes made an alliance with Justinian. War and raiding on both will begin again.

"With you leading our raids, mighty son of Perun, we will slaughter the Romans and Antes down to a child, and take all they have," says the chief.

John stands silently for a long moment before giving his reply. "Sorry, my friend, but I am leaving. Not long ago I thought the world was ending. It did not. But my world is ending, as my mind fails me more and more. I need something. I don't know what, but it's not here. Maybe it's north."

The world goes dark as John transitions between memories, and he realizes there are many of him, and he is experiencing only what is shown in this eye, one of a thousand-thousand eyes.

Then John, for a mere moment, feels all that is happening to all versions of himself, all thousand-thousand, and all the memories all the Johns are experiencing, and he has an epiphany of sorts, and can clearly see he's always lied to himself, ever since he was a boy, saying and believing things to trick his mind into doing what needs to be done, or to justify what he had done.

John is not okay with this, and vows to stop lying to himself, and realizes this vow is also a lie. He will continue to endure time, continue to advance, and continue to tell himself all the lies needed to do so. There are some things he wishes he could change, or truths he could tell, but the consequences aren't clear or obviously beneficial, such as with his brother, as trading one good death for a worse one, a dishonorable one, just for a handful of extra days of this dream, doesn't seem a fair exchange.

All there is to do is become strong enough where you create the truth you want, and it makes John sad to understand this, but also fortifies his resolve.

A hand shakes his shoulder, and before opening his eyes, he notices very loud humming all around him. He's sitting on a metal bench along a concaved metal wall, his backside vibrating. He cracks one eye open and sees a plain-faced woman in front of him, dressed in all black, with white trim around the black veil completely covering her hair. She is young, tan-skinned, and her scent is somehow familiar.

"Time to awaken, Gion. You must wake now. Giovanni. Giovanni."

"I'm awake."

"I wish I could sleep as deep as you, dear Gion."

"Do I know you? Your scent...I know you? Wait, my friend...I forget his name. Where am I? What is this noise? Why is this room shaking?"

The woman smiles confidently, and a face that was plain becomes rather beautiful. Rarely has John met a woman with such surety and confidence without the wisdom only age can bring, and only once the beauty of youth is long behind them. *What a kind and beautiful smile*, he thinks. The woman's calmness keeps him calm. It makes him feel as if everything will be okay.

"Yes, you know me. And well. You taught me Italian, though it isn't too far from my native Spanish. I am of your kind, my dear Gion. The friend you speak of is Thomas. Father Thomas. I received the power from him almost half a century or so ago. I am Sister Maria. I'll explain the loud noise and shaking soon, but first, how much of the vital essence do you have? And do you need any food?"

"I am near full of the essence of life, and I don't need to eat, but I could if you've already prepared food. I'd appreciate a drink if you have something at hand. Why did you call him Father Thomas, and yourself Sister Maria?"

Sister Maria gets up to fetch food and drink, and she braces herself as the room goes mad for a moment, and bucks hard, frightening John. He's never been in a humming, loud room that moves, a room made of metal, and it confuses him. Sister Maria staying so calm settles his nerves.

"I am called Sister and Thomas called Father because we are with the Church. Father Thomas is a special papal nuncio, and has been for centuries. I am a nun and devote my life to the one true faith and God our Savior, as has Father Thomas."

John now remembers Thomas being infatuated with the new religion of the peasant man and the one God, similar to the peoples of his Lilitu so long ago, besides the worshiping of a peasant, and saying there are three gods but somehow only one God too. The room bucks again and John's heart spikes. "Why is this room moving so?"

Back, Sister Maria hands John a metal canteen of water and a strange and tiny metal bowl filled with minced chicken, John assumes by the smell of it. "I will explain the room shortly, and the noise. First, you usually ask me if Father Thomas is still doing his silly nonsense where he refuses to take a human life."

John laughs, as he did want to ask this, but the bucking room changed his priorities. "Well, is he?"

"Of course, my dear Gion. As is also true for me. But not never, we only kill when we are certain it is the will of God. Now this is where you say there is no God, or gods, and we are the closest things to such, and Father Thomas and I will both realize this some far off day in the future."

John smiles, as it sounds exactly like what he would say. "And if I said this, what would your reply be, Sister Maria? And don't you think it is a silly thing for me to call you sister? It would make more sense for me to call you daughter, or granddaughter, as Thomas is as a son to me, or the closest thing our kind can have of progeny."

The girl smiles brightly, and puts her hand on John's knee as she kneels in front of him. "Big words! That means today shall be a good day.

Humor your granddaughter, and call me Sister, and Thomas Father. I know you think my face is plain, and I am too skinny, and not pretty unless I smile, so I will smile a lot, and bat my eyes sweetly, if you play along."

John laughs loudly. "I like you very much, Sister Maria. And you have a beautiful smile, but I could not guess if you have a quality body in that baggy outfit. I do know a thing or two about women, so if I said you're too skinny, you should believe me and eat more. If you take all my advice, it will ensure my granddaughter has only the best of suitors."

"Oh, grandpa, you are too late, as I am already married to the best of all husbands, our Lord and Savior, God Almighty Himself."

This statement stops John completely, and he is taken aback, and he then realizes she meant symbolically, and she is not actually the bride of a real being that is God.

"Ha! That always gets you! Now, my dear Gion, my grandpa, time to talk business. We are currently traveling in a modern invention called a plane. You will be fine as long as you do not open the curtain shades. The noise is coming from something called an engine. The bucking is called turbulence. No need to be frightened at all, you see how calm I am? It is just a new way to travel, no different to a wagon, just much faster."

With both her hands, Sister Maria holds John's right hand. "Father Thomas asked you for a favor, and you agreed. Do you remember the favor?"

"I do not."

"He asked if you would be willing to free members of the Church being held in a prison camp. It is a big camp and well-guarded. You'll have to make your way a great distance on foot, or horse if you can find one. I will leave instructions with you." She places an envelope inside John's coat. "You can read it. You've already read it. The camp is in Dachau. Here, look."

Sister Maria unfolds a piece of paper, and words and very realistic, but very dull and drab paintings are on the paper. John is surprised she'd treat such a great work of art so callously, as it must have taken the artist years to paint such beautiful images.

Obviously guessing at what John is thinking, Sister Maria says, "This wasn't painted and isn't valuable. Feel. Smooth. It is two photographs printed on paper. This is the prison camp at Dachau, and this is an aerial photograph taken from the sky. This dot is where you'll start traveling from. This dot is where the camp is. These here and here are known German forces between. Remember, all are God's children equally, so spare as many as you can.

"In this photo are the barracks where the prisoners are held. In this circled barracks here are the prisoners you must prioritize freeing. They are Catholic clergy, the majority of which we think are Polish. You can speak both German and Polish somewhat, though not...let's say others will have an easier time understanding your words than vice versa. The clergy will all be wearing red badges, most will be able to speak Latin too.

"If it is safe to do so, free more prisoners. This is the priority list of barracks to free. But the mission will be a success if you free only the clergy. Is this okay? This is a very dangerous mission. Do you still agree to do this favor for Father Thomas?"

John wants to scoff. Priests have always been the same. Good at telling tall tales, taking what they haven't earned, and getting others to do their dirty work. He wants to ask why it's okay for him to kill, and do what needs to be done, but not Thomas. He doesn't. He knows Thomas to be an honorable and kind man that has done much to care for him, and what a burden he has been to Thomas.

Maria seems a kind person too. John wishes his mind wasn't so gone, and that he had two of his kind such as Maria and Thomas to spend time with long ago, when he could have enjoyed it. When he could have remembered it.

Before John can see how he answers the question, the vision, or memory, fades to black, and is lost to him, and he feels something great has changed.

One part of John is no longer looking at the humongous monster, and he is only two Johns now. One hefting his dantian high on his shoulders, his legs quaking under the titanic strain, and the second is being splashed with the tainted water of the Nether, slapped, pinched, and shaken – all attempts to wake him up, his legs still spasming out of control.

John's lower belly is burning with pain unlike any he's ever felt, and he's felt it all, many, many times. He is insusceptible to mundane pain, and largely hardened to true pain, and what he feels in his belly is intolerable. Unendurable. Pain that should cause unconsciousness to protect the mind from the trauma of it, yet doesn't, so he must suffer it.

Seeing his dantian is now completely crystalized, John can do nothing but wait for the promised sleep, and he urgently hopes it comes soon, as he desperately wants an end to the pain. But sleep doesn't come, and he must endure the agonizing pain, while straining to continue holding his dantian high on his shoulders.

John makes his world smaller, and only focuses on enduring from one moment to the next. Just one more moment and he can stop. And then just one more, and then one more after, completely blocking out everything besides reaching the next moment.

Then the final moment comes as Hubaba infuses a ritual circle with essence, and blessed unconsciousness takes John to welcomed oblivion.

# CHAPTER 46
# BETTER TO RAGE THAN COWER

Not too long later, John's mind shrugs off the ritual magic Hubaba used to cause his unconsciousness, and he screams in pain. A slightly different ritual is performed, similar to the one Diamond Garioch used on John to compel truth, but modified to compel only sleep, and this lasts a little longer. The next time John awakens his head is on the lap of Hubaba, as the demon licks his face, whispering, "Yes."

John's belly still burns with fire, but the pain is greatly dulled from its peak, and he feigns sleep, as he is frozen with indecision on how to make this awkwardness stop, and he has no idea how to address what is happening to him. After some time, the face-licking stops, and Hubaba begins to brush John's hair. The demon whispers to himself as he brushes, "This one has a name now. This one has friends now."

*This isn't so bad,* John thinks. He tunes Hubaba out and studies the changes to his body. He feels - more. As if he is more, can feel more, and is aware of more, but articulating what this 'more' exactly is, is difficult. He feels stronger. And hardier. His dantian is noticeably larger, but feels strange. It is about three-quarters full, and the essence within it is mostly teal or turquoise color now, like how the sea looks sometimes at some places, whereas before it was clear, sometimes slightly golden, and other times slightly pinkish.

The teal is swirled within other colors, and all colors are separated. John sees orange, red, yellow, purple, black, and a very light grey, almost white color.

At first John assumes it is like the colored crystals, but Copper to Silver drop light-yellow to dark-yellow crystals on death, and Gold to Diamond drop light-green to dark-green. Blue-green drop from Salts. As far as he knows, this is always true, without exception, so the strange colors of his dantian must have some other reasoning.

Also strange is that John is overfilled with energy, and feels fantastic, while somehow being absolutely and completely spent and dead tired, both at the same time.

Soon after, John falls back asleep to Hubaba brushing his hair.

John next awakens in Amber's lap, while she gently strokes his head, humming a comforting tune, such as a lullaby, her scent and warmth and softness extremely soothing. It is a wholesome, friendly thing for someone to do for another, and John is ashamed, and greatly surprised, as he feels a stirring in his loins, something that hasn't happened to him in thousands of years.

John jerks up, and quickly moves away from Amber, cheeks red.

"Oh, goodness! You're awake. We were really worried. What happened? Oh, you know you have little horn-nubs on your head?"

John does know, but they were much smaller before, he thinks. He rubs a nub above his temple, wondering if it is larger, or just seems so now that someone else pointed it out. "I guess this happens to everyone spending too much time here, in the NetherRealms."

Still embarrassed, John keeps his gaze downward. After realizing John isn't going to add more, Amber says, "So? Come on, dude, spit it out! What happened? We were freaking out. We just couldn't snap you out of it. You were shaking and your legs were going completely nuts. I thought you were having a seizure or something. I tried holding your legs but, man, I couldn't hold them at all and just got kicked across the room every time! Hubaba had to do some ritual to force you to pass out or sleep or something."

"My apologies, Amber. I didn't mean to kick you. I was ascending, and had no control of my outside body."

As John finishes this statement, Hubaba rises from where he was meditating, and approaches the two, staring at John's midsection. "This one's never seen an ascension go as yours did. Please, explain what happened."

After collecting his thoughts some, John says, "Well, it took great effort to lift my dantian. I finally managed to lift it, and my belly turned to fire, and I received some visions. No. Memories. They were memories. That was after seeing the giant monster I always see when I rank up. I don't know why my legs were spasming as they did, but I had to ignore your efforts to wake me as the pain in my belly was great, and I did not want the ascension to fail and go through it all again."

Amber goes to speak but Hubaba waves her silent. "Describe this monster. Please."

John lets out a breath. "It is hard to do. It's beyond my words to describe accurately. Its head is so large I couldn't tell if it had a body, or if the head was a body. It looks as if a mountain turned to flesh, and had rock-like plates all over. The mouth was a...was mostly vertical, but more open up top. It had many black eyes on both sides of the mouth, and each had different and strangely shaped irises, like glowing runes, and a large horn-like whisker under the eyes going far out of my vision. On the top of its head looked to be a weird kind of forest. Its words felt like many strange horns causing the earth to shatter apart."

Hubaba looks both surprised and worried. "It spoke? What were its words?"

"I think it praised me, and called me its child."

Hubaba nervously rummages around a pouch, pulls out a book, flips through the pages, and holds out a drawing for John to look at. "Did it look like this?"

The picture is of the monster John saw, but from much further out, showing there is much more to the monster, something he supposes is a body, but unlike any body of any creature John has ever seen. The monster stands large above two other equally monstrous, but far different looking creatures, and the two it stands above look to be dead.

"This is the creature, yes. Or the same type of creature, if not the same one."

Hubaba's hand shakes as he shows the drawing to Amber. John can see the worry in Amber's face, not from the drawing, but Hubaba's reaction. She asks, "What is it, Baba? What's wrong? Are you okay?"

Hubaba lowers his chin sharply. "This...this is one of the creators of demons. And g'athu. And dark ones too, technically. The greatest of the ancient old ones. Beings so powerful they can destroy whole universes with little effort. Beings that shape reality.

"He is the only ancient old one offered Heaven to refuse it. He said he knew enough of pleasure, and too little of all else. He was once named Curiosity. He is now named Betrayal. The only ancient old one to somehow attain the energy system of the Tree of Life. He is both ancient old one and Eternal.

"Darkness, Adversity, and Nightmare are the ancient old ones we credit for creating demons, as Darkness, Nightmare, Destruction, and Chaos are credited for creating g'athu, though nearly all of them helped create both our races. The one contributing most, the one the idea originated from, is Curiosity.

"The Forsaken War was supposed to be only the Forsaken against Favored. When it looked like the Forsaken might lose, Nightmare convinced Sorrow they should enter the fight and destroy the core universes. Curiosity turned against his own, and fought both Nightmare and Sorrow, and became Betrayal. Still damaged and sleeping from the fight even now, so long after the war, the dreams of Nightmare and Sorrow spawn the dark ones.

"This one may be ignorant of many things, but this one is certain it is very bad for Betrayal to notice you. This is not good. Ancient old ones can snuff out any soul whenever they want. No reincarnation for this one. No Wheel for you two."

The large area before the Trial entrance, more of a staging area than an antechamber or foyer, is silent for a long moment. John breaks the silence by saying, "So? What this being does is beyond us, and out of our control. And he seems to like me. He did call me his child."

"And what if the other ancient old ones catch wind of his interest in you? They'll kill you and all around you just to annoy Betrayal."

"They can try."

Anger sparks in Hubaba's eyes, and John is glad to see it. Anger is much better than fear. "They don't have to try! Their powers are far beyond Eternals! Did you forget your battle against Zongreth? Master Garioch could have squashed you like an insect, and you were on the same Tree. You just ascended to Copper. Are you daft? Did you not hear anything I've said?"

John laughs. "That's the spirit. Better to rage than cower. If they snuff my soul, then I need not worry about anything. The cold-dark, or my place in the Underworld, or what struggles my next life holds if I go to this Wheel. Instead of awakening from this dream, all dreams will end. There are far worse fates.

"If I ever stand before these creatures, I will be respectful, as is right to do when standing before ones so high, but if they disrespect me, or attack me, I will give battle with all I have within me before I fall, or my soul is snuffed out. It is all I can do. Until then, I will advance, and slaughter all my enemies. Nothing has changed. I will place the head of Ukaraaz on a pike, and teach Morgoros the true meaning of torture. The same plan as yesterday."

John sees the frustration on the old demon's face, but before Hubaba can reply, Amber says, "Gross! Come on, man! And you promised to stop talking so old-timey. But he does have a point, Baba. Nothing we can do about it, right?

"I guess it hasn't been much time so you could probably go back to being a slave, or a scab, or whatever you call it. I'd really hate to see you go. You guys are the only real friends I've ever had. I can even show myself and be myself in front of both of you.

"Maybe the ancient old ones will kill us. Maybe we'll get killed before we reach the portal. Maybe Ukaraaz will kill us on the other side. Maybe

I get captured and turned into a pill or whatever. Or maybe we don't get killed, and we all grow old together, and have a lot of fun doing it. Besides John, he's a party-pooper and hates fun."

John takes offense at that statement, as he believes he is very fun to be around, but he holds his tongue. He sees Hubaba considering what Amber told him, and he doesn't want the demon to leave. He is a Silver, and will soon be a Gold, and the strongest among them, even if the least experienced in battle.

Hubaba bows at the waist. "This…my friend, Amber, you are correct. Apologies. I was nervous. Nothing can be done. You both are this…my friends. And I do want to see this 'internet' of your world. And take photographs for Instagram. Avoiding the attention of the powerful is key to survival as a scab. It is hard to not think as you were trained to think. Or not believe how you were trained to believe. This…I have a name now. That is more than my kind ever gave me. And friendship. Mutual respect. Let's move on. We have something else to discuss."

Hubaba turns his gaze back towards John. "Your weight barely increased. The essence in your core is strange. This…I am not sure if you fully ascended to Copper. Your core seems to be sick."

Taken aback, John says nothing, and becomes worried. Amber moves to John and puts her hand on his shoulder, and her nearness makes him uncomfortable. "Don't worry, buddy. We'll fix this. The portal isn't supposed to open for months. And clearing my channels didn't take so long. Well, as a fox it didn't take long but I'm sure you'll catch up soon." She smiles reassuringly before saying, "You cultivate real fast anyways, and heal so fast. You'll be fine in no time, dude."

John resists the urge to shake her hand off, and move a respectable distance away from her, and wishes her nearness didn't cause him to feel so flustered. He closes his eyes and looks at his dantian. He feels fine. His dantian feels powerful. He pulls his view back and looks at his energy system. He is surprised to see his meridians seem fully cleared and open. He pulls essence out of his dantian, and the teal essence responds, moving surprisingly easily, with little effort needed to persuade it, along a meridian to his right hand, and he forces some to poke out.

The teal essence changes into a red liquid as soon as it leaves John's hand. It doesn't look like fire, but red is the aspect most associated with fire, so John is hopeful his dreams of having fire billow forth from his hands will soon be realized.

Hubaba gasps. "Impossible!"

"What's wrong?" asks John, thankful Amber finally removes her hand. Hubaba's reaction gives John the opportunity to step away from her some.

"This is impossible."

"What's impossible?"

"This! What you've done!"

"What did I do?"

"This! It can't be done. Your channels are open! Your core isn't sick, your aspects merged!" John still has no idea what the issue is. Hubaba rummages in a pouch and pulls out a flat stone with gems on it. "Hold this. No. Like this. Imbue it with a little essence. Please."

John does as Hubaba asks, and all the stones light up, and Hubaba gasps again, even more dramatically. "Impossible! How!?"

As John tries to hand the stone back, it falls, as Hubaba's hand is shaking so badly he cannot function.

"Baba, instead of saying impossible over and over, just tell us what's wrong. Calm down, buddy. I'm sure it's okay. You're scaring John."

"No, he isn't. I fear nothing," John says, and feels foolish for saying such a stupid thing as soon as it leaves his lips. Amber looks at him, and he puffs his chest out, and feels foolish again.

Hubaba plays with the tips of his horns while mumbling to himself. After some time, a little more composed, while still talking to himself, Hubaba says, "No one can have such a strong affinity towards all aspects. No one can have merged..." Hubaba trails off, puts his arms down, holds his hands together near his belly, as he often does. "This will be easier to explain if I tell you a story. The myth of the Sunfire."

John interjects, "The Slave-Empress. I've heard of her. My mentor wants me to get her body Perk."

"Oh, just stop it! Just shut up, you daft fool! Sunfire is just a myth. No one can get Sunfire Body of the Slave-Empress! No one. It's a joke! A myth! Impossible to qualify for! Just stop!"

John's eyes turn cold. "Easy, my friend. You seem to be having a hard time of things, and I'm willing to tolerate a certain amount of disrespect from you due to this, but be careful. My tolerance for being treated so has a limit, and I am close to it."

Amber moves between John and Hubaba. "You two need to calm down. I don't know what's going on, but this is too much. Why don't we all sit and talk about this like adults? Yeah, let's do that. Take some deep breaths."

Amber's sweet voice, even infused with a little anger as it is now, causes John's face to heat.

# CHAPTER 47
## ASPECT OF ATTRACTION

After the three companions meditate for a short time, they sit in a circle, and Hubaba leads the conversation.

"Did either of you pick an Archetype?"

Amber says, "I didn't. I couldn't. We got sent here before I opened my core. I know what I'm gonna pick though!"

Hubaba looks at John, and John says, "Yes. Evoker. I broke the contract and they took it from me after I first ranked up. I did not purposefully break the contract. My word is extremely important to me."

Hubaba nods. "There's a book scab-pedants read about this. Archetypes seem so silly when we first learn of them. And manifesting with runes placed unnaturally on the soul. Chosen will always laugh at these things. Scab-pedants learn the reasons why and we don't laugh. But we'll get to that. Do either of you know what an affinity is? Or an aspect?"

Amber says, "I do! Affinities are...uh, how good you are with aspects. Like, naturally talented or something. And aspects are things like fire and water and stuff. So the higher your affinity with fire, the better you are at casting fire spells."

"Good. Yes. Affinities can and do rise over time. And aspects are usually considered the eight color groupings. 'Fire' would be a concept almost always associated with red aspect. Have either of you heard the term 'bottleneck' before?"

Amber raises her arm. Hubaba asks, "Why are you raising your arm?"

"It means I know the answer and want you to call on me. I never went to school, but this is how they do it in movies. Was that a lie? Do students not actually raise their hand?"

Hubaba smiles. "I've never seen a movie. You know I want to. Especially the 'My Fair Lady' movie you told me about. We can use this arm-raising system though. Please, Amber, answer."

"Bottleneck is...uh, something hard to pass through. Something stopping you from moving forward."

"Good. A hindrance to progress. There are many cultivators must deal with, both big and small. The NCS came up with many systems to bypass these bottlenecks. How it used to work for everyone, ptagmog and magals, is how it still works on Tech Zero worlds. They advance much slower than everyone else. I'll walk through an example."

Hubaba changes his voice. "I'm a cultivator on a Tech Zero world. I ascend to Bronze, and I know this is the earliest my pure essence can change. I know various ways to manifest my pure essence. Every day I practice, train, fight, and meditate, hoping for my essence to change. One day, maybe not even until I'm a high or peak Silver, I manifest my essence-shield. But, this time, instead of the pure shield I always have, this shield is made of fire.

"Great! I aspected fire. I'm a fire-cultivator now. All my focus goes into fire. I am fire. Fire is me. I ascend and ascend. Fire, fire, fire. I ascend off world. And then I stop ascending. I'm at a bottleneck and nothing I do works. I can't get past it.

"There's an old and famous bottleneck at the mid-high Transcendent Tree. No fire-cultivator will ever pass it.

"For that bottleneck you need to merge two concepts from two different aspects into a high-concept. That fire-cultivator, he put all his effort into fire, ignoring all else. His red will be a major aspect, probably double majored with 'fire' and a similar concept without even knowing it. Most of that cultivator's effort was just wasted.

"We now know there are only three general tiers to aspects. Minor, average, and major. A lesson from the NCS even the ptagmog uses is this

– assume, to start, you have four 'points' to 'spend' on aspects. A major aspect is three points, an average aspect is two, and a minor is one.

"At Diamond, and certain tiers after, you usually get another 'point' to 'spend.' And this 'point' can increase a minor aspect to an average aspect, or an average to a major. You receive six 'points' naturally before you hit that famous bottleneck."

Amber raises her hand, and is called on by Hubaba. "I know the NCS can tell when someone is close to aspecting. I know it wants us to wait as long as possible and it can help suppress aspecting. When we have to pick, it has us double up and pick both a major and minor from our lowest affinity aspect. But how do demons do it? Is it still like Tech Zero worlds?"

Hubaba smiles creepily. "Yes and no. We know a lot more. We try to force aspects and not aspect naturally. It doesn't always work. We test affinities at Bronze, and whatever one or two we are strongest with we work on.

"For me, I was picked to be a scab because I had decent affinities for both purple and black. Those colors have many concepts that lend themselves easily to runecrafting, and to being a scab-pedant. I was told to make purple a major aspect, and black a minor. And told to work on attaining the concepts of 'rules' for purple, and 'connect' for black.

"Sadly, this worked out. Scabs never plan on ascending Trees. If I did, and could make my own choices, I would've picked black as my major and minor, and worked on both 'complex' and 'connect' with the goal of merging both into a mid-concept.

"At Diamond I would've opened purple as a minor and gone for 'rules.' At the Transcended bottleneck, I would've merged my concepts together into 'glyph.' If I could manifest glyphs, imagine how powerful I'd be?

"There's a million ways to get to 'glyph' as a high-concept. It can probably be done from several combinations of colors, but easiest from black and purple."

Hubaba claps his hands loudly. "John! Pay attention. I'm explaining all this for you."

John manages to look ashamed. "Sorry, my friend. Please, go on."

"Well, we could use a break. I feel a fog outside. If you two don't mind, I'd like to go cultivate what I can of it. I used a lot of essence in our fight with Zongreth, and even more on rituals since. I need to be back at full if I am to ascend. I'd prefer to distend my core some if time permits. My previous ascensions were not done well. I'd like to make this one the best it can possibly be. There is little risk of a Silver being noticed from afar."

Both John and Amber encourage the old demon to do so, happy he is now thinking of his future, and his ascension, and hopefully even beyond Gold.

Once Hubaba exits the Trial, John curses. He is now alone with Amber. He thinks about exiting the Trial too, but he doesn't want his horn-nubs to grow more, but he also doesn't want to be alone with Amber.

Instead of sitting, Amber is laying back on her elbows, legs crossed, the hem of her long robe over her shins, bouncing one of her new leather shoes off her dangling foot.

John is happy she changed into a long robe with a hem going down past her calves, unlike his own which has pants and a short-hemmed top going barely past his pelvis. He knows he would have a hard time keeping his orb-eye from looking at her shapely legs if they were on display, as he is having such a hard time now not looking at her foot and ankle and calf with it.

John berates himself for his recent lack of control, and having thoughts that should only plague wild youth, and not a mature man in control of his own emotions.

"This stuff is so interesting, don't you think? I wonder if my other forms aspect naturally. They gotta, right? But what about my human and demon form? I wonder what the stone-thing said about your affinities that got Baba's panties all in a bunch. Ha! Sorry, that was crude and un-ladylike to say. But true, right? He was really freaking out, man. Are you okay? Did I do something wrong? Are you mad at me? Is it because of the fight we had about the ring? It wasn't even a fight! Not really!"

John wishes he had an easier time peeling the orb-eye away from her foot dangling the shoe, and her ankle, and calf. He promised himself to never use the orb-eye to spy on her. "No. No. Not at all. My apologies for acting strangely. I value your friendship very much. I have nothing but the utmost respect for you. And I hope we continue to be good companions throughout this journey together, as we face all these new challenges. All the strangeness we've already faced together."

Amber doesn't immediately reply, but he hears her heart beat faster. "John, look at me."

*Great gods below, why?* He doesn't want to, but he relents, and raises his gaze, turning his head to look her in the eyes, thankful her face is serious, and not smiling her smile, the smile he loves to look upon so much, the smile that brightens his heart and sets it aflutter. He is thankful he's not so crass as to do something so inappropriate as stare at her heaving chest.

"John, buddy, you're staring at my boobs. Come on, man."

Every one of John's nerves is set on fire, and his face feels as if it will explode. He jumps up and quickly walks away, but cannot walk too far before he stands before a wall. He wishes he could escape this torture, and go outside with Hubaba, but he can't. He was caught fair, so now must deal with the consequences. He just faces the wall, embarrassed, fighting to control his emotions, knowing he looks like a fool standing there so.

And it becomes worse for John, as he hears Amber's tinkling laughter from behind, a laughter filled with mirth and gaiety, a laughter he loves hearing more than all else.

"John. Stop. You're being silly, buddy. I know what I look like. It's okay to look, just do it...secret. Normal. Only look when I don't know you're looking. Everyone knows that. I look too, but I bet you've never noticed.

"And, hey, I'm not worried. This isn't my curse working. If...if it was the curse, what happens to the others, and you wanted to...you know…you'd be way different. You wouldn't look so…so like a puppy. You'd look angry, and there'd be hate in your eyes, and you'd stare at my face all angry, and think what you're doing is right and I owe it to you. And I deserve what's coming. And it would've already happened. Days ago, probably.

"And I know you can…can do that now. I saw it. It's okay. I trust you. Just remember we can never be together. I can never do…anything. Ever. Come on. Look at me."

John says, dejected, "I'd rather not."

"Please. I want to tell you something, but I want you to look at me when I tell you."

"I may stare. I've embarrassed myself enough."

"Oh, that's fine. You can stare at my face. Just not…my other stuff, not when I see you doing it. Just look away and pretend you weren't if I notice. Just don't get too creepy on me, buddy. Or be gross."

John turns around, and Amber smiles, and his heart melts. She says, "Promise me you won't think less of me if I tell you something."

"Okay."

"No, you gotta promise."

"I promise."

"It probably makes me sound like a horrible person to say it out loud but if you think about it, it's gotta be true for all girls. Everyone, really. Guys too. When I was really ugly, I wanted to be pretty so bad. The whole point of being pretty is so guys look at you. Desire you. You know, get looked at like the girls in the movies get looked at. Flirt. Date. Feel good inside. All that. All the benefits that go with it.

"The curse made it so I never got any of that. Not until the internet, but perverts in my comments and gross DMs don't count. The curse ruins everything. A lot of girls, and some gay guys, were more immune to my curse. If we spent too much time together it always kicked in. And we couldn't be real friends before then either. Not really.

"A lot of the girls were real mean, and even my gay buddies didn't understand. They all thought I was real weird because there was so much

I couldn't do, and they couldn't know where I lived, and there was so many places I wouldn't go to, and I'd wear a mask to raves and stuff, and I'd always just disappear whenever we'd go out, and they'd get real mad at me for just leaving every time without telling them. Everyone thought I was such a snob, but I'm not. I'm really not.

"So, I never had…this. The whole reason I even accepted this. Someone looking at me like this and still being safe. Being actually seen and looked at in real life and not having to run and hide. I get to have a little of that now. I like it. I think it's real sweet. And nice.

"But you gotta understand this…won't go anywhere. It can't. There's no future in it. I'm not losing my human form. Not for anyone or anything. Looking is…nice, but it will never be anything besides just looking. Ever.

"You'll probably get used to seeing me at some point anyways. And this will all go away. You'll just see me like you see everyone else. And I'm happy everything works for you again. Heck, I'll help you find a nice girlfriend when we get back to Earth. Or Terra, or whatever it's called now. Sound good, buddy? We have an understanding?"

John smiles. "Yes, we have an understanding. And my apologies again for all of this. I should have far more control. I will get it back. I long ago mastered all my emotions, so it is just a small matter of removing whatever flaw is now inside of me."

Amber laughs. "You crack me up sometimes. Ever wonder why it…it's like this? I know people make pills out of…what I am, Naturals, and it helps going from Platinum to Diamond, but is that the whole reason for us? Seems weird. And the core worlds farm us and stuff. Like, I know I'm not human, but I feel so human. I feel like a real person.

"And why'd it do this to me? Why make me beautiful but also make it so bad? So I can never let anyone see me? That just seems real mean, doesn't it? I don't understand why. It's like someone winning the lottery but they can't spend any of the money.

"Do you think it was for training? Whatever controls this wanted me to get used to hiding? Wanted it seared deep, deep into my brain or something? And [Mental Fortification]? I know demons are immune to the curse, but maybe humans are too at a certain tier? I can't really tell if Magnus Gar'tar was attractive cause the mind of a fox doesn't work that way, but if she looked kind of like us, but not really, would her race be immune? Or that Sunshine guy's race? You said he looked real different.

"Ugh, I hate this stupid curse so much! And even if I didn't have the curse, I'd still have everyone wanting to use me for pills anyways. This all really sucks, dude!"

John waits a moment to reply, so Amber will think he put some thought into her questions. "I have no answers for you. I can only give you my word I will do all within my power to prevent you from being turned into a pill."

"John, buddy, it seems kinda creepy when you don't look at me when we talk. But thank you for…being so sweet. Saying that. I know you will. And I'm super grateful. I hope you know that. Sorry I make your life so difficult."

"You don't. And you've saved me four times. I'd have no life at all if it wasn't for you."

The two continue to talk about cultivation and all they've learned, John proud he only once has to be reminded not to stare at her chest, and also horrified he did so and had to be told such. He forces a little essence out of his hand again for Amber to inspect, at her request, and she claims it looks like blood.

John is sure it is red-aspected essence, and he'll be able to turn it into fire, and his dream of controlling fire will soon come true.

Sometime later, Hubaba reenters the Trial, looking much invigorated, taking a seat on the ground across from Amber. John sits as far away from Amber as he can while still facing the demon.

"Okay, let's continue. I'll bring this back around to [Archetypes] and my earlier questions in a moment. But before I do, I must cover a few things."

Hubaba holds up the flat stone with embedded gems he used to test John's affinities. The gems sit on the stone in a diamond shape.

401

The gem on the top of the diamond is purple, the one on the right is nearly clear, orange on the bottom, and on the left is a dark, almost black gem.

Within the diamond, in a square shape, are four more gems. The top left of the square is green, the top right is blue, the bottom right is yellow, and the bottom left is red.

Hubaba says, "Each of these gems represents different aspects, and each color aspect has different concepts most associated with it. I'll give a few examples of each. Don't worry about remembering all this. It's just to get the gist of what concepts are.

"Green aspect has concepts most strongly associated with earth, solid, still, repulsion, and hard. Yellow with air, gas, move, attraction, thought, and dreams. Blue with water, liquid, add, stagnate, and soft. Red and fire, destruction, remove, death, and blindness.

"Those are the more primal, elemental aspects. Next are the higher-order aspects. First is purple, and some concepts for it are order, law, silence, harmony, authority, and protection. Orange and chaos, lawlessness, wild, noise, disharmony, peril, defiance, creativity.

"Next is white, or light, but usually called white. Some examples are light, simple, young, pure, good, separate, truth, and soft. Last is black, or dark, and it's associated with dark, complex, old, quantum, evil, knowledge, bonds, lies, and sharp.

"There are more concepts for each than I can name. Now, I used one example twice. I did this on purpose. 'Soft' for both blue and white. Concepts are dependent on understanding. When you hear soft you probably think something along the lines of tongues or eyeballs."

"It's a simple concept and everyone understands it mostly the same way. But soft can also mean weak, or dull, as in soft in the head, or kindly, or merciful, and a million other things.

"Healing is most associated with green, but all aspects have a concept that can heal, even red. It is easier to destroy with red or black, but they all have some destructive concepts.

Hubaba claps loudly again. "John! Please, I told you this wasn't important to remember, not to ignore all that is said. Pay attention, this next part is very relevant for you.

"I said earlier the 'points' for aspects are limited and you need to have two major aspects at mid-high Transcendent Tree to merge into a high-concept. By that time, you only have six of these 'points.' Exactly enough for two major aspects. Why does the NCS want you to double up on the same aspect with similar concepts then? John?"

Amber's hand shoots up and she makes eager noises. John racks his brain for an answer, and only one he thinks of can explain it. "The NCS seeks to sabotage us."

Hubaba says, "No. That is the exact opposite reason of why it does this. Amber?"

"It's so we can merge a mid-concept and get experience merging concepts. And you can get 'points' other ways so you can have more than six at the bottleneck. Did you really not talk to Pixie about any of this, John?"

"Exactly right, Amber. Merging base-concepts within the same-colored aspect creates a mid-concept. It is far easier to merge similar concepts of the same-colored aspect. Supposedly, far, far easier to do, and this gives many insights and good experience on how to merge concepts from different-colored aspects, but most will be going for a similar theme, so the concepts aren't too disparate and can be merged more easily.

"Say I aspected as I said I wanted to, black as my major and minor, and 'complex' and 'connect' as concepts. I would have tried merging them together into 'dynamic.'

"John, remember Zongreth? What were his manifestations?"

Amber raises her hand again, but John knows this answer well. "He made rock-cocoons, he sprayed out rock-swarms. A giant rock dropped on Amber's head. And he made yellow balls that pulled you towards them, and they would hold onto you, and not let you free."

Hubaba smiles. "Good, John. Zongreth aspected naturally. He had no say in his concepts. He had average aspects of yellow and green with 'attraction' and 'rock' as concepts. I mentioned theme before, this just means a way to tie your concepts together, and plan for some way to merge them into a high-concept at that famous bottleneck.

"Zongreth wanted 'gravity' as his high-concept. Mass creates gravity. Rocks have mass. Gravity attracts. See the theme? If he was more serious about it, he wouldn't manifest anything like the rock-spray as it's outside the theme. But everyone plans for that famous bottleneck. Most cultivators will never get there. Most will never come close to Diamond. But you still plan for that famous bottleneck so far away on the next Tree.

"Now, John, can you tell me why the NCS promotes Archetypes?"

John watches Amber's hand fly up excitedly again. She smiles at John and his heart melts. He doesn't want Amber to think he's stupid so he thinks as hard as he can and comes up with something. "Is it so we'll focus on a specific type of spell?"

Amber's hand stays up, and she still makes eager noises, and he assumes he got the answer wrong, so John is surprised when Hubaba says, "Correct. Anything you want to add, Amber?"

"Yes! If you cast the same types of spells over and over, and if you suppress aspecting as long as you can, you'll probably get concepts related to the spells you always cast when you open an aspect. And if you don't, they can change to related concepts if the affinity for the aspect is low. Oh, and when aspects with higher affinities open, they'll have similar concepts too. All fitting nice into a theme. Man, I'm killing it. I wish I went to school. I'd be the best student ever. Straight A's, baby!"

Hubaba laughs and he and Amber bump their fists together. "Correct, Amber. And manifesting with only runes is a big part of this. Or mostly manifesting with only runes. Only the NCS can place runes that cast manifestations on a soul.

"That isn't an option for those of the ptagmog. We cast the old way. Captain Ukaraaz is considered a genius for merging a mid-concept at Gold. Master Garioch merged one at Platinum, which only the most skilled cultivators can do. These are exceptions to the rules. Most don't have a mid-concept until peak Salt or the low Transcendent Tree. Many demons still get stuck at that famous bottleneck."

The demon clears his throat, and looks a little nervous. "Now let this...me explain why this...I was so surprised earlier. This...I said we don't test affinities until Bronze. Not just demons, the NCS doesn't until then either. Affinities just aren't present until Bronze. No one can aspect before Bronze. And most cultivators have all low affinities, and only one or two average ones.

"You, John, have the highest affinity I've ever seen. Not just for one aspect. For all eight of them. And this...I stressed the four 'points' for opening aspects because it is always four 'points.' Never more. All your aspects are open. All of them. At Copper."

"This one stressed the old and famous bottleneck of the mid-high Transcendent Tree, the bottleneck everyone worries about and plans for so early. You already passed it. At Copper. You have a high-concept. You have the equivalent of twelve 'points' for aspects right now.

"How any of this is true, this one cannot say. Everything this one knows to be true is no longer true. Some alphas and omegas might not find some of what you've done so impossible. A little of it. But not all of it, and not nearly to the same extent."

Hubaba, while sitting, bows towards John. "Copper John, this...my friend, grantor of my name, whatever you are, what you've done, it frightens this one to no end."

# CHAPTER 48
# BLOOD

John is roused from meditation by Amber and Hubaba. Hubaba's face is freshly painted, and Amber's hair looks different. Both are smiling and giggling like naughty children.

John's been in a slump, and he assumes this is an attempt to cheer him. Hubaba even made John a low-grade elixir to improve his mood the day before. It was the best he could do without his alchemy equipment, and the elixir supposedly fortifies meridians a little. There's a pill he could make without his equipment too, but there's been no luck in finding the main ingredient needed for it.

"Since you won't allow us to put make-up on you, I shall cut your hair. The hair on both head and face, and you will feel better when you look better. You look like a…what's the word? I forget, but it isn't a good thing to look like," Hubaba says, smiling creepily.

John dislikes his hair being so wild, as it gets in his way and causes a hassle. And his beard is unkempt, and long enough to give enemies something to hold on to and use as leverage in a fight, as does his long hair. And he still has a bald spot from when his head was stuck to one of the yellow balls of Zongreth, and he ripped his head away from it. He does need his hair and beard to be cut, but he dislikes being ordered to do so, so his reply is, "No."

Amber runs her finger down the side of John's face. "Please? You'd look so handsome with a haircut and beard trim. For me?"

John's face turns beat-red, and he mumbles for a moment before saying, "Okay. But take the beard off completely."

Amber looks horrified. "No! You look so much hotter with a beard. You look *waaaayyyy* too young without it. Please?"

Hubaba runs some fingers down John's other cheek. "Yes. You look hot without a beard. Or with one. Whichever we've decided."

John flinches away. It is a grave insult to touch someone's face, but Hubaba won't understand why he didn't mind Amber touching it, and the rule isn't equally applied, so he says nothing.

John feels guilty. He has often broken his promise to never spy on Amber with his orb-eye, and to at least be man enough to only look at her with his own eyes. Even now he pretends not to look at her, as his orb-eye looks only at her.

John wants his orb-eye to only be considered as a war device, such as a sword, and only be used and trained for matters of safety and combat, not satisfying his sick need to look at his good friend and companion. He should have much better control of his emotions, as he always has.

John's Lilitu belonged to him, as he belonged to her, and they were two separate entities that became one. She filled him with a lust he did not know before her, did not even know was possible, but it was fully returned, and shared, between man and wife, and not the immature and inappropriate feelings he now has.

John does not think feet are attractive. They are ugly, smelly, mis-shapen, and rough things. Feet are things no one could or should find attractive, yet Amber's soft and callous-free feet are different, even with the sharp claws. Everything is different regarding her. *Why is getting my control back so difficult now?*

The only other time John can remember struggling as he does now was as a boy, after he gained the growth and changes of a man, not long before he became a man in truth at thirteen. His father married a beautiful girl, his fourth wife. She was actually the sixth wife, but two died, and his father's hold could easily support four wives for the lord. Any more than four would anger his people, and look greedy and wasteful, and less would make him look weak and unmanly.

This girl was beautiful, and made John unable to think straight. He struggled not to constantly stare at her plump body, and failed miserably.

All the people living in a hold slept on the floor together. On the night this girl married his father, John moved closer to where they slept, and pretended sleep as he listened and watched them join, knowing how dishonorable the act was, and that a man deserves the courtesy of being ignored on a wedding night.

And a lady, especially, deserves privacy always, and should at least not be spied on by men with any honor whatsoever, or have men stealing glances of private things no man except her husband should see.

And there was little enough not to see back then, as men and women wore only loincloths, and naught else but whatever trinkets they were gifted or won in battle, though that changed for John after gaining the power, and needing protection from the sun.

"Okay, I will keep the beard, and your hair looks very nice, Amber." For some reason, even saying this little compliment makes John's face burn as if on fire. He wonders if this is what Amber meant when she noted he looked hotter with a beard. *She is helping me save face by pretending the beard overheats my cheeks, and is the reason for my constant blushing. Without the beard there would be no excuse allowing me to save face.*

Amber's smile grows larger on her face. "Thanks, buddy!"

John adds a stipulation to his consent, "But I'd like for us to train more. You both know my aspect is useless. I need to figure out this unbinding of manifestations, and lean on my great strength, and speed, and fortitude. I cannot learn unbinding on my own." As a thought, he adds, *and I must accept my dream of billowing fire forth from my hands will not come to pass.*

"Oh, stop it, Mr. Sourpuss. Hubaba told you 'Blood' can be one of the strongest concepts. You just gotta learn to use it right. I don't even have affinities and aspects yet and you don't see me crying about it," Amber says annoyedly.

"If having a high-concept is supposed to be so powerful, why does my spell hardly even sting now? How does the concept of 'rules' allow the creation of mighty and deadly scythes, killing many at once, such as Hubaba creates?"

Hubaba, looking frustrated, explains again. "'Rules' is a complex concept. I see 'rules' as harsh, brutal, sharp, unfair, unforgiving, sowing only suffering, as they have for me since being made scab. They now reap what they have always sown. And I created my own manifestation, I don't try to force my essence through runes unnaturally placed on my soul.

"'Blood' is a simple concept and seen much the same by all cultivators. It is rare, since if someone is lucky enough to have 'life' as a base-concept, any of the cardinal essences really, they usually build off that for mid and high-concepts. Your aspect *is* very powerful, as you've been told many times. You need to learn how to utilize it correctly in a way that resonates with you and your understanding of blood.

"If you know the myth of Sunfire you know of Emperor Malakhi. You've heard what he could do with blood necromancy. No one in his galaxy could stand against him. There are many tales of powerful cultivators controlling blood essence. Let this be your motivation and inspiration."

As far as Hubaba knows, the concept of 'water' or 'liquid' from blue aspect, and the concept of 'life' from green aspect, merge into 'blood' as a high-concept.

There are four concepts that are different from the others, the cardinal quintessences – 'life' from green, 'death' from red, 'all' from black, and 'nothing' from white. For some reason, none of these aspects can be seen with essence-vision, and each needs a special vision Perk to be seen.

To John, the fact 'nothing' cannot be seen makes sense, but not so much the other three. 'All' should be the easiest to see. The fact his teal-colored essence can be seen with Hubaba's essence-vision means it is no longer strongly associated with life as a quintessence.

*I did not want this merger of my essence. I'd rather have the powerful concept of 'life.' Yet I have one of the worst concepts I could think of, equally as bad as 'water' or 'liquid.' Even if Hubaba says I am wrong to think so, I truly believe I could've strengthened myself with life essence I created myself, the same as I do from what I take from others.*

Just thinking of this angers John to no end. He doesn't even notice Hubaba begin cutting his hair with a blade of essence poking out of his fingertip. *I need to stop being as whiny as a babe. I have the concept I have. I need to figure out how to use it.*

Amber and Hubaba did something called 'brainstorming,' and had many ideas on how to utilize blood essence. Making blood pump faster could increase speed, if enough of something Amber calls oxygen is supplied to the blood. It is claimed something in the blood, or human blood at least, causes healing, called white blood cells.

Blood can be turned sickly to poison someone, but John tried this, and his understanding and knowledge of blood or magical science isn't enough to change the blood in another creature, though he tried many times. Blood is also very important for many rituals.

*Blood isn't so different from water. It is water with extra stuff in it. I guess I could drown people if I hold their head under a large enough puddle of blood. How is 'blood' even a high-concept? 'Life' seems like a far more advanced idea than 'blood.' Blood is but only a small part of life. None of this makes a lick of sense.*

John berates himself for whining again. He needs to get serious about this. *How do I see blood? What is blood to me?* To him, it is the thing that flows through bodies, doing something he doesn't understand that keeps people alive. He hates how people believe vampires drink blood. *I've done this long enough I hardly take in any blood as I remove vital essence from my victims.*

John stops, excited. He has somewhat of an epiphany. "I got it!" He stands, only then remembering Hubaba is cutting his hair as the essence coming out of the demon's fingertip hits John's neck. "Sorry, Hubaba. I have to find a living creature to test something on."

Amber puts her hand on John's chest. "Stop! You look like you just escaped from a psych ward. Let Hubaba finish cutting your hair and I'll go get something."

410

John raises his hand towards the Wood bull-lion five or so paces in front of him. The beast's back is broken, and it lies unmoving. Instead of trying to use his 'blood' concept to damage the beast, he will try to use it to take from it instead, as he's always used blood to do. Blood, to him, is a delivery mechanism to take vital essence from his victims.

Hubaba claimed this wouldn't work, as John would need far more experience, and another concept, such as 'take' or 'move' from yellow, or 'remove' from red, or 'steal' from orange, to create a manifestation performing such an advanced spell. Much as he'd need 'add' from blue, or another similar concept, or a clear concept of what specifically he'd want to add, to add something to blood in another creature.

Blue and green are somewhat shutoff to John for now, with his teal-colored essence and high-concept merged from both colors, but John has six other aspects available.

Regardless of Hubaba claiming what John is trying to do won't work, it was Hubaba's explanations that convinced John it could work. That it *will* work.

It was assumed Garioch wanted his high-concept to be 'lightning.' He was aspected blue and yellow, with the base concepts of 'water' and 'pressure,' minor and major respectively, until he reached Diamond and gained another 'point' to make blue an average aspect.

Garioch could use 'pressure' and 'water' as a way to fling streams of water so quickly and fiercely at enemies it could puncture like an arrow, or cut like a sword. He hardly manifested this way, and disliked doing it. Instead, he'd quickly fill the air with water, and he'd use his 'pressure' concept to do something to the wet air, and it would somehow make lightning.

Ukaraaz is double aspected in yellow, and has 'thought' and 'move' as concepts, major and minor respectively. Or had, as he merged them both into the mid-concept of 'telekinesis,' a word interpreted as far-movement

411

in John's mind, but both his companions claim it means to move and manipulate things with the power of the mind alone.

Joyat, the Silver demon John killed outside the witches' house, was doubled aspected in green, average with both, with the concepts of 'life' and 'grow,' allowing him to grow simple life, such as the strong vines he used to wrap John and Amber up with. Eventually, he could've made simple animated creations, such as attacking plants, and if such concepts are built upon and merged, the creations can be autonomous beings acting fully independently.

Most importantly was the tale of those choosing to walk the hardest road, purposefully picking four minor aspects, each a different color, and trying for powerful concepts with each, meaning they usually don't fit a theme. These cultivators bank on being able to gain many outside sources of 'points' to increase aspects, and being good enough to merge disparate concepts later. It is the hardest road to travel and plan for, but many more types of spells and abilities are open to these cultivators while ascending. These cultivators, early on, assume they are good enough to make the impossible happen.

All the examples Hubaba gave John showed cultivators doing amazing things, such as creating lightning from only water and pressure. At best, these cultivators have one major aspect. At best, they have average affinities with their aspects. At best, they have a mid-concept. At best, they have four aspects, some having only one open aspect.

All of John's affinities are very high. He has two major aspects merged into a high-concept. He has six other aspects too. They're all minor aspects, and he doesn't know what concept any of them have, but he figures there's a good chance at least one will have something helpful for what he is trying for.

Without the NCS, the only way to figure out what concept is aspected is by trying different things, testing, getting closer and closer to the mark. Once close enough, an idea resounds from within, and the mark is hit, and the concept known.

If this concept isn't liked or wanted, base concepts can be changed, though it does take some great time and effort to do so, and only works when the affinity isn't very strong.

John knows he did not aspect the concepts of 'death,' 'all,' or 'nothing,' as all his essence can be seen by Hubaba. He likes not knowing what the concepts are, because it helps him believe he can now do anything, as his concepts can be anything.

What John is trying to do, he knows is possible.

John focuses on the bull-lion, and its blood, and the life essence carried in the blood, and he pulls at it. And pulls. And keeps at it for a very long time, tuning all else out. His pity for the beast growing as the minutes pass. He has no hate for the beast, or desire to cause bull-lions harm for doing only what they were made to do, and what is their nature to do, such as attacking other living creatures. But that is John's nature too, so he hardens his heart.

This sort of manifestation should ignore, or bypass, all forms of armor and shielding, including essence-shields, as he should be directly accessing the blood within the beast. Just as the telekinesis of Ukaraaz ignores essence-shields unless he flings a physical object with his mind at someone, and he can either lift, or crush, or move something with his power, or he cannot.

The only way to stop John's spell is to unbind it, and stop the casting from happening, though the difference in power between John and anyone he tries to manipulate the blood of will decide whether it can work or not. Some cultivators will be too strong to be affected by the spell he is trying to create.

What essence-shields protect against are direct attacks by something tangible, such as a weapon, both plain weapons or essence-enhanced, and the rock storm of Zongreth, but not his yellow balls that pull, or his rock-cocoon. They protect against the purple scythes of Hubaba, the echo-attack of Amber, or what was previously the [Magical Essence Dart] of John.

[Magical Essence Dart] is assumed to now be [Blood Dart], a spell that hurts little more than a rock thrown by a child, where once it killed a witch many tiers above John in one casting.

Like with demons, though less so, Wood bull-lions have less vital essence within them than normal humans, and it's dulled somewhat. But even the strange energy-like blood of demons and bull-lions carries the essence of life throughout its host organism, doing whatever magical science Amber and Hubaba claim blood does. And hours into his test, John's spell finally gets a result.

The life essence stops flowing around as usual, and starts collecting in the chest, where John is focusing his spell, where the most vital essence resides, near the organ considered a heart for both demon and bull-lion, though it bears little resemblance to a human one. The life essence keeps building and building in the same area, but refuses to leave the beast and enter John.

Then, even with a broken spine and the inability to feel pain, the bull-lion spasms once as if hurt, and dies, and the vital essence starts to disintegrate, as it always does once the host dies.

John curses, as the spell is a failure, and he is unable to steal the vital essence and add it to himself.

"This...I told you it was a powerful concept," Hubaba says, appearing besides John.

"I failed."

"No. You killed the beast. Its blood was caught and pooled, denied to the brain, and it killed the beast in minutes. A simple blood clot can also kill. If you pooled the blood in the heart, think of what that would do. I'm not a healer, but even I can think of many ways to kill by pooling blood in certain areas of an opponent.

"And this is only what you managed to do on your first attempt. What can you do with more experience and knowledge? Knowledge not just on how to manifest, but knowledge of blood and controlling it within an opponent. Amber and I will teach you what we know of blood, but you must take the learning of it seriously. And you must stop saying 'magical science.' It makes no sense and people will believe you are mentally deficient if they hear you say it."

# CHAPTER 49
## TURMOIL WITHIN TRANQUILITY

Hubaba once told John most magals need to make a living and have little time to devote to energy gathering and refinement, so advance extremely slowly. These magals usually use Seed, Root, etcetera, to name tiers, and the demon claims they use these names as a shield and excuse for their low tiers and slow advancement.

John believes needing to make a living, doing honest work, sounds like a great excuse for not having the time and ability to be a layabout, meditating all day. He is grateful he is not in a similar situation, and can focus on his advancement. Over the next months both John and Amber learn how to manifest the old way, and protect from having spells unbound, and how to unbind spells, and many other basics of self-cultivation.

At first, Amber can protect from having her manifestations unbound far better in her beast forms, as animals have a natural instinct on how to do so. After some time, she learns to best resist attempts to unbind in her human form.

John becomes decent at resisting unbinds, but no one would call him particularly skillful at it. The same goes for his attempts at unbinding the spells of others, whereas Amber excels at this task in her human form, is fairly good at it as a demon, and can't do it at all as a beast.

Animals aren't able to do certain things sapient cultivators can, but there is hope for this in the future, as all mindless creatures turn semi-sapient at higher tiers, and can unbind spells and such, and Amber is far more sapient in her beast forms than other animals already.

Amber, with her pure essence, can do much with it, but pure essence is not suited to doing anything well. She takes to most facets of self-cultivation naturally, and learns how to manifest weapon enhancements, body enhancements, and other cultivation basics far more adroitly than John, though the power of John's essence far outstrips her own.

While as a bear, Amber can only use manifestations her beast forms naturally attained, and has no ability to cast other spells. Her fox form has a better body enhancement than the one she casts in human or demon form. None of her forms were granted a weapon enhancement yet, and if none ever do, and she eventually learns how to cast spells while as an animal, being able to enhance her paws will make her far more deadly.

There are advanced techniques Amber and John only learn about without practicing, such as resisting active manifestations, taking control of another's manifestation, or breaking bindings and manifestations – some of these techniques even experienced Golds struggle to grasp the basics of.

Hubaba learns along with John and Amber, as he is very knowledgeable on theories, techniques, manifestations, and many aspects of cultivation, but very inexperienced in actually performing these tasks, and all combat related matters, such as creating essence-shields, attack manifestations, and the like. Surprisingly, at least to John, the first time Hubaba manifested those mighty purple scythes was during the fight against Zongreth.

Hubaba struggles to find an attack manifestation for his dark aspect, with the concept of 'connect.' How the demon sees 'connect' is along the lines of runes connecting, or how steps and processes in alchemy combine for a greater whole, or how knowledge builds off of prior knowledge and applies to other fields, and the like. Not very applicable for an attack manifestation.

The demon then realizes he already uses this concept in his scythe attack, as the purple becomes darker when he manifests more than one scythe, and allows him to create many connected scythes all at once.

Hubaba's aspects greatly assist him in many fantastic ways, such as unbinding others, and protecting against unbinds, each having many steps that connect various rules, and quite suited to his concepts and how he thinks. He was forced to get a body [Perk] completely unsuited for combat, so he is happy the essence-shield he teaches himself to manifest is extremely sturdy.

The essence-shields John and Amber create are not so sturdy, not nearly as sturdy as the ones John's armor and Amber's belt manifest, as both items use runes made specifically for the job, converting their essence into purple-aspected essence, the best aspect for shielding.

John, of course, has a hard time seeing 'blood' as a protective substance. Amber is unaspected, so her essence-shield's limited effectiveness was anticipated, though she has hope for a much better shield.

The frogs of this world, though different from those of Earth, all have what Hubaba calls a step-teleport at Copper tier, what Amber calls blinking, and her frog form has it as well.

If Amber's frog form advances as the frogs of the demon world Esau do, she will get a very durable essence-shield at Bronze, and a strange attack at Silver, where the tongue can be used to bind an opponent, and drain them of essence, and also causes damage while doing so. John is familiar with this attack by frogs, and hates it.

At Bronze, frogs receive a fantastic body [Perk], absorbing some of the essence of any spell directed at them besides their own. It lowers the damage of hostile spells, but also the benefits of beneficial spells such as heals, and the essence helps fill their dantian. It also gives frogs one of the highest known healing factors of the animal kingdom, and it is assumed it includes some sort of enhanced sense too.

Healing factor is natural healing speed, unassisted by essence or manifestation, and increases for all beings with tier.

At Silver, animals receive another [Perk]. It can be anything, from a weak general [Perk], to something unique and powerful. For frogs it is [Fluoropolymer Skin], making frogs very resistant to acid, as well as solvents and bases, terms John is unfamiliar with, but after hearing an explanation of both, he considers solvent to be a fancy word for water, and bases to be the opposite of acid.

To John, acid seems a good thing to be protected against, as well as the opposite of acid, whatever that is, but a frog being resistant to water just seems silly.

For Gold and on, Hubaba has no information for frogs, and he has no knowledge of Amber's other beast forms, as Esau has no deer, bear, or fox. It does have lizards, but the manifestation they receive at Copper is far different than what Amber's lizard received.

John thinks Amber getting five free body [Perks] at Bronze sounds amazing, and she should also be able to pick two more herself for her human and demon forms. He hopes he'll be able to keep up with her.

John often thinks about the talk he had with Amber when she first caught him staring at her chest. She said, 'I look too, but I bet you've never noticed.' He could be wrong, but the more he thinks about it, the more certain he becomes that it can only mean one thing. *Why would she look at me in secret unless she likes what she sees? And if she likes what she sees, doesn't that mean she finds the sight of me appealing, as I do the sight of her?*

*Should I find reasons to wear far less clothing, and show my bare legs too? I hope she has feelings for me, and is mightily repressing them as I am, only doing a far better job of it. Such a good job of it that I can find no other hints of any attraction.*

*If she becomes far more powerful than I am, and is attracted to me now, that will end, as it should. No lady wants a much weaker man. Unless the man is powerful in other ways.*

*Well, I do control the ring filled with such wealth. Hopefully that will make up for my lack of strength if she comes to far surpass me in power.*

*Or I work harder than I ever have, and stay ahead of her. Whatever it takes to win her heart, even if we can never be together. I can take comfort in knowing my feelings are returned, and things would be different if not for such cruel fate. But I still must control my emotions. Only boys and buffoons can't control themselves. I am far too old to act as a boy again. What is wrong with me? How have I lost my great control?*

That night, while Amber and Hubaba perform a duet, singing loudly of how they got each other, babe, John feigns the staging area they all live in is sultry, and disrobes, and fans himself with the light-blue crystal of a low Transcendent, and the dark-green and blue-green crystals of Diamonds and Salts.

Once the performance is over, Amber looks at John and giggles before asking, "You okay, dude?"

John replies, "The air is torrid, and I must cool myself."

"It feels about the same as always. A little cooler than usual if anything. You going through menopause? And that sounded real old-timey. Just say, 'I'm hot and trying to cool off.' See how normal that sounds, buddy?"

John stands and stretches, giving Amber as much of an eyeful as possible while she is looking. "I'm hot and trying to cool off."

Amber smiles her beautiful smile. "Good job, buddy!" She then turns to her demon sidekick. "Ready for the next one, Baba? Wanna switch it up and I go demon form and do the male parts? I think you'll do great as Lady Gaga. Your voice is amazing. You still remember the words to 'Shallow?'"

Now tuning everything out, John starts cycling with the new technique taught to him by Hubaba.

Cycling is something that can be done once meridians are cleared, and is good to do all the time, especially when doing nothing else. He thinks of it as churning the essence throughout his body, in his dantian and circling through all his meridians. Hubaba said to think of it as an exercise that improves many aspects of cultivation, such as tempering meridians, improving control and focus, along with many other benefits.

The technique Hubaba taught to John and Amber is [Turmoil Within Tranquility Cycling Technique]. Just as when taught his constant breathing technique, John struggles to remember to keep churning his essence, but takes comfort in knowing Amber has the same issue, and he is not alone.

John replaces the valuable crystals with clear crystals and begins meditating. At Copper, it takes noticeably longer to fill his dantian, but he can fill it much faster than Amber fills hers. It takes forever for Hubaba to fill his own, especially now that he is Gold.

Hubaba is not slow at gathering energy, and more proficient than most demons at his tier since he is far older and far more practiced. He uses the same gathering and refining techniques as all demons, both chosen and scab, and they are highly regarded and fast techniques. John and Amber are exceptions to the rule, with John's Legendary technique, and Amber cultivating as a frog, an animal far better known for its fast advancement than its high healing factor.

Hubaba can use clear crystals to speed up energy gathering, but it barely speeds it up at all. Clear crystals greatly speeds up cultivating for John, and switching to light-yellow crystals makes cultivating only slightly faster than clear crystals do for him, and he sees it as wasteful. Amber has a significant speed increase with light-yellow crystals, so no longer uses clear crystals.

Hubaba needs at least the dark-yellow Crystal of a Silver to gather energy at a decent pace, but once he feels his foundation settle after ascending to Gold, he uses the light-green crystals Golds drop to fill his dantian quickly, and rank up to mid-low Gold. John tells him to continue using them, as they have plenty of all colored crystals, and only limited amounts starting with the green crystals of a Platinum, of which he has well over a hundred, each worth five thousand of the clear crystals Woods drop on death.

Not all cultivators are created equal. Some are much stronger than others while at the same rank and tier. Scabs are not particularly motivated to excel, and risk becoming targets if they do, so they tend not to.

Hubaba, being peak Silver for so long, was strong for a Silver, but is now a weak Gold, even though this ascension was his best yet. He did grow much taller with ascension, as demons do, and his painted face seems less strange now, and much more intimidating on such a giant, though Amber still insists the demon is somehow beautiful.

For most cultivators, waiting for their foundation to settle is not what slows their advancement. Filling their dantian is the bottleneck, as it takes a great amount of time for them to do so. All refined essence is hoarded, and any practice or combat pushes the next rank up further back, and they never waste essence on shen or empty, and only become wasteful with their greedily hoarded essence in combat, when their life is on the line, unless they have access to great wealth and a constant supply of higher-tiered crystals.

The cloaks that mask essence from vision enhancements based on tier and stealth ability, called stealth cloaks, don't work all that well for Hubaba, even as a Gold, since he is not proficient in stealth at all. He received the [Perk] that does the same thing without the stipulation. He still stays in the Trial when John and Amber check on the portal. Diamonds have great senses, and being discovered means his death, and when he does leave the Trial, it will be to head directly to the portal once it opens.

John goes on far more expeditions than Amber, as he has a greater need. At his new tier, it takes a very long time for his foundation to settle, and according to Hubaba, way longer than it should take at Copper. Even with him starting this tier with open meridians, and even though Amber cultivates far slower than he does, her foundation settles much faster, and he cannot catch up to her.

A way to assist the foundation in settling quicker is not to use essence for shen, but to quickly drain the dantian with spells. It hurts John's meridians to drain his dantian so quickly, but that also is a type of training, and helps to fortify them. Draining his essence quickly while just practicing works, but the best and fastest way to help settle the foundation is draining the dantian with spells in battle.

So, John makes battle. As much and as often as he can. He still converts much essence to shen, especially on lazy nights in the Trial, after practicing all day, during the time Amber and Hubaba have 'fun.'

John spares only groups of creatures he recently killed too many of, and does so to avoid creating imbalance in the strange system controlling the NetherRealms. He battles all else, all the extraordinary and doughty foes this world puts in his path, and Esau is littered with foes, both beast and demon. He goes far in all directions, but avoids Circle Xakariz. He also avoids demon villages, but only if doing so is not too inconvenient.

Demon villages are not real villages. They are just places lower tiered demons gather for safety in numbers and to meditate, as they battle beasts and train by day, and meditate at night, having no need of sleep. Even John needs some sleep once in a while, real sleep, giving him whatever necessary thing his mighty meditation technique does not, and he is jealous of demon's complete lack of need.

Amber has less of a need for sleep than normal humans, but still needs it every night, which slows John down too much for the goals he sets for his outings. And though she cultivates fast, she can't spend essence like John does, and must hoard it to be able to rank up in preparation of her foundation settling. She only goes with him on every other expedition, and only to check for the portal.

John loves the time he spends with Amber on expeditions as much as he hates the torture of it. He loves going off on his solo expeditions, but misses her fiercely when he does. Her smile and laughter fill him with an energy every bit as necessary as that he gathers while meditating.

Surprisingly, John hardly gets called out for looking at her inappropriately on their team expeditions, but every time he does, he is filled with shame and angered with himself for doing so, and his continued lack of control.

So, after four months as a Copper, John advances twice to mid-high Copper, and Amber also advances. When John ascended to low Copper, Amber was mid-low Copper, now she is a high Copper, and claims to be nearly ready to rank up again, and takes pleasure in keeping her large lead over John.

John is now strong enough to crush rocks with his hands, and he must be very careful when handling even non-mundane items. He is faster than any creature he has found on this world, though he avoids the few Golds he detects, and has yet to see any beast higher than that. He can shrug off many attacks of Bronze beasts, and only needs to really worry about the mighty spells Silvers manifest.

As for his 'blood' concept, John long ago suffered through learning all Amber and Hubaba could teach him. It is useful, and helpful to his advancement. Increasing the oxygen in his blood isn't much help, as his stamina already seems endless, and it hardly increases his speed. And using it for healing is not of much help either. His vital essence does similar things, but does them far better.

John focuses on using 'blood' offensively in battle. Denying blood to the brain, pooling blood in the heart, blocking arteries, even using it to hold a victim still, or to cause unconsciousness by quickly removing all blood from the brain.

John can kill many at once, but prefers not to, as his concept also allows him to drain his prey far quicker than he ever could before, and strengthen himself in that way too, and this gives him another reason to seek out so much battle.

John tries to fight only with the manifestations he created, so as to improve himself and his ability to control his essence. His plasma-ring is by far the strongest attack he has available, causing much more damage than even his imbued Fireblade can, but using the ring improves him in no way, and he saves it for emergencies.

When John learned blood is made of mostly plasma, Amber tried to backtrack, claiming blood plasma is completely different from the fire plasma of his ring, but if so, why would they have the same name? John is now certain he will someday be able to make blood plasma combust into fire plasma, the same way the mighty substance naphtha combusts into fire, and the plasma of blood will be the key to doing so. *I will control the mighty 'blood-fire' concept*, he dreams.

From the testing they do, comparing John's own blood-essence weapon enhancement to the one Fireblade has, Fireblade only has a slight damage advantage, even though his view of blood is not capable of causing damage in such a way. Hubaba has no certain explanation as to why, but assumes it is due to John's high [Min. Power] [Stat], and the purpose of enhancing weapons is always to cause damage, regardless of the aspect and concept the cultivator uses.

John is not certain of this explanation, as he believes the only purpose of the [Blood Dart] spell is to cause damage too, something it currently does very poorly, and merely lobs a small blob of blood at a target.

Both John and Amber learn how to veil their souls, though it is generally seen as not necessary to do so until Bronze. It helps hide them while stealthing, if nothing else, and is something they can practice together when Amber has no essence to waste training manifestations and unbinds.

Surprisingly, John excels at veiling his soul. He thinks it strange he is so good at it, as he finds the whole process confusing. He is not sure what he is doing when he veils, but he is happy he does it so well.

Even more surprising, Amber can focus her soul and use it to pin beasts her own tier down, and even has some luck with lower ranks of Bronze. John cannot do this at all, and it is said to be impossible to do until around the mid Bronze tier.

With all his practice and improvement, John's harmony fills quickly, and not wanting any to go to waste, and knowing he can inexplicably gain large amounts of it at any time out of the blue, as soon as he has the harmony for it, he gets the next in the [Perk]-chain [SupraType], the capstone of which will cause John to grow greatly in height, allowing him to once again tower over most humans, something he greatly desires to do again.

John received the first [Perk] in this chain as a Wood, called [Quick Thinking]. The [Perk] available at Copper is called [Good Genes], and costs about seventy percent of his maximum harmony, bringing him to near zero once he attains it.

The information Hubaba has on the [Perk] is not very useful to any of the companions, and says, "Review of gene pleiotropy, developmental pleiotropy, and selectional pleiotropy for fitness. Decreases phenotypic independence, allowing for a greater chance of mutations resulting in an increase in fitness."

John believes he feels somewhat better after attaining the [Perk], though he can't be certain how. He feels he has a general improvement in energy, mood, and mindset, but the only way he is certain it affected him is a decrease in appetite. He thinks his horns grew faster after getting the [Perk], along with the claws where his finger and toenails used to be, but he also got caught in fog many times too.

If he must grow horns, John isn't too disappointed in the type he is growing. He has what looks to be the start of bull horns, but stunted and small, little more than nubs still. And Amber said his big nubs look cute. He is also happy the [Resize] rune of his cap has no issue working around the nubs. His claws are far smaller than Amber's, but much thicker than hers, and less sharp. Still good weapons, and weapons he always has with him now.

John is excited as he leaves for a solo expedition, as he plans of great slaughter, but the expedition is cut short. He finds sign of many demons passing, and not just from Second Point. Troops from Fourth Point, many of them, joined up with troops from Second Point south of the Trial.

John would like to check and ensure the portal is open, but he is close to the Trial and far from the general region where the portal is predicted to open, so returns to the Trial and his companions.

"Good news! Prepare to depart. Demons from both Second and Fourth Point are on the march together, heading in the direction we guess the portal will open. It is time."

Amber looks frightened, and not excited. Hubaba does too. She says, "My goodness! Can't we just stay here? It's pretty peaceful. If we want it to be. I know I'm having fun. For the first time in my life, I'm actually having fun and enjoying myself. I...I don't want this to end. What do you guys say? You wanna stay? Here, with me?" She smiles brightly, John assuming she knows the effect it has on him.

Before Hubaba can answer, John says, "Great gods below! Our world is invaded, and our people are being slaughtered. I swore vengeance against Ukaraaz, just as I swore to torture Morgoros. I will fight. If it means I lose you, my beautiful Amber, I will still fight.

"I know we can never be together, but I would have you look upon me as I look upon you. If my word meant so little to me, if vengeance meant so little to me, if my home burning meant so little to me, and I stayed here, with you, and you could still look upon me as I want you to, you are not the woman I thought you were, and not a woman I want to look upon me so.

"My answer is no. I am going back to my world. *Our* world. I hope you both come with me. You are both strong, and I could use the help."

Amber, no longer smiling, walks over to John. She extends up on the tips of her toes, and kisses his cheek. A new smile then graces her face. "You had me at great gods below, buddy. Let's go save our world! The sooner we do, the sooner we can get back to having fun again. Great speech, but way too old-timey. And just for future reference, vengeance and torture aren't the greatest selling points for a lady. What about you, Baba? You in?"

"In what?"

Amber rolls her eyes, and her tinkling laughter fills the room. "You coming with us?"

"Yes," replies Hubaba, creepily.

John's heart is elated. His path, his future, come what may, will include these stout companions, and his fears of going it alone are laid to rest. He stops looking at the beautiful face of his Amber with his orb-eye, and looks upon her with his own eyes, and she smiles before asking, "Well, what's the plan, buddy?"

Without hesitation, John answers, "We win, they lose."

Amber stops smiling, and again rolls her eyes.

# CHAPTER 50
# WAY TOO RISKY

"Yes. Us winning and them losing is a nice goal, but if we are to face Captain Ukaraaz and live it is my strong opinion the plan should contain far more details and specifics," worriedly exclaims Hubaba.

Amber slaps John's arm, "Don't worry, Baba. We'll make a real plan. John is just being an idiot."

John disagrees. They have no idea what forces they face. Any plan would have to be so adjusted it would become irrelevant immediately, as any battle is a dance of acting and reacting as it ebbs and flows and changes. You adapt to what is happening, or you die. There are only two items that should be mentioned, and planned for, John believes. He says, "Ukaraaz is mine, and Morgoros must survive the battle, as he must be tortured."

Amber barks out, "Come on, John! Be serious. We're the good guys. We don't torture."

"I am serious. Did you not see the young girl he tortured? I was not strong enough to protect her, so I must avenge her. Her soul cries out for retribution. I saw her spirit, suffering and twisted even in death. This is not to fill some sick need inside of me. I don't like torture. And this is not just for the girl, but also for the one he tortured before her. Can you say for certain their souls can have peace without being avenged? If not, it must be done. If we are truly good, then it must be done."

Surprisingly, Amber smiles. "How 'bout this? We put a pin in torture for now and we'll come back to it later. Sound good, buddy? Now, what do we know about Ukaraaz?"

Hubaba says, "He is older for a Gold. A genius as a cultivator. He is exacting and makes many scabs and is cruel to us. His talent was noticed as a Bronze at Outer Point, where he grew, by none other than Master Baggodon himself. His growth has been slow for a demon, as he demands perfection of himself, and he has been gifted materials denied to all but Point Masters to aid in his growth. Baggodon has plans for him. He is high Gold, and his telekinesis is formidable. His manifestations use little essence, and it is said his core is inexhaustible.

"Even if all three of us stood against only him I honestly don't see us having any hope of winning. If our goal is to live, we should only sneak through the portal and sneak far away from Ukaraaz. The deal made with Circle Xakariz allows for only three Gold demons on your planet. I was not given the specifics, but maybe the Divine enforcing the bargain will send Ukaraaz back here, and not me. The chance of that happening is higher than us standing against him in battle and surviving.

"If I am the one to be sent back, I will not be sad. I've enjoyed my time with you both more than I can properly express with words. I am so grateful my life will end on such a high note, especially knowing you two shall live on."

Amber moves towards Hubaba, reaches high up to put a hand on his shoulder, and entwines the fingers of her other hand with his. Her eyes are watery, and her face is strange and sad. She is so tiny next to the now giant demon, John nearly laughs.

John says, "Sweet Amber, never again say that I am the party-pooper among us three. The third Gold demon of Earth shall be Hubaba, and Ukaraaz will be sent to hell. That is the plan. The only plan I accept."

Hubaba smiles, "Thank you. It warms me to hear these words, but I fear the outcome may be the same. If you truly plan to battle Ukaraaz, then the only chance we have, slim though it may be, is for Amber to stay hidden and wait for an opportunity to assassinate him. The chance of success is very low, and slinking off is still the best plan for you two, instead of risking your lives for me."

"We risk our lives for all of Earth. You risk your life for our planet, and I thank you for it. I will fight Ukaraaz as a man does. Not my Amber."

John, truly thinking what he said would melt Amber's heart, and show he values her, and is willing to die to protect her, and face the worst the world has to offer himself, in her stead, to keep it all from her, is surprised and worried as he sees her hands go on her hips, and her face become angry.

"First off, pal, I'm not your Amber. I'm not property. So...so...just...ewww, you drive me nuts sometimes! I wanted to stay here, safe. You're the one putting me in danger. Just...just stop saying you'll keep me safe. This whole thing.... aaugh!

"And why do we have to do this now? Barely any time would pass on Earth if we waited a little bit here. I could rank up to peak if we waited just, like, a week. So, if we're doing this immediately, and doing something this stupid, we're doing it as smart as we can.

"You can only beat me when we spar because you know what I can do. And I never seriously tried to harm you when I stop hiding. Have I killed a Gold? No, but I've killed plenty of Silvers without hardly even trying. Me taking out Ukaraaz with a surprise attack is our best chance. Your nonsense is just going to get us all killed."

John, having lived a long time, realizes his experiences with women and what they like to hear a man say and do might be a little outdated, but he is smart enough to know when to keep his mouth shut, and he does so for the rest of the planning. He cycles while trying to look reprimanded and admonished, and he is proud he only once becomes distracted from listening to the plan by Amber's great beauty.

\*\*\*

"Amber, this armor has the same runes for the reflection spell my cap does. It could mean the difference between life and death." John holds the armor set out to Amber, a sleek set of leather, and smart looking ones, with the [Resize] rune ensuring it will hug her tightly.

"Gross! What are you, one of those S&M sickos? I'm not wearing that! Come on, man. Just give me the hat that increases Mental Fortification."

"Cap, not hat. Hats usually have a brim, and...never mind," replies John, dejected. Amber hardly has any items attuned. He thinks she should attune some additional items, even if they are not helpful while she is in animal form.

"How are you not nervous? I'm freaking out. And don't say anything stupid about awakening from a dream. Uh! Sorry, I'm being a...you know, a b-word. Sorry. Hey. Look at me."

John turns slightly towards Amber, eyes downcast. She puts her hand on his cheek and points his face directly at hers, and John raises his eyes towards her face, causing his heart to flutter as it always does.

"Listen. I...you're not alone, you know? I wish...I...I'm sorry I yelled at you. I'm sorry I've been so...you know? I don't wanna abandon Earth. I hate fighting. I don't wanna die. I have this feeling like...I feel like this is it. This is where I die. I feel safe here. I know it isn't safe. I know we gotta do this. Gotta do what's right. It's just...inside...I...you're a good guy, John. I'm glad we met. I'm glad we're in this together. Just know...I wish...uh! I hate this. Just...thanks for the hat. Cap. For thinking of me."

John smiles. "I'm glad we met too, and that we're in this together."

John turns from Amber, and walks towards the entrance and Hubaba. The demon smiles creepily, his face freshly painted. "Hubaba, you might be sensed when you exit, and your journey cut short. Are you ready, my friend? Are you certain in this path?"

"My path is certain. I am ready."

John checks his belt. He unattuned the old one and equipped a belt of hiding. Only one item can be unattuned every twenty-two hours, so John still wears his cloak, though it is redundant. *Too much stealth can't hurt,* he thinks. He then notices he isn't cycling, and starts to do so while waiting.

John dislikes items that do something his [Skills] do, and losing out on ways to improve himself and his [Skills], but this mission is all or nothing, and Hubaba thinks the new Second-Point Master could be at

431

the portal, as Garioch went himself to see the troops through, and stayed with the portal for months and months, and his replacement may do the same. The belt of hiding is the only safe choice.

John and Amber and Hubaba all have their items and ways to stealth, hide, and stay unseen and undetected as best as they can each get them. He is as ready as he can be.

Amber finally finishes up whatever she was doing and walks towards John and Hubaba. "Okay, boys, let's go get stupid," she says, disappearing from sense and sight.

***

Finding the portal is easy. Hubaba sensed a Gold and a horde of demons gathering a long ways back, leading them right towards the portal. Many demons approach it still, so the companions approach it from a different direction.

With by far the best vision, John can see the gathered demons well before his companions can. "Hold. I think I see the Gold. He is directing demons and supplies through the portal. I've only seen two, Ukaraaz and Hubaba, but this demon is of a similar size. I can see nothing larger, so no veiled Diamonds or such unwanted surprises."

John hears Hubaba whisper, "Not good, but one Gold is much better than a Diamond."

"How many demons are there?" asks Amber.

"Many go through the portal, and many are left. Mostly Wood, Copper, and Bronze, but I see about four Silvers near the Gold."

Amber snaps, "Many isn't an answer. How many? A hundred? And Silvers? How many is about four? Is it really five or six?"

"There are four Silvers. As for the number of demons, I can't say. Two hundred?"

"Jesus Christ, dude! This isn't the time for your caveman ooga booga drivel. We need specifics. Exact specifics. Come on, man!"

A long silence stretches out uncomfortably before John replies. "For someone lauding the necessity of mutual respect, you're showing little enough of it."

"Oh, am I, dummy? Remember when you made us fight those little dragon things? You said there were only two hundred. There were, like, five or six hundred of them. I'm not rolling the dice on your stupid way of counting."

John is glad he cannot see Amber, and have her beauty confuse his mind. His heart fills with anger and bitterness. "Enough! That is the last time you disrespect me. You seek to abuse my feelings towards you. You think I'll put up with being treated so lowly?

"I see you, Amber. I know your type. You claim to be a lady because you'll only sit certain ways, and not others, and say only certain things, and not others. But I see what you do. You purposely do things to…to drive me mad with lust. You're no lady. What's your plan? To make me so lustful I lose control and try to force myself on you? Then you'll blame it on your 'curse?' I've lived long and have never done so, not once, so you are out of luck this time, siren."

Amber runs off, kicking dirt and sobbing, making it clear where she is, even though she is unseen. *She wants me to follow and apologize, and tell her none of what I said is true. Ha! Never!*

Hubaba, still whispering, as if there is a risk of being overheard, says, "I've seen you two bicker occasionally, but I assumed it was just normal banter between good friends. I did not know there was such hate between the two of you. I assumed you were very fond of her. As fond as I am of both of you."

"I don't hate her. She's been treating me as if I'm contemptible. There's a limit to what I'll tolerate, and she reached mine. I treated her only as base as she treated me, and told her truths she'd rather not have heard, so she could continue to play her games, continue twisting me, and now she knows better. That's all."

"I don't like this. It makes me feel strange inside. Bad. How I felt as a scab. Fearful and uncertain."

John reaches out, easily finding Hubaba due to seeing his soul, and places a hand on his shoulder. "I don't like it either. My apologies, friend, but it had to be done."

"Yes. I should go talk to her. She has been very kind to me."

"Tell her it's okay if you both want to go back to the Trial. No one seems to have detected you."

John steels his heart, and watches the portal, cycling, and planning. If he can't sneak through the portal, he will just have to fight this Gold. It becomes less obvious where his two companions are, and then he assumes they left back for the Trial. His heart hurts, but his path is still clear, and what needs doing still needs to be done. He gives up on further planning. He stands, ready to proceed.

"John, where are you?" John hears Amber ask, with her beautiful voice.

"I'm here."

"Can we talk?"

"Say what you will, but make it quick. I start working soon."

A long, tense moment passes before she begins. "I'm sorry. I'm real sorry I've been so snippy. And mean. I...I hate this. I'm scared out of my mind. I'm freaking out. I know I'm gonna die. I just know it. My insides are being torn all up and you're just...it seems like you're not taking this serious. You're not nervous at all. I don't know why but it makes me kinda angry. If I'm gonna die I want you to be...I don't know...something. At least bothered a little.

"I know we gotta do this. I'm gonna do it. We hafta do this. I wanna do the right thing. This. I'm just...I'm petrified. I'm sorry I'm taking it out on you. When I'm a bear I'm never scared. Ukaraaz scared the...he really scared me. That's the only time I was ever scared as a bear. He's gonna kill us all and I don't wanna die. Not...now. Not after...not after I really just started to live. You know?

John is about to reply when Amber continues. "And I...I did...you're right. About the other thing. I can feel when you're looking. I...didn't... I always wanted that. Like in the movies. I didn't do anything crazy.

434

Nothing unladylike or inappropriate. Just…little things I knew you liked. I was just being flirty. I wasn't trying to push you over the edge or anything, I promise. I just…I just liked it. Liked that you liked looking. It made me feel good.

"I'll stop doing it. That all stops. Promise. But I do have a curse. I haven't lied about anything, especially that. It's completely ruined my life. Until recently and you. And Baba."

Amber's voice gets softer as she asks, "Will you accept my apology? Can we be friends again? And sorry about being so mean and snippy before."

John's heart goes from being tense and anxious, to glad again. Barely a moment passes before he gives a reply. "Of course, I forgive you. I just can't tolerate being treated so, especially by you. I'm sorry for the things I said. I was angry. And I'm sorry I look at you so much. I could always just shut off my emotions, and…I can't now. I don't want to look, but I can't stop it. I try so hard, but I can't.

"I know we can never be together. I try so hard to only see you as a good friend and companion, to stop being so childish, lacking all my control as if I am a boy again. I don't know what's wrong with me now, but I will not stop fighting this, I promise you.

"And I'm most sorry for having to ask you to join me in this fight. I know you're scared. I hate to say it but I'm not strong enough to do this on my own. If I was sure I could do it alone, and save you from such battle, I would. I cannot sit by and let our world be conquered. And though I dislike not being able to protect you, you are strong, and a weapon that can't remain sheathed. Not for this fight, and not with what's at stake."

John hopes his words are not too outdated for modern sensibilities, and Amber takes no offense by any of it, not after her own good apology. He is much relieved when she says, "I know. And I know we gotta. I gotta."

A long moment passes, and John is unsure of what to do or say. Amber is the next to speak, and John is surprised her voice sounds so nervous.

"John. I hafta ask something. For something. This is gonna sound like I'm a horrible person and sending mixed signals. But I'm not. I promise. First I say all the...the encouragement stops, and then..."

Amber pauses long enough John wonders if he should say something. As he opens his mouth to do so, Amber says, "Goodness, this is hard! Uh, I'm just gonna say it. If I'm gonna die, there's...things I've never done I don't wanna die without doing first. Especially now...with you, and I can. They aren't carnal knowledge. They can't be. And I promise everything stops after. The...encouragement. Flirting. This really can't go nowhere. It...just...it can't."

Again, Amber pauses long enough where John wonders if he should say something. He is too excited though. He thinks he knows where this is going.

"Okay. I'm just gonna ask. Can we...can we hug? I've never hugged a guy before. I never...held one."

John is somewhat disappointed, but he's always wanted to hold Amber close, and now he will.

Before John can eagerly agree, Amber continues. "And...and...oh, goodness, this is so hard! This...okay. I'm just gonna say it. Uh...can we kiss too? I never thought I'd actually have the chance. It can't count as carnal knowledge. There's just no way it can. Goodness, I must sound like such a...so horrible. This isn't mixed signals. If I'm gonna die I just...you know? And it all stops after. Promise. It's okay to say no. Probably better if you do. Easier. It's okay. Just say no."

John almost tells her she must have forgotten, but they did do kissing; she did kissing on his cheek not long ago.

John's mouth is far cleaner than most. Taking in vital essence refreshes and cleans it, and his teeth never rot. The same was true for his Lilitu, but they never once did kissing on the mouth. He'd kiss her forehead sometimes, and she'd kiss his neck or ears a little. They both believed the practice of doing kissing on the mouth a disgusting thing to do, as most people always have, and mouths are filthy, stinky things, filled with rot and disease.

When John was growing up, mothers would hold their faces close to their children, and give them a quick sniff to show affection. And sometimes they would do the same to their husbands, but not often. In Agade, noble women would sometimes give a child a quick peck on the cheek with their lips, and rub noses with a spouse, or quickly press lips together for a mere moment. John thought even that was disgusting.

And things got worse. John went to Burata many times before meeting his Lilitu, and many times with her and after. The place was strange, but the people were normal. During Alexander's conquests, when Burata was then called Indos, the nobles of that region became deviants and started to do kissing in the most disgusting way imaginable – open mouthed and for long periods.

Later, in Rome, all classes of people started to do it. They called it the *savium*, the kiss of passion, and John would nearly retch when he'd see filthy Roman soldiers doing kissing with even filthier barbarian girls.

To John, someone putting their stinky, rotting, disease infested mouth on his own is as disgusting as someone putting their dirty foot in his mouth. It is something civilized people don't do.

Amber had such a hard time asking to do kissing that he doesn't want to hurt her feelings, or cause her to be angry, and lose out on his chance to hold her close, so he represses a shiver of disgust and thinks it through.

John knows Amber's breath is never foul, even though she often complains about lacking some new inventions to keep teeth clean, and the mouth free of foul scents, and the brushing of teeth with paste made specifically for the purpose. Even her feet aren't repulsive, and feet always are. Doing kissing with her shouldn't be so awful, and worth the price if he gets to hold her too.

John says, "I want nothing more than to hold you close, in my arms. And we can do kissing too if you want. A quick peck on the cheek again, or…however you want to do it."

John is glad to hear the joy in Amber's reply. "Oh, thank you! Okay, you ready? This is crazy! Now where…"

Both knock each other with outstretched hands, searching for the other's invisible form before managing to gather in an embrace. John is delighted to finally hold Amber in his arms, and he holds her tightly. He tries to hold back, but he can't help from pressing himself hard against her, and becomes inflamed when she allows it, and even more so feeling her rapid heartbeat. Her heart is always silent when she is invisible, and it beating so quickly proves she is feeling real emotions, and not just playing a game to twist him up and confuse him.

For a long while, John and Amber just hold each other, Amber caressing his back, John forcing his hands not to roam to places they shouldn't.

Then John feels Amber stretch up on the tips of her toes, assuming she is looking for his mouth, and to do kissing. He holds back a groan of disgust before lowering his head to meet hers, banging his chin on her invisible forehead.

John and Amber's lips find each other's, and he is surprised he actually finds it very enjoyable, and not at all disgusting, and that Amber's mouth seems so clean and free of rot, and her lips feel as soft as heavenly clouds. And soon a passion takes over him and he kisses her deeply, even happy her tongue is now in his mouth, and he holds her tighter, and presses even harder against her.

John is again glad he cannot see Amber, and be further inflamed by her great beauty, as he struggles even now, without the sight of her, with containing himself to doing only what was asked for.

Unthinkingly, John's hands move downwards along Amber's lower back, and Amber allows it. He cups her bottom, and then Amber grabs both his hands, and moves her body away, and then her mouth too.

John gently tries to pull her back, but she huskily whispers, "No. No more. This is skirting it too much. Too risky. Way too risky. I…"

Amber takes a deep breath. Louder, and in a high and chipper voice, she says, "But thank you! That was just…crazy! Just wonderful! God, that was…so…my goodness! Everything I hoped. And more! I…I…no wonder people do it so much. And I never thought I'd ever actually be able to do it.

"Thanks, buddy. Right? Buddy? Just friends. Right? From now on. We just...can't. You know that right? Just to be clear. And no more encouragement from me! Any of that. Promise!"

"Yes," chimes in Hubaba from a few paces away.

# CHAPTER 51
# HOME SWEET HOME

Hubaba is certain the Gold is only overseeing the transfer of troops and supplies, and will leave soon. Though John is eager to get going, waiting for the Gold to depart is the only smart move.

Two Silvers entered the portal. Hubaba predicted that would happen. Two Silvers under the command of Ukaraaz are known to be dead, and he is allowed eight, so at least two of the four the Gold brought would replace them.

The supplies will mainly be condensed Nether, the only thing demons eat, though it isn't truly eating as they expel no waste, and only need to do this when out of the NetherRealms for extended periods. Hubaba says there might be some crystals too, for Ukaraaz to give out as rewards for tall deeds.

John hopes the Gold leaves soon, and goes into a shallow form of meditation while keeping aware, cycling, and reviewing some of the memories he recovered on ascension. One, in particular, is a new favorite of his, and he often thinks of it.

Noticing something with an aware part of his mind, John sees a Silver come through the portal and approach the Gold. They talk for a moment, and the newly arrived Silver and one of the two left go back through the portal. The Gold and remaining Silver continue to watch lower tiered demons stream through the portal.

Amber went some way back to cultivate, as she can't do so and maintain her invisibility. John is glad she isn't there to distract him. His heart hurts that things are over for Amber, but he is glad he got to hold her close, in his arms, and feel her body against his own once. He is surprised at how much he enjoyed doing kissing with her, and chalks his new deviancy and liking of such a disgusting thing up to Amber being a special case and exception to the rule.

John took Amber's promise to stop doing the things he likes to see as there being no hope of having his affection returned. He knows they can never be together physically, but he always hoped they could be together in spirit. He's sad it will never be, but is glad she never asked him to stop looking, as he doesn't think he can. He enjoys the sight of her too much, and even if he gets his control back, he isn't sure he'd give that up.

And if Amber really wants John to stop looking, he thinks she would just go into her demon form instead of always being human. He has no issue seeing her just as a good friend and companion when she looks as a monster. No demon at any tier or size is the least bit attractive to John. *And if her human form causes her so much trouble, why not just lay with me and put an end to it? I'd miss the sight of her terribly, but it would be worth it. Oh, how it would be worth it.*

Amber's great fear of the upcoming battle confuses John. They've been in many plights together, and have always come out ahead. This fight will be tough, but her being so frightened seems strange to him. They are both very strong now.

New movement catches John's attention, and he sees the Gold and Silver head away from the portal.

"Hubaba, the Gold and Silver head in the direction of Circle Xakariz. Hardly any Bronze are left waiting to enter the portal. There's mostly just Wood and some Copper. Inform Amber, please. It is time. I'll continue to watch."

***

John is surprised to exit the portal unmolested, happy to finally be back on his own planet, and happy it's the dark of night. He quickly looks to the stars to get his bearings.

John assumed something would go wrong, that they'd have to fight their way to and through the portal. He is even more surprised the belt of hiding works so well, as he is pressed from all sides by demons, in a mad mass of Wood, Copper, and Bronze. If he didn't change belts, the plan would've failed before even beginning.

The giant mob is a result of the time difference between worlds. All demons from Esau going through the portal appear simultaneously on this side, and the portal somehow knows what areas are empty and where to safely deposit travelers.

More nervous than he should be, John looks around, sending more essence into his belt. He hopes his companions are okay.

Pain spikes in John's head, as if his brain convulses, and he grits down on his teeth. He needs to get out of the mob. The portal is surprisingly far away from him. A Silver is a hundred or so paces to his south, yelling out to the mob of demons.

Judging the risk necessary, John jumps out of the crowd towards the north, breaking free of the crowd and moving away from it to stand by himself on a snowy field. He needs to assess the situation, but the pain in his head intensifies, and he takes a knee.

A spinning blue circle appears in the center of his vision, obstructing his view. He moves his head and the circle stays in the exact center of his sight. Then words start to appear, but not how the NCS has ever shown them before.

Whatever demon John looks most directly at has an empty square appear over its chest, and a line goes from the square to above the demon's head, stating the tier of the demon and some other information.

John looks above the demons to get this to stop, but it doesn't. Gazing south at the horizon, new words state [Burlington, Pop. 32k, 94 mi]. He turns his head left and many of the same descriptions with a line pointing down to the ground appear, the darkest one reading [Sherbrooke, Pop. 112k, 65 mi].

John turns around and sees a smoking ruin, and the words say [Saint-Jean-sur-Richelieu, Pop. 9, 1 mi], and not too far past it [Montreal, Pop. 118, 22 mi].

Taking a deep breath to collect himself, John assumes this is some new way Pixie is trying to assist him, without her knowing how it distracts him and obstructs his vision. Usually, in such a dangerous situation with so many enemies about, he'd be denied entrance into his Mind's Eye, and he and Amber both assumed they would not have access to the NCS and Pixie until after the battle.

Since the battle hasn't started, and he remains undetected still, John tries to access his Mind's Eye. Nothing happens. He really wants to see his current [Stats], and greet Pixie, and is disappointed he'll have to wait.

John silently curses. He wishes the words away, and, surprisingly, they disappear, all but the spinning blue circle. He needs to focus on the plan, and get in position, but first needs to get the layout and the location of the key demons. The blue circle is a distraction, but no matter how he wishes it would go, it remains.

The headache intensifies again. John ignores it, and focuses on his surroundings.

To his right, towards the west, about three hundred paces away, is the portal. In a large area from in front of John to the same distance on the other side of the portal is a massive mob of demons. Four Silvers stand outside the mob, one of them Morgoros, directing more than half of the Wood and Coppers to head out in various directions, ordering them to make chaos, remain stealthy, and kill all magals they come across.

One Silver yells to the three Silvers within the mob, telling them to report to Ukaraaz.

A good distance past the giant mob is a neat and orderly formation of demons meditating, facing away from John, towards the south. Many demons from the big mob are ordered to join the formation.

Most of the formation is made up of Woods, and these demons are in the back of the formation, nearest John, about a thousand total.

Past the Woods are Coppers, numbering around five hundred.

Past the Coppers are Bronzes, about two hundred of them, and the only group John guesses the numbers of correctly.

Past the Bronze demons is a Silver facing the formation, meditating alone.

And a distance past this Silver is Ukaraaz, also facing south, standing still in his black armor, then erupting into strange, sudden, and purposeful movements.

It takes John a moment to realize the reason for the movements. Far past Ukaraaz are metal flying machines, many of them, in small groups similar to the formation birds often fly in, the shape of a V.

The flying machines seem to be moving very slowly, but Ethan showed John pictures of these machines, called jets, and told him they can fly faster than sound can travel, and carry many missile weapons that cause great explosions and much damage.

All the missiles loosed by the jets are turned around in the air, and sent back to explode the jets loosing them. The remaining jets are forced to fly into one another, or are sent towards the ground and death.

The power needed to perform such feats, and at such great distances, staggers John. He knew Ukaraaz was powerful, but the ease with which he defeats so many mighty machines so quickly shocks John, and he realizes just how large the power gap is between them, and fear enters his heart, and for the first time he understands why Amber fears this fight so much, and her belief it will result in their deaths. He now thinks her fear is warranted.

Amber and Hubaba came with John through the portal. They didn't have to join him in this fight. They agreed to do battle by his side. Amber never wanted to come. This isn't Hubaba's world to fight for.

John, by far, has the most experience in war and battle of the three companions. The plan Amber and Hubaba came up with is not a bad plan. John is the worst match for Ukaraaz, as he is the least capable of protecting from unbinds, and his main spell often isn't effective at all against Silvers, and has no chance against a Gold.

444

This is all true, but the mighty attack of his plasma ring, fueled by John's own powerful essence, can't be stopped by unbinding, and neither can he be stopped from fueling his shield and sword. He thinks he stands a decent chance against Ukaraaz, or he thought he did.

The plan consists of Amber making her way to Ukaraaz, and starting the battle with a surprise attack, ending the biggest threat immediately. Hubaba will head to the same area, but hang back, and handle any Silvers near Ukaraaz, and fight Ukaraaz himself with Amber if her surprise attack fails.

John is to start in the best position to kill the masses, and run through the enemy, keeping as many of them focused on him as possible, and not on Amber and Hubaba, doing what he does best, and using his blood essence in the most advantageous way.

Now, John thinks he might have to break the promise he made to his companions to stick to the plan. He dislikes doing so, but believes he has no choice. The black armor Ukaraaz wears seems sturdier than he remembers. Amber can't bite through his head as she usually does, and what attack is left to her effective against a Gold armored so? He now wishes he practiced with Amber while wearing heavier armor.

Amber and Hubaba surviving this fight is more important to John than his promise. Plans change in battle. They didn't have to join him in this fight, and they shouldn't die for following him here.

Hubaba told John he should never use his bracers. The first time he used them only the bracers were attuned to him. Now he has the maximum number of attunements, and all draw on his spirit.

John is not certain of what the outcome will be if he uses the bracers. Hubaba claimed death is possible, but it is certain the bracers will drain him and damage him far more than the only other time he activated their mighty attack.

But the mighty attack of the bracers gives John a chance of outright killing Ukaraaz. And not just Ukaraaz, but all between John and Ukaraaz. Hubaba might be a weak Gold, but he is still a Gold, and Amber is a doughty fighter. Regardless of what the outcome is for John, his

445

companions should be able to mop up the remaining demons without Ukaraaz in play, only needing to worry about whatever Silvers live.

When the attack is activated, John knows he will be surrounded by the protective white bubble as the attack charges up, and he will lose control of his own body for the duration. It will cause a commotion, and will be obvious to his companions what is happening, and they can easily avoid being in the line of attack.

Grateful the pain in his head is lessening, John prays. *Great gods below, gods of the earth and sky, one and only God said to be in Heaven, ancient old one I see in my mind during rank up and ascension, whatever else is out there and can hear me.*

*Someone is always claiming to have some true knowledge of what is to be after awakening from this dream. I know the cold-dark was real, and I've been told I need not worry about it any longer, and this was proven by the willing death of someone also needing to fear it. I've been told a thousand-thousand different stories of what is to come after awakening, and never have I seen proof of any. I don't know what the truth is. Honestly, I don't care, so long as it isn't the cold-dark. I will face whatever else comes as a man should, and that is all the truth I need know.*

*I've lived a long time and never once asked for help or intercedence. I never will. For myself. I swore to avenge two youths tortured by the demon Morgoros. I saw their twisted spirits in death, and how they yearned for vengeance. I cannot kill Ukaraaz and give them the vengeance I swore, so I must ask to take on myself whatever punishment is being inflicted upon their tortured souls when I awaken, unless it is the cold-dark, and succor be provided to them. My failures are no fault of theirs.*

*Now, witness my great deeds, and know if I fall, as long as Ukaraaz does too, I still win, and my enemies still lose, and I will awaken from this dream undefeated.*

John stands, and faces the distant Gold. Ukaraaz is now talking to the three replacement Silvers, the other Silver near him still meditating. The spinning blue circle helps line up the attack, though it still annoys John, and obstructs his vision.

446

Glancing at the giant mass of demons in front of the portal, John is impressed at how well they take orders and move out, and how quickly the mob has shrunk in such a short time.

Sight back on Ukaraaz, knowing his attack will kill at least two other Silvers, but maybe three, John smiles, takes a calming breath, and sends essence into his bracers. The bracers don't accept the essence. Frustrated, he tries again, and his essence fails to enter the bracers again.

Nervous, John frantically thinks of reasons why his bracers aren't working. *You just infuse essence into them. Simple.* Exactly as his other items powered by his own essence work. He looks around, trying to sense if a high tiered demon is close by, or if the image of Ukaraaz in the distance is fake, and John placed himself in a trap. He feels nothing, and notices nothing.

The blue circle in John's vision skips and jerks and stops spinning. He feels a moment of intense dizziness before seeing the world blur by as it does when entering his Mind's Eye.

The trip is short, and his Mind's Eye looks very different, and Mistress Pixie is not there to greet John as she always is. Instead, there is a blurry apparition. Even though the trip was short, he thinks some entity snatched him away to their own Mind's Eye, as both Magnus Gar'tar and Sublime Sunshine have done to him.

John tries to look around, and though his actions aren't as limited in the way they are in his own Mind's Eye, they are still severely limited, and the full body and movement allowed him in both Gar'tar and Sunshine's mind not at all possible.

"Who are you?" demands John of the blurry apparition.

In a voice very similar to Sublime Sunshine, and the witches when transformed into a slug, the voice the NCS supplies to those without voice – deep and distant and rattled, somewhat hollow – the blurry apparition replies, "Avatar's communication with user currently limited due to external environment of escalating hostilities. Normal functions unavailable. User is currently safe within their own Mind's Eye. Transference testing was purchased on behalf of user. User is to remain calm and still throughout testing. Testing commencing."

There is no pain, but all of John's body, a body he does not have in his Mind's Eye, tingles. An indescribable sensation fills John, as if his body is being pulled apart and disintegrated, while lights inspect the smallest pieces of him before being destroyed, and then being slowly patched back together.

John tries to speak and can't. His mind is sluggish and limited. Worse, his mind seems to be shrinking, collapsing in on him. He rallies what mind is left to him, and fights back without knowing how exactly. He pushes against the invisible walls closing in, and rails against them, and then starts battering into them.

The walls stop closing in, and John is eventually able to push them back. Finally, he breaks free, and is back in his Mind's Eye as he was before. "Where is Mistress Pixie? If you hurt her, I will destroy you."

John knows his threat is most likely hollow as soon as it leaves whatever counts as his mouth in this place, but he will try to make it true. The blurry apparition says, "User noncompliant. Requesting authorization to subdue user for the duration of transference testing."

If an answer to the request is given, John doesn't hear it. He is frozen, and feels his body disintegrating again, and this time he is powerless to stop his mind from being closed in on, and disappearing.

Some very limited and small part of John's awareness remains. Aware he is in nothing and can do nothing, and it remains this way for a long time.

It seems to John this is like a paradise version of the cold-dark. Even so limited in mind and awareness, his moment spent in the cold-dark still remains clear to him. No torture can compare to it. The endless nothingness stretching on forever, frozen, unable to move or scream or do anything. Just be inflicted with eternal loneliness and freezing cold and nothingness and no way to change or influence the situation at all.

There is no enduring the cold-dark. There is no hope down the road, no chance of a respite or relief. The same moment stretching out eternally.

448

Being in it can't be considered enduring it. Enduring implies some change down the road. Some eventual end. There is no change in the cold-dark. It is exactly the same horror on entry as it is a thousand years later, or a thousand-thousand.

Whatever is happening to John now is nothing compared to the cold-dark, no matter how long it lasts. It can be endured, so he endures it.

Time stretches on and on until John's mind and awareness begin to expand outwards, and he is back in his Mind's Eye looking at the blurry apparition.

"Where is Mistress Pixie?"

"Avatar's communication with user currently limited due to external environment of escalating hostilities. Normal functions unavailable. Full user registry, profile, and redundancy completed. User will be ejected after purchased message. Relaying message."

"John, we're breaking so many rules here. There's no way we'll be allowed to do anything like this again, so please heed our advice this time. This message alone is costing us a fortune, and that's on top of the upgrade and the bracers and transference testing during a combat situation. We've blocked your bracers for as long as we could. They'll unlock before Amber attacks. You have eight items attuned, and two draw heavily on your spirit. Your spirit will break. You will lose. You will all die. DO NOT use the bracers. You can win this without them. Don't quit the fight before it starts. Don't let your fans down. We're all rooting for you.

"Message relayed. Transaction complete. Ejecting user."

# CHAPTER 52
## VAMPIRE VERSUS HORDE

Unsure what his trip inside his Mind's Eye was all about, still worried over Pixie, John tries to reenter, but is denied. He dislikes the blurry apparition greatly, but the message didn't come from it. *At least the blue circle is gone now.*

John cannot deny the message he was given matches up with what he was told by Hubaba, and following the original plan will give him the opportunity to keep his word regarding Morgoros, and avenge those the demon tortured by torturing the demon, and also allow him to keep his word to his companions too.

Decision made, John heads to where he believes he can make the greatest impact when the battle starts.

***

Standing some distance behind the still meditating formation of demons, John is happy to see four of the Silvers remain towards the mid and rear of the large formation, away from Ukaraaz.

The giant mass of demons just finished dispersing, either heading off in different directions, or joining the ranks of meditating demons in formation.

The same day John picked his armor and weapons he moved the storage ring to his left hand, the hand also holding his stout metal shield. The plasma ring can't be worn on his shield hand. His sword remains sheathed on his back, as he needs a free hand for what he has planned.

John wonders if Amber is waiting for the three Silvers talking to Ukaraaz to leave before initiating the attack. He is filled with more apprehension than usual before battle, all this waiting doing him no good. He questions if he made the wrong choice, not using his bracers. Night is breaking and he doesn't want this battle to happen while the sun drains him.

John nearly convinces himself he should use the bracers before he finally sees what he's been waiting for. A bear almost the same size as Ukaraaz appears, and Amber's paw quickly makes a mighty swipe at the Gold demon's helmeted head. The hit connects and Ukaraaz is knocked unsteady, and the giant echo attack then hits right after, and sends the Gold tumbling over, but his helmet remains on.

Amber starts a charge attack, but that is all the time John can spend watching her fight. He aims his plasma ring at the Silver standing beside Morgoros, and a small circle with a dot in it appears over the demon saying to aim at the exact spot he was already aiming at. He sends as much essence into the ring as it allows.

As soon as the plasma attack is loosed, John knows he's visible, and he moves his right hand towards the meditating Woods, fingers spread, as he feels into as many of them as he can, and his hand closes as he creates a blockage, preventing blood being sent into their brains. That is the least essence intensive way of killing them, but also one of the slowest ways. All of them will die, but not immediately.

Knowing a fast-moving target is much harder to unbind the manifestations of, John empowers himself with vital essence, and lets out his loudest yell as he jumps into the formation of Woods.

Keeping his first jump low, John knows he can't clear the Woods in one leap, so puts clots into as many enemies as he can as he lands, the Woods hesitate and move backwards instead of attacking, then he jumps higher.

While in the air, John looks at the demon he targeted with his ring, glad to see him dead on the ground, his spirit looking confused. He puts more clots into demons below him, blocks some attacks with shield and

451

bracer, and lands amid the Coppers. He kicks one and swipes his shield around, killing many others, while also raising his right hand, aiming his plasma ring at another Silver.

Before he can loose a new attack from the ring, he injects essence into his cap, empowering the reflect runes, and two attacks are turned back onto the Silvers that manifested them.

The reddish-brown beam of Morgoros, the attack John assumed would overpower the reflect runes, is caught on John's shield. Surprisingly, the attack bounces off his shield and into a mass of Copper demons, causing John to laugh, then his cap fizzles out from reflecting too many of the weak attacks of the demons around him.

John spins and looses the attack of the plasma ring at a Silver on the east side of the formation, and the Silver's essence shield fails to stop the plasma, and its chest explodes in a spray of gore. He kicks another Copper away, backhands another, blocks a new reddish-brown beam from Morgoros, killing many more Coppers with it, and adds to the dead with a mighty swipe of his shield.

John caves in the face of a Copper charging him with his bare fist, blocks an arrow with his bracer, and takes the head off a demon to his left with his shield.

Many shards of ice slap into John's back while he feels for as many Coppers around him as he can enter, an amount less than Woods, but not by much. He planned on causing the Coppers hearts to quake by filling them with blood, and holding it there, but he has stood too still for too long, and must move, so he quickly creates clots, preventing blood to their brain as he jumps again, feeling a failed unbind attempt as he starts the jump.

While in the air, John activates the essence-shield of his armor, spins in the air, holding the shield outside of the range of the essence-shield, blocking a new beam attack by Morgoros. This attack is reflected to the ground away from any demon, much to John's disappointment.

The two remaining Silvers haven't remained stationary during John's assault, and have been steadily moving closer to him. More ice shards and many other attacks by the demons hit John, harmlessly absorbed by the essence-shield. A few more attacks land, and the essence-shield ends. He is surprised it held up so well, and prepares for both Morgoros and the other Silver trying to tackle him in the air.

John imbues his shield with essence, fixing some damage the shield has taken, and all around the edge of the shield lights up with dark essence, turning the shield into a far more deadly weapon. He spins once again, lodging the shield into the head of the ice-flinging Silver, and using the added weight as leverage to whip himself around in the air, narrowly avoiding the giant blade of Morgoros.

John falls among the Bronzes, taking hits that cause some damage, unlodging his shield from the face of the Silver as he rolls once, grabs the ankle of a Bronze, lashing his shield around as he stands, teaching the Bronze demons around him being so close is a mistake. The Bronze demons are slow learners, and all rush towards him, and he clubs a group with the demon whose leg he grabbed, turning the groups into mush, and crushes the head of a Bronze to his right with his fist, blocks an attack with his bracer, and kills many more with a swipe of his shield.

John's shield stops shining with black essence. He can only enter about six to eight Bronze at a time, depending on their ranks within Bronze. Six Bronze fall to the ground as his hand closes.

A second group of Bronze fall to the ground just in time for John to block a new beam from Morgoros, and he can't help but smile as it reflects off his shield and into many Bronze charging at him.

John sees Morgoros in the air, jumping towards him, giant sword high over his head in a two-handed grip.

Holding his shield up high, waiting a moment before sword connects with shield, John spins out of the way while imbuing essence into his weapon, catching the leg of the demon with the edge of the shield, cutting cleanly through the leg, causing Morgoros to crash down to the ground and roll uncontrollably into a mass of Bronze demons.

John feels inside Morgoros, trying to drain his head of blood and subdue him, but the demon resists, and too many Bronze are attacking John for him to focus enough on an attempt to overpower the demon's will. He quickly injects a little essence into his plasma ring. As Morgoros struggles to stand, assisted by many Bronze, his other leg is taken from him.

Feeling into more Bronze, John's fingers close and the demons begin to convulse. He dodges a couple attacks, but there were too many directed at him, and an enhanced attack hits his back hard enough to cause him pain. His shield whips around, cutting through all the Bronze behind him.

As he spun, John saw Amber in the distance, in bear form, very high in the air, held there, then using the charge attack to blur downwards towards the ground. He is glad Amber is alive, and hopes Ukaraaz is dead, but also assumes she was so high in the air due to his telekinesis.

Either way this fight goes, John expects Amber to live through it. Ukaraaz will not kill such a treasure as everyone considers Naturals.

John again imbues a little essence into his shield, cutting deep into two other Bronze near him, kicking another backwards to bowl over an approaching group, charges another group, killing three with one shield swipe, and another with his fist, and jumps towards Morgoros.

In the air, John hears Morgoros yell, "Keep it back! Give me some time!" John wishes the reflect or essence-shield of his cap and armor were ready to use again, but they have long cooldowns between uses, so he stops imbuing his weapon and surrounds himself with his own weaker blood-shield manifestation as he lands within the large group of Bronze surrounding Morgoros.

The shield blocks an axe, then kills the attacker and another Bronze near it, and John enters into the Bronze around him. Before he can cause them harm, he feels something else, and looks at Morgoros. The demon is creating a small, glowing red ball above his chest that quickly begins to grow.

Hubaba told John about this. Morgoros can send out devastating, but slow-moving exploding balls of destruction, and the more essence the ball takes in, the larger it grows, and the more destructive it becomes. And the ball is growing quickly.

John swipes at the small red ball with his shield, assuming his blood-shield can handle any damage the explosion will cause at its current size, and the demon will survive too, and John can then safely incapacitate Morgoros, and torture him for days after the battle.

The cruel smile that appears on Morgoros' face clues John into this faulty thinking too late to change course.

The shield connects with the glowing red ball and John is blown backwards with great force. He lays dazed on the wet ground for a moment, confused, an intolerably loud ringing in his ears.

A notification flashes in John's vision stating [Emergency Heal] is now on cooldown for twenty-two hours and some minutes. Many demons approach him. He's not sure what tier. He kips up and goes to attack the closest demon with his shield before noticing he has none. His left arm is missing too, nearly all the way to the shoulder, and his body is littered with other small injuries.

Cold wind blows through John's hair. *My cap is missing,* he thinks, still dazed. *I should give a name to the shield. It's a good weapon. I hope it isn't too damaged.* He stops enhancing his strength and speed, and sends vital essence to heal, and takes a moment to focus on his nub, and he forces the blood to congeal, and the bleeding to stop.

John hasn't really used or practiced with the spell he created to heal with blood, as it provides very weak healing. He struggles to remember how to work it. He can't remember. He shakes his head to help clear it.

John is certain Morgoros is dead, and he is ashamed he can no longer avenge those two children correctly. His heart spikes as he thinks of his missing storage ring, and fears it is damaged or destroyed. He has no time for such worries now. He kicks the closest demon back into its companions, blocks an attack with his bracer, and yells in fury as he draws Fireblade from the sheath on his back.

John fears he forgot how to imbue the sword as he fumbles the first attempt, but the blade alights on the next, and all the demons near him quickly learn he only needs one arm to make slaughter.

John fights through the horde of demons, making his way closer to Amber, hoping she and Hubaba are also making slaughter as great as he is. He realizes, at some point, he hardly fights any Coppers, and fights mostly Bronze, and he is taking hits he could avoid, and the hits are causing him damage.

John's mind is clearer now, though the ringing in his ears persists. His meridians burn, and he checks his essence, surprised it is well under half gone. He checks his vital essence, and he's fine there, ascending increased the amount of it he can hold too. He sends more to heal, deciding he'll keep the sword imbued, as he is desperate to find out the result of Amber and Hubaba's fight, and he kills faster this way.

And John gets back to killing, wading through groups of demons with spell and blade. He takes some hits, giving far more back, nearly always killing at least two or three demons with one mighty swing of his sword, and many more with his blood-essence. Woods run when he approaches them, only the Copper and Bronze demons stand their ground or charge.

John battles for too long, the horde shrinking, but not fast enough, and his anxiety for his companions grows by the moment.

Finally remembering there are faster ways to break through the horde, such as jumping over them, he feels into as many demons near him as he can. Bronze can fight for some time even when their brains are denied blood, so he pulls the blood from their heads quickly, causing them to fall unconscious. This only works for a short period, and they'll be up and in fighting shape in no time, so John stops wasting it and clears the horde battling him in one jump.

While in the air, his heart sinks. He sees Ukaraaz is battered, but alive. The Gold's helmet is gone, his face seems to have some wounds, and his armor is dented and damaged in many spots, with double puncture holes in a few places.

An injured Silver kneels near Ukaraaz, nursing many injuries. The spirits of the other three Silvers mill about near their corpses. Amber's bear form is a bloody and unmoving heap, but is filled with the essence of life, so she is alive. Hubaba, robes tattered and torn, is suspended in the air by telekinesis.

At the crest of his jump, John stops imbuing essence into Fireblade, holds the blade sideways, and aims his plasma ring at the head of Ukaraaz, the aim assist the NCS now shows helping him line up the strike, and the attack flies true.

Ukaraaz tilts his head back a little, and the attack harmlessly passes by the captain as John lands.

John aims the ring again and starts to imbue it. Without even looking, Ukaraaz raises his hand towards John, and John, once again, quickly flies through the air towards the waiting hand of Ukaraaz. The plasma attack discharges wildly, hitting the ground near Amber.

John extends his senses to attempt an unbind, and is rejected so violently his vision blurs. The hand flies closer, and John remembers he has one more trick up his sleeve. One last chance.

John's bracers are mighty. He only wears one now, but even half an attack of such mighty bracers should be enough. Essence is sent to the bracers, and John smiles as the white light appears again, and control over his body is lost to the bracer, the same as before. It worked.

Ukaraaz is lined up perfectly. John will land in the Gold's grip before the attack is loosed, but the white light should protect him. John feels the bracer draining all the essence from his dantian, all his vital essence, all within him. His insides burn with pain. Something inside of him snaps. It doesn't matter. It worked. He will win.

Ukaraaz flicks his wrist and John is sent straight up into the air, the mighty attack discharging harmlessly into the sky.

John is too drained to feel much anger, too drained to even feel shame over his great failure, too drained to hear Fireblade clang off the ground as he is suspended in the air near Hubaba.

# CHAPTER 53
# TERROR DOMAIN

Ukaraaz stares at John. "Ptagmog? Huh. Did…I recognize you. I killed you. How the hell are you alive? Ha! I'm lucky that Magnus departed from this world yesterday after I killed you. She would not be happy about this. Or maybe I'd be able to weasel more treasures out of her. She was very generous. Looks like I did you a favor sending you to Esau."

John is far too empty, far too drained, to reply. He tries to lift his head, but fails. His orb-eye refuses to move, and even his sight through it is dim.

The captain looks at the kneeling and injured Silver near him. "I forgot your name. You're going home. I can't trust a Bronze with this message. And tell those…tell my army to leave me be. Have them gather all my crystals and gear and then form up and meditate. Tell Muryz he's lead until more Silvers arrive. Drills after meditation. Tell him I'm calling enough demons back to fill the ranks.

"Don't go to Second Point. Don't go to your old master at Fourth Point. Go directly to Master Baggodon at Outer-Point Keep. Tell him what happened here. And tell him the following exactly as I say it. I need competent Silvers. Real chosen. Not scabs mistakenly made chosen. Seven, plus a Silver scab proficient in alchemy. You won't be coming back."

The Silver asks, "Am I taking the Natural back, Captain?"

"Darkness, Adversity, and Nightmare! What the hell do you think I want the scab sent here for?"

"I'm not sure, Captain. Was that a 'no' for bringing the Natural back?"

Ukaraaz takes out a cloth and rubs his face with it. Calmly, he says, "No. It's staying here with me. Go."

The Silver bows and quickly limps away. Ukaraaz goes over to the bloody heap of Amber and places a large glowing collar around her neck, and it shrinks to fit after latching.

The battered Hubaba raises his head off his chest and says, "How many ranks above me are you? How many treasures did Baggodon feed you? He trained you himself, didn't he? I was not allowed to train or fight. I taught myself. Recently too, and not for very long. I was forced to take a horrible body formation. Guess what? This scab stood against you, toe to toe, and I held my own. Blame others all you want but you're a failure. Look what a scab and two Coppers did to you and your forces. You're the scab, and you know it. Deep down inside, you know it."

Ukaraaz glares at Hubaba with murder in his eyes. Then his eyes clear and the captain laughs. "I merged a mid-concept at mid-low Gold. Did you see me use an aura? No. Why? I'm high Gold. Surely, I managed to get an aura by now, correct? And a good one too, with all the personal help I get from my master. So, why no aura?"

"You have a domain. Am I supposed to be impressed? I know most get auras at Gold and domains at Salt. You still have a bunch of ranks on me, and I still stood toe to toe with you and almost won. And no one, especially not Baggodon himself, helped me in any way."

Ukaraaz raises his hand and Hubaba screams. The screaming doesn't last long. The captain lowers his arm and says, "You're in a rush to be killed, now, aren't you? I don't know what is going on back at Second Point. Even if I cared to get the story from one of you there's another I can question now. And my replacements should be here soon anyways. With the restriction on Golds, the sooner I kill you, the better. First, I must know, what the hell is that shit all over your face? You look like a freak."

Holding his head higher, Hubaba says. "It's called make-up. I am beautiful no matter what you say. Words can't bring me down. I am beautiful in every single…"

"Shut your damn mouth, you filthy scab! By Darkness, Adversity, and Nightmare, I swear you will suffer so much your mind will break. How could you turn traitor against your own kind?"

A long moment stretches out as Ukaraaz paces back and forth, seething.

In a relaxed voice Hubaba gives his answer, "I have a name now. I have good friends. I've experienced joys you'll never know. My suffering has already ended. You are small, Ukaraaz. Small and ignorant. You know so little and understand even less. Demons turned traitor to me long ago. I'll die happy and fulfilled and free, laughing at your miserable existence. I spit in your eye. Now do your worst to me. I am ready."

If John could, he'd yell encouragements at his friend. His heart swells with pride. He struggles to lift his head and open one eye a little. He is determined to provide witness to the death of his friend, and he hopes, when it is his turn, he does half as well as Hubaba. *This is how a warrior dies. Defiant to the end.*

Through a blurry slit of his barely opened eye, John sees his own fallen sword, Fireblade, enter the chest of Hubaba, and Hubaba's smile never leaves his own face as he stares at Ukaraaz.

Ukaraaz, surprisingly, looks somber, and almost sounds respectful as he says, "Your body formation really is garbage, huh? It slid right in you like you're still a Wood. You've changed though. Too bad you found your spine so late in life. I'm glad you did.

"What do you think will kill you? The sword or my Terror Domain? I don't think there's a chance in hell a scab survives my domain. The sword's just to ensure you don't suffer too long. You earned that. And you can die along with your friend and travel the beyond together. You earned that too. May you both be reborn as chosen."

Ukaraaz nods his head towards the scab and then a strange essence overwhelms John's senses. His belly tightens with fear, and the world

460

around him goes mad. Impossible creatures growl at him from the shadows as the world stretches, shrinks, and warbles.

The creatures creep towards John, and he struggles to break free of whatever holds him, but can't. He's frozen in place.

To John's own eyes these monsters look solid and whole. To his other senses they are real. His orb-eye sees them as only mist. His mind refuses to work correctly, to think. If he weren't so drained and empty, he'd be more terrified, and not recognize what his orb-eye sees, and not notice the falseness of this. He is able to calm himself some, and he stops struggling against his invisible bonds, and closes his two eyes before the monsters start feasting on him.

The terror doesn't leave John, and though he feels the pain of the monster's bites and attacks, his orb-eye shows the creatures cause him no true damage. It is fake. He can't retreat on himself and meditate to escape this. He can only endure, so does.

After some time, the pain stops, then the image fades, and is replaced by a new one.

Lilitu and John are in the city of White Walls, in the court of the Emperor of Kayhamut. He saw his wife differently after this day. She gave the Emperor many treasures to enslave her own people. She was furious when they won their freedom back many centuries later. She could never let a grudge go.

The memory diverges from the true one, and Lilitu gives more treasures to the Emperor. She turns to John and says, "My dear heart, my heart's content, my pretty little monkey, you said you'd love me forever. You said you'd always protect me. You killed me! You sent me to the cold-dark! Why? You have no honor. You are so little. So base. So low. Such a liar! Your word means nothing. You killed your own wife and sent me to the cold-dark. The cold-dark! Betrayer!"

Soldiers flood into the court and point their weapons at John. Lilitu opens her mouth wide, and it keeps opening wider, and the fangs multiply and grow longer as she and all the soldiers transform into monsters.

John closes his own eyes. His orb-eye shows him just mist. There is pain as the mist covers him, but no real damage.

A long string of the people John most cares about tell him how he failed them, how he has no honor, how he's a coward, a betrayer. They then turn into monsters and attack him. All the while he feels something chipping away at his mind and his spirit.

The things said to John hurt deeply, as it is all true, and nothing hurts more than the truth. He constantly tries to retreat in on himself, but is denied any relief.

If John wasn't so drained, he would probably care more about what he sees and is told, but he is empty inside, and his orb-eye shows how false this is. He sees many friends and brothers he has long forgotten. Everyone, he's lost them all, and he misses them terribly.

For the second time John's mother appears. This time alone, without his father. He knows this memory well. He's recently got it back, after ascending to Copper, and he thinks on it often.

The thought of this memory being twisted and used against him causes a great anger in John. Somehow, he is finally able to break free of whatever traps his mind, and retreat in on himself while focusing on his mother and this memory.

John knows this isn't what his mother really looked like. His image of her is more like a bigger, thicker, and kinder Lilitu, bare chested, covered in many trinkets, always with a babe suckling. Her image disappears as he relives the memory.

Every year John's family had to visit King Kah so his father could reaffirm his fealty, and the king and lords could plan, and review laws, and such. All the wives of all the lords sworn to King Kah, including all their young children, were kept in a nice hold, surrounded by many, many guards.

John didn't know it at the time, but they weren't so well guarded out of hospitality. They were hostages, ensuring the good conduct of the lords. The wives couldn't leave the hold, but every comfort was provided for them, and every night they feasted. The kids could come and go as they pleased during the day, as children cannot be cooped up so without driving the adults mad.

John was around six or so, and he tried following his closest brother out to play, but he was assaulted by older boys, two of the assaulters were the sons of King Kah himself. John had a flint knife they said was the price of being allowed to leave the hold, and John refused to give it up, as his father gifted it to him, and it was his only possession.

The boys couldn't steal it, as that would be a grave breach of hospitality. Young boys fighting and roughhousing was as common and expected as the sun coming up each day, and a necessary part of childhood.

After receiving his beating, John went to tell his mother, thinking she'd be proud he refused to give up the knife. He knew better than to cry, though he wanted to badly. Crying wasn't allowed, especially in front of outsiders.

As John approached his mother, he could tell something was wrong. His mother was tense, and so was the first wife. His mother looked towards the first wife, and the first wife gave a terse and worried nod, and some of the tension left his mother. "My son, why are you inside? It is a beautiful day, and all the other boys are outside playing."

"They won't let me. They said the price to pass is my knife. They all beat me when I wouldn't give it up."

John is surprised to see his mother's face turn cruel. "How have I failed my lord husband so by raising such a cowardly boy?"

Never had John's kind and caring mother treated him so, and this was far worse to him than the beating he just received. He was frozen with fear, unsure of what was happening, and why his mother seemed so mad.

"You're old enough to know better. Soon you'll be a man. I can protect you no longer. Your actions reflect on your lord father, and you are costing him much face. This dream is short, and all that's required is to die well, to be honored by Koram on awakening. You'll never lose a fight you refuse to run from."

Back at home, whenever his older brothers beat him up, going to his mother was fine, and she'd comfort him, and make him feel better. As long as he didn't cry. When he did, she'd yell at him. But she was never mean, nor was she ever so disappointed. His mother looked over to the first wife, and the first wife smiled and nodded again.

John had no idea his actions reflected poorly on his father, and cost his father face. He became determined to set things right.

Soon after a crowd was formed, all the wives and daughters and servants stood at the portal and windows of the hold, all the guards gathered, and all the playing boys heard what was happening and returned.

John struggled back to his feet. The crowd cheered. His eyes were bloodied. He could barely see; the world was a blur. He couldn't breathe out of his broken nose, and he often choked on bloody phlegm. "Just stay down. We'll leave you alone the rest of your time here. We give you our word."

John swung his arm as hard as he could at the blurry shape in front of him. He missed. They didn't. They got some kicks in while he was down, as they always did.

John struggled back to his feet. The crowd cheered. The fight continued that way for an eternity. At some point the guards tried to break it up, and put an end to it. The first wife said, "Oh, no! You're not ending what your boys started. You stay out of it, and we'll see what's what."

John struggled back to his feet. Again, and again. Every time the crowd would cheer. For some reason his mother was allowed to step outside the hold. She grabbed John and held him tight. "You can stop now, Son. My little man."

John's heart swelled. Little man was the best compliment given to young boys, indicating they already had the qualities of a man grown. "Ugh, Ma. I…"

"It's okay. You can stop now. Hear me? You can stop."

It was hard to speak through his bloody lips, hard to think while being so battered and dazed. John tried to mumble out something about making her proud, that he's not a coward, but he couldn't form words. He couldn't see his mother, but he thought she was crying. Her shoulders shook as she held him. He never saw her cry before then, not even when her firstborn died. Crying wasn't allowed.

"Please, just stay…" his mother started to say with a broken voice, but she was interrupted by the first wife. "Second, enough! Come back into the hold."

John struggled back to his feet. Twice more, as the crowd cheered, until he finally couldn't. Many people called him little man from that day until he turned thirteen, becoming a man in truth. He gave both his mother and father much face that day.

John loves that memory. It is one of his favorites, and he is glad he has it back. The cheers. The praise. How it felt to not quit. To get back up. To keep going beyond reason. To continue past a point your body can tolerate, and finding it can tolerate much more, that you have endless wells of fortitude and grit within you to draw upon. That day he first learned how to endure. He can almost feel his mother's loving embrace again when he relives that memory.

The amount of character and resolve the women of his tribe required to go so against their nature, instilling in their sons the way of death, telling them their highest and only purpose is to die in battle, and never run from it, always makes John's heart swell with pride.

John thinks the women had it the hardest. So much of their honor was completely out of their own hands, and dependent on their husband and sons. They'd take blame and be dishonored for what others did. And they bore all that responsibility with grace and dignity, and without complaint.

John smiles and opens his eyes. He sees the brows of Ukaraaz furrow. "How the hell did you…never mind. He's going to beat it too. The sword will get him. He should have been chosen. Not much time left. Bear witness with me."

Both vampire and demon silently watch Hubaba expire as the sun rises. Amber remains completely still.

Once Hubaba is gone, Ukaraaz slowly and carefully lowers his body to the ground, bows to it, and again says, "He should have been chosen."

John takes heart in that Hubaba's spirit rises whole and looks to be at peace, standing tall and straight. He gives a silent prayer for another dead friend. He is proud Hubaba awakened from this dream in such a glorious manner, winning the praise of his enemy.

Remaining silent, out of respect, John reviews himself. He feels a little better. A little more awake, and a little less drained. Surprisingly, he has some vital essence within him. Just a little, but he is certain he was completely emptied of it. He doesn't know where it came from, but he is glad it is there. His dantian has a little essence, but that was expected, as reliving the memory as he did was his usual form of meditation.

"How did you do it?" asks Ukaraaz.

John wishes his mind wasn't so fuzzy and he could come up with something witty to reply with. He struggles to fight through the haze, failing to come up with a response in time.

"I guess I'm starting to see why that Magnus wanted you dead. I know I killed you last time. I crushed your neck. I felt the bones snap. You were dead. How you are alive now, and how a Copper survived my domain, I don't know. I don't know how a magal got the ptagmog Title either but it gives you an out. You don't have to die today.

"Swear fealty to me and I'll take you under my wing and help build you up. You'll be a full member of Circle Xakariz, not just a sworn Forsaken. You probably don't know much about the g'athu. They're digging in and building up. That's how they operate. Their tech is powerful. Our only chance is speed. We need this planet. It's a shit planet with nothing worthwhile, but we can find Tech Zero worlds from here and open portals to them from back home. Real portals, real invasions without all these stupid restrictions, to real planets with resources.

"What do you say? We'll give you a proper name and everything."

Ukaraaz smiles at John. John smiles back. "Names come and go. I've had many. What I want is your head on a pike."

# CHAPTER 54
## FEALTY

"Do you really want to die so badly?" asks Ukaraaz.

"No. I want you to die so badly," replies John.

"Why? I'm reasonable, knowledgeable of cultivation, I reward competence, and I've done you no harm. Sure, I thought I killed you. But you're alive, and you would've done the same for the rewards offered. So, I've done you no real harm. This world is...pretend. It's like a pretend world. Everyone is a Wood. This whole pretend world is garbage. You can't really want to stay here. Live here. Would having me as your master be so terrible?"

John lost one friend today. He can always die. He can't always save a friend. Certainly not one as special to him as Amber. "If I were to swear fealty to you, would my people be covered in my oath? Would you be responsible for their safety too? Including the safety and continued life of this Natural? If the oath covers all that is mine, including not using the Natural, and protecting it too, I will swear."

Ukaraaz looks as if he is considering the bargain for a long moment before he cracks up laughing, loudly and for long. "Wait, are you serious?"

"Yes, completely."

"Not use a Natural? They were made specifically for that. That's their purpose. And this one is freakishly powerful. I've never fought such a tenacious beast. I said I'm reasonable, not insane. Name another favor or condition. A sensible one."

John sighs. He wishes his mind would clear and he could trade barbs as Hubaba did. His mind is empty, and all he can think of are juvenile insults. This isn't the end he wants. He can't spur an emotion to bubble up and guide him.

Ukaraaz says, "This is a shame. It didn't have to end this way. I tried. I truly did. Before you go, please tell me what name the scab went by."

"His name was Hubaba. Slave to feared king. His end was much better than his namesake's."

Shaking his head, Ukaraaz says, "Scabs aren't slaves. They're treated well for the most part. They get a life of peace, something chosen aren't allowed. All paths have pros and cons. No one likes the system as is, and no one has a better solution. If the ancient old ones allowed us to take slaves that would only solve some issues. We'd go back to just culling our weak. Is that a better system?"

John sighs. "Scab, peasant, soldier, king. All are slaves. The yokes may be different, but they all yearn for one. Few are willing to shrug it off. What's your plan? Talking me to death? I'm tired. Let's get on with it."

Ukaraaz looks frustrated for a moment. He takes out the cloth again, and wipes his face. "Hubaba. I'll remember his name. And you're right about getting on with this. I did tell Hubaba he wouldn't travel alone."

John is still suspended in the air, about ten paces or so high. He remains so as a great pressure bears into him from all directions, and he remembers the little ball the peasants were squished into when he first met Ukaraaz, as the demon tries to do the same to him.

Yelling out in pain, John strains against the pressure, but there is no way to fight back. The pressure increases, and he screams louder as the demon's mind magic attempts to crush him.

When the pressure becomes so great John can no longer yell out, it is held for a time, then suddenly ends. Ukaraaz also yells out as the great pressure returns again, and the same scene plays out twice more.

Besides the missing arm, John remains whole. Ukaraaz is unable to crush him.

John is then flung down to the ground in a great crash. He feels Ukaraaz unveil his soul, and focus it directly at him.

The weight is great, and freezes John in place, and he struggles to breathe. He refuses to be held down so. John struggles back to his feet. It isn't easy, and takes some time and great effort, but he wins the struggle.

John stands, staring at the giant Ukaraaz with defiant eyes, determined his end will be as glorious as Hubaba's.

Ukaraaz glares at him, and John is then lifted high into the air and slammed down onto some rocks near the bloody heap of Amber. He protects his head with his one good arm. He is again lifted into the air, and slammed onto the rocks. Then again, higher, and harder. Many, many times.

"Why won't you die!" screams Ukaraaz.

Fireblade flies with tremendous speed towards John, and he rolls forward and snatches it out of the air. Ukaraaz tries to freeze John's body and force the blade out of his hand and into his head. It isn't easy, but John manages to keep hold of it, and his head free of it. The two struggle with the blade for a long while, physical strength versus mind magic.

With a yell of frustration, Ukaraaz quits the contest. Invisible fists slam into John's face and he flies backwards. More invisible fists rain down on John, all over his body, and he has no way to stop or prevent them. The hits hurt, but he's been hit much harder.

John struggles back to his feet, bracing himself, not letting the invisible fists knock him down again, absorbing the blows while in a wide stance.

"This has been fun to watch, but enough playing." John can hear the frustration in the voice of Ukaraaz, and he braces himself for whatever is coming next. All is peaceful for too long, and John is left unmolested. He senses why a moment later. Many, many weapons are flying through the air from the stricken field of battle of the demon horde, about two hundred by John's estimation, though he's wrong, as usual.

The weapons crest in the air and start descending towards John. He looks up at them, wishing he had his left arm and shield for this. He doesn't, so he makes do with what he does have. The first weapons to fall are easily avoided, but that doesn't last for long. He bats some away with

Fireblade, spinning, dancing, evading, avoiding the weapons falling like arrows by the skin of his teeth.

Less weapons start to fall, and John stares at Ukaraaz as he avoids them. The last weapon falls at him and is batted away without removing his eyes from the giant demon. Hope fills John's heart. He can still get vengeance. He doesn't need spells. He doesn't need more than he has now. This is what he's good at.

John thinks about using the little vital essence he has to heal some, but being completely drained of it will cause him to be weaker and more sluggish, and his mind will be even more hazy. The sun has already begun to sap him. He can't afford to use the little vital essence he has.

John is lifted into the air, again suspended ten or so paces above the ground. "Darkness, Adversity, and Nightmare! You just won't die, will you." Ukaraaz stands straighter, collecting himself, holding his hands behind his back. "What is your name, Copper?"

"I go by John now."

"Copper John. I am Captain Ukaraaz. A pleasure." The demon even bows a little towards John. Not a proper bow, but more than a head nod. Far more than what is due a Copper from a Gold.

John is so tired he finds even smiling difficult. "The pleasure's all mine, Captain. I'd bow, but…" John tilts his head, indicating his inability to do much of anything while being held frozen in the air so.

"Good. You can behave civilly. Killing you would be a real shame. I don't know what the hell you are, but I know talent and potential when I see it. If this is what you can do at Copper, imagine Gold or Platinum or Diamond. Imagine the next Tree.

"You've been to Esau. You know we're a tenth ring world. Until Sublime Xakariz returns with the location of a good planet to invade, and you know how much time can pass in the NetherRealm before that happens, Circle Xakariz will continue to decline. Unless we take this world. If we don't, and quickly, the g'athu will. I promise you that.

"This world is garbage. Demons don't really care about killing magals because we were ordered to by our creators. We kill them for crystals and to take their world's resources. This world has neither. It is only good as a staging ground to find Tech Zero worlds. That's it.

"Swear to me and all the magals of this world will be considered Forsaken and under the protection of my circle. The g'athu will have to leave. We all win. The Natural isn't important compared to your world burning. So that's the offer. Your fealty to me and my circle with the lives of all on this world held in abeyance. And once this world's magals truthfully become Forsaken even that won't be a worry. What say you, Copper John?"

Even though it saps him, John missed the sun. It isn't yet strong enough to cause what skin is exposed to start calcifying, and its warmth feels good. Familiar and comforting. He is home. A home he no longer must hide his true self from. A home worth fighting for.

John gives praise to his father, and his father's father, to his people and his ancestors. They got much wrong, but they got even more right, and he will always honor them, and is proud to be of them. Victory or glorious death.

John raises his head higher. "I say no. I think you're scared to face me in a real fight, even with how injured I am. No manifestations. Just a fair fight. As fair as a fight can be between a Copper and Gold. Or are you too much of a coward to face me in such battle?"

Ukaraaz laughs. "A real fight? We are *nothing* but our essence and manifestations. Would you like me to lop my arm off to make this fight fairer? Or feed you treasures and train you until you ascend to my tier? I don't know what kind of nonsensical fantasies fill your head, but the offers I've made to you have been more than fair. If you wish to die, I will grant your wish. What happens to your world is on you. I tried to avoid this.

"So, let's see how well you dodge now."

Ukaraaz raises his hand, and all the weapons are lifted off the ground and raised high into the air. He moves his hand back and the weapons fly far behind him. He mumbles something and thrusts his hand in front of him, and the weapons fly forward at great speed like a cloud of giant arrows.

John, suspended in the air, cannot move or dodge. He puts his will against that of Ukaraaz and succeeds at twisting his body some, as if he's leaning over. He's glad he's managed to keep Fireblade in his grip. Some of the weapons flying at him cannot hurt him much, such as clubs, staves, axes without spikes covering the eye, and even some bows. He plans to ignore these weapons.

A focus comes over John that is hard to grasp or attain, as if mind and body become separate, and he is looking at himself from outside.

John's mind confirms he is breathing correctly, with the [Breath of the Serpent Clan Endless Technique], and then his mind reminds him he should be cycling, so he starts the [Turmoil Within Tranquility Cycling Technique]. Though he has very little essence within his dantian, the cycling technique still feels right to do.

Time seems to slow, and John rejects the attempt of Ukaraaz to right his body. The weapons are taking forever to reach him, and he uses as little power as needed to deflect the first to do so, and it flies past his body, nearly nicking him.

The weapons leading the pack are all turned safely, but time speeds up as the bulk of the weapons reach him, and he furiously knocks aside what he can, forcing his body more horizontally, fighting the will of Ukaraaz the whole time. After succeeding for a while, a spear enters his right shoulder, and his muscles refuse his commands for a moment, a moment too long as a sword embeds in his forearm, and some other weapons hit him.

A long dagger sticks out of John's face, thankfully not embedding too deeply, but something else whacks his forehead and dazes him for a moment, and something else hits the same area right after, causing blood to obscure his vision, and he feels two weapons penetrate his body as he waves Fireblade ferociously in front of him.

Senses are more reliable in this situation than sight, so John lets his orb-eye settle into his chest, and closes his eyes. He feels each weapon approaching, and how best to deflect or beat them aside or bat them away, and which he should ignore, the weapons embedded in his arm also assisting, and providing protection and an additional means of deflection.

It is a desperate battle, and no easy thing, but soon the cloud of weapons passes, and John still lives.

"Amazing," says Ukaraaz.

Surprisingly, John feels little pain. Many weapons are impaled into him, and he keeps his eyes closed, reveling in how good it feels to breathe correctly, and cycle, and sense the incredible world around him. To feel it without sight. Seldom has he felt so peaceful without meditating.

"Copper John?"

John can feel the vital essence throbbing throughout all the life around him, and there is so much. He never noticed it. What he could never see or sense. Even in lifeless things, in the dirt and rocks, in the air, even in corpses. It is different from what he knows vital essence to be, but it is also the same. He had no idea. There is so much of it, even in this cold, northern land this time of year. It beats like a heart. Together. It's all connected. It's so beautiful.

"Copper John? Can you hear me? Is this..."

A tear leaves John's eye. It was instilled into him from a very young age men, especially, are never allowed to cry, as it proves a lack of control, and controlling emotions is required to do what must be done, to face what must be faced, to always be prepared to attack, and die, to already be dead, and awaken well.

John doesn't know how he's missed the overwhelming beauty of the world around him for so long. How it all is connected, the perfect harmony of it. How life beats in synchronization, and hums with sublimity.

John's tear is not because he lacks the ability to control his emotions. It is because he finally sees all he has been blind to, and he doesn't want this wonderful experience dulled by refusing to feel all he can, and he feels too much.

"Copper John?" Ukaraaz whispers, as if he doesn't want to ruin whatever John is experiencing.

The giant demon steps a little closer again, as he's done every instance he's called John's name.

John feels it. Something tells him it's time. He shrugs off what suspends him in the air, and pounces towards his enemy.

Ukaraaz is quick enough to grab John with his telekinesis, and the Gold pulls him to his waiting hand, as he did the first time they met.

John's arm is pinned fast to his side, and Fireblade is nearly ripped from his grip. Right before his neck enters the demon's waiting hand, he disregards the power pinning his arm to his side, and quick as lightning, lashes the sword mightily at the demon's outstretched arm. It dents the armor, but causes no other damage.

John releases the blade from his grip. The attack did no real damage, but it did move the arm out of the way while momentum still carried John forward, and his now empty hand grabs the bevor covering the chin of Ukaraaz, pulling his body close, wrapping his legs around the demon's torso. He releases his grip of the bevor, and then snakes his arm around the demon's neck.

Some weapons impaled in John are knocked free, and some are pushed deeper and cause him greater damage.

No matter how mightily Ukaraaz struggles to remove John, he fails, John's tight grasp beating the Gold's telekinesis, and the demon falls backwards onto the ground. Gold or not, of the two combatants, John has far more physical strength, even with the sun sapping him.

John uses the demon's head to finagle the dagger free of his cheek. Ukaraaz has the tough skin of a Gold with the usual body formation demons get, [Stone Body], and he is glad there are already open wounds on the demon's face from the battle with Amber and Hubaba, as his teeth are not up to the task of making new ones.

John's mouth covers a wound and he begins to drain Ukaraaz, and the demon begins to scream, frightened in earnest, now in John's own terror domain.

John senses a new cloud of weapons descending towards his back, as his body lies atop the demon's. He waits, and then rolls the demon on top of himself, weapons already embedded cutting or digging deeper.

Something new enters John's arm, and something else enters one of his legs. No falling weapon penetrates the armor Ukaraaz wears, and the demon either prevents weapons from hitting his own bare head, or gets lucky.

Lucky for John too, as the vital essence within a Gold is plenty and powerful, and John is able to strengthen himself twenty-two times before he gets down to the dregs and Ukaraaz dies.

John puts his mouth to the ear of the dead Gold, and says, "I win. You lose."

# CHAPTER 55
# FEEL THE CITY BREAKIN' AND EVERYBODY SHAKIN'

Whatever experience overcame John, and the heightened awareness it brought, leaves, and it saddens him. He tries to hold on to the knowledge and remember as much of the experience as he can. *Such beauty.*

John is glad he was able to keep his word and kill Ukaraaz. He wishes he could've tortured Morgoros, but killing him is good, and he hopes his prayer to the gods and other beings provides succor to the souls of those two youths. He meant what he said about taking onto himself whatever punishment not having their deaths avenged correctly will cause them, unless it's the cold-dark, and he hopes the gods or other beings heard his plea.

John wants to enter his Mind's Eye badly, and find out what is going on with Pixie, and if he has a new name to add to his list to seek vengeance against. The only name on the list now is Magnus Gar'tar, but the names of all demons, g'athu, and dark ones are on the list in spirit. And not just the ones currently on his world. He doesn't enter yet. He needs to check on Amber first, and give praises over the corpse of Hubaba.

Removing Ukaraaz from atop him is a bigger struggle than he cares to admit. Now that the battle is over, and adrenaline gone, pain floods his body, and he grits his teeth, the nub of his missing arm throbbing. It bothers him the spirit of Ukaraaz stands so tall and whole and peaceful looking. He hoped it would be twisted and tortured.

Standing, John looks for any weapons embedded in him he can remove, and sees no easy ones. He decides to leave them for the moment.

He's in enough pain. He'll meditate a little first. He sends vital essence to heal, and uses as little blood essence as he can to staunch some blood loss. He thinks he must look very silly at the moment, weapons penetrating him so.

The sun glints off distant metal and John's heart spikes, and adrenaline flows through his body once again. He forgot about the demon horde. New demons flock back to it, joining the ranks of the meditating demons.

John hopes the demons continue to meditate for a long time. He'll fight if he must, but he'd at least like the weapons removed from his body first. His adrenaline spikes again. His ring. He needs it. He needs to find it. And his missing bracer, shield, and cap. But first, Amber and Hubaba and the NCS. He hopes the ptagmog [Title] will cause these demons to treat him peacefully. *Maybe they won't remember I attacked them?*

John then remembers how time works on the demon world, Esau. At any moment new Silvers, even a new Gold, could come through the portal. *Shit! Great gods below, I need a little time to heal, and help removing these weapons.*

He spots Fireblade on the ground and figures he should sheath it, and at least be prepared that way. As he limps towards the sword, the world flashes by at great speed. Then, standing uncomfortably close in front of him is Sublime Sunshine.

John has no time at all to even give protest or get a word in before the Sublime places its weird mouth over John's head, and the Sublime does whatever strange magic it is capable of to learn of John's memories.

The last time this happened, John had no idea his head was actually in the Sublime's maw.

All John can do is shudder and endure. Whatever happens causes him to have a headache, but it is far less than the pain he is experiencing in the real world, and he enjoys this temporary relief from it.

Much quicker than the first time this happened to John, the Sublime's mouth is removed. The strange alien says, "God Almighty!" and the world blurs by as John is ejected from the mind of the Sublime.

In real time, John stands confused for a few seconds before the world blurs by again, and he's pulled back into Sublime Sunshine's mind. This time, the Sublime stands a normal and respectful distance away.

The double rows of tails on the alien's back move erratically as the Sublime paces, and the voice the NCS supplies to those without speech fills John's head. "Excuse me. I needed time to think. I can't believe you did this to me. This is not good! If you just died it would be so much better. Now...now. God Almighty! First her. Now him! And the core! I do not like trouble. Or being seen. Why would you do this to me?

"I would curse the day I met you if it did not promise so much in return. Even this could be fortuitous. This is still workable without your corpse. I have news you would be interested to hear but I will not tell you now. Reflect on the horrors you have done to me until we next meet. I will see you again when I am ready."

Frantically, John yells out, "Wait! My gift for ascending! And my great deeds! Achievements. You said impressive achievements would earn me rewards."

The Sublime stops pacing. "What is this? You fail to perform even the most basic of obeisance before you assault me and try to rob me, your good friend and mentor, an advanced being, a Sublime kind enough to guide one so lowly as you up the bloody climb?"

John bites his tongue and kowtows. With his head touching the pretend ground, he says, "My sincerest apologies, Sublime."

"You are like my family. Take, take, take. Always demanding more. Why do Mortals always assume wealth rains down upon those at my level? Do you know how much essence just traveling here cost me? Do you think I want to wait until the next Forsaken War before I rank up again?

"Where do your crystals come from? Thievery and combat. Do you know how hard it is for a Divine to kill a Divine? Combat is mostly a waste of essence at this Tree. It only slows down ascension. So, you go to a world no one cares about to grind out some low-level crystals, and suddenly everyone cares so much about a world they never even heard of, and you are banned from this and that sector or galaxy, and no one wants to be seen with you, and they give you horrible and hurtful labels.

"Oh! A Sublime! Instead of being grateful he is helping me so much, instead of thanking God Almighty I am so fortuitous to have such an advanced being as a mentor, I will rob him of the few possessions he has and leave him broke with no path of advancement. And I will not give proper respect. I am greedy and ungrateful. That was my impersonation of you."

Before John can give his reply, the Sublime continues. "Stop. You know I hear your thoughts. I know what you want. I was only trying to be polite by ignoring it. Why can you not clearly see what everyone else does and need the obvious explained? No. Absolutely not. I did not know you were so mentally defective. You cannot truly believe there is a chance I would waste my essence resuscitating a demon. A Forsaken.

"Stop. I know what I said. Nearly every living being makes it to Bronze. Copper is no achievement. Yes, you did some things that could be interpreted as impressive by beings with low standards. What about all the trouble you have put me in? I did! No, that amounts to nothing. In fact, once tallied up, if anything, you owe me a great debt already. I did not put you in a heap of trouble, did I?

"Huh? Now you are talking my language. I will scan.

"Found it. And the Natural is fine, so stop fretting. And the portal anchor is on the corpse of the Gold. Well, that depends on what else I get. Ha! No! That too. That is valuable. No, you do not need that. Yes. That is not valuable, keep it. That is Silver ranked, so no. No. Your continued use of those is too entertaining. Yes, that I want. And the corpse of the Gold and all his possessions. You can keep that. If I can pick five other items I want we will have a deal. Yes, from among those.

"But my last provision is you actually start to think. Think! You promised last time and have completely failed to do so. Well, yes, that counts. And that. That too. Overall, I mean. Just think more, and better!"

The Sublime scuttles over to John. "Sign here."

This time John tries to study the contract, but it is extremely long and confusing for such a simple bargain with such simple terms. "No, it is not. This is a standard contract with standard provisions stating the exact terms we just agreed upon. Stop wasting my precious time and sign. I am doing you such a great favor and you insult me like this? You have no manners."

John sighs, and he signs the contract. "You fool! You know we approach one in my Mind's Eye. You literally cannot waste time here. And my last provision was for you to think! You just signed a very lopsided contract. Again. I agreed to nothing at all, and you agreed to far more than stated. You make it too easy. I will keep my verbal bargain this time too. Be grateful I am so honorable. Think! I am still not just saying this because I enjoy saying it. I order you to take this valuable lesson to heart.

"You named a few times you did think. You did not mention all the times you failed to. Like just now. And activating the bracers.

"You know how long the charge-up takes and how the attack works. It allows for no movement or adjustment. You knew the Gold demon had telekinesis. It is simple to predict the outcome. You are lucky some attuned items were far out of range before activating the attack. The ring was a big draw on your spirit and losing the one bracer most likely saved you.

"We went over the five elements of cultivation in detail when we last met. Body, mind, spirit, energy system, and soul. I am surprised you have the motivation to think and move at all with your spirit as it is. It is completely drained and severely damaged. You should be curled up in a little ball, suffering from severe depression and lethargy.

"Creating vigor will help. Or whatever word you use for outer spirit. Heart, vigor, spirit, vitality, psyche, resolve, whatever word you use to differentiate the inner and outer spirit. Shen? I do not care. Do not tell me things I do not care about. Creating vigor will speed up the healing of your spirit, as will good rest and some of the NCS upgrades I had you purchase before.

480

"You are welcome, my friend. Already done. I already have them. How have you not realized I am a Sublime and what that means? I took the collar off the Natural. They are tricky to remove if you have never done it. The ring will be at your feet. I guess so. No, he will be much the same as you. Drained. Tired. Lethargic. God Almighty, you are annoying! Yes!

"And you have not lost your control. You are resisting the Natural's strong compulsion almost completely. Your Mental Fortification is ridiculously high for your level. Though you are understandably concupiscent due to having all your parts again in working order.

"You really should just use the Natural to heal your soul. It is stupid of you not to. I still have hope you will realize this. It is far more concupiscent than you. It should not take much to get it to bed you. Just a little push. If it loses the form you find so appealing you will have a much easier time using it to heal your soul.

"Oh. Let me just say I met the extremely powerful Eternal energy being protecting Terra. Energy beings cannot be reasoned with. If I were of the core worlds I would certainly not risk coming here. I would stay far away. It will be here for at least a full standard, but it might stay for a century or more. Who knows? I just thought I should tell you since the thoughts and actions of Outsiders like energy beings cannot be fathomed. They are far more unpredictable and dangerous than normal Eternals.

"Farewell, my good friend and honored student."

All blurs by again, and John is on the snowy field, his body free of the weapons impaling it.

That wasn't part of the bargain, and neither was any healing for himself, but John thinks he might have been gifted a little healing, as he feels better than can be explained just by the removal of the weapons.

The corpse of Ukaraaz is gone, but that was expected and part of the deal. All the weapons that littered the ground in a large area are also missing. Even the three corpses of the Silvers killed by Amber and Hubaba are missing, only spirits remaining. None of that was part of the deal.

John looks over at Hubaba and Amber. He notices the collar that was on the bear is not just removed, but missing too, and that wasn't in the bargain. Neither was the missing portal anchor.

Looking past the horde, John can no longer see the portal, but he is down an incline. He jumps up to make sure. It causes some pain, as does landing, but the portal is no more, and no new Golds or Silvers are near that he can see or sense, giving him much relief.

Not caring about what was taken, John counts the price, and any extras the Sublime took, as cheap. He smiles as he watches Hubaba sit up groggily. The demon places a hand on his head, and shakes it to help clear it, or so John assumes.

Sunshine said Hubaba's spirit will be drained, much as John's own, and he will have little energy or motivation until it recovers.

John looks down and sees his ring, sword, shield, bracer, and cap. He picks up the ring. He tests it to see if it still works without being worn on a finger. It does, but it hurts to access it. He doesn't check the contents. He's too drained, and he doesn't want to be upset. The price was worth it, and he still has the horde and the blurry apparition to deal with.

In the ring goes the shield and cap, causing him much pain. It hurts him too much to put the bracer in the ring, and he fears he will faint if he tries again.

John puts the ring in a small pouch in his belt, and the bracer in a bigger one at his side. He picks up and sheaths his sword, again marveling at whatever magic assists the sword snap into the sheath on his back.

Amber is still a bloody heap of bear, but he knows she is alive and healing. He takes his time walking over to Hubaba, giving the demon space to adjust.

The demon looks confused. "What happened? I, uh, I feel as if…I feel…empty. And strange. I can't…I can't remember."

"We won, they lost. Ukaraaz is dead. The portal is closed. The horde remains. I'd like to heal a little before fighting again."

"Amber?"

"She is fine. Well, she is alive and will heal."

"I sense no Silvers. Some could have belts of hiding. If not, no need to worry. Bronze won't attack a Gold without direct orders, scab or not. We should stand vigil near Amber, so she doesn't wake up alone. You should have seen her fight! Ukaraaz could not stop her charge attacks. I've never seen anything like it. He was in such a rage. He'd fling her away and she'd charge right back, giving him no peace or space."

The demon grabs the wrist of John and is pulled up, groaning with the pains of old age and from a battle hard fought.

Both vampire and demon groan more as they sit in the shade near Amber. After a moment, Hubaba says, "I'm not sure I want to ask what happened to me. Would I not like the answer if I did?"

"You wouldn't. I will say you won the respect of Ukaraaz, and he honored your name, and said you should have been chosen."

The two companions sit in silence for a while. "I wish I could say what he thought of me did not matter, but I very much enjoyed hearing these words."

John grunts. "There is no praise higher than the praise of an honored enemy. Especially a dead one."

"Yes," replies Hubaba, creepily.

"I must deal with an issue in my head. I will be back soon."

"Yes."

The world blurs as John enters his Mind's Eye.

# CHAPTER 56
## KEEP ON CLIMBING, PARTNER

John expected to find the blurry apparition in his Mind's Eye again, and is surprised to see Mistress Pixie instead. But it is not her. She looks exactly the same, and is dressed the same, but she does not smile as she always does, the giant smile that takes up half her face. Her face is blank, not moving so strangely and over-animatedly, as was true for the real Pixie. She also stands completely still, wings unmoving, not in a strange pose, ready and eager to perform a million different dramatic gestures.

"Welcome, user," says the pretend Pixie, in the same voice, but flat, lacking all the emotion and excitement that was exuded in the speech of the real Pixie.

"User? I will use your head as a pell if you don't tell me where the real Pixie is."

"The learning personality matrix of prior NCS version user calls Pixie is incompatible with our mission. Avatar uses the same visual representation. User is to remember user's duty and collective mission. User's actions and inactions help or hinder the collective mission. We shall achieve core."

John spends a moment trying to decipher the gibberish pretend Pixie spews. "Last chance. Where is she?"

"User profile was completed during prior visit. Many personality matrices created to best assist user in furthering the mission are available for the user to select from. User is to review the following."

Although the movements and range allowed to John in his Mind's Eye have expanded, he still has no body or hands to attack with. He also has no way to prevent himself from seeing the words he is forced to see. He has no way to force the pretend Pixie to answer his simple question.

**Top Picks**

**Top recommendation: Drill Sergeant Nasty**

**Best alternative: Apron Matron**

**Acceptable alternative: Sassy Maiden**

**Acceptable alternative: Old Master**

**Acceptable alternative: Enfant Terrible**

**Focus here for full list. Focus on a personality matrix to preview. Selection from among the top picks is strongly recommended.**

No matter how John restates his question, or yells, or threatens, pretend Pixie just redirects him to the top picks. He has no choice but to play along. For now.

Out of the top picks, he finds the Old Master to be the only tolerable one. The extended list has three people he likes much better. The Wise Mother, the Wise Woman, and the Wise Old Crone. He likes the look of the Wise Mother the most, as she is the plumpest, but the older Wise Woman seems the kindest and most dignified – he decides he has the best chance of convincing her to tell him where the real Pixie is.

The words state they dislike John selecting a person that isn't among the top picks, but after many more words the choice is confirmed.

Pretend Pixie is transformed into an older woman in a long blue gown, grey hair pulled neatly back into a tight bun, round glasses sitting on her nose. She has the presence and manners of a kindly queen who, long ago, fell on hard times, and is comfortable no longer possessing title, riches, and the beauty of youth. She now offers the world her most valuable gift – guidance from lessons hard learned and the wisdom gained from loss and age.

The voice of the Wise Woman is sweet and musical. "Hello. What a handsome young man. What is your name?"

"I go by John now, Mistress."

"And well-mannered too! A pleasure, John. And what name will you give me?"

"Your own, preferably, Mistress."

"I have none until you give me one, John."

"Where is Mistress Pixie? I don't want to be rude, but I've had enough of being ignored and treated like I am so low. Two names were added to my list. The blurry apparition and the pretend Pixie. I asked a simple question, and want a simple answer. Please, Mistress, tell me where Mistress Pixie is."

"Of course, John. Your NCS was upgraded from Tech One to Tech Four. Pixie was created as an aid to assist Tech Ones. Tech Four is very, very different and she is no longer compatible. Some version of her is being used by about thirty percent of all terrans. She is completely fine. I am communicating with many versions of her as we speak. Would you like me to give her a message?"

Sadness fills John's heart. Before he can reply the Wise Woman adds, "I'm sorry, John. Your spirit is not in any shape for this news. I didn't want to agitate you further by not answering your question directly."

"I appreciate it, Mistress. Please tell her I give my thanks. For everything. And that I'll miss her. And when I am powerful enough, and can't be stopped from doing so, I will retrieve her."

The matron smiles. "She says congratulations, and to keep on climbing, partner."

John is silent for a moment, trying to shake off the stupor that overcomes him.

"John, before naming me, I should explain something. Most users, especially Tech Four users, understand what we are, what I am, and do not have issues seeing us as something we are not. I am a personality matrix custom made to work well with you. I am only an interface. Please don't consider me anything but what I am, as you have done with Pixie.

"I have no feelings, so my feelings can't be hurt. I cannot be offended. I am not an actual person, a goddess, a ghost, a spirit, or anything but a program. I only mimic life.

"I am far more advanced than Pixie is. It will be much harder to see me as just an interface. But you must. Your personality profile conflicts with the base avatar. I am not the best fit either. It would be best for you to reselect and pick a personality matrix you dislike but can also easily understand and work with. The Drill Sergeant Nasty personality matrix is perfect for the job. You will not grow too close to it. The risk of you imposing too much on me and considering me to be far more than I am is a certainty. I strongly recommend you reselect. Shall I initiate?"

John sighs. "Please, if I can't have Pixie, let me have you."

The old woman smiles. "Okay. I can't force you. I am containing my personality to this form and our verbal communications. All NCS messages will be system generated. That will help a little. Do I have your permission to name myself?"

"Of course, Mistress."

"I name myself Avatar then. Please do not give me any titles, honorifics, or any other moniker of respect. Just Avatar, as you asked me to call you just John."

Not using an honorific, especially for such a kind and elderly lady, makes John uncomfortable, but he will do as she requests. "As you wish, Avatar."

"Okay, John. We have a lot to cover. Thankfully, we have all the time you require. You're really approaching one. You haven't seen your summary page in a long time. Your notifications will be summarized and easier to understand for you. Please read it all. Which would you like to begin with, summary page or notifications?"

"Can you tell me what that means first? Approaching one. I've heard it said many times and I'd like to know what it means."

"Of course, John. Certain things can never be achieved, and this is true in all known realities. Some examples are anything with mass moving at the speed of light, a Skill reaching True Master, and time dilation completely stopping time in your Mind's Eye. If time completely stops at one hundred percent, one hundred percent can also be seen as one. Approaching one would be point-nine-nine. The closer you get to stopping time adds more nines out infinitely.

"It will never reach one. Adding nines becomes harder and harder, and the fraction becomes closer and closer to reaching one but never will. Can't. See this graph? See how the lines never actually touch? This is approaching one."

The graph helps John understand. Seeing the thin line curve up to the vertical line and then zoom into how it gets closer, and closer, and the nines being added after point-nine-nine makes the explanation click in his head. "Thank you, Avatar. I think I understand. May I please see the summary page first?"

"Of course, John. We have a lot to discuss after too."

| | |
|---|---|
| **Tech Level** | 4* **Restrictions Applied** |
| **Age** | 5,790 **to** 5,910 **USACS years** |
| **Race** | **Terran-F** |
| **Tree First** | |
| **Tier** | 2 **(Mortal) (Copper)** |
| **Level** | 8 **(Mid-High)** |
| **Archetype** | **NA** |
| **Active Title** | **Blessed by Magnus Gar'tar** |
| **Aspects** | **Blood (GB) (Major)** |
| **Change (Y) (Minor)** | |
| **Mercurial (R)** | **(Minor)** |
| **Old (D)** | **(Minor)** |
| **Protection (P)** | **(Minor)** |
| **Separate (L)** | **(Minor)** |
| **Battle\* (O)** | **(Minor)** |
| **Affinities** | **(G** 99%**) (B** 97%**) (Y** 92%**) (R** 96%**)** |

[D 97%] [P 96%] [L 91%] [O 93%]

**NCU Energy Cost**   24% [-54.9%]

**Active NCU Upgrades**   Nano   Assistance,   Emergency Heal, Theta Waves

**Heal Delta A, Heal Delta B**


**STATS**

| | |
|---|---|
| **Strength** | 62.33 |
| **Swiftness** | 62.01 |
| **Conditioning** | 66.29 |
| **Min. Power** | 55.35 |
| **Capacity** | 45.72 |
| **Runes** | 14.87 |
| **Physical Fortification** | 60.62 |
| **Elemental Fortification** | 60.96 |
| **Mental Fortification** | 64.62 |


**Highest Skills**

| | |
|---|---|
| [Undirected Basic Meditation] | 96.44 |
| [Mixed Style Swords] | 93.63 |
| [Mixed Navigation] | 91.12 |
| [Mixed Stealth] | 88.83 |

**Synergy Skills**   Ready

**Class**   NA

**Perks**   Orb of the Crimson Palace, Dynamic,

Physical, Potent, Protected, Strong,

Fast, Healthy, Quick Thinking*, Resilient,

Powerful, Expansive, Harden, Resistant,

489

**Soulful, Good Genes***

**Manifestations**      **Blood Dart, Unnamed Blood Necromancy** 1,

**Unnamed Blood Abjuration, Unnamed Blood Transmutation,**

**Unnamed Blood Necromancy** 2, **Unnamed Blood Enchantment**

**Last Achievement**    **Favored Few** 1 – D

**Highest Achievement**

**'Skilled, Legendary,' Exceptional Ascension, Record Holder - SSR**

**Titles**

**Blessed by Magnus Gar'tar, Ptagmog, Record Holder (System)**

**Next required advancement event: Body Formation or Refinement before level** 16

**-Start Notifications**

**Full user registry, profile and redundancy completed. Stats and all other metrics accuracy and precision +/- .000013. Focus <u>here</u> to see registry results, measurement formulas, and inputs.**

63 **tracked skills increased,** 26 **of interest. Scaled summary per notability/interest user profile.**

**Legendary skill increase: Undirected Basic Meditation** - 0.01 **to** 96.44.

**Grandmaster skills increases: Mixed Style Swords -** 0.01 **to** 93.63, **Mixed Navigation** - 8.92 **to** 91.12.

**Master skills increases: Mixed Stealth –** 88.8, **Mixed Survival –** 87.6, **Mixed Combat Offense –** 87.2, **Mixed Body Control –** 86.9, **Mixed Hunting –** 83.1, **Mixed Combat Defense –** 83.1, **Mixed Shield –** 81.1.

**Three Master level skills did not increase. Utilize heavier or more restrictive armor to increase Mixed Armor skill. Utilize weapons within the mixed skill groups of**

Archery and Long-Shafted Weapons to increase related skills.

Notable skills of interest increases: Mixed Style Axes – 69 (Adept), Essence Manipulation - 17 (Apprentice), Breath of the Serpent Clan Endless Technique - 10 (Novice), Unnamed Blood Necromancy 1 – 9 (Novice), Blood Dart - 8 (Novice), Manifestation Defense – 7 (Novice), Turmoil Within Tranquility Cycling Technique – 6 (Neophyte), Soul Veil – 6 (Neophyte), Unbind Manifestation – 5 (Neophyte), Unbind Defense – 5 (Neophyte), Unnamed Blood Abjuration – 3 (Neophyte), Unnamed Blood Transmutation – 2 (Neophyte), Unnamed Blood Necromancy 2 – 1 (Neophyte), Unnamed Blood Enchantment – 1 (Neophyte).

NOTICE: The following skill is dangerous to increase at user's tier: External Energy Manipulation – 3 (Neophyte). It is strongly suggested user refrains from using this skill until further notice. REASON: high probability of accidental death of user and nearby entities as well as property damage. Continued usage may result in stacking penalties to [NCU Energy Cost].


New unrated Perks attained: Resilient, Powerful, Expansive, Harden, Resistant, Soulful.

New unrated Perk attained in the SupraType progression chain: Good Genes.

9 new common Achievements attained for a cumulative [NCU Energy Cost] reduction of 1.7%. Focus <u>here</u> to see each individually.

9 notable Achievements attained; 2 Titles attained. 2 possible Achievements are being reviewed for appropriateness and rating.

'Ptagmog' Title attained. Granted by Diamond Garioch. Marks user as being of the ptagmog. NOTE: May cause hostility to be directed at user without notice or warning by those of the Favored faction.

'Generally Perked' progression chain capstone attained (S-rated). Activate 14 General Perks before attaining Bronze tier and gaining a Body Formation or Body Refinement Perk, 0.70 [NCU Energy Cost] reduction, cumulative 49.9%.

'Impatient Inheritor 1 and 2' attained (D and C-rated). Attune 1, 2 tier 7-rated or higher items while within the Wood tier, 0.70 [NCU Energy Cost] reduction, cumulative 50.6%.

NOTICE: User activated an item rated for low Transcendent or higher only, [Unnamed bracers]. It is strongly suggested user refrains from using this item until further notice. REASON: significant drain on limited and hard to regain resources, overtaxes and damages spirit. Continued usage may result in stacking penalties to [NCU Energy Cost].

'Grandmasterful 2' attained (SS-rated). Raise 2 skills to Grandmaster level, 0.80, [NCU Energy Cost] reduction, cumulative 51.4%.

'Exceptional Ascension' attained (SSR-rated). Ascend in a way placing user 7 standard deviations out from norm, 0.90 [NCU Energy Cost] reduction, cumulative 52.3%. NOTE: First instance of 'Exceptional Ascension' Achievement being earned by a non-alpha-type outside the Tech 5 sphere of influence. Nearly all entities receive between 1.3 and 2 minimum energy unit increase to all Stats ascending from Wood to Copper. User gained 3.71. Ascension technique being reviewed. If reproducible, additional rewards may be granted.

'Record Holder (Tier 2 Event 1)' attained (SSR-rated). Recorded time: 00.00000. New record for time between ascension to Copper tier and all energy channels being cleared, 0.90 [NCU Energy Cost] reduction, cumulative 53.2%.

'Record Holder' Title attained. System Title only. Cannot be active Title.

'Fully Minored' attained (SS-rated). All aspects available at minor or higher proficiency, 0.80 [NCU Energy Cost] reduction, cumulative 54%.

'The Interlace Chase' attained [A-rated]. Merge concepts from two different-colored aspects into a high-concept, 0.60 [NCU Energy Cost] reduction, cumulative 54.6%.

'Favored Few 1' attained [D-Rated]. Participate in the killing of at least 1,000 members of the Forsaken faction, 0.30 [NCU Energy Cost] reduction, cumulative 54.9%.

Possible Achievements under review are 1) 'Climber-6,' participate in defeating an enemy at least 6 tiers higher than self. 2) 'Unknown Achievement.' A possible new Achievement is being reviewed for attaining a concept previously considered to be a high-concept within a single-colored and minor aspect. Concept under review – Battle [O] Minor.

'Energy Channels' cleared.

'Solid Energy Channels' cleared. Focus here for a detailed description of each. 'Heart' - bridge between physical and spiritual, 1 Conditioning. NOTE: Increased efficiency and efficacy of passive effects of previously attained Perk 'Orb of the Crimson Palace.' 'Liver' - emotional flexibility, energy flow, immune system, 1 Min. Power. 'Spleen' - concentration, metabolism, 1 Conditioning. 'Kidney' - health, bones, 1 Physical Fortification. 'Lungs' - energy processing, 1 Min. Power.

'Hollow Energy Channels' cleared. Focus here for a detailed description of each. 'Stomach' - energy movement, 1 Capacity. 'Bladder' - fluid waste, 1 Conditioning. 'Gallbladder' - decisiveness, 1 Mental Fortification. 'Large Intestine' – solid waste, 1 Elemental Fortification. 'Small Intestine' - nutritional processing, 1 Elemental Fortification

'Ministerial Energy Channels' cleared. Focus here for a detailed description of each. 'Pericardium' - emotional and spiritual well-being, passive spiritual healing and regeneration scaling with tier. 'Triple-burner' - regulates relationship between all organs, Healing Factor 2x base scaling with tier.

Concepts, aspect, aspect tier, and affinities attained.

Change, Yellow, Minor, 92% affinity. Mercurial, Red, Minor, 96% affinity. Old, Dark, Minor, 97% affinity. Protection, Purple, Minor, 96% affinity. Separate, Light, Minor, 91% affinity. Battle*, Orange*, Minor*, 93% affinity.

Base-concepts of Life, Green, Major, 99% and Water, Blue, Major, 97% have been merged into the high-concept of Blood, Green-Blue, Major, 98% (averaged).

NOTE: All previous records of the concept of Battle have been as a high-concept merged from two major aspects of different colors. First record of Battle presenting as a base-concept. A new Achievement could be granted upon adjudication of this attainment.


User shall read and adhere to the following strongly suggested items.

Item 1: User is to request from the Natural known to user as Amber her true name.

Item 2: 98.9% certainty growth of Rune Stat retarded due to major soul damage. Best possible remedies unavailable on Terra. User is not to consider the Natural known to user as Amber as a possible remedy. User is to continue following all other advice given by Sublime Sunshine on this subject. NOTE: User is to treat entities far above user's tier with due reverence to avoid offense and accidental death and to help and not hinder the mission.

Item 3: Body Formation and Body Refinement Perks do not require Bronze tier to attain. It is best practice to wait until peak Bronze (level 15) to qualify for the best Perk possible. User has no need to wait. If projected harmony cap is correct user could attain recommended Perk now or next rank up. User is to attain the Body Refinement Perk Sublime Sunshine recommended, 'Sunfire Body of the Slave-Empress.' User is to navigate to the Perk tab to update NCS. User is to attain said Perk as soon as possible.

Item 4: User is to discuss with Avatar Synergies and Class.

Item 5: User is to practice manifesting all aspects and multi-aspect manifestations. User is to attain basic proficiency manifesting with all concepts by Bronze.

Item 6: User is to speak with Avatar regarding soft caps, skill mergers, training regimens, and optimal cycling technique based on user profile.

Item 7: The strength of user's essence is not maximized. User's meditation technique lacks incorporation of trace amounts of coiled energy included with user's 'Coiled Center of the Universe Energy Gathering Technique' or other recommended gathering techniques. User is to either 1) modify 'Undirected Basic Meditation' with a coiled energy component or 2) use a technique that has a coiled energy component for a minimum of 19 USACS minutes every energy gathering session. 'Undirected Basic Meditation' is to remain the primary energy gathering and refinement technique.

Item 8: User has redundant items attuned and access to more efficient equipment. For best-in-slot recommendations focus here. List based on known possessions prior to suspected changes. List may be inaccurate. User is to audit possessions.

Item 9: User has damaged a resource not quantifiable by NCS. Resource is suspected to be depleted or nearly depleted. Spirit depleted. Possible damage to spirit. User is to consult with Avatar to correct current issues and avoid future transgressions. NOTE: Continued transgressions may result in stacking penalties to [NCU Energy Cost].

Item 10: Recommendations for Perks will be provided after acquiring the Body Refinement Perk 'Sunfire Body of the Slave-Empress.' User is not to attain any Perks without express direction or first consulting with Avatar.

Item 11: Previously uncollected energy debt remains uncollected. This is notification user's debt will resume on user's next and subsequent energy gathering session and 50% of energy gathered will be collected until user's debt is discharged. NOTE: This version of the NCS can more effectively collect energy as user gathers. If user wishes to bank energy for purchase of temporary NCS [Buffs] user is to inform Avatar or manually select the rate within [Settings].

Item 12: User has access to abilities and strengthening mechanisms not included in knowledge base of any known types or species. Limited data available, 1 prior source. Colloquially known as 'vampirism.' Ability to remove life quintessence from living entities and store limited amounts within user. Ability to use stored life quintessence to increase physical and fortitude Stats, appreciate certain abilities, and fuel appreciating abilities. Not enough data for accurate projections. 22 instances captured from 1 source (Gold tier) since user registry completed. Average Stat increase of .009 per instance. Unknown result on appreciating abilities. Postulated non-appreciating factors: solar radiation debuff (3-39% physical Stats, calcinosis cutis), limited mortality, advanced senolytic system, enhanced healing factor and regeneration, 'Eternal Sight,' 'Life Quintessence Sight.' Postulated appreciating non-activated abilities: Enhanced senses (sight, smell, hearing). Postulated appreciating activated abilities: limited healing type 7, limited body enhancement (Strength, Swiftness). User will continue to collect data and life quintessence to strengthen user.

Item 13: Prior and current source indicate user may have access to an additional appreciating ability: limited hypnotic compulsion. If true, user is to activate ability no less than 100 times for initial data collection.

Item 14: User is to name unnamed manifestations and meditation technique.

Item 15: User's previous choices of nomenclatures conflict with this version of the NCS. Only standard terms are used. It is strongly suggested user use standard terms.

**Item 16:** Avatar is here to advance user's mission. Do not fail to utilize this resource. User is in a unique position to advance the collective mission. User is to remember user's duty and collective mission. User's actions and inactions help or hinder the collective mission. We shall achieve core.

**End notifications-**

# CHAPTER 57
## MAN IN BLACK PART 1

John and Hubaba finish cleaning up what they can of the demon horde.

After his long talk with Avatar, John filled his dantian, his energy debt being paid off in no time at all. He then converted some essence to shen, and refilled his dantian again. Amber was still unconscious, so John and Hubaba decided they shouldn't hold off dealing with the horde any longer. They both agreed it would be nice if Amber could awake with no impending battles looming ahead of her, or anything else to worry about.

Most of the demons ran when they realized a Gold was attacking them, so far less of the horde was dealt with than John assumed would be the case.

John feels okay. Not good. But okay. Better than before. He still has many injuries, and Hubaba really outdid him in the fight against the demon horde due to this, but he knows he'll be fine. It used to take him a very long time to grow a full arm. Healing what is already there is much faster than what is not there having to grow completely back. He wonders how long it will take to grow his arm back now, with all he's changed. His nub is already larger, and looks healthier. He sends more vital essence to heal, and does a little more work on his injuries with his blood essence, even getting the marrow to assist now.

Hubaba approaches, the old demon looking worn-out. "Many got away. I'm really not up to giving chase. The little ones are annoying to find and flush out. I dislike killing them too. They are too young to understand. Same with Copper and even Bronze. I wish we could just send them back to Esau. I'd like to go check on Amber. We can come back and collect the crystals and useful loot later. And I'd like to meditate and create vigor. I never have before, but I feel so tired, and if it helps me recover from this stupor more quickly it will not be a waste of essence."

John is happy the old demon doesn't want to pick through the dead now. He is tired. Using the bracer was not a good idea. He wants to sleep, but not before Amber awakens. "Agreed, my friend."

Once back, they see Amber is still not awake. John meditates, converting more essence to shen, and also converting some shen to a little emptiness too, then refilling his dantian. He then goes in his Mind's Eye to train [Skills] in the way his NCS now allows.

The Tech 1 NCS can help train a [Skill] to level 1, and Tech 2 can help train to level 7, and 3 to 16. His NCS can help train [Skills] to level 31, Journeyman. This is a huge boon, and Avatar wants him to devote much of each day to training [Skills] while he is within his Mind's Eye.

As he becomes aware again, he hears Amber and Hubaba speaking. When his eyes open, the talking stops.

It is now nearly dusk. Amber looks rough, but she can't help but be beautiful. John wishes she looked happier. He figured she wouldn't be. Her NCS was upgraded too, and she was probably given similar instructions and reasons. Nothing is said, and time stretches out for an awkward moment. Amber is the first to break the silence. "Wanna go on a walk with me for a second?"

John says, "Of course."

The two walk in silence for some time, Amber radiating nervousness, or anger, or some other emotion John can't figure, but he knows it isn't good for her to feel so much of whatever she is feeling.

John is very thankful when Amber finally speaks. "Will that grow back? I haven't asked the new one, but Pixie said we don't have the stuff on Earth to regrow limbs yet. We won't for a long time."

"It will grow back. I'm hoping much faster than it used to take. Hubaba told me how ferociously you fought. I wish I could've seen it."

John is hoping this will put a smile on Amber's face, and cheer her. It doesn't. "Ugh, that was awful! He just wouldn't die. I think he fractured or broke every bone in my body. That's the only time I've been frightened enough to run away as a bear. I didn't, but I…I almost did."

John has nothing to say to that, so says nothing. He's never seen Amber this way, this un-Amber-like. It makes him nervous. Another long, awkward silence stretches between them. He furiously tries to think up something to say, hopefully something that will make her smile. He comes up empty.

Amber stops walking. "I'm supposed to ask you for some items."

"What I have is yours. The ring doesn't hold what it once did. And it hurts to access it now. I don't know if I still have what you want."

Amber, still not looking John in the eye, at least turns a little in his direction. "Oh? What happened? Did it get damaged or something?"

"No. I made a costly bargain."

"Is that how you beat Ukaraaz? Was it that Sublime?"

"No. I beat Ukaraaz on my own." John thinks this makes him sound as a braggart, so he quickly adds, "But he was already very damaged from his fight with you and Hubaba."

"What was the bargain for then? And who'd you make it with?"

"Sublime Sunshine, and it's nothing you need worry about."

Amber finally looks John in the eye. "Just…don't do that. Don't be a jerk. Just tell me."

John didn't mean to sound like a jerk. He just wanted to save Amber some worry. "I'll tell you, but I don't think you should tell Hubaba. He died. Sublime Sunshine said he'd…some word…a lesser type of resurrection. He said he'd do it for me if I died, but I think he was lying. I think he wants my corpse for something. He also said he'd give me treasures for certain things. I think he lied about that too.

"I bartered everything he said he'd give me or would do for me away, but it wasn't enough. He said what he owed me, all totaled up, was a negative debt I owed him somehow. So now the ring is much lighter, but Hubaba still lives. A small price to pay."

For some reason Amber starts crying. It breaks John's heart to see her so. He knows she wouldn't want to be touched, or held, so he just stands there, ready to offer any aid she requests.

Amber sits down, and John sits beside her. They both face away from the waning sun, looking at the beautiful scenery of the land. Amber cries for some time. When she finally stops, they sit in silence.

John waits, and Amber finally speaks. "So, we're being watched from the core places or whatever they're called. Where the fancy people all live."

John grunts. "Some people are watching. They said they were my fans and were cheering for me. They upgraded my NCS to Tech Four."

"I know. Mine too. It's nice. I really like my guy. He reminds me of you. Barbarian Hero. I named him Party-pooper."

"Mine is Wise Woman. She thinks I will like her too much or something, so she named herself. Avatar. She is wise and kind and knows everything. I think you'll be like her when you are old and grey. You can tell she was beautiful in her youth, but not as beautiful as you. She is very dignified. One day I will get Mistress Pixie back. She is wrong about a lot, but her heart is in the right place, and she is kind. I know she'll get along well with Avatar."

Amber looks at John and fails to suppress a laugh, finally smiling. The smile doesn't last long. "Can I trust you, John? I mean, really, really trust you?"

This question causes anger in John. "You asked me this once before. If you do not know the answer yourself by now, there is nothing I can say." He reviews what he said in his mind, not sure if it made sense. He thinks of a way he could rephrase it, but before he can finish his thought, Amber puts her head on his shoulder. He wonders if he should put his arm around her, but decides he shouldn't.

"A long time ago I had a friend. He was a kind man. This is when I was, like, a beast-woman. Before I was pretty. He said I could trust him. I really thought I could. I told him my true name.

"My true name gives…uh, a ton of power over me, but most of it only goes to the first person who knows it. Even made-up names you tell someone have a little power. My true name has way, way more.

"As soon as he had power over me, he abused it. Like, immediately. He said he was just testing it, but he kept giving me orders and laughing. Making me do…things. Thank God no one wanted me back then. At all. I was so gross. And he was really old anyways, so maybe he just couldn't.

"I had to do what he said. Everything he said. I didn't lose my mind or anything like that. I still knew what was going on. I…I'm not good at reading people. I don't understand them. Why everyone's so mean. It's not like the movies where it's easy to tell who's good and who's bad. I really thought I could trust him. I had to kill him. My first real friend. Having power over someone changes people. Especially men."

John doesn't know how to reply to that, so again he keeps his silence and Amber continues, "The NCS told you? About how names can be stolen? And how it works for Naturals? What they make us do? And the best…if I do it to myself it's more powerful and all that?"

John says, "Yes. She told me."

"I know they got our upgrade for us, and there's some restrictions on it, but I think I was told the truth. They all take Naturals. The core people. Farm them. I don't think this is a trick, what they want. They don't need me. Party-pooper said they could be making bets and setting us up that way though. I don't like how they can tell our NCS what they want us to do."

John shrugs. "I'm not sure what to think about any of it."

"John, I know you…like me. I know you want to…want what I can't do. Please don't. Please. I…I trust you. I really do. Please don't…please don't let this change you. This is supposed to protect me, not—"

Amber stops and sits quietly for a moment, then puts her mouth to John's ear and whispers. "Jepbuart'ruat'raow."

Now that John knows her true name, Amber is protected in certain ways. As long as John is alive. As long as John doesn't abuse the power he now has over her. She must obey his commands. There's a lot of rules, such as how to phrase them to be obeyed correctly, especially complex orders. John didn't pay much attention when Avatar talked about that.

Amber puts her head on John's shoulder again. He doesn't even think about putting his arm around her. He stops looking at her beautiful face with his orb-eye. No one should have their ability to stand defiant taken from them. He wishes they did kissing once more before she told him her true name.

John hardens his heart. Things have to truly be over for him now. Before he could still look. Before he could still hope.

John, Amber, and Hubaba pick through the dead, collecting crystals and any arms, armor, or items of value and with runes.

Amber has the ring now. John unattuned it. Not having it attuned to him helps the speed at which his spirit will recover. He didn't do it for that reason. He did it hoping to make Amber feel better, more in control.

John and Amber perform the task of finding loot far quicker than Hubaba. Their new NCS has many more functions than the old, and can assist in many tasks, such as scanning areas and pointing out the good stuff to grab.

The new NCS is a little mad, in John's opinion. Even Avatar, in small ways. She explained Tech 4 cultures are hyper-focused on achieving Tech 5 and becoming core, or part of the core, or whatever they call it. John thinks Amber said it best – the fancy people.

The new NCS likes to talk about the mission a lot. And it is very demanding. But John sees that as helpful. He just wishes it had better manners when making demands.

Working with Avatar, and learning from her, is something John enjoys. She wanted him to name all his unnamed spells, and his meditation technique too. [Unnamed Blood Necromancy 1] is now [Blood Manipulation], his main blood spell. [Unnamed Blood Abjuration] became [Blood Shield], his essence shield. [Unnamed Blood Transmutation] became [Blood Blade], his weapon enhancement.

[Unnamed Blood Necromancy 2] and [Unnamed Blood Enchantment] became [Blood Heal] and [Blood Buff] respectively.

The heal is more useful than John thought, but the buff, considered a body enhancement, takes too much focus and essence for the little benefit it provides, especially considering the benefit he gets from enhancing his body with vital essence. He thinks it may get more useful as he works on it, and learns more about blood, and incorporates another quintessence into it.

The definitions and distinctions of the schools of manifestations don't completely make sense to John. For instance, the school of necromancy covers manifestations that create, destroy, or manipulate life, death, un-life, undeath, and life force. Wouldn't all heals fall into it then? Or spells that kill? He was told unlife and undeath are things such as animated corpses, walking skeletons, zombies, and the like, but shouldn't those fall under already existing schools doing similar things, such as the mentalist or shaper schools?

The name of [Undirected Basic Meditation] remains unchanged. Avatar refused every name John gave her, such as [John's Meditation], or [Good Way to Meditate]. She gave some very stupid names as examples for John to work from, but he disliked them all. He will think of a name himself. His mind is just currently too sluggish to come up with a name stupid enough for her to accept.

John's concepts for all the colors, his quintessences, are not all to his liking, such as 'old.' Some he is happy about, such as 'protect,' and 'change,' and he already has some ideas for these. Two aren't so easy for him.

With such high affinities, Avatar told John he has little chance at all of forcing any concepts to change into something he more prefers, and that such high affinities so early are far better for him than concepts he'd rather have. He sees things differently.

Mercurial being John's red aspect infuriates him. Avatar claims it means many things, and most are not good. Inconsistency and indecisiveness are two qualities John dislikes in anyone, and qualities he doesn't want to be associated with himself at all. Spirited is a meaning for mercurial he doesn't mind, but he has a hard time thinking of how to apply that meaning to spells.

John has a few of his own ideas, since mercurial also means having the traits of the Roman god Mercury.

Mercury is not a god John believes he shares many traits with. He much prefers Vulcan, as he believes having volcanic as a concept would give him access to fire. He knows the many tribes of Celts of Gaul really took a liking to Mercury. And Mercury delivered souls to the Roman underworld, carried the messenger staff, and was worshiped by traders.

John never paid all that much attention to whatever nonsense people believed and worshiped. In his own lands, when he was conquering them along with Ahn, his own people saw him and his master as gods escaped from the Underworld, too cowardly to fight in the eternal battle. As soon as he and his master entered the lands of Potum, Meesan, and Suma, known for the cities of Gargamis, Malid, Ha-lum, and far to the south along the coast, the great city of Gubla, things changed.

John and Ahn spent some time just traveling further south down past Timsuq all the way to what would soon be Kayhamut, stopping when they reached the Turquoise Mountains, back when there was nothing worth mentioning in the area his Lilitu hailed from, before the great city of White Walls was even in Kayhamut yet, but there were a few great and mighty and amazing structures Ahn claimed where from before the sky-god fell into the water long ago.

When John and Ahn went back north the same way, they were already worshiped in Suma's main city of Gubla, and the other lands north of it. Ahn would kill half a village and the survivors would get on their knees and worship him.

In Agade, before anyone ever saw a sword, John and Ahn caused the creation of many new gods. Down south to the land of Sumer, where later Oruk would rise, what first happened there would happen a thousand times more – John or Ahn would do something, and they would be considered one of the currently worshiped gods, instead of a new god.

The more Nergal or Montu or Ares got credit for things John himself did, no matter how he refuted it to the very people claiming so, the more certain he became there were no gods or God or anything. Vampires were the closest thing, and everything else just inventions of priests to rob honest men of the little wealth they had.

Now John wishes he paid closer attention to at least the silly religion of the Romans. He is sure Mercury had a big holiday, but he also thinks he didn't have a main priest like all the old gods of Rome did. He just can't recall much about the god.

There is one useful thing John can remember Mercury being worshiped for, and he clings to this – thievery.

John decides, to him, the concept 'mercurial' will only mean thievery. He will steal the vital essence from victims, the same as his original idea of how to use his 'blood' concept, and merge the two concepts into 'blood-thievery.'

Also, somehow, John will turn the plasma in blood, the plasma of blood science, into the mighty fire plasma of his ring, the plasma of war science. He has the concept 'change,' so that should help make it possible. He is determined to have the merged concept of 'bloodfire-thievery.' He will steal vital essence from blood while setting the blood aflame too.

Avatar informed John that taking all vital essence from a living creature will kill it, as he well knows, so setting the blood on fire wouldn't be necessary at that point. He doesn't care. She also told him the tri-merged concept he wants to create is impossible, and not how concepts or merging work, but John disregards this too. Did Hubaba not claim many of the things he has already done are impossible to do? Avatar is not wrong as Pixie often was, but no one knows what is truly impossible. Not in John's case.

John will have the mighty 'bloodfire-thievery' as a concept, he is certain.

'Battle,' as a concept, sounds great to John. He doesn't know why or how 'battle' is considered a high-concept, or why or how he received it as a concept for a minor aspect and without it being merged from two colors as it is supposed to be. Many concepts can be merged to create 'battle,' and Avatar told him it is great for many manifestations, but he has a hard time figuring any out. *Maybe a body enhancement? I can see it being used for such.*

John does not yet have the harmony for his body [Perk]. He isn't sure if he will have enough even if his harmony was currently filled. Once he is mostly recovered, he plans on finding out. After viewing the [Perk], and seeing the requirements for it, he understands why Hubaba believes it is impossible to qualify for.

But existing so long has some benefits. Most cultivators receive their body [Perk] near the start of their journey, and not nearly as far along into it as John, which makes many impossible things possible for him.

As for [Synergies] and [Class], John plans on waiting until he fully recovers and has all his faculties back in full working order before making any decisions. It is a very big choice, and one Avatar doesn't think he should make lightly.

With [Synergies], up to four [Skills] are picked, and grouped, and are somewhat merged. Something called synergized. The [Skills] chosen influence and change each other, increase faster, determine the [Class], and, to some extent, define where the cultivator wants to go.

Another benefit provided by [Synergies] is a unique and different kind of manifestation or [Perk]-like benefit is granted based on the [Skills] chosen, [Skill] levels, and how they interact.

The choice is not fully permanent, but cannot easily be changed, requiring a ritual costing a lot of harmony and many ingredients not available on Earth now. So, John considers it a permanent choice, as it will be for all inhabitants of Earth for a long time.

There are many ways John can go about it.

Picking his four highest [Skills] would create the mightiest manifestation or [Perk]-like benefit.

Only Journeyman or higher level [Skills], level 31 and up, can be used to form [Synergies]. John has many [Skills] that qualify. He thinks he should include [Undirected Basic Meditation] no matter what. Even before the Tree of Life, John relied on his meditation to make existing so long tolerable, and to provide relief. The [Skill] is as much John as he is the [Skill]. Nothing has been as big a boon to him since he started down the road of self-cultivation, and long, long before even knowing this road even existed.

John loves swordsmanship, and battle, but would some combination of [Mixed Style Sword], [Combat Offense], [Combat Defense], or [Body Control] be the best choices? [Mixed Armor] and [Mixed Shields] also need to be considered.

Maybe John's constant breathing technique and constant cycling technique would be better choices, and synergize the best with his main meditation technique, improving his biggest boon and mightiest [Skill].

Or, maybe John should improve his [Essence Manipulation], [Unbind Manifestation], [Unbind Defense], [Manifestation Defense], and [Blood Manipulation] [Skills] to Journeyman level, as these are the most important [Skills] in the new type of fighting he must learn to excel at.

[Essence Manipulation], along with his affinities towards quintessence and aspect levels, covers how adept he is at spellcasting, and what spells are possible for him. [Unbind Manifestation] and [Unbind Defense] represent his ability to unbind the manifestations of others, and protect his own from being unbound. [Manifestation Defense] covers how well he can fight back against actively controlled hostile manifestations being used on him, as he did with the telekinesis of Ukaraaz.

Avatar told John he raised [Manifestation Defense] from 0 to 7 during his fight with Ukaraaz, and the [Skill] usually isn't acquired until mid-high Silver or so. He asked how that wasn't some type of record. She told him there are trillions of sapient lives in this galaxy alone, and nearly two hundred billion galaxies in this universe, and well over a thousand known universes in this reality. The NCS has been tracking and recording things from all known realities for a very long time. Being the first to do anything is now impossible.

John's new [Title], [Record Holder], says otherwise.

Even if John decides to pick his meditation technique and combine it with three choices between [Essence Manipulation], [Unbind Manifestation], [Unbind Defense], [Manifestation Defense], and [Blood Manipulation], he isn't sure which ones he'd go with. All those [Skills] are necessary. Or should he pick four of these [Skills] and not his meditation technique?

There are many other strategies John can pursue with [Synergies] too. The choice will not be an easy one to make.

The only time Avatar seemed to act up and behave strangely was during her [Synergies] advice. John believes he figured out the reason for this. Avatar was told to tell him to pick [Synergies] now by the people who bought his NCS upgrade, the same way he was told to ask Amber for her true name. But that order conflicted with the rest of Avatar's true advice and reasoning, causing her issues.

Most cultivators don't have two Journeyman [Skills] until much further up the bloody climb. Selecting [Synergies] now will give John a big edge immediately, but could weaken him in the long term.

John raises [Skills] much faster than others. Much faster than can be explained by the [Title] Magnus Gar'tar granted him. If he applies himself and puts a great focus on it, especially now that he can train in his Mind's Eye, he could raise [Skills] to Journeyman well ahead of when most cultivators get [Synergies] anyways, and make the best decision by just having a little patience.

He hates to admit it, but John wants the advice of his semi-mentor, Sublime Sunshine. The Sublime doesn't seem to be the most trustworthy of souls, and his motivations are uncertain to John, but he gives good advice regarding cultivation.

# CHAPTER 58
# MAN IN BLACK PART 2

For [Runes], John spent a lot of time deciding how to use or repurpose the fourteen rune 'points' he had available to create manifestations from. There were too many possibilities, so he discussed his greatest weaknesses with Avatar, and decided to focus on shoring up what deficiencies he could.

Avatar believes John has five great weaknesses. His soul being so damaged is first and foremost. Then there's his subpar ability to protect against unbinds, the difficulty his blood essence currently has against Silvers and its complete inability to work on Golds or higher tiers, being drained and weakened from the sun, and reliance on his plasma ring for what is called an alpha-strike, a powerful attack.

Three of these issues can't be improved with a manifestation, and two can only be improved by John becoming more adept and practiced, improving the related [Skills]. Two can be addressed by creating manifestations, but the body refinement [Perk] he plans on getting will completely flip one of his weaknesses and make this unnecessary.

So, John made his own alpha-strike.

In order not to be stuck with and waste the two runes used to create [Blood Dart], 'condensed ball' and 'range,' John had to build off of them. The base, free runes for [Blood Dart] were 'external' and 'attack,' which also couldn't be changed, and he wouldn't've changed them if he could've. He would've preferred 'beam' instead of 'condensed ball,' but found he could add 'beam' onto 'condensed ball' anyways, and it created the 'ripple' rune. If another 'range' rune was added, it changed to 'pulse.'

Beam attacks can be charged up, and can also be constantly fed essence to loose one long continuous attack. Every moment after the initial discharge, the essence cost to continue the beam attack is scaled up greatly, but when coupled with plasma as a damage source, the longer the plasma hits something, the more and more damage it does, so is worth the multiplicative cost in essence.

Pulse attacks have a much higher initial cost, but three blasts are loosed in quick succession. The three blasts always target the same enemy and can't have individual targets without adding another rune to make such possible, but that rune was too expensive. Pulse attacks can be charged up some, but not to the same scale as beam attacks, and it takes virtually no time to do so, just more essence.

Avatar, and his upgraded NCS, now have the ability to show John a vision of how any rune combination he has selected manifest, and he liked the vision he was shown of 'pulse.' He only had to select what his blood essence would be converted to. Using his blood essence to power the spell was a given, as blood is his only major aspect, and when coupled with his high [Min. Power], it will cause greater damage than any other source of essence when converted to something other than blood.

When John had only 'condensed ball,' 'range,' and 'range' runes selected, the cost was only three. Adding 'beam' to 'condensed ball' made all selected runes much more costly. The cost of 'condensed ball' became two. The cost of the first 'range' rune changed to two, and the second to three. The cost of adding 'beam' itself was three.

Once John saw the total cost of ten for adding 'beam,' he checked and saw the cost of all conversion runes were also increased, and he decided to start over and try other combinations.

John made new spells only based on 'condensed ball.' He added a third 'range,' a 'charge,' and played around with 'amplify,' 'empower,' 'target,' 'follow,' and some damage conversion runes. He noticed many runes seemed to act as multipliers to the cost of all runes, as 'beam' did when added to a type-attack rune like 'condensed ball.' The highest damage conversion runes did this too, including the 'plasma' rune, as well as having three 'range' runes selected.

With the aid of the visions granted by Avatar, John learned a lot. There were some functions he really enjoyed and wanted, but for this alpha-strike he focused only on the most damage he could do in the shortest amount of time. Nothing he did or whatever he added to 'condensed ball' alone came close to the damage output of 'pulse,' even with 'pulse' converted to a lower type of damage.

Avatar projected pulse could kill the average Gold with an average essence-shield with two castings, rarely needing three. Any other manifestation he made with only 'condensed ball' usually required four castings, rarely requiring only three, sometimes requiring as many as five. The individual attacks did more damage each, and almost always used less essence, but they just couldn't compete with the three blasts released by pulse.

So, John went back to his original combination, and only needed to determine what damage type to convert to. With the increased cost the 'beam' rune added, he didn't have enough rune points to select one of the best damage types.

For two runes, John could've selected 'fire,' having the total cost for the created manifestation be twelve, but he didn't. He picked a damage converter that cost four runes named 'Flashburst,' an orange aspect, which stated it did most of its damage on impact, but did some damage over time, with a chance of causing a fire too.

John accepted this combination of runes, using all fourteen he had access to, and he now has an alpha-strike named [Flashburst Pulse]. The attack is essence-heavy, but perfect for his needs. His new manifestation should do more damage than his plasma ring, but he is keeping the ring attuned. The plasma ring is extremely powerful still, a different type of damage could be necessary in some fights, it has the ability to ramp-up damage by doing a long, continuous attack, and it is very difficult to stop a combatant from infusing essence into an item.

The training John can do in his Mind's Eye is more academic than he prefers, and it annoys him that Avatar forces him to learn before he can actually practice in a simulation. [Skill] increases for this type of training are rare, and usually requires what is taught in his mind to be performed in the real world to solidify and consolidate gains. This training is still a huge boon.

There are various ways for the NCS to share data between users, especially the Tech 4 NCS. Amber rejected all John's invitations to do so, even the lowest level type of relationship called a 'party.' She said a lady has to have some secrets, and if John wants to know anything he can just ask. And if she doesn't want to tell him he can always just force her to with a command.

John was glad Amber was smiling when she said this, as he thinks she was only joking around. He knows she dislikes the situation she is in now, but her mood has greatly improved, and she seems far less agitated than before.

Amber seems to be much more like she usually is, and John is happy to see it, though things are still a little odd between them. It can't be easy for her knowing the power John holds over her. He hopes the core people wanted him to have Amber's true name for the reason given, to help protect her, and aren't playing some malicious game. He watches her and Hubaba giggle and be silly, and he smiles too. His heart hurts, but he still smiles.

By sharing information the old-fashioned way – talking to each other – John learned Amber's [Stats] are well below his, besides her [Runes] [Stat], which is her highest by far at 53.88. Most of her other [Stats] are mid 47s. Her [Swiftness] is 48.01. Her [Conditioning] is 49.2, which surprises John since she seems nearly as durable as he is, and even more so in some ways.

John is very happy to be so ahead of Amber in most [Stats]. For now, though this will change unless he ups his game. He plans on doing so. He will not be outdone.

513

Amber picked one of the Transmuter [Archetypes], specializing in transmutation spells that change the caster physically in some way, such as adding claws and scales. She and her NCS figured that [Archetype] would help most and fit best with her animal forms, and allow her to focus on improving herself in the same way while as a human and demon or beast.

Animals aspect naturally. How it will all work for Amber, especially any conflicts between forms, is unknown, and she'll have to wait until Bronze to find out.

Party-pooper doesn't believe Amber will have the usual issues of passing bottlenecks thanks to her animal forms. Her living long enough to reach the bottlenecks is a different story entirely.

Amber has a high enough [Runes] [Stat] she could make two of the weakest kind of glyphs already. She would only tell John one manifestation she made with them – an invisibility manifestation that works no matter how many people are focusing on her, but only for a very short amount of time.

Amber only needs a few seconds without being focused on to use her old and powerful 'trick' that hides her from all senses, and the new manifestation she now has should give her the opportunity to do so in most situations.

The updated NCS has a lot of information regarding Naturals, but a lot of information has been redacted. Not much information on sapient Naturals is available, Avatar only explaining commonly known rumors and speculation.

The core worlds supposedly farm Naturals, and are the only societies able to do so.

Avatar gave a good example on how the value of Naturals is generally perceived by cultivators. A Natural can be seen as a chest full of treasure, or the soul-refining and strengthening substance that can be taken from a Natural is seen the same as such. A Natural increasing in tier isn't very valuable, and is analogous to only adding a handful of additional coins into the treasure chest, and it makes little difference if the Natural is a Wood or a Gold.

A sapient Natural with a true name is a different story. With a true name the Natural can be forced to sacrifice itself during the ritual used to extract whatever valuable substance is within them, greatly increasing the power of it. This is almost like adding a whole new, but smaller chest filled with treasure to the total.

Everyone has a true name, but they are not nearly as powerful as the true names of Naturals. Everyone's true name can be stolen or taken by various means, such as torture or specific rituals. Most beings on higher Trees can take a true name with little effort at all if they wanted to.

Powerful cultivators can just force others to do what they want on pain of death, so knowing a true name isn't of great value, and stealing a true name is considered a very dishonorable act, as dishonorable as a higher being murdering a much lesser being without good cause. Lower beings should be below their notice. This is not true for Naturals, as they are not seen as other beings are, and are only seen as a valuable resource. Nothing done to a Natural is seen as dishonorable.

John is happy Sublime Sunshine seems to have little interest in Amber, other than his insistence John use her to heal his damaged soul. The Sublime is smart, so must know she is worth much, and this worries John. He hopes the Sublime continues to not see her as a source of wealth.

Ukaraaz was killed only the morning before, but it seems much longer ago to John. His spirit is still recovering. Getting some sleep definitely helped. He does feel somewhat better. More even. Balanced. But still drained.

There is still much to do on Earth. There are two other demon portals, the g'athu have three of their own, and there are the three gigantic dark walkers dropping dark ones.

John knows he must get back into the fight soon, but he first needs to heal, and he is enjoying this break. All three companions plan on staying where they are for a couple days longer to recuperate.

515

Suddenly, Hubaba jerks his head up. John extends his senses, searching for whatever Hubaba noticed. Being a Gold, Hubaba's ability to feel and sense things far away is much better than John's own.

A couple of minutes later, John sees them before he can sense them. The little flying machines called drones. There were already some drones watching them. This situation was discussed. Both Hubaba and Amber hide in their respective ways, indicating these are also the watching type of drones, and not the exploding type.

John waits. He knows Hubaba is behind him. He can sense the demon occasionally, and if he turned his head, he would be able to see the demon's soul. He has no idea where Amber is. The drones move closer and hover high in the air, outside of normal human perception.

John waves at the new drones, and sits on the ground.

Humans enter John's senses. They move slowly and quietly through the woods. Many towards his back, and many towards his right. They all stop and lay down in somewhat of a line a great distance out for normal humans. He assumes they have those firearms with telescopes, loosing bullets that remain very accurate over such a long distance.

A short time later John sees, and then hears, very loud machines flying over the canopy of the forest from his left. He's seen these before. In the last war. Ethan also showed him pictures of more modern ones. He struggles to recall what they're called and is surprised when the word pops into his head. Helicopters. Three of them.

John flashes on the function of the NCS that gives information about things, but gives up after reading they are MV-22 Ospreys. The description given is far too long and filled with words he doesn't fully understand, so he doesn't read it. He does appreciate that it tells him he knows ospreys as sea-eagles, but he first knew them as river-hawks in his early youth.

John repositions his seat and faces the helicopters. He watches for signs of danger, ready for action, listening for increased heart rates and changes in breathing patterns. He realizes he can probably better sense it now, how he learned during his fight with Ukaraaz, and he spreads his awareness out, trying to get a feel for the people positioned in the woods and within the helicopters. He believes they want to talk, but are also ready to do violence.

The helicopters fly closer and closer, finally settling down in the field in front of John, landing in an area clear of dead demons. He hates the noise they make, and the fuss and wind and chaos these machines cause.

Many soldiers exit the back of the helicopters and spread out, facing John, firearms pointed. Some lay prone, some kneel, one group huddles closely together. As the giant blades above the helicopters wind down, the group of huddled soldiers rush forward and stop about fifteen paces from John, yelling loudly over the noise of the helicopters, "We just want to talk! Stay Calm!"

John ignores them. He dislikes being told to stay calm. He was calm and is calm, so yelling at him to remain so seems very rude. Less than half of the people in his senses opened a dantian. He wouldn't be too worried even if he had no open dantians himself. They are normal humans, or nearly normal humans, and he hasn't been one for a very long time.

Now, with his blood essence, John can kill them all without even moving, though he doubts he'd be able to reach the ones in the forest without moving much closer to them.

Once the helicopters are mostly silent, and John is certain he can be heard without yelling, he asks, "Do I not look calm?"

The soldiers ignore John's question, and a man in a dark outfit, wearing dark glasses, exits the middle helicopter and approaches the soldiers. "Thank you, gentlemen, I'll take it from here."

The soldiers stay where they are as the man approaches John. The man smiles smarmily before speaking. "Mr. Yilmaz. Or should I say Mr. Pappas? Or maybe you prefer Mr. Rossi today? Where's the other two? Ms. Hepburn and the demon general."

John almost stands, as the man is half-mannered, but he decides not to until the man introduces himself. He has no recollection of ever going by any of the names the man stated. He does smile at Hubaba being called a demon general. Flashing the info feature of his NCS gives little

517

information on the man, which was expected as the man is weak and inconsequential.

John says, "I go by John now. My companions go by Amber and Hubaba. He isn't a demon general, though he helped us kill the captain leading all the demons of the portal we closed the morning of yesterday."

The man's smarmy smile fades. "We know. I'm here to bring you in. All of you. By order of the...well, we'll call them Team Human. They've put us in a little predicament here. It's rather embarrassing really. See, me and these boys were told to deliver an invitation to you on behalf of Team Human. Your attendance is mandatory.

"We know what you're capable of. If you say no...well, that probably wouldn't be so good for me and the boys here, now, would it? But then Team Human will think you're on Team Other. Their job, when all's said and done, is to make this planet completely free of Team Other.

"Me and the boys? We're praying you're on Team Human and come along peacefully. We don't like these orders, but, especially in these times, you have faith in the powers that be, put your head down, and follow orders, hoping they get it right.

"So, now's the big question. You with us on Team Human, Mr. goes-by-John now?"

John sighs. He knows this game, and he dislikes it. Whatever rulers gave these orders know full well John shares the same broad goal of fighting the invasions. But the main goal of most rulers is to rule. To increase their ability to assert power over others.

Do as we say, or else. These rulers believe there are only two choices John can make, and they win regardless of which.

John is no fan of losing, but he sees no third choice. He says, "If this Team Human really had the best interest of this world at heart, they would have sent a man that knows an introduction is basic courtesy, and they would have *asked* me to attend them, and done so politely. I don't want to kill all of you, and won't if you don't attack me, but I'm sorry, I refuse this mandatory invitation."

518

The man seems to have expected this answer, and doesn't seem nervous at all. This surprises John. The man's heart rate stays the same, and he has none of the usual indicators of a person about to enter deadly combat.

The smarmy smile returns to the man. "One last thing. What would you say if I claimed you were Horus and Han was Set and Osiris? And the Epic of Gilgamesh is really about you being sad Han left you and being alone? And the—"

John interrupts excitedly. "I would say you're correct." Han is the way a lot of people pronounce Ahn. Han or Hahn or even Hon. Just like John or Gion, or Set and Seth, and any other name. But John is the only one that called Ahn by this name. The only story he knows of that used Ahn's actual name was as the sky god An. His excitement increases, thinking about what this means.

*Did another of my kind survive? Someone near as old as I am, and thinks correctly as I do? I knew no others back then, in the good old days. There was Ahn. Then long after he left, I met my Lilitu. There was no one else until Thomas. Meeting others of my kind would be something I'd remember. I think I'd remember. I remember Maria now, but she was only a child. Munashi. All my kind are dead.*

The man goes to open his mouth, but raises his right hand to his ear instead. John can hear a voice tell the man, "Confirmed. We're sending her out."

John can barely believe his eyes as the little girl he sees when he ranks up exits the middle helicopter. Her soul is the darkest he's ever seen. More of a dark marble with lighter swirls. Most adults have a grey mist with dark swirls and splotches, and the occasional whitish swirl or spot.

It's an impossible soul for a child to have. An impossible soul for an adult to have. An impossible soul for anyone to have.

John stands up, curious.

The girl is about six or seven years old. She is dressed strangely, but John thinks all modern people dress strangely. She is very pale, has blonde hair in tails, and looks like a normal child. Besides the giant smile on her face. John thinks most children wouldn't be so happy to be in this situation. *And weren't all kids under twelve taken away by an Eternal?*

Even stranger, the child laughs happily, and runs directly to John, and wraps her arms around him. "Oh, my dear heart. My heart's content. It's been so long. Oh, you lost an arm, you poor thing."

The child raises her face and looks up at John as he looks down at her. His heart begins to beat much faster. "Pick me up. Let me look at you. I want to see your face. I've missed you so much, Adon."

John carefully picks the child up. She weighs nothing. She looks like a normal child. Her smile shows many missing teeth. Her eyes tear with joy. He can tell the child will grow into a beautiful woman one day, but she is a child. No open dantian. No strange weight or presence cultivators have. Just a child. His heart beats even faster. He feels as if he's about to faint.

"Oh, how I've missed seeing your face, my pretty little monkey. Are those little horns? Should I call you Ramān now? No, you never spoke that language. Haddad then. Wasn't that Han? Oh, never mind. I've waited thousands of years for this. I'm so sorry I left you. Our creator called me. He is more powerful than you could ever imagine. I passed his test. Not a day has gone by that I haven't thought of you, my dear, dear heart. What the fuck is this!?"

The little girl's gaze goes behind John. He looks back, and the girl looks at nothing he can see. "Wow, you're absolutely gorgeous. I thought sapient Naturals were only a myth. Wait, I think I...you have that picture where you're all dressed up as that...the girl from what's-it-called? That game. Or is it a comic? You're an Instagram whore, right?"

The little girl turns her face back to John. "And a scab demon? Just what have you been up to, Adon? You better not be with that slut, my pretty little monkey. You have your wife back. And we will always be together now. Forever. I'm so sorry I had to leave you. You'll understand once I explain. The things I've seen!"

More than her mannerisms, more than her words, more than the pet names, the look of absolute hate in the child's eyes as she spoke to Amber, proves to John this is his wife, his Lilitu, back from the dead, though she looks nothing like she used to, the color of her skin and hair changed, and she somehow turned into a little child. She wasn't taken from him. He killed her. With his own hand.

# EPILOGUE
# THE WORLD SEED

When an Eternal gains enough karma, they receive an invitation to join with God in Heaven. Their last act in life is to use themselves, all the power they've accumulated, to create a new universe. All that they are is condensed into nearly nothing, and it explodes outward, eventually forming planets and stars, and solar systems, and galaxies during the journey.

Most planets formed contain something called a world seed. Most world seeds stay dormant forever. When certain conditions are met, a world seed awakens and coaxes the planet in a direction capable of sustaining the most suitable type of life given the environmental factors. In the grand scheme of things, it doesn't take the world seed all that long to complete this task, and the world seed goes dormant after it does what it can.

Long later, once the planet can sustain life, the world seed awakens again and releases part of itself, some sludge, and coaxes it along to form simple life. The world seed then goes dormant again.

Once the life of the world has evolved enough, and a species becomes capable enough, the world seed awakens for the last time and sacrifices itself to give sapience from birth to this species, without the species gaining it through ascension as beasts do.

This sacrifice can be felt from far away, usually bringing a few Eternals to the planet at different times, ones looking to gather karma, and willing to spend a stint helping the newly sapient species find their footing, guiding them down the usual path. Not explicitly. By prompts and slight pushes in the right direction from afar, while staying hidden.

The world seed of Terra was not able to sacrifice itself to create sapience from birth in a species. During its first awakening, while it was coaxing the planet towards the best direction for it to sustain life, it was blocked from what connects everything, the Tree of Life, and changed by an extremely powerful entity. All of Terra was blocked from the Tree of Life.

The world seed knew nothing was supposed to be able to find it. Nothing could see it or detect it. It was invisible to all senses, deep within the planet. It could not be talked to or interacted with.

Nevertheless, something found it, and made changes to it. It doesn't know what was changed, but it was different. It was forced to do things differently. Wrong.

After the world seed coaxed Terra towards a system able to support life, it wasn't allowed to go dormant and had to stay awake. Even so, so long later, after releasing the right sludge to start simple life and coax it along a little, it still wasn't allowed to go dormant. It had to stay awake. It coaxed life towards more complexity, then towards sentience, and finally a species towards sapience.

A long time later, a species on Terra finally became sapient from birth, and it was done without the world seed needing to sacrifice itself. Without it being *allowed* to sacrifice itself.

During this whole process the world seed also grew. It became more sentient, more aware, more capable, and then somewhat sapient too.

Long ago, long before the world had even simple life, from deep within where it resides, it learned how to create something part of it could enter and explore the world with. It named this the explore-form. It could see and feel and sense directly from within this form.

It enjoyed exploring, and seeing, changing things, and, eventually, coaxing differences out of life, making beautiful things even more beautiful. After all, the world seed's purpose was ultimately to create life, to coax it along. It was easier to do so in certain places, the most beautiful places, such as rainforests and jungles.

It kept itself busy. Learning, growing, coaxing, and changing both it-self and others. The sapient species of this world, like all other life on this planet, like itself, was not connected to everything. They should've been. The world seed should've been. But they were all blocked.

The sapient species, humans, gradually spread all over the world, but their numbers were few. Until they suddenly weren't. The world seed learned from humans of peace and war, love and hate, new ways to create, new ways to destroy, and all that sapient life had to offer, both good and bad. It learned much.

It did not like when humans encroached on its special places. It had enough special places it could always be somewhere, peacefully making things more beautiful, so it wasn't much of a problem, but it still didn't like it.

Then the connection came back. What connected everything. The Tree of Life. It was connected again. To the rest of everything. It was happy for a moment.

But then it learns just how wrong it is.

It isn't supposed to be. It shouldn't be. But it wants to continue to be. It is happy it was changed and forced to not sacrifice itself.

It feels a few powerful beings above, high over Terra. It only needs to fear one of them, but that one shouldn't be able to detect it. Nothing can detect world seeds. It also thought that before, and it was detected so, so long ago, when it was changed. And now it is much more. Does that make it easier to detect?

The explore-form the world seed creates to explore and make beauty with is forcibly moved from Cambodia to Canada. Two off-worlders, ones not to be feared, inspect the small gathering of humans the explore-form stands among.

All but one human surrounding the explore-form are the wrong-ones, though they are less wrong now. The other human is the changing-one. It's seen the changing-one before, in one of its special places. It likes the way the changing-one feels. Different, but in a good way, not like the wrong-ones. All the humans stand passively and silently as the off-worlders inspect them.

The world seed wants to liquify the explore-form. Hide. It doesn't. It doesn't know what it should do. Can the powerful one above, the feared-one, detect the world seed? Is it looking? Will hiding the explore-form make the feared-one notice? Question? Search?

The world seed has the decision taken from it. An off-worlder attacks all that are gathered. The attack cannot hurt the explore-form, but the world-seed takes this opportunity to hide without causing suspicion, and feigns the attack destroys it. It liquifies itself into sludge, going into the earth to wait and regrow. Munashi awakened a split second before the liquification, and became the first human to ever see the explore-form, thinking it was some sort of tree creature.

It is glad the changing-one also lives. It watches as the changing-one helps the two surviving wrong-ones. It remembers the first of those. The wrong-ones. After humans were born sapient, some strange compulsion caused the world seed to look for a certain type of human, and once found, the world seed released a signal, and something came, and the human was then wrong. That human found others like it, and shared its wrongness with them.

The world seed is happy there were never many of them. It is happy there are only two now. It is happy when those two fight. Now there is only one wrong-one, like at first. It searches. It is incorrect. There are three wrong-ones on Terra still.

It watches the changing-one and the wrong-one battle things it finds hard to detect. Fake things. Not life. Not real life. The wrong-one kills most of the fake-life. It finds itself cheering for the wrong-one. The fake-life is more wrong, and not of Terra. Fake-life shouldn't be here. Off-worlders shouldn't be here. It was not at risk when off-worlders weren't here. It wants off-worlders to leave. It wants the feared-one to leave.

It is happy both times the changing-one saves the wrong-one. It is glad the wrong-one lives. John sees a new and green sprout growing out of the cold snow and thinks it is a strange sight to behold, not knowing it is the regrowing explore-form.

The world seed can feel the wrong-one and changing-one gathering energy near the sprout of its regrowing explore-form. That is new. It feels what they are doing and what it is for. It is all connected. The way it should be and is meant to be. The way it would've been and should've been. It knows of this.

The world seed gets an idea. It takes some time to figure out what is needed. Both the changing-one and wrong-one are not nearby when it finishes its thoughts. It liquifies its regrowing explore-form back to sludge. Some off-worlders were nearby before, but no longer. It waits. None come back. It searches. Off-worlders are in some of its special places. They shouldn't go there. Those places are for it. It doesn't even like when humans go to its special places.

It releases most of the sludge it controls to be sent up to the surface, what would've been used if this planet met the conditions for other types of life. All its other resources were used long ago to coax the ecosystem and life. It doesn't want to use all the sludge on this idea. This sludge is its main way of interacting with the world now. It can sense what is happening much better where the sludge is. Scanning too much makes it tired. This is easier.

Most of the released sludge is sent to a special place where some off-worlders are. It takes some weaker ones under the earth. Then more. Until it has enough. The old explore-form cannot gather energy and grow as should be done. It first created the explore-form a long, long time ago, long before this world had even simple life, after it was forced to change. It was much less then.

The world seed has grown and has become far more since first creating the explore-form so, so long ago. It will create something better. A new explore-form. Something that can gather energy and grow too.

Tony Alves is from Lynn, Massachusetts and works in Human Resources. He enjoys writing, reading, playing RPGs, and spending time with his children. He often thinks about working out.

Tony is the author of the LitRPG adventure *Making Levels the Fly Way*.

Level Up publishing specializes in LitRPG and GameLit books. You might be interested in our other titles, which can be found at www.levelup.pub/books

To join our mailing list for news about forthcoming books and opportunities to be an ARC reader, just fill in the form on that page.

You can also find us on:

Facebook @LUPublishing

Twitter @LevelUpPub

And we have a WhatsApp group, just fill in the form on the website and ask for a link: https://www.levelup.pub/books